··*The Pulse of Passion*··

Everything in the moon-silvered world seemed to stop. Merial could hear nothing but the pounding of her own heart and Rayn's ragged breathing. Nothing mattered, nothing existed but his arms and his mind-drugging kisses.

Rayn felt the yielding of Merial's soft body, and passion blazed through him until his bones and nerve ends seemed on fire. Desire hammered white-hot through his loins, dazing him, driving every other consideration from his mind. He began to caress her hair, her slender throat, the curve of her breast.

His mouth sought her lips again, drinking from her mouth, breathing her breath, consuming her. Merial felt herself disintegrating, dissolving into him. She no longer knew where Rayn began and Merial ended.

In the drum of his white-hot blood, Rayn sensed her surrender . . .

SILKEN TIGER

CYNTHIA LEIGH

CHARTER/DIAMOND BOOKS, NEW YORK

·· *For my Book Club friends* ··

SILKEN TIGER

A Charter/Diamond Book/published by arrangement with
the author

PRINTING HISTORY
Charter/Diamond edition/November 1990

ISBN: 1-55773-412-7

Charter/Diamond Books are published by The Berkley Publishing
Group, 200 Madison Avenue, New York, New York 10016.
The name "CHARTER/DIAMOND" and its logo are trademarks
belonging to Charter Communications, Inc.

PRINTED IN THE UNITED STATES OF AMERICA

10 9 8 7 6 5 4 3 2 1

·· *Prologue* ··

India, 1856

"WE'VE STOPPED AGAIN," Lady Elizabeth Ashland fumed. "My God. What's wrong this time?"

Seven-year-old Meri Ashland peered through the curtains of their horse-drawn carriage. "Something's wrong with the cart behind us," she said fearfully. "Will the bad men catch us now, Mama?"

Lady Elizabeth glared back toward where they had traveled. "I'll never understand why your father insisted on bringing that cart along. But then, I don't understand why he took this post at all. Commissioner of Sri Nevi—bah! A miserable post in a godforsaken country."

She raised her voice so that Sir Edward, who was riding toward them, could hear her last words. Meri saw the irritation in his pale gray eyes. "The cart's wheel is stuck in a rut," he brusquely informed his wife. "Nothing to worry about. We'll still make Gandari by nightfall."

"Nothing to worry about when a mob was storming our residence?" Lady Elizabeth's voice was shrill. "You know what's been going on in Delhi and the Punjab. The natives are murdering anyone with English blood, even children!

And this is the third time that damned cart has slowed us down. I insist that you leave it behind, Edward."

Meri looked fearfully at her father, but he paid her no attention. "Nonsense. Colonel Malcolm is in perfect control of Sri Nevi, and there's nothing to fear from a few ruffians. You're becoming hysterical, Elizabeth."

He rode away before his wife could speak again, and Lady Elizabeth glowered after him. Then she rounded on Meri. "For heaven's sake, Merial," she snapped, "sit still. Your squirming is intolerable."

Meri sat bolt upright on the hard seat. She had been doing her best to stay motionless in the rocking, jolting carriage, and her skinny backside, legs, and arms were almost numb. Worse, her mother's words had made her remember stories she had overheard her old nurse, Jassmina, whispering to the cook. Jassmina had spoken of English memsahibs who'd watched their babies butchered before their eyes. . . .

Heavy footsteps approached the carriage, and Captain St. Marr, the ranking British officer in the commissioner's party, peered through the window. The big blond man looked exasperated. "It'll be some time before we can get yon wheel unstuck, marm. Perhaps ye ladies would like ter stretch yer legs a bit."

Meri gladly lifted her arms to St. Marr, who gave her a comforting squeeze as he swung her down from the carriage. "There, now, bairn," he told her softly. "Don't ye worry. My lads will soon have us on our way."

Lady Elizabeth caught the end of that remark. "If you'd let an Englishman drive the cart instead of that Indian driver, this wouldn't have happened," she snapped. "The natives are too stupid."

Meri saw the big captain's eyes narrow. "If ye'll excuse me, I'll be about my work."

He strode back to where sweating, swearing English soldiers assisted the driver of the bullock cart. Lady Elizabeth followed him, but Meri stayed where she was. For the first time since early morning she could move and breathe freely, and that was a blessing. She stretched and looked around her, her turquoise eyes widening as she saw the Pir Panjal mountain range so close by.

Since leaving her father's small district of Sri Nevi, they had been steadily climbing. Far, far below them lay the river-ribboned, tawny plain while above, rising sharply out of thick forests, the peaks of the Pir Panjal mountains shimmered in the afternoon sun. Once they reached the mountain garrison town of Gandari, the mob from Sri Nevi could not hurt them. But supposing the *budmarshes*—ruffians—caught them? She thought of what her mother had said and could not keep back a shiver.

"Tired, Meri?"

The familiar voice behind her began in a manly baritone and then cracked into a boy's treble. With a glad cry, Meri turned to greet Niall St. Marr, her best friend.

"I wanted to look for you this morning before we left, but Mama and Father were in a hurry and wouldn't let me. I was afraid you'd stayed behind with the garrison."

"Colonel Malcolm gave me the choice of staying or going with my father." Niall St. Marr's eyes were snapping with excitement, and his carefully casual tone didn't mask his pride. Meri knew that her friend's dearest wish was to ride and fight at his father's side.

At twelve, the captain's son was already taller than many men, and his shoulders and chest had begun to fill with muscle. In this and in the line of his jaw he resembled his Scottish father, but Niall was darker in hair and skin, his features cut finer than those of the bluff officer.

Meri beamed up at him in happy hero worship. "I'm

so glad, Niall. Maybe now your father will let you go to the military school in Lucknow. You'll be a wonderful officer."

The pride in his eyes dimmed a little. "Maybe not," he said.

Meri understood. Niall might not be given a commission in his father's regiment because of his mixed blood. Niall hardly ever spoke of his dead mother, Princess Lakshmi, one of the many daughters of a minor Indian prince, but there were many who did.

The Ashlands had only tolerated the friendship between their daughter and the captain's son because as yet there were no other English families in Sri Nevi. Meri had often heard her father deploring the fact that St. Marr had actually married a native woman, while Lady Elizabeth added contemptuously that no blacky-white could ever be fully accepted in an English community.

Meri said stoutly, "You'll be a brave soldier, then, the best there is." She added for emphasis, "The *very* best. You won't be scared of anyone. Not even of *budmarshes*—"

Then, suddenly, she remembered why they were running away from Sri Nevi. As the fear returned to her heart-shaped face, Niall put a big-brotherly arm around her thin shoulders. "Don't be scared. Father says that our sepoys in Sri Nevi will never mutiny. We're only going to Gandari because Colonel Malcolm thought things would calm down if the commissioner and his family left for a while."

Meri nodded, but her small, homely face twisted with the effort of keeping back tears. Poor scared kid, Niall thought. She'd had precious little comfort from those parents of hers, that was for sure. He tightened his arm around her shoulders and tried to think of some way to cheer her.

Suddenly he grinned. "Look, Meri, you can wear my amulet as far as Gandari."

"Your *mother's* amulet?"

Tears forgotten, Meri held her breath as Niall drew a heavy golden chain from under his shirt. Affixed to the chain was a magnificent moonstone set in a golden nugget. The amulet had belonged to Princess Lakshmi, and he valued it more than anything in the world.

"It protects all who wear it from harm," Niall was saying. Meri nodded raptly, unaware that Niall had switched from English to the liquid Hindustani they both spoke fluently. "Only those with royal blood can wear this amulet."

"I know," Meri breathed.

Niall settled the heavy chain around her thin neck and sketched a salaam. "Now you are a princess, and princesses aren't scared of a few *budmarshes*. Don't worry, Highness, I'll protect you. My life for yours."

"Niall!" the captain shouted. "Come over here, boy, and put your shoulder to this wheel."

Niall hurried to obey. Meri would have followed, but her mother stopped her. "What were you two talking about in that heathen language?" she asked suspiciously.

"Niall was telling me he wants to be a soldier," Meri said, and her mother clicked her tongue.

"The regiment would never give that chi-chi a commission. I think you see too much of young St. Marr, Merial."

"But he's my friend," she protested. "My very best friend."

Lady Elizabeth frowned, but before she could reply there was a cheer from the men who had at last freed the cart's wheel. As the echo of that cheer died away, a soldier who had been on watch came riding up. "Sir!" he cried to St. Marr. "If you'll look down along the road . . ."

Meri looked with the others, and her heart bumped with fear. Not too far below them were many small moving dots. Sir Edward swore. "The Sri Nevi mob—they've followed us."

St. Marr turned to the women. "Back in the carriage, and quickly. We've still got a good start."

Bundled into the carriage, Meri remembered what Niall had said about princesses not being afraid. She bit her lower lip and clenched her small hands and tried not to cry. She thought of her nurse, Jassmina, rocking her to sleep. She thought of last spring when Niall had taught her to ride.

She must have fallen asleep. The next thing she knew, her mother was shaking her and saying urgently, "Wake up, Merial. We must get out." Had they reached Gandari? But then Lady Elizabeth hissed, "Wake up, do you hear? We've come to a mountain pass, and they're going to lead the horses across. It's too dangerous to ride in the carriage."

Sir Edward helped his wife and daughter out into the dusky twilight. No one had lit lanterns for fear of discovery, so Meri could hardly see, but even so she realized that her father was terrified. "Hurry," he snapped, "they're close behind us. For God's sake, hurry."

The *budmarshes* were near. The ruffians were going to catch them and kill them. A cool wind from the mountains gusted down, so strong that it made Meri stagger. She clung to Sir Edward's hand for support, but he shook her off impatiently, and it was the captain who steadied her. "Go on with Niall, bairn."

Then Niall was taking her hand and leading her across the shadowed path that was only a scant two yards wide, barely wide enough for the carriage and the cart. On one side was mountain; on the other lay an abyss that began and ended in windy blackness. As the native driver and the British soldiers struggled to guide the carriage horses across the narrow pass, Meri heard a rock dislodge itself and plunge downward. She listened to it fall and fall.

"Niall . . ."

"It's all right. We're in the mountains and this is the Gujjar Pass—the Goat Pass. Just keep walking and don't look down."

But she did, and she nearly screamed. Not far below them were specks of light that flared in the wind and burned like beasts' eyes. Torches. "The *budmarshes,*" Meri whimpered.

Niall's hand tightened on hers. "My father will get us out of this."

His voice held excitement but no fear, and her terror lessened for an instant before she heard Lady Elizabeth's voice. "Edward, we must leave the cart and hurry on. We must, to save our lives. Please listen to reason."

"I'll be damned if those ruffians get what belongs to me. No, I tell you." Sir Edward's voice rose stubbornly and then snapped a question. "Captain, how far off do you judge our pursuers to be?"

"They're closing fast." St. Marr's tone was blunt. "Yer lady's right, Sir Edward. Without the cart we could reach Gandari much more quickly." Sir Edward was silent and the captain urged, "We could leave the cart blocking the pass. Ye and your lady and Meri could ride on ahead. My men and I would follow as a rear guard."

"Please, Edward." Nothing frightened Merial so much as the humble note in her mother's voice. "Will you risk our lives for your ridiculous cart?"

But Sir Edward was obstinate. "St. Marr, you forget

yourself. As commissioner of Sri Nevi, I give the orders. To leave the cart here would be to admit defeat—and an English gentleman will not be defeated by mob violence."

"But damn it, man—" the captain shouted, protocol forgotten.

"Your idea of a rear guard is a good one, Captain. As soon as we get the cart across the Gujjar, we'll proceed to Gandari ahead of you. Deploy your men at the pass. Give us half an hour's head start, and we'll reach Gundari and send reinforcements from the garrison."

Merial glanced down at the bobbing lights. They were closer now. How many *budmarshes* were there? She could not count. St. Marr was protesting hotly. "We are only six men, Sir Edward. There are at least fifty of them down there."

There was a sneer in Sir Edward's voice. "Are you afraid of the odds? Come, man. An Englishman is worth twenty wogs any day."

"I'm no' afraid of the odds, but this is stupidity." In his agitation St. Marr's Scottish burr rumbled like thunder. "Ye're saying that the life of my men are wur-rth less to ye than that damnable cart—"

Sir Edward interrupted, "If you'll hold the rear guard, we'll take your son with us."

Merial felt Niall stiffen. Next moment he had dropped her hand and had pushed forward to stand beside his father. "I'm staying with my father."

"Nonsense, boy," St. Marr snapped.

Niall's voice cracked as he added furiously, "I'm nearly thirteen. I'm a man."

"More of a man than some I know of," St. Marr spat. He faced Sir Edward, and though his voice was low, every word cracked with contempt. "I'll do what ye say because there is no choice. Take my son wi' ye and go."

"I'm staying," Niall retorted.

The cart had at last made its way to the other end of the pass. "Get into the carriage," Sir Edward ordered his wife. "Take Merial. Hurry!"

But Meri dodged her mother's hand and ran to Niall. "Please—come with us," she begged.

She felt his hands on her shoulders. In spite of the chill of the pass, his touch was warm, and his voice was oddly gentle. "Go on, Meri—go with your father." Then he added in a sharper tone, "Hurry or the *budmarshes* will get you. Can't you hear them?"

She could—oh, God, she could. Over the eerie wail of the wind she could distinguish distant voices. Her father was cursing her as he strode toward her, and in a moment he would reach her. But she could not leave her dearest friend here alone, unprotected.

Grasping the amulet he had given her, she yanked it over her head. Desperately she pressed it into Niall's hands. "It'll keep you safe. . . ."

Her words trailed off as Sir Edward caught her by the arm and dragged her back to the waiting carriage. To the driver he snapped, "Drive on. Hurry, idiot!"

As the carriage began to creak away from the pass, they could hear shouting on the wind. "Oh, hurry, they're coming," Lady Elizabeth whimpered, and then all fell silent, straining to listen for sounds above the whip of the wind and the sound of plodding horses' hooves. For a while there was only dark silence, and then they heard the crack of rifle shots.

"The mob," Meri's mother breathed, but Meri wasn't worrying about the *budmarshes* anymore. She was listening to a clear young voice that rose above the sounds of the wind and the tumult of combat.

"St. Marr, *ki-jai!*" Niall was shouting—long live St. Marr. "St. Marr, *ki-jai!*"

··*One*··

India, 1872

"JUST WHO THE devil does this Narayn of Baranpur think he is?"

Sir Edward's querulous tones cut through the noise of the departing train, the shouts of harried porters, and the babble of passengers that crowded the station at Armitsar. He added, "This so-called prince seems to have frightened half of India."

"Hardly that, sir," Lieutenant Hammond protested. "All the same, he's not called the Tiger for nothing."

Merial frowned a little. Since she'd first heard of the warrior prince in Delhi three nights ago, she'd been almost constantly reminded of him.

"The people we stayed with in Delhi warned us about Prince Narayn," she said. "It was the same with travelers we met on the train. I don't understand why the man is such a threat to us. All we want to do is get to Sri Nevi."

"To do so you need to travel southwest of Srinagar. That's close to Baranpur's southern border," Hammond explained. "Prince Narayn considers anybody traveling too close to Baranpur an enemy—especially if the traveler is English. He and his father, the Rana Khem Raoshad, hate the *Angrezi,* as they call us. The rana's older son was killed fighting us, you see."

Sir Edward snorted derisively, and Lieutenant Hammond stifled a sigh. Hamilton Perce, commissioner of railroads at Sri Nevi, had written to his commanding officer asking him to send someone to meet the Ashlands' train and help them on their way. Perce hadn't added that Sir Edward had a way of antagonizing everyone he met.

Perhaps it was because he'd had a hard crossing from England. Ashland looked sickly, far older than his fifty-six years. But then, there were also rumors that this former commissioner of Sri Nevi had come back to India to escape his creditors. Though heir to his late wife's fortune, Sir Edward had apparently lost it all in unwise speculations.

Lieutenant Hammond glanced at the tall, slender young woman who was waiting patiently beside her father. Now *she* was a different matter altogether. Creamy skin, coal-black hair, a softly curved mouth that promised both sweetness and fire—Miss Merial Ashland had all those plus the brilliance of direct, dark-lashed turquoise eyes.

It was for her sake that the young officer tried to have patience with the father's complaints.

"It's the same old story I used to hear fifteen years ago," Sir Edward was sputtering. "These hill princes think they're God Almighty. Can't the army take care of this beggar, Hammond? But then, I suppose it's a case of no guts and no leadership. Always is in these remote areas."

Seeing the young man's painful flush, Merial hastened to change the subject. "You were very kind to meet us, Lieutenant," she said gently. "Perhaps you can help us find a reliable guide?"

"Know just the fellow—Walid Mohammed. Used to be a *shikari*—a tracker—very reliable. He can get you safely through." Hammond snapped his fingers, and a man stepped forward. "Walid Mohammed can help you round up ponymen, cook, horses—everything you'll need for your four-day journey."

Weather, sun, and wind seemed to have stripped Walid Mohammed of every ounce of fat and left tough, gnarled skin behind. It was impossible to guess at his age, Merial thought. Even the years seemed to have been burned from him.

Sir Edward sniffed disapprovingly. "*Shikaris* were always a thieving lot. You, Walid Mohammed—are you afraid of this so-called Tiger?"

"Yes, sahib, but I have guided many Englishmen safely past his borders. I know the country as well as I know my own hand."

The man spoke without expression, but Merial saw the fear in his hooded brown eyes.

"This is foolish," she protested. "Even if we do come close to this Narayn's borders, he'd only have to warn us away. Why should he want to harm us?"

"Or dare to," Sir Edward added.

Hammond shrugged. "The Tiger is a daring bastard— sorry, Miss Ashland—and he's also a law unto himself. Baranpur is a remote kingdom and English rule doesn't carry any weight there. The old rana is as proud as Lucifer. He believes he's descended from the sun, no less. And it's common knowledge that no Englishman who's gone against Prince Narayn—or Prince Rayn, as he's usually called—has lived to tell about it."

The bustling, sun-drenched station faded, shadowed by the menace of those words. Merial had the queasy feeling of being seven years old again. She could smell and taste the fear of those nightmares. Then into that dreaded vision came a clear, laughing young voice. "Don't worry, Meri. . . . My life for yours. . . ."

They'd never recovered Niall's body. When reinforcements from Gandari had reached the Gujjar Pass, they'd found Captain St. Marr and most of his soldiers hacked to pieces. It was surmised that the Sri Nevi mob had heaved the bodies of Niall and two other soldiers into the abyss below, but no one knew for sure. It hadn't been possible to scale the sheer cliff walls in search of the missing dead.

Niall. Her heart still ached at the thought of him.

"Prince Rayn is supreme commander of his father's standing army," Lieutenant Hammond was continuing. "He has fifty handpicked *bhaldars*—lancers—who ride with him and have the devil's own reputation." Then, seeing the look in Merial's eyes, he added somewhat hastily, "But don't worry, Miss Ashland. The prince may hate us with the hate of hell, but he knows that an attack on a British district would bring the army after him. You'll be safe in Sri Nevi."

They had to get there first, Merial thought, but she didn't voice her concern aloud. Her father was already unhappy enough. He was furious that Hamilton Perce had not met them personally at Armitsar or at least sent a military escort to guide them into the hills.

"After all, I *was* the commissioner of that godforsaken place," he sputtered to his daughter. "And, damn it, I'm to be deputy commissioner of railroads over there. But I suppose I couldn't expect any better treatment from Perce. He's from low stock, I've heard—his parents were common shopkeepers. Blood always tells, Merial."

"I'm sure Walid Mohammed is reliable, father," Merial soothed.

The guide truly seemed efficient as he went about hiring

ponymen and a cook, acquiring horses for Sir Edward and Merial, and ponies for himself and for the baggage. None of this was to Sir Edward's liking.

"Cheeky beggars," he complained. "Don't trust any of them. Make sure you keep your belongings securely about you, Merial."

It was an unsightly procession that took to the road next morning. Sir Edward swore at his horse and his servants, and complained unceasingly of his own discomfort, but Merial's spirits rose as soon as they were clear of Armitsar and riding higher into the hills.

A good horsewoman, she didn't mind long hours in the saddle. As they rode she delighted in the cool greenery of deodar pine and the glossy clumps of rhododendron that cloaked the lower reaches of the mountains. The high peaks themselves she greeted, like old friends, by name.

"Great Kabru, Little Kabru, Kang Peak, Jannu . . ."

Walid Mohammed was riding behind her. "The Miss Sahib knows the names of the mountains?" he asked, surprised.

"I remember them from my childhood."

He had spoken in his faulty English, but she had replied in Hindustani. He looked even more surprised, but then remarked, "The mountains have spirits that are unfriendly to the English, Miss Sahib."

"You're speaking of Prince Narayn," she charged.

He cast a fearful look around him. "I have never seen him, but I know his power is great. Some say he is in league with all the jinn. He is a fearsome fighter, a mountain of a man. If I were English, as you are, I would be afraid of him—especially since you are going to Sri Nevi."

Was he warning her? His eyes were narrowed against the sun, and his gnarled, whipcord-hard face was difficult to read. "Why 'especially'?" she asked.

"The Tiger is greatly opposed to the railroads that Perce Sahib is building near his border. He wants to keep Baranpur free of all *Angrezi* influence. Besides which, Perce Sahib is a hard man to the people in his district. A very hard man."

There was much unsaid behind the brief words. "Surely there are laws that could protect them," Merial protested.

"Ah, but Sri Nevi is far from Delhi. Perce Sahib's word is the law. It is said that he only fears Prince Rayn of Baranpur—and with good cause. The Tiger's hatred of the *Angrezi*—and their servants—is well known."

Fear harshened the guide's voice, and it was contagious. Merial found herself looking about her, suspecting every shadow that fell across the road, startling at unexplained noises. Even the sun seemed less bright than before.

When they camped that evening, she told Sir Edward what Walid Mohammed had said. He wasn't impressed.

"Good for Perce if he keeps a tight rein on things. Merial, I wouldn't have come back to this godforsaken country if the railroad weren't important. At the time of the mutiny there wasn't any track linking Sri Nevi with the rest of India. If there'd been a way to bring troop reinforcements to my district, we'd never have had to run from that mob. Our lives would have been very different."

He was silent a moment, his pale gray eyes gazing back across the past fifteen years. Then he added sharply, "Don't take anything a native says at face value, Merial. Liars, all of them. There's nothing dangerous about this place."

Merial looked around the upland plateau Walid Mohammed had chosen for their campsite. Surrounded by mountains that were turning rosy with sunset, the place was scented with wild jasmine and the thick, white stars of wild coffee blossoms.

Her heart lifted at all this beauty, and she smiled. "You're right," she told her father, "there's no danger here."

The ponymen had set up the Ashlands' tents. Sir Edward went to his, but Merial stayed where she was. The roseate glow on the hills had turned to ash gray, and now the swift Indian night fell like a velvet curtain. The warm air was soft, the sky studded with huge white stars. Merial felt something in her heart swell with inexplicable joy. "Fifteen years," she whispered, "and nothing's changed."

Then a cool night wind rose out of nowhere and curved about her like a living hand, and she knew she was lying to herself. India might still be the same, but everything else had changed. She was no longer the wide-eyed child, Meri, and those she'd loved were dead. Even this beautiful place was not secure, for the shadow of Narayn Raoshad lay over it.

She did not sleep well that night, and next day she was silent and subdued as they went on. They made good time up the now-steep path, and by noon they had crossed a suspension bridge over a foaming river gorge, the halfway point to Sri Nevi.

The sky was so clear and blue that the rainstorm that blew up toward sunset caught them by surprise. The servants scurried to erect shelters in a hastily chosen campsite, but by the time they were under cover, Sir Edward complained of being chilled. "I'm soaked to the skin," he said, aggrievedly. "I need some hot tea and brandy, Merial."

Before Merial could go in search of the cook, Walid Mohammed coughed at the flap-entrance of the tent. He looked unhappy.

"This is bad country, sahib," he told Sir Edward. "There is a safer place a little further on. We must go there as soon as the rain stops."

"How can we go anywhere in the dark? Impossible," Sir Edward snapped. "Here we're camped, and here we stay. Merial, tell the cook to boil up that tea and be quick about it."

She followed Walid Mohammed out of the tent. "Are you afraid that *he* is close by?"

"We are very close to Baranpur's southwestern borders. It is doubly dangerous because here Afridi—Afghan—raiders often cross into India and Baranpur in search of loot. The Tiger's men patrol this area regularly against those raiders." He repeated earnestly, "We are in danger here."

His fear was almost palpable. It took all Merial's control to remain calm.

"It isn't possible for us to go on tonight," she said. "Tomorrow, early, we'll break camp. And don't worry, Walid Mohammed. My father has a rifle, and so do you."

"What are rifles against such as the Tiger?" the old man muttered.

That night she dreamed of a tiger the size of an elephant. It had a man's face and a cruel beast's smile, and it chased them to the edge of an abyss. Then the Tiger laughed and pushed them over. She fell and fell—

Merial sat bolt upright on her narrow cot and stared into the gray dawn. She still had the sensation of falling, could still hear the Tiger's snarls. Then she realized it was the sound of her father coughing in the next tent.

She found Sir Edward sitting fully dressed on his camp cot. His face was putty-colored and he was sweating heavily. "You're ill!" she exclaimed.

"It's just a chill—I'll shake it off." But he could not swallow his breakfast and his hands shook so that he could not even hold his teacup. He insisted he could ride, but after an hour he slumped forward into his saddle.

When Merial insisted that they make camp, Walid Mohammed looked stricken. "Not here!" he exclaimed. "I went out before the dawn and saw the tracks of many mounted men. The Tiger is close by, Miss Sahib."

She felt as if she were falling from a great height. Fear made a roaring echo in her ears, and light and darkness undulated before her eyes. From far away she heard her own voice say, "You don't know that the tracks were made by this Narayn."

"If it's not the Tiger, it is a band of lawless Afridis, and that is just as bad. We must leave immediately."

Merial clasped her hands to keep them from shaking. "My father can't go any farther."

Sir Edward was very sick and grew even sicker during the day as his fever rose. Merial tried everything she had in their small camp medicine kit, but even quinine did not help.

Later, when twilight fell, she went to draw water from the spring nearby and realized how isolated they were. The mountains that had been beautiful only yesterday now looked alien in the dusky twilight, and the wind that had come whipping out of the northeast wailed like a damned soul.

"Suppose the sahib is not able to travel tomorrow? What then?"

The sound of the wind almost blotted out the frightened whisper that came out of the darkness. Merial saw that some of the ponymen were squatting some distance away. Walid Mohammed was with them.

The guide said, "It is a sudden fever and will pass."

"But if not? Shall we stay here and be killed by the Tiger for serving an Englishman, or maybe gutted by Afridi raiders?"

Not wanting to hear more, Merial walked out of the

darkness and faced them. "No one will go anywhere if my father cannot travel," she told the startled men. "If Ashland Sahib is ill tomorrow, one of you must return to the nearest village for a doctor."

A jackal began to bark somewhere nearby and other mocking jackal voices gave answer. "Maybe the Tiger's *bhaldars* are mocking us," one of the ponymen whimpered.

"Peace, fool," Walid Mohammed snarled, but in the faint light of the campfire his eyes were terrified.

Merial was scared, too. All that night she sat by her father's side with his rifle across her knees. Once she dozed and woke with a start because something was rooting around in the woods that surrounded their camp. She jumped to her feet, heart hammering, but nothing else happened and the night became still once more. It was only in the morning that she realized who had made that noise.

All the men, even Walid Mohammed, had left during the night. With them had gone the horses and ponies. Merial, looking at the empty servants' tent, saw all their abandoned baggage and knew that she and Sir Edward were helpless—helpless and trapped in Tiger country.

"Oh, damn them," she groaned. "Damn the cowards."

"Merial. Merial!"

She hurried back into her father's tent and looked down on him in despair. His face was drawn and haggard, and he was shivering so hard that the camp cot shook. "Water," he implored.

As she gave him water, she forced herself to think rationally. There was little she could do for her father. If she didn't get him medical help soon, he would very likely die, but she was miles from the nearest village. Meeting someone on the road who was willing to find a doctor was her only possible hope.

A small, despairing voice in her mind asked who would dare incur the Tiger's wrath by helping English people, and suddenly she was furious not only at the Tiger but also at Hamilton Perce. Why hadn't he sent someone to guide them to Sri Nevi? Probably because Perce hadn't wanted to take a chance of meeting the Tiger face to face.

"Oh, my God!" she exclaimed. "What am I going to do?"

As if he had heard her involuntary cry, Sir Edward began to mutter deliriously. The unintelligible sounds cut through her fear and her anger and left her clearheaded. Gently she took his hands.

"Father, I'm going to get a doctor for you. I'll leave water here, near you." Would he have the strength to drink water by himself? Or perhaps he would die while she was gone. He didn't even seem to hear her, and when she bent to kiss his forehead, her lips felt singed. "I'll be back as soon as I can," she promised.

She didn't look backward as she hefted Sir Edward's rifle and began to walk back along the way they had come. The way led mostly downhill, and she kept a steady and resolute pace. As she walked, she found herself making a bargain with God. If she could only find someone who could help her father, she would never ask for anything again. If God would be good to her and help her now, she would do anything. "Anything, God," she whispered. "Without question, I'll do what You say. . . ."

There was a rustle in the trees that edged the mountain road, and she glanced to her side. She stared. Where had so many mounted men come from? They had bandoliers on their shoulders and wicked curved swords at their sides, and their rifles were pointed directly at her.

This much she saw in one blink-flash of time, and then the image of the men seemed to haze. In place of all of them was one man who sat on a cream-white stallion a short distance away. Though he was dressed like the others in a simple tunic and white jodhpurs, she knew instinctively that he was their leader. He was a big man, much taller than the others, with broad shoulders that rippled with muscle as he moved to control his restive mount. Under the sweep of snow-white turban that emphasized his bronzed skin, his face was hard-planed, strong-boned, square-chinned. It was an arresting face, but his tawny eyes were what made her catch her breath. They reminded her of a hawk about to strike. . . .

A hawk—or a tiger.

Merial felt dizzy as realization hit home. Dark spots danced before her eyes, and her legs went to jelly. There was a humming in her ears. But when she saw the Tiger put his hand to his curved sword, despair made her bold.

"Are you the one called Prince Narayn of Baranpur?" she demanded in her perfect Hindustani.

There was a ripple of astonishment among the prince's *bhaldars,* but their leader remained unmoved. "Drop your rifle at your feet," he instructed her. "So. Now, who are you, and why are you here in my hills?"

His voice was deep, measured. There was no real threat in it, but it set her heart leaping and thudding. Defiantly she said, "I didn't know the hills belonged to you. I thought they belonged to everyone."

The Tiger's eyes remained colder than rain-washed stone. "Why are you here?" he repeated.

Remembering what Walid Mohammed had said, she didn't dare mention Sri Nevi. "My father and I have come from the north—from Armitsar," she explained. "He became very ill, and our servants deserted us because they were afraid of you. I was trying to find a doctor to help him."

Unexpectedly his firm mouth quirked into a smile. "And instead you found me."

A dark-faced youth with bold eyes and a white scar puckering one cheek laughed aloud. "Truly, my lord, your reputation grows. It's said that *Angrezi* mothers use your name to frighten their babes into obedience."

"Peace, Deen." The Tiger did not take his eyes away from Merial. "You have not told us where you are going—or why you speak our language so well."

"I was born here. I learned the language from my nurse. Please let me go. If I don't find help for my father, he'll die."

The Tiger shrugged. "An Englishman's death wouldn't trouble me," he began, but before he could continue there was the sound of galloping hoofbeats and a rider burst through the trees and onto the road.

"Lord!" he exclaimed. "You were right about that band of Afghans. The Afridis are making for a small encampment a mile or so away."

She watched his attention switch away from her, saw the hard face become even harsher. "Good. Deen—" The young man with the scar backed his horse into the woods and took a dozen men with him. "Rassul." Another man, older and more deliberate, disappeared in the other direction, also followed by a dozen of his comrades. "The rest, with me," the Tiger commanded.

They were going to ride away. They weren't going to kill her. For a moment relief was so strong that she felt sick, and then she realized what the Tiger's *bhaldar* had said. There couldn't be another camp within a mile of them. . . .

Desperation made her forget her fear. Hardly realizing

what she did, she ran forward and caught his stirrup. "That band of Afghans—they are riding into our camp, aren't they? They'll kill my father."

"As I told you before, a dead *Angrezi* means nothing to me." He frowned down at her and she forced herself to meet the steady amber gaze. Her heart was beating wildly, and when she tried for a bracing breath she drew in his scent. Clean, vital, touched with leather and the outdoors, it made him seem more human, more approachable.

"Please," she begged, "take me with you. I can try to help him—" He was shaking his head and she tried to think of something she could say, some appeal she could make that would change his mind. Suddenly she thought of something Jassmina had said years ago. "It is written that there is no hem or border or fringe to the mercy of God. Be merciful, also. . . ."

Dark eyebrows arched up in surprise and something like respect. He seemed to hesitate for a moment. Then, with a quick, decisive movement, he pulled her up behind him and spurred his horse so that she was flung forward against the powerful musculature of his back. Instinctively she put her arms around his waist and felt against her palms his whipcord-lean, tight-muscled belly. Such close contact was disturbing, but she had little choice but to cling to him. And as they galloped back along the way they had come, he spoke in a cool, deliberate voice.

"I don't make war on sick men or women. If you've been honest with me, you have nothing to fear. But if you're lying, not even your God will be able to help you."

·· *Two* ··

WIND SHEARED AWAY her breath. Her hair had come undone, and the black mass whipped across her face, making it difficult to see. When Prince Rayn checked his stallion's furious gallop, she didn't realize at first where they were.

Then she saw the Afghan raiders. At this distance of a hundred yards, there appeared to be an army of them. Like ravens in their rough, dark clothing, they were busy looting the camp and had dragged the Ashlands' supplies into the center of the clearing. Seeing the sunlight glitter on their rifles and on their wicked curved swords, Merial couldn't suppress a gasp.

"Be still," Rayn whispered.

He could feel her soft-curved body go rigid against his back, but she made no further sound. He hadn't been wrong about her courage, he thought grimly.

Now one of the Afghans pushed aside the flap of Sir Edward's tent and yelled for his companions. "He's found the *Angrezi,*" Rayn commented.

Merial tried to slide down from the horse, but a steely hand around her arm kept her where she was. She tried helplessly to free herself, protesting, "Let me go. *Please.* They'll kill him—"

"My captains aren't in position yet. Wait."

The Afghan raiders had gathered around Sir Edward's tent. One of them, a ferocious-looking man who wore a goatskin coat and breeches, shouted an order, and there was a spurt of flame. Derisive laughter hooted through the clearing as one of the raiders set fire to a corner of the Englishman's tent.

The prince caught Merial's wrists and swung her to the ground. "Stay here," he commanded, then urged his stallion forward. Simultaneously his followers burst from opposite sides of the clearing and plunged down on the unsuspecting raiders. The crackling sound of the fire masked their approach. The Afghan raiders didn't even look up until too late.

Merial saw the first raider go down as she ran toward her father's tent. The fire was beginning to fan out when she reached it, and she snatched up a horse blanket that lay nearby and began to beat out the flames.

An Afridi raider bore down on her as she worked but was cut down by one of the Tiger's *bhaldars.* Merial ignored them both. Coughing, choking against the roiling black smoke, she concentrated on her task. "Father," she called. "Father—"

There was no answer. They'd killed him—or else he'd suffocated from the smoke. Mindless with fear, she beat down the last of the flames, then ran into the dark, smoke-filled tent. "Father!"

This time a racking cough answered her. Merial nearly fainted with relief when she saw Sir Edward struggling feebly to sit up on his cot. "Where did those beggars come from?" he croaked.

She ran across the dirt floor, bent to slip an arm under

his shoulders. "We must leave, Father. Quickly." He blinked at her as she helped him swing his legs over the side of the cot. "Put your arm around my shoulders—lean on me. That's it."

"*Angrezi* pigs!"

Merial looked up at the guttural snarl and saw one of the Afridis standing silhouetted in the tent opening. He looked enormous as he strode forward, sword raised.

Pulling away from Sir Edward, Merial snatched up the first thing she could find to ward off the raider's blow. His savage attack knocked her to her knees, but when his sword bore down a second time, she managed to parry once more. This time her flimsy "weapon" shattered. Defenseless, dazed, she looked up and saw the raider's face, crazed with blood lust, suspended over her. She closed her eyes as his sword went up for the kill.

There was a sound at the tent entrance, a yell of pain. Merial snapped open her eyes in time to see the Afghan raider pitching groundward. A few feet away Prince Rayn was sheathing his sword.

He motioned to her to rise, but, nauseated and numb, she remained kneeling on the blood-soaked earth until he reached down to draw her to her feet. As he did so, he began to laugh. "*Shabash*—that was well done," he told her.

What was there to laugh about? Then she realized that she was holding the stump of Sir Edward's umbrella. "Oh, my God," she murmured, "I tried to stop him from killing us—with this." Laughter, tinged with hysteria, rose to her lips, but she forced it down. This wasn't the time to fall apart.

The Tiger was saying, "The Afridi are dead. There is no longer anything to fear from them."

But Merial knew that their greatest danger didn't come

from the Afridis. In the smoky gloom of the tent she could feel the Tiger's keen eyes watching her.

"What? What's he saying?" Sir Edward mumbled. "Can't understand his gibberish—"

"Father, be quiet," she whispered in frantic English. "It's Narayn of Baranpur." Sir Edward subsided, and she said in Hindustani, "Thank you for our lives. Now I beg you to leave us be. You can see that we're no threat to you."

"There may be more raiders in the area. What then?"

"We'll manage."

Rayn's eyes went to the broken umbrella, and his firm mouth quirked a little. "Can you ride?" he asked.

When she nodded, he went to the tent entrance and called an order. One of his men came running. "Saddle one of the Afridis' horses," the Tiger commanded, "and fashion a litter. We take these two with us."

"*Where* are you taking us?"

The fearful cry seemed wrung out of her. Turning, Rayn saw that she had put a protective arm around the sick man. Something in that gesture reached a part of his heart that he'd forgotten about long ago. He knew that the fear in her voice was not for herself, and this also touched him.

He said almost gently, "You'll come with us. Later I'll send you on your way with an escort."

Reacting more to the change in his voice than to his actual words, Merial sank down on the cot beside Sir Edward. Relief had made her legs feel rubbery. "Do you mean you'll help us?" she whispered. "Really?"

One dark eyebrow arched. "I respect courage wherever I find it. You have my word."

The prince's *bhaldars* worked swiftly. By the time Merial had helped her father out of the tent, a saddled horse was waiting for her. A litter, fashioned from tree branches and covered with a blanket, had been attached to a horse's saddle so that the sick man could be dragged behind one of the riders.

The young lancer captain called Deen helped Merial lift Sir Edward onto the makeshift litter. "We carry our own wounded this way," he explained. "It may not be very comfortable, but it's better than walking."

He sounded sympathetic, so Merial ventured a question. "Where are we going?"

His sympathy faded immediately. "Wherever our prince wants you to go," Deen replied shortly.

She didn't ask any more questions, but as they rode away from the camp and into the forest beyond, Merial felt instinctively that they were heading away from Sri Nevi.

They rode all morning and by afternoon were climbing into a fir-scented wilderness where black-faced monkeys scampered among the deodar pines and wild-eyed Kashmiri stags guarded their gentle does. Merial, riding behind the rider who dragged Sir Edward's litter behind him, had by now lost all sense of direction, but as they went higher, she noticed that there was a change in the Tiger's warriors.

The wariness they'd shown earlier was gone, and they appeared relaxed and jaunty. As they rode, Captain Deen burst into a rollicking love song and was joined by a gigantic *bhaldar* lieutenant whose name was apparently Big Fanji. The two were still singing when the trail they were following broadened into a clearing. It was set with a large tent and several small ones. Near the center of the campsite an old man waited, leaning on a gold-topped staff.

"I knew you were coming for a full fifteen minutes," he scolded. "Only Deen could make a noise to scare the monkeys. I don't know how you put up with him, my prince."

"It's not easy." Rayn's hard face had relaxed into a grin. Dismounting, he threw his arms around the old man, hugged him, and lifted him off the ground. "It's good to see you again, Baju," he said.

The smile softened his hard face, smoothing the harsh lines around his mouth and making him seem younger and much more human. Merial felt more hopeful about his promise of safe conduct.

But would that promise be in time to help her father? Merial dismounted and knelt down by the sick man's litter. As she wiped Sir Edward's forehead, his gray eyes questioned her fretfully. "I'm sorry about that terrible ride," she told him, "but we've stopped now. You can rest, Father."

"Damned *dooli*—shook my bones loose," Sir Edward muttered. "Hell of a way to get to my district. Your mother will be angry I'm so late, Merial."

He had been fading in and out of delirium all day. If he didn't get medical attention, he might sink into a coma from which he'd never recover. Merial looked over her shoulder and saw that Prince Rayn was standing nearby, speaking to the old man, Baju. She bit her lip. Nothing ventured, she thought, nothing won.

The men broke off their talk as she came closer. Was she breaking some rule by approaching him this way? Without waiting to find out, Merial put palm to palm and bowed deeply.

"My father's condition is much worse, and there's nothing I can do to help him," she said. "If you know of any way I could find him a doctor or medicine, I beg you tell me."

Rayn said, "Baju is a physician."

A doctor—here! She swung around to face Baju, but before she could entreat his aid, the old man said, "Some of Prince Rayn's men were wounded in their skirmish with the Afridi. I must care for them, child."

Baju's voice was mild and kindly. Deep-set, twinkling brown eyes under tufted gray eyebrows smiled at her. Looking into them, Merial found the courage to argue. "But those men are not badly hurt," she protested. "My father is desperately ill. Surely—"

Baju turned questioningly to Rayn, who said, "My men must come first."

With a nod he dismissed the old doctor and went on, "It's my rule that my fighters are attended to even before I am myself. When Baju has finishing caring for my men, he'll help your father."

"He might be beyond help by that time!" she cried.

Broad shoulders shrugged. "That's as the gods will," he told her.

With difficulty she bit back the arguments and entreaties that rose to her lips. Knowing how he felt about the English, she knew they'd be futile. At least so far he hadn't forbidden them medical help, and she had to be grateful for that.

"I've had a tent readied for you," Rayn was saying. "You must be tired. It was a long ride and not an easy one."

"I'm more worried than tired," she said frankly, and he smiled and put a hand on her shoulder.

The impulsive reaching out surprised Rayn almost as much as it did her. She startled under his hand, and he could feel the delicate bones of her shoulder go rigid as tension thrummed through her. It was as though every muscle in her slender body was poised for flight, but he knew that she wasn't going to run. As scared as she was, her eyes still went to the litter where her sick father lay.

"It's all right," he told her.

There was something in his deep voice that was strangely reassuring. His hand remained on her shoulder and conveyed strength and, strangely enough, safety. Remembering everything that Lieutenant Hammond had told her about the Tiger, Merial doubted her own sanity. Why should anything Prince Rayn said or did be comforting?

"There's nothing to worry about," Rayn continued. He could feel the tension drain out of her as her eyes swung up to meet his. She had unusual eyes, he thought. Just now they were dark with the effort of controlling her fear, but if she laughed they would probably be the color of a warm, sunwashed sky. Suddenly, irrationally, he wanted to see her smile.

"May I take my father to the tent?" she was asking. She spoke so softly that he had to strain to make out her words. She was exhausted. He'd meant to question her—as of now he didn't even know her name—but that could wait. Rayn gave the slender shoulder he held a gentle shake.

"Go and rest," he said.

He nodded to Deen, who came forward to lead her to her tent. As Merial followed the jaunty officer, she glanced over her shoulder and watched the Tiger walking among his lancers. She couldn't miss the way their fierce faces brightened at their leader's attention and thought, they're like sunflowers turning to the sun. That surprised her. Somehow, she hadn't expected Narayn of Baranpur to be so loved.

What kind of man *was* this warrior prince? She wondered about this as Deen helped settle her father on a pile of blankets and brought her a basin of water. Though unquestionably a man to fear, Prince Rayn wasn't the demon she'd pictured. And though the big hand that had clasped her shoulder had been strong, it had also been unexpectedly gentle.

A gentle tiger? Merial's tired mind grappled with that incongruity as she sponged her feverish father down and got him to drink a little water. Time passed, and the sunlight that crept through the tent flap changed from pale yellow to dusty gold, then took on ruddy sunset colors. Now, outside, she could hear the Muslim chant—*lā ilāha illa Allāh*—there is no God but God—mingling with the ritual Hindu prayers attending the lighting of lamps.

Hindus believed that light was a manifestation of God, and "bringing on the light" was a nightly ceremony as lamps were lit to replace the dying sunlight. Merial wasn't at all sure what she believed in, but she closed her eyes and spoke to Whoever was there. "Please," she begged, "help my father. Send the doctor quickly."

As if in answer to her prayers, footsteps approached the tent. But instead of the doctor, Deen stood in the tent opening. "Prince Rayn wants to speak to you," he announced.

"Why?"

The *bhaldar* captain shrugged.

"I don't want to leave my father," Merial persisted. "Can't this wait until the doctor comes?"

"It's wrong to keep the prince waiting," Deen pointed out.

It was also dangerous. Merial got to her feet and was suddenly aware of her appearance. Lacking comb or mirror, she'd pulled her heavy, dark hair into a knot at the base of her slender neck, but her clothes were beyond help. Her once-white shirt and dark, dusty riding skirt were singed and torn. Since she'd left all their baggage at the campsite, there was no way to change.

Nervously Merial smoothed her skirts and touched a hand to her hair. She saw that Deen was watching her impatiently, and a spurt of irritation made her ask in English, "Do I look ready for a royal audience?" He stared at her uncomprehending, and she lifted her chin. "To the devil with all of you. I'm ready."

Outside, her defiance weakened, and by the time they'd reached the Tiger's tent, her heart had begun to thump in a cowardly way. When Deen motioned her to enter the prince's large tent, she hesitated.

Perhaps because of the danger she was in, this twilight seemed more beautiful than any she could remember seeing. The sky above them glowed like a dark opal, and the air was full of the scent of campfires and oil and spices and incense. Surely, *surely* if Rayn had wanted to harm them, he'd have done so before this?

Merial squared her shoulders and walked into the Tiger's lair. There was nothing luxurious or princely about the royal tent—she saw this immediately. A smoky torch lit its spartan darkness, showing a carpet that covered the earthen floor, bedding of furs and woven blankets. The prince's weapons—dagger, sword, rifle—were stacked neatly against a near wall. For furniture there was only a simple wooden table set with fruit and surrounded by thick cushions and chairs.

Prince Rayn was sitting on one of the chairs. He'd changed into a loose-fitting, white kaftan that covered the expanse of his broad shoulders and chest and flowed almost to the ground. Instead of riding boots he now wore shoes of soft dark leather. There was the glint of a gold ornament around his bronzed neck.

The change in clothing did nothing to soften the force

of the man, Merial thought, but it altered that power somehow. Before, he'd been a warrior prince, rock-hard and implacable. Now there was an added dimension to him. She hadn't been aware, before, that Rayn's eyes were the color of honeyed wine or that his fine lips held a sensuous curve.

Torchlight spun a silken sheen across the gold of his bare arms and throat, shadowed the beginning of crisp-curling dark chest fur, still damp from a recent bath. He was the same man who had terrified her back on the mountain trail, and yet he was different. Merial didn't know what this difference meant, but she was sure of one thing. The silken Tiger taking his royal ease before her was as dangerous as the one made out of steel.

"You asked to see me," she began.

"Sit down." From the wary way in which she obeyed and from her pallor, Rayn could tell that she feared him and that she was determined not to show that fear. "How long has it been since you ate?" he demanded.

"This morning—last night—it really doesn't matter."

"I can't have you sickening, too. Food will be ready soon. Meanwhile . . ." He indicated the fruit. She looked away. "Are you worried about breaking bread with an enemy?" he asked.

"*Are* you our enemy?"

He smiled at her flash of spirit. "Try some fruit and see." She swallowed hard as he selected the largest apple and offered it. "Perhaps the English have told you I poison my guests?"

There was a new note in his voice. Afraid that he'd be insulted if she didn't take the fruit, Merial reached for it. Her fingers grazed his as the apple changed hands, and the impact of that touch was disconcerting. Though only a shadow-touch, the warmth of his strong fingers seemed to seep through her skin and tremble through her blood.

She covered her reaction by taking a cautious bite of fruit. It was sweet and crisp. In fact, it was delicious. Merial took a much larger bite of the apple.

Rayn nodded approvingly as he watched her devour the fruit. When she'd done, he offered another, and this time she didn't hesitate. "I didn't realize how hungry I was," she apologized.

She looked very young sitting there and apologizing for being hungry. In spite of her rumpled attire, there was a freshness about her, a youthful vitality that made her untidiness somehow endearing. A wave of blue-black hair had escaped the heavy knot at the base of her neck and hung across her cheek, and Rayn found himself wanting to smooth back that silky lock and trace his fingertips over the cream-white skin. When she licked the juice from her lips, his eyes followed the curl of her pink tongue against the curve of her mouth.

A desire to kiss that mouth came out of nowhere and hit him hard. Rayn felt as if he'd been knocked sideways by a lightning bolt. No stranger to desire, he was astonished at the explosive force of the heat that coursed through him. The fact that this was an *Angrezi* woman made no difference.

Merial felt the intensity of Rayn's gaze. She wanted to look away from him, but wasn't able to do so. Watching the play of powerful muscles under his kaftan, she was reminded of riding pressed against his hard body.

It was an uncomfortable memory. A slow warmth, never before imagined or felt, seeped through her and left her shaken. Good Lord, what was the matter with her? But of course she was hungry and exhausted. Before she became even more light-headed, she'd better learn why he summoned her.

"Your *bhaldar* said you wanted to see me," she challenged.

Rayn reminded himself that this woman and her father were under his protection and that the law of hospitality couldn't be violated even for English people.

"I need to know more about you," he said. She looked so frightened at this that he hurried to explain. "I must know where you are going if I am going to send you on your way."

Merial wanted to weep with relief. For a moment she'd feared he was going to go back on his promise. She began to tell him where they were going and then stopped. She'd forgotten how much Prince Rayn hated Sri Nevi and Hamilton Perce and his railroad.

"My father is too sick to travel," she hedged.

"Baju will take care of that. When he is well enough to travel, where will you go?"

More frightened than she'd ever been, she searched desperately for a lie. She couldn't find one. "We are going to Sri Nevi," she told him.

She should have lied. She knew that the second she'd spoken. Immediately the warmth in his eyes flickered out and was replaced by a chill wariness.

"Is your father connected with Hamilton Perce?"

Unwillingly, she nodded.

"He's to work on Perce's railroad, then."

"My father used to be commissioner of Sri Nevi before the rebellion. Mr. Perce thought that his knowledge of the people would be an asset—"

She broke off as, with a swift catlike movement, he swung to his feet and stood glaring down at her.

"What is your name?" he demanded.

She told him and watched his face change again, saw the astonishment and disbelief in his narrowed eyes give way to an expression that terrified her.

"I've heard of *Commissioner* Ashland." Suddenly, with a swift, catlike movement, he swung to his feet and stood glaring down at her. "He was corrupt and incompetent. A criminal, in fact. If I'd known who he was, I'd have let the Afridi burn him alive."

Even in her terror she was stung by his contempt. "You gave me your word to help us!" she cried. "Does your honor mean so little?"

"Honor!" he roared. She flinched as he walked toward her, then gasped. His kaftan had shifted, and she could see clearly the ornament he wore around his throat.

She'd have known the amulet anywhere. That rough golden nugget and that exquisite moonstone had pursued her through a thousand dreams. "Where did you get that amulet?" she cried.

"What in hell's name are you talking about?"

"That amulet—it belonged to my friend Niall St. Marr. He wore it always." Forgetting her fear, she pleaded, "Where is he? Do you know what's happened to him?"

There was silence for a heartbeat's space. Then—"I took this amulet from a dead *Angrezi,*" the Tiger said coolly.

Dead, dead—the echo went on endlessly in her brain. It stirred memories awake. Once again she felt Niall's strong hand guiding her across the pass, heard his clear young voice. All this time she had known he was dead, had to be dead, yet now it was as if she'd heard the terrible news for the first time.

Pain surged through her and drove out common sense. "You stole from the dead!" She flung at him. "Oh, *sha-bash,* Prince. Well done, indeed."

Angrily he said, "I don't rob dead men. I took the amulet from a man I killed in fair fight near the Gujjar Pass. When he saw me, he lifted his rifle to shoot me—but his aim was bad."

White teeth glinted in a fierce smile. "After I'd killed him, I saw this amulet around his neck. No Englishman has the right to wear this—it's meant only for princes. He must have been a thief."

"Oh, dear God," she sobbed.

That explained why Niall's body had never been found. They'd all thought him dead, but by some miracle, Niall had survived. Survived, that is, until he'd met the Tiger.

And the Tiger had killed him. He was proud of it. His face glowed with a remembered satisfaction. Anger such as she'd never known before shook Merial. She had only one thought in her mind as she lunged toward the wall where the weapons were stacked.

She was quick, but he was swifter still. Before she could snatch up the dagger, he was beside her. One big hand grasped hers in a viselike grip, twisting it so cruelly that she cried out in pain.

"Not so fast, Lady Ashland."

"You murdering bastard!" she cried. "You said you killed a *man*. Niall wasn't a man, just a wounded, frightened boy. How brave you must be to attack boys and sick men and women—"

"All this virtuous indignation from Edward Ashland's daughter?" he jeered.

"How dare you speak like that? You aren't good enough to wipe Father's boots." She saw the warning flash in his eyes but wouldn't stop. "My father is an honorable man, but you'd never understand that. You're just a *budmarsh*. I hope the English catch you and hang you like the ruffian you are—"

"Be silent!"

She saw murder in his eyes and something else that frightened her even more. She'd angered the Tiger, roused his instinct to kill. Well, damn him to hell, *let* him kill her as he'd killed Niall. She wouldn't give him the satisfaction of so much as a whimper—and she'd fight him to the end.

She tried. She kicked and pounded against his hardness until her fists ached, until his arms tightened so cruelly that she could hardly breathe. Then, sobbing for breath, she hung half-fainting in his grip.

"Your father I may kill," he told her. "But women have other uses."

His voice was a soft, feral snarl. It made her spine crawl. Then she saw the heat in his eyes. Black terror made her cry out—once—before his lips came down on hers and drowned out the sound.

·· Three ··

SHE COULDN'T TWIST free. Couldn't move. One of his hands was riveted to the base of her skull, while the other arm gripped her around the waist, and this strangle-hold made it almost impossible to breathe. Instinctively Merial sought oxygen by parting her lips, but instead of needed air there was the invasion of Rayn's tongue. That ruthless violation created shockwaves that penetrated to her bones.

There was a roaring in her ears and her surroundings began to dim. Merial prayed that she could faint, but even this questionable mercy was denied her. As the rest of the world faded, *he* became more real. There was nothing else in her universe but the flex of hard-muscled arms, the tense, powerful body, the pitiless demand of his mouth.

Without slackening his hold on her, he'd undone the knot at the nape of her neck. Released, the dark silk fell about them both, and Rayn began to caress Merial's cheek and throat and shoulder until his fingertips just grazed her breast.

His touch brought madness. It seeped through the flimsy barriers of cloth and skin and invaded her veins and nerves. When the shadow-caress was repeated, Merial felt as though her bones were beginning to disintegrate. With her last fragments of sanity she willed herself to die.

He could sense what she hoped for, but death would be too easy for Commissioner Ashland's daughter. Anger such as he had never known before was coursing through Rayn. He had never wanted to destroy anyone as he wanted to crush this *Angrezi* woman. When he thought of the contempt he'd seen in her eyes, he wanted to make her suffer.

She was no coward, he'd give her that. She'd tried to resist him, but now there was no fight left in her. When he caressed her breasts again, she didn't struggle, and as his stroking fingers became more insistent, a low moan escaped her. Rayn knew that he'd broken her will, and that she was now his to kill or enjoy.

By now beyond conscious thought, Merial still sensed the change in him. His savage grip eased, and for the first time he took his mouth away from hers. Released from that terrifying kiss, she gulped for air and drew in his clean, vital scent.

"Please," she whispered, "don't."

As though he hadn't heard that craven whimper, Rayn began to trace kisses along the corners of her mouth, her temples, then move down to the hollow of her throat. Lightly he brushed her bruised mouth with his lips.

In response to his tantalizing caresses, Merial's body seemed to change. Her breasts, pressed against his hard chest, felt heavy, and her breath came in shallow gasps. She felt as dizzy as if she'd been drugged.

"You are a rare flower." Rayn's voice was a deep purr. His tongue tip traced the periphery of her mouth, and her powerless lips parted. With tantalizing slowness, his tongue relearned the satin of her inner mouth.

She didn't have any resistence left to offer. She was trapped in a maelstrom of sensations she'd never before guessed at. Dark fire whirled through her veins, stroking her quivering nerve ends until she actually craved the pitiless, wonderful invasion of his tongue. She no longer fought for air but was content to draw in the air from his lungs.

Rayn felt Merial trembling and intuited that she wasn't shivering from fear. Leisurely he let his hands glide down her body, exploring the slope of her shoulder, the slender line of her waist, the gentle rounding of her hips.

"Yes," he murmured, "a beautiful *Angrezi* rose."

Something in the tone of his voice slashed through the muzziness in Merial's mind. Prince Rayn had murdered Niall. He had broken his word to her. A few moments ago she had wanted to kill him.

His deliberate seduction of her was just one more act of the Tiger's hate, and yet she lay a willing prisoner in his arms—horror blasted through her like a cleansing wind.

"Let me *go*—"

He released her so suddenly that she stumbled and nearly fell backward. Recovering, she backed away from him until she felt the coarse cloth of his tent against her back. Then, stopping, she swallowed the lump that blocked her throat and forced herself to face him.

Rayn had no idea why he didn't simply stride across to her and pull her back into his arms. His powerful body pulsed with unslaked desire. He had wanted to crush Merial Ashland, humiliate her, but when he'd held her slender, proud young body against him, he had come close to forgetting who she was or how much he hated her kind.

Every nerve in his powerful body ached for release, and yet he had allowed her to break away from him. Rayn frowned, caught in emotions that he didn't care to analyze.

"Wh-what do you intend to do with my father?" she was asking.

He was grateful for the returning rush of anger. "What we always do to *Angrezi* criminals," he replied harshly.

The moonstone at his throat glowed like a cat's eye, and Merial's heart clenched like a fist. "*You* are the criminal." She tried to shout out the words, but they came out in a strangled whisper. "You murdered him."

He glared at her for a moment, then shouted a command. Deen must have been standing with his back to the flap, for he appeared on the instant. "Take this woman away," the Tiger snarled. "She and her precious father will return to Baranpur with us. The rana will know what to do with his *Angrezi* prisoners."

Furiously Merial cried, "I should have known that your word meant nothing."

Deen's hand flew to the knife stuck into his belt, but Rayn stopped him. "We're at war," he told Merial. "All's fair in love and war—as you *Angrezi* say."

Muttering under his breath, Dean grasped Merial by the wrist and hauled her out of the prince's tent. Darkness had fallen, and the campfires glowed like feral eyes. When they reached the Ashlands' tent, Merial saw two *bhaldars* standing guard. One was a small, leathery little man. The other was the oxlike lieutenant, Fanji.

Deen jerked open the tent flap and snarled, "Get in."

She pulled her hand loose from his grasp and faced him. "I suppose we're to be killed in Baranpur," she flared.

"It is for the rana to say," the scarred youth snapped back. His eyes blazed as he added, "If he hadn't stopped me, you'd be dead already for questioning Prince Rayn's honor."

"Merial? Is that you, Merial?"

Responding to her father's feeble cry, Merial turned her back on Deen and went quickly through the tent flap. It was then she realized that Sir Edward wasn't alone.

The old doctor, Baju, was seated beside the native string cot on which Sir Edward lay. He was dressed simply in a clean white tunic, his staff lay at his feet, and he smiled a pleasant welcome at Merial.

She hadn't expected that the doctor would be there. Nor had she foreseen that there would be a simple meal of curds and lentils and cups of buttermilk. The thought touched her mind that a prisoner in Newgate Prison in England might receive far worse treatment.

Then she remembered what awaited them in Baranpur. Biting her lower lip to keep it from trembling, she concentrated on her father. Sir Edward's eyes were closed, and he appeared to be asleep. She also noted that he'd been laid on a mattress of what appeared to be thin slabs of wood.

"What is this, *hakim?*" she whispered.

The old man's face wrinkled into a smile. "No, do not call me 'doctor,' child. I am known as *Baju*—grandfather—to all. There is no ice here, so I ordered a young banana tree to be cut down. Sliced thinly and soaked in water, the stalk can be used to cool fever." He paused. "But your father is a very sick man. He was not well or strong before the fever came, am I right?"

She was so tired, so heart-sore and worried, that Baju's gentleness brought tears to her eyes. She knuckled them away before nodding.

"Then why endure a long sea voyage?" Baju wanted to know.

He patted a stool beside him, and she sat down wearily. "After my mother died, he was restless. And he was not lucky in speculations. Soon there was no money left, and we had to sell our properties, one after another until nothing was left. We were desperate when Mr. Perce wrote, offering my father the position of deputy commissioner of railroads."

Remembering Prince Rayn's hatred of Perce, she stopped abruptly, but the old doctor only said, "I do not ask out of idle curiosity. A doctor must know his patient, for if a man's body ails, his soul is often also ill. What troubles your father?"

"He was sick because there were so many debts and no money to pay them. Mr. Perce's offer put new life in him. He used to be commissioner of Sri Nevi before the uprising. He knew here was a chance to prove himself."

Baju mused, "Your father has no love for India. His ramblings have told me as much. But you feel differently, my daughter."

Eyes, hooded as an old turtle's, seemed to look deep into Merial's heart. They reminded her of her old nurse, Jassmina. "Sri Nevi was the first home I knew," she replied. "I sometimes feel as if I never had another."

The string bed creaked as Sir Edward turned. Merial tensed, but Baju said soothingly, *"Nini,* child, rest. I have made an infusion of herbs and honey which will make him sleep and sweat out the infection."

"Then he'll recover?"

He nodded, and her heart eased momentarily before despair returned. Given Khem-Rana's hatred of English people, it really didn't matter whether Sir Edward recovered or not.

Bluntly she asked, "Why should you heal my father when Prince Rayn intends that we both be killed in Baranpur?"

"It is not for you to question your fate—or the prince's

will." A stern note crept into Baju's voice as he added, "He does nothing without a reason."

"Oh, I'm sure of *that.* "

Ignoring the bitterness in Merial's voice, Baju continued, "Prince Rayn is many things. He can be as fearless as a young tiger in battle, but he is also wise. His enemies fear him, but he gives his people justice and love."

In the shadows thrown by the flickering, smoking torch, Baju looked almost reverent as he continued to extol his prince's virtues. According to the doctor, the prince was loved by his people even more than was his father.

"The King of Kings is just but hard. He is a rana made of iron. In his time victory could only be gained by battle, and so he still follows the way of the sword. Prince Rayn realizes that that time is over and is wise enough to want peace for his people."

From what she'd seen, Narayn of Baranpur didn't strike her as a peaceful man. "He hates the English," Merial pointed out, "and the English control India."

"You *Angrezi* will come—and go." Dismissing British rule, Baju snapped his fingers. "There is a legend among us foretelling the coming of Prince Rayn."

He began to tell Merial that once Baranpur was a beautiful place and all the beasts of the mountains and jungles wanted it. They fought against one another until it seemed as though Baranpur would be drowned with blood.

"Then," Baju recounted, "a great tiger came out of the Pir Panjal mountains. His pelt was gold, and he was the most powerful animal that had ever been seen. He subdued the other animals and ruled them wisely, and ever after there was peace." He paused to add significantly, "Many consider Prince Rayn to be the golden tiger who will bring peace and prosperity to our country."

As Merial wiped the sweat from her father's face, she

remembered the expression in the prince's eyes when he learned who she was. No matter what he might want for Baranpur, she thought bleakly, peace was the last thing the Ashlands were likely to find in the Tiger's lair.

"Sun, Anger, and the deities presiding over Anger, save me from sins committed through anger—"

The two *bhaldars* outside the tent were reciting the morning prayer. Listening, Merial knew that prayers were useless. She had prayed her heart out for Niall that day of the Gujjar Pass, and yet he'd died at the Tiger's hand.

The tent flap was pulled back, and Big Fanji shoved his bullet-shaped head through the opening. "The prince has commanded that we leave at once. Best you get ready, *Angrezi.*"

Big Fanji looked ferocious in the predawn darkness, and it took all her courage to ask, "How long a journey will it be?"

"That depends on how swiftly our lord wants us to travel. We've covered the distance in a day during emergencies."

Such speed would kill her father. Sir Edward was sleeping now, lulled by Baju's herbal drink, but he was still hot and feverish. She wanted to fill the tent with her protests but knew they would be useless.

Meanwhile, there was a favor she needed to ask. "I've used up the water," she said. "Can you get us some?" The big lancer hesitated, and she added, "If we faint along the way, it'll delay you."

"There's that." Big Fanji shrugged mountainous shoulders, tramped into the tent, picked up the bucket, and strode away.

Merial closed her eyes against the ache in her temples. She had snatched a few moments of sleep last night, but fear had followed her into her dreams. "I mustn't show fear," she whispered to herself. "That would make things even worse. And perhaps it will not be so bad."

Her words slid away as the tent flap was flung back, but instead of the big *bhaldar,* Rayn stood silhouetted against the faint gray light. Lamplight winked fire along his tulwar, but the curved blade wasn't any more menacing than the look he turned on the sick man. "So," he said, "he has lived through the night."

Any hope that Baju's words may have given her died. In the Tiger's eyes his English prisoners had already been tried and condemned.

What their sentence would be, she didn't know. Imprisonment for her father—or perhaps he would be held for ransom. Merial didn't want to think of the next possibility, but the word forced itself into her mind. Sir Edward could very well be dead soon.

Despair gave her courage. "If only he could rest for a day—"

He glanced at her, and that speculative golden look silenced her. Whatever happened to Sir Edward, his sentence would be easy compared to what awaited her. Prince Rayn had demonstrated, last night, that death wasn't the ultimate evil that could befall a woman.

Remembering last night, Merial felt her cheeks flame. Instinctively, as though this gesture could expunge what had happened, she scrubbed her mouth with the back of her hand.

"God have mercy on us," she whispered.

"Amen," he replied gravely. "We are breaking camp in fifteen minutes," he added. "Even though he deserves to be dragged to Baranpur in chains, I am going to allow Ashland a litter."

Was she supposed to thank him? "May I ride beside my father?" Merial asked woodenly.

"Why not? You'll be easier to guard that way." His teeth flashed in that white, hateful Tiger's grin. "It will be a long ride. Perhaps your father won't survive it."

"You bastard." But she didn't dare do more than whisper it as he strode out of the tent. "Oh, you mocking, murdering bastard. I hope the English soldiers catch you and hang you someday."

But for now that was a forlorn hope. Prince Rayn was invincible. And, as she mounted a horse and took her place beside her father's litter some minutes later, she realized how completely powerless she was. Narayn of Baranpur would murder them, and not even the bravest Englishman would dare to bring the Tiger to justice.

The thought stayed with her as they followed a trail into the mountains. As they climbed higher, the air turned cooler, and the terrain became more rugged. Was Baranpur built on the very top of the mountain?

Perhaps so, for they kept on climbing. As they did, they met many of the prince's subjects. Goat herders greeted them along the way, rangy, sun-darkened people who bowed respectfully to the prince and his party. Even higher, turbaned men in dark clothes and women in colorful, open-necked tunics and enormously wide pantaloons shouted greetings and blessings. "Welcome home, *Yuveraj*—crown prince," one woman called. "The hills have been lonely for you."

Rayn stopped to talk for a moment, and the people crowded close, respectfully touching his booted foot in gestures that were as much loving as reverential. Merial was surprised when she heard Rayn speak to them in friendly fashion, often calling people by name and asking questions about their families. When they rode on at last, blessings followed the prince.

This scene was repeated again and again. People held up their babies so that they could see the Tiger and gazed wide-eyed at the English woman who rode beside the litter. "Is she your woman, Prince Rayn?" one toothless old woman questioned impudently, and she hooted when the older lancer captain, Rassul, bade her hold her tongue. "Why? The prince is a fine, hot-blooded young man, and the *Angrezi* isn't bad to look upon except for those blue eyes."

They rode until noon when they stopped to water the horses at a small village nestled high on the side of the hills. While the horses drank at a nearby stream, the villagers left their terraced farms and vied with one another to make their prince welcome. The headman, a short, self-important little man in a turban too big for him, came out to plead that Prince Rayn and his *bhaldars* rest and eat.

"Stay, Shield of the Kingdom, and do us honor," he begged. "We heard of your arrival hours ago, and the women have been cooking and cooking."

The air was indeed full of the delicious smell of curry and savory steamed rice cakes. Merial's empty stomach rumbled, and she was grateful when Deen stroked his faint mustache and sighed, "Lord, the gods would not like it if so many beautiful women were disappointed."

"You mean that you'd like a chance to seduce the prettier ones," Big Fanji growled. "But please, lord, let's stop anyway. I'm so hungry I could devour my own horse."

Merial had never felt so grateful when she heard Rayn give the order to dismount. She had lost her hat long since, and her skin felt blistered by the hot sun. And if she felt badly, how must Sir Edward be?

"Is it permitted for me to dismount?" she asked her

guards. The small *bhaldar,* Chetak, ignored her. Big Fanji nodded indifferently but made no motion to help her dismount.

As she slid down from her horse, Merial realized that all of her limbs ached. They protested even more as she led her father's horse into the shade of a thicket of pines. As she did so, he opened his eyes and tried to focus on her face.

"Water, for God's sake."

Prince Rayn's men were already drinking heartily from water jugs proffered by the village women. Merial hesitated only a moment before approaching the nearest group of *bhaldars.*

"Sister," she said to one of the women, "will one of you lend me a jug so that I may give my father some water?"

A little girl moved as if to offer her jug, but was instantly checked by her mother. The woman drew the child closer while hissing warnings about those devils, the *Angrezi.* "They are wicked people who killed Prince Bikaner, don't you remember?" she muttered.

"*Angrezi* are rich," a man's mocking voice added. "She should pay for the use of a pot."

Glancing over her shoulder, Merial saw that a burly young man was standing near Sir Edward's litter. "Look at this feeble specimen," the young fellow jeered. "He looks like a plucked chicken instead of a mighty sahib."

As a small crowd gathered around Sir Edward, the sick man's voice rose in broken Hindustani. "Mutinous blackguards. Keep your hands off me or you'll be punished."

Rayn looked up at the jeering laughter that followed this remark. He was seated on a pile of cushions under a huge deodar pine, and a woman was holding a basin of water so that he could wash his royal hands. Merial hadn't thought she could hate him any more than she already did until she saw the mockery in his eyes.

"Are the proud *Angrezis* reduced to begging?" the Tiger drawled.

"My father is sick and needs water. You'd give as much to a stray dog on the road." She'd hurled that defiance at the Tiger, but it was the older of the lancer captains—the one called Rassul—who responded. Taking a half-full water jug from one of the women, he handed it to Merial.

"In the name of God, the All Compassionate," he said gravely, "ease your father's thirst and your own."

"Leave go of me, you—get your hands off me!" Sir Edward's hoarse shout cut short Merial's thanks. "Give it back, you *dacoit,* you filthy thief!"

Struggling to sit up, he pointed to the burly young man who had taunted Merial earlier. "That fellow stole my watch," he accused.

The young fellow scowled. "Stop lying, *Angrezi.*"

Was Sir Edward delirious? But Merial saw that the chain from which his watch always hung was bare. Anger flared in her as she faced the grinning young man.

"You robbed him."

The man she'd accused balled his big hands into fists. "How dare you speak to me like that? You *Angrezi* dogs lie whenever you open your mouths. Best be quiet, or I'll shut you up for good."

His voice was thick with menace, but Sir Edward was too sick, or too stubborn, to hold his peace. "I'm not going to let that wog get away with it, I tell you. When I tell Perce Sahib, he'll be flogged."

"What is the meaning of this commotion?"

Everyone went silent as Prince Rayn strode into the center of the rapidly growing group. "Rassul, did you see what happened?"

The middle-aged *bhaldar* shook his head. "No, lord. The prisoner says that this man has stolen his watch, and the accusation was denied. That's all I know."

The accused thief slapped his chest. "I, Aliwar Gangur, would never steal from even an English pig."

Sir Edward stuttered, "Tell him, Merial. When you were over there asking the women for water, I felt his hand on me—"

He broke off, coughing, and Merial begged, "Leave it, Father. Please."

"No one's going to steal something that's rightfully mine," Sir Edward whined. "Thieving wogs—can't trust any of them." In Hindustani he added, "You're all thieves and murderers."

Something cold and deadly seemed to flash in Rayn's eyes. He took a step toward the Englishman, and his arm arced back as if to strike. Merial wedged herself between the Tiger and her father.

"He's a sick man," she pleaded. "He doesn't know what he's saying."

For a heartbeat's time tawny eyes held hers, and she felt almost physically sick with fear until the Tiger turned to the assembled villagers. "Did any of you witness this supposed theft?" he demanded. "Speak the truth."

No one moved or spoke, but Merial noted that almost everyone avoided their prince's eye. His expression hardened as he said, "Even stealing from an *Angrezi* is against our law. You are my people. Your actions touch my *izzat*—my honor."

The burly young fellow had turned pale. He began to edge away, but Rassul and another *bhaldar* caught him by the arms. "Search him," Rayn ordered.

Swiftly he was stripped and searched. A low murmur ran through the villagers as Rassul held up something that glinted in the sun. "The *Angrezi* didn't lie, lord. Here is the watch."

In the deathly silence that followed, Merial heard a woman begin to wail. The thief had lost his insolent look and was stuttering explanations. He hadn't taken the watch—he would not do such a thing—he had merely leaned over the Englishman. Perhaps his cursed watch had fallen into the folds of his tunic—

"Silence," Rayn commanded. "This affects the honor of your village, too," he told the headman.

The little man fell on his knees. "Heaven Born, he is my sister's worthless son," he stammered. "Have mercy, Shield of the Kingdom. He has a wife and child."

"He should have thought of that before he broke the law." Hearing that stern voice, the thief fell on his knees and knocked his head against the earth.

"I didn't steal from one of us. He's just a prisoner. Have mercy on me."

Inexorably, Rayn drew the wicked, curved tulwar from his side. "A thief loses a hand," he decreed. "Is that not the law?"

The villagers murmured, "It is the law," and the headman began to weep.

"It is the law," he moaned.

Merial's heart was thumping so hard that it seemed ready to burst through her ribs. She watched in uttermost horror as Big Fanji rolled forward, threw the thief on the ground, and pinned him down. Rassul then knelt down beside the man, grasped the thief's right arm, and extended it.

Into the horrible silence that followed, the little girl who had moved to help Merial earlier wailed.

"Father—"

The pain in that one word got through to Merial, and,

picking up her skirts, she ran toward the prince. "Please, stop this."

Rayn didn't even look at her. "Don't interfere."

"I'll *give* him the watch. It's not important—"

This time he half turned so that she could see his face. His eyes were hard, and yet for a moment Merial thought she could see regret in them. "The watch has nothing to do with it," Rayn said. "He has broken our laws."

"Surely justice must be tempered with mercy," she argued. "That man would never think of stealing from you or your men. Because you hate the English as you do, he thought it was permissible." Rayn didn't react to this, and she snatched at something Niall had once told her. "Isn't it the code of your own lawgiver, Manu, that you may not wound others or do others an injury in thought or deed?"

Rayn paused. Then, so swiftly that it seemed only a flash of light, he raised and brought down his curved sword. The thief yelled as the prince's tulwar sliced off his right ear.

"You will carry the mark of your dishonor always," Rayn decreed. "Thus everyone will know that you are a thief and a fool." He added to Rassul and Fanji, "Let him go."

The man crawled away, bleeding and blubbering. As the wide-eyed villagers parted to let him pass, Rayn spoke sternly to the whey-faced village head. "If he breaks any other law, he must die. You'll see to it that my will is carried out."

The headman groveled in the dust. "It will be as you have said, Great Prince. I thank you for your great mercy, Favored Son."

Merial realized that she was trembling uncontrollably. She'd been sure that Rayn had been about to cut off the thief's hand. Had he been merciful because the man had stolen from English prisoners and not from his own kind?

As if he'd read her thoughts, the Tiger turned to her. "What I did was for my people—so they wouldn't become criminals like you *Angrezi,*" he said sternly. "Otherwise, I wouldn't have lifted a finger to help either of you."

He tossed Sir Edward's watch into the dust, then turned to his grim-faced *bhaldars.* "Mount up—we've got prisoners to deliver to the rana."

·· Four ··

THAT AFTERNOON THEY climbed a winding road that led higher into the Pir Panjal mountains. Sir Edward dozed intermittently, then woke to curse his jolting litter, the hot sun, and his daughter for not bringing him water. Merial ached in each separate bone. Drained by the scene she had just witnessed, it was all she could do to sit her horse as it plodded up the trail.

He had no such problem. Merial glared at Rayn's broad back, resenting the arrogant ease with which he sat his stallion. He was riding some distance ahead with his captains and looked to be as vigorous as when he'd started this morning. So did his men. "Does he intend to ride all day and night?" she muttered.

"It is most unlikely since there is no need for haste." Baju had dropped back to check on Sir Edward's condition. "The prince will probably order that we make camp after we cross the Bridge of Winds."

As he spoke, the path before them widened, and the hills seemed to part. Merial drew a deep breath, scented with deodar pine and wild roses, as she looked down the sheer cliffside. Miles below them, surrounded by a range of snow-topped hills and threaded through by a river, lay a valley. An aquamarine lake sparked at its heart.

"That is Baranpur," Baju said with obvious pride. "Rasgani, our capital city, is built around the lake you see. The river is the Azara, which is a tributary of the mighty Jhelum River."

For an unthinking moment Merial was enraptured by the beauty of the emerald valley. Then Baju added, "And here is the Bridge of Winds."

The winding mountain path they had followed for so long came to an abrupt end some three hundred yards away and was resumed on a downward spiral on the hillside directly opposite them. Connecting the two peaks was a bridge made of rope and wooden logs. It looked to be four or five yards across and nearly three hundred yards long. As Merial stared at it, it swayed slowly in the wind.

The bridge was a place of nightmares. "The horses will never cross that—that thing!" Merial exclaimed.

"Not ordinary horses, maybe, but Prince Rayn and his *bhaldars* ride Kumari-bred steeds."

Rayn called an order, and his *bhaldars* dismounted. Leading their horses, they followed their captains onto the bridge. It rocked alarmingly, and Merial closed her eyes.

"The prince crosses last," Baju was saying. "It is his way to see to the safety of his men before his own."

"Apparently, the great Prince Rayn can do no wrong," she snapped.

As if he had heard, Rayn turned his head and looked directly at her, and Merial flinched before the impact of that hard look. It held both mockery and challenge, and she realized that by some demonic telepathy the Tiger sensed her terror of heights.

Deliberately he trotted his stallion closer to her. "So," he drawled, "you've lost your nerve."

She clenched her hands, and Rayn's teeth flashed in a white grin as he watched her bosom heave with emotion. "If you're going to faint like a useless memsahib bitch," he taunted, "I'll leave you here for the tigers and jackals."

"You can go to straight to hell."

She had spoken in English, but he'd evidently understood her tone. His grin disappeared, and he commanded sharply, "Then get on with it."

Glaring at him, she said, "I want to see my father cross first. How do I know you won't abandon him?"

Baju looked horrified, but Rayn only motioned to one of his *bhaldars,* who took the bridle of the litter-drawing horse and led it toward the bridge.

Knowing there was now no hope of reprieve, Merial still couldn't move. Baju said kindly, "My prince, some of us are afraid of high places. It is no sin. Didn't the gods make all of us different? I will go first and show her how safe the bridge is."

"As you wish." Rayn dismounted and held out a hand to help Merial dismount. She would have liked to ignore his offer of help, but long hours in the saddle had left her stiff and sore. Involuntarily she clutched at the hard, sun-browned arms that lifted her effortlessly from the saddle. For a fragment of a second she felt the iron of his grip and was pressed against his powerful body. Then he let her go.

"Well?" Rayn prodded.

She had been so intent on the Tiger that she had forgotten about the bridge. Now it loomed ahead of her again, and the old fears that had tormented so many nightmares came gibbering back. The black night, and the narrow pass, the *budmarshes* at her back. "Hurry, Meri," Niall had said, "or the ruffians will catch you." And now they had her.

"Oh, my God," she muttered, "I can't do it."

"Your father's litter is nearing the center of the bridge."
Baju's voice broke through her memories. "Come, lead
your horse like this. You mustn't anger our lord."

Your lord, not mine—but defiance died as she stepped
onto the bridge. What if the ropes broke? What if she lost
her footing and fell through the openings in the side of
the bridge? Merial glanced down—and wished she hadn't.

A wind gusted up and shook the planks under her feet,
and Merial's stomach lurched. She almost turned to run
back and then heard Rayn laughing at her back. That
hard, ironic bark of laughter made her realize she had no
place to run to. Gritting her teeth, she concentrated on
the mountainside at the other end of the bridge and took
another step forward.

"That's it," Baju encouraged over his shoulder.
"There's nothing to fear."

As he spoke, a wail arose from mid-bridge. "God help
me," Sir Edward howled, "we're at the Gujjar Pass. I've
got to get out of here!"

Shouting incoherently, he sat up in his litter and attempted to get to his feet. Startled, his horse snorted and
stamped, and the bridge rocked alarmingly. Baju, who had
been talking to Merial, lost his balance and fell to his
knees.

"Look out!"

As Rayn shouted, the bridge tilted, and Baju slid downward toward the abyss. Instinctively Merial reached for
the old man. Her scrabbling fingers caught his arm seconds before he slid off the bridge.

Next second she was yanked off her feet by Baju's
weight. She heard Baju yelling and screamed herself as she
was dragged across the bridge into the void. Still clutching

Baju, she clawed for something to cling to and could find nothing. She was falling, falling—

A viselike grip clamped down onto her arm. "I've got you," Rayn said. "Hold on a moment longer."

She gasped with the effort of clinging on to Baju's sweat-slippery arm, cried out with pain as Rayn dragged both her and Baju back onto the swaying bridge. There she collapsed onto the rough planks.

Strong hands lifted her up; an arm went around her in support. "Look at me," Rayn said.

If she opened her eyes now, she'd be sick—but the deep voice compelled obedience. Merial blinked into a flinthard golden gaze as Rayn continued, "Are you hurt?"

Mutely she shook her head, and the movement made her feel so dizzy that she closed her eyes again. "Baju?" she managed to question.

"Safe, thanks to you."

She was now aware of Baju coughing someplace nearby. "And my father?" she asked urgently.

The arm that held her grew rigid. "It was his fault that this happened. I should kill him here and now."

Her cry of protest was sheared away as he got to his feet, dragging her up with him. Terrified, she looked about until she saw that Sir Edward's litter had safely reached the other side of the bridge. He was sitting up and looking wildly about him.

"He's delirious," she pleaded. "He doesn't understand where he is."

"Don't you *Angrezi* always say that ignorance is no excuse?"

Hating him for the sneer in his voice, Merial pulled free of his supporting arm, but the planks beneath her feet rocked sickeningly. She stumbled forward and would have fallen if Rayn had not caught her around the waist. "Go slowly," he told her. "There's no danger now."

Merial wished she had the courage to walk alone, but she was too afraid to shake off his arm. Her legs felt boneless by the time she reached the other side, and unable to go farther she sank down on the rock-strewn mountainside.

Some distance away Deen was giving Baju some water. *"Shabash, Angrezi,"* he told her, "that was well done."

His scarred face was friendlier than she'd ever seen it, and he offered her the water flask almost as though she were a comrade. As she drank thirstily, Rayn came over to them. "We'll rest here until you're able to move on," he said.

He put a hand on Baju's shoulder, and the old man quickly covered it with his own. He was still very pale as he said, "I thought that my death hour had come. But for *her,* I would now be waiting to be reborn."

When Rayn said nothing, Baju continued formally, "My prince, you'll bear witness that my life is forfeit to this woman."

He was interrupted by Sir Edward's howl of terror. "Must get away from here!" he cried. "Must reach Gandari and the English garrison. St. Marr, damn you, didn't I tell you not to let those *budmarshes* near my cart?"

It wasn't just Rayn's face that changed. Merial sensed the transformation in him, a metamorphosis of bone and blood and skin that altered him completely. The stance of his powerful body, the rigid line of his jaw, and the icy burn of his eyes—in that moment he completely resembled his namesake.

Merial had never seen such ferocity in a human being, a savagery made even more terrible because it was held in check. She saw him put his hand to his sword, saw the knuckles of his fist turn white as he grasped its hilt.

This was the end, then. He was going to kill Sir Edward. Merial wanted to plead, to protest, to offer her own life instead of that poor sick man's. But her tongue wouldn't move, and her lips had gone numb, and she could only wait in mute horror as Rayn turned pitiless eyes on her.

"Your father's raving again," he said harshly. "Best take care of him before I close his mouth for good."

About ten miles past the Bridge of Winds, the mountain path broadened into a glade, and here Rayn called a halt. The clearing was bordered with wild rhododendron and cedar saplings and made fragrant by wild roses. A spring, fed by melting snow from the mountains, trickled amongst the rocks.

Merial had no eyes for the beauty of the place. Her adrenaline had ebbed away, leaving her too exhausted even to be glad that they had stopped moving. All she wanted to do was to sleep—but rest was far away. Sir Edward, convinced that they were back at the Gujjar Pass, kept rambling about his precious cart and the ruffians from Sri Nevi.

"St. Marr will hold them off," he mumbled. "Good man, St. Marr. I'll mention his bravery to Colonel Malcolm."

She was too tired to do more than soothe him mechanically and give him more of the sleeping draught Baju had provided. When at last he dozed off, she lay down on the string bed next to him and slid a thousand miles into sleep.

And she dreamt. She dreamt she was falling from the Bridge of Winds. Twisting, clawing, she spiraled into a vortex of black wind which rushed to meet her. Down and down she plunged until she woke to find her father calling her name.

"Wake up, Merial," he was hissing. "We've got to get away."

Wearily she sat up and pushed back her tumbled hair. "Father," she said, "we're safe. We're not at the Gujjar Pass."

"Who said anything about the Gujjar?" he demanded, and she realized that his voice, though weak and querulous, was lucid. When she got up and went to him, she saw that his eyes were sane and clear.

"Thank God," she whispered.

"I know I've been sick. I seem to remember that our servants left us and that we were captured by Narayn of Baranpur." He caught her wrist and gave it a feeble shake. "Was I dreaming?"

When she shook her head, he exclaimed, "You mean that we've fallen into the clutches of the Tiger? What does he want with us?"

"He's taking us to his father," she told him dully. "We're his prisoners."

"An outrage! Peaceful English people can't be kidnapped by this—this _budmarsh_. I'll have the army on the Tiger's trail. He'll be sorry he ever set a hand on us."

"The army is far away," Merial said dryly. As Sir Edward frowned, she added, "You must understand that we are miles away from the nearest English garrison. Threats will do us no good and will only anger these people."

"Then we've got to escape."

Sir Edward had no recollection of the long mountain road, the Bridge of Winds. "How can we escape?" she parried. "You can't walk or ride."

"We can give the beggars the slip in the dark and hide in the forest. We'll wait until I feel better, eh?" He tried to sit up and then sank back on his cot, cursing the fever, his weakness, and Narayn of Baranpur. "The rana may kill me. It's common knowledge that the blackguard hates us English. But you—you're in even greater danger. *You* must get away."

She took his hand and held it tightly, saying, "Even if I could, you know I wouldn't leave you."

With a smothered curse, Sir Edward gripped her arm. "Girl, listen to me. You don't know, can't know what these bastards can do to you. An Englishwoman amongst these barbarians—you must get away, I tell you."

As he spoke, the tent flap was thrown back and Baju entered. He still looked pale, but his smile was warm and he gave Merial a deep ritual bow. "I came, daughter, to renew my thanks and see how you and your father are feeling," he said.

"Who's this fellow?" Sir Edward interrupted. When Merial explained, he frowned. "I don't want any ignorant *hakim* mauling me and feeding me rubbishy potions. I want a proper doctor."

Though she had no idea whether Baju understood or not, Merial felt mortified. "In common decency, be still," she whispered. "He saved your life."

Sir Edward lay down again but said in a surly voice, "I don't want any kindness from him or his master."

When Baju had gone, Sir Edward's brief spurt of energy burned itself out. He dozed off, and Merial lay down on her cot once more. Though still weary, sleep was the last thing from her mind. Was it possible they *could* escape?

The trouble was, she couldn't focus on a plan. Like smoke, like shadows, senseless images filtered into her weary mind, touched her, and then melted away. She remembered Prince Rayn as she'd seen him for the first time, relived the moment when the Afridi warrior rushed at her with sword upraised. And then came the memory of that evening in the Tiger's tent.

He had saved her life today, and he hadn't murdered Sir Edward, but he hadn't been acting out of kindness. He was probably waiting to give his father the pleasure of killing the *Angrezi* man, and as for her—Merial shivered. Sir Edward was wrong. She *did* know what lay in store for her.

As she turned restlessly on her narrow cot, a breeze belled the cloth entrance of the tent. Tiredly she got up and went to push the flap back. Tonight no guards stood outside the tent.

Before she had fully registered this fact, a clear tenor voice began a love song. "My beloved is anointed with heavenly fragrance," Deen sang. "Roses twine in her dark hair. But I have lost my beloved, and my arms are empty. Where is my beloved tonight?"

Deen was sitting nearby at one of the cooking fires, and many of the *bhaldars* were grouped around him. Amongst others Merial spotted Big Fanji's bulk. Neither he nor any of the others were looking her way.

Merial looked swiftly about her and noted that darkness lay beyond the gleam of the cooking fires. *Was* it possible to drop into that velvet blackness and escape?

Experimentally, she stepped through the tent flap and paused, holding her breath. The men around the campfire seemed oblivious to her. Holding her skirts tightly against her legs, she slipped away from the tent toward the dark that surrounded the camp. A twig crackled underfoot and her heart nearly stopped, but again no one paid any attention.

A hundred yards away from the campsite, she stopped, listening. At first she hardly dared to breathe, but when no challenge came from the blackness beyond the camp, she began to hope. Beyond the clearing there was nothing but inky-black forest. "We can hide there," she told herself. "If Father leans on me, he can walk this short distance. And then—"

She was interrupted by the unmistakable sound of a leopard's cough. But the big cat wouldn't dare to come so close to a camp, Merial told herself sturdily. And anyway, leopards were no more dangerous than the Tiger.

"What are you doing out here?" a deep voice demanded.

For the life of her she couldn't answer. Movement and thought and breath itself seemed to stop. In the absolute silence that followed Rayn's question, she heard the leopard snarl again.

"How did—how did you know I was here?" she whispered.

"My *bhaldars* saw you leave the camp," he replied, adding impatiently, "This is not the English countryside. It's not safe to go walking alone."

All she could think of to say was, "I dreamed of falling from the Bridge of Winds."

"That's understandable." Incredibly, he actually sounded sympathetic, but there was no softness in his expression. The spare moonlight harshened the already hard planes of his face as he continued, "Understandable, but not wise."

"I meant no harm."

His appraising gaze made her wonder if he knew about her pathetic plans to escape, but all he said was, "I've been talking to Baju this past hour. He was reminding me of the law that cannot be broken—that a life must be given for a life."

It took some time for this to sink in. When it did, Rayn watched the hope flame into her eyes. Turquoise eyes, silvered by moonlight, so honest that they showed every nuance of emotion—incredible that they could belong to Edward Ashland's daughter.

Merial had clasped her hands together as if in prayer. "Do you mean that you're going to let us go?"

"Before I learned who you were or where you were going, I promised you safe conduct." A sob of relief broke from her, and Rayn was plagued with conflicting emotions. His deep tones were more clipped than usual when he resumed, "I told you that I respect courage wherever I find it. I'll send you on your way tomorrow."

"My father, too?" When he didn't answer, she cried, "You said it yourself—a life for a life. You've already killed one person I loved—Niall St. Marr. Please don't murder my father, too."

Almost absently he touched the amulet around his throat, and its moonstone glowed with reflected moonlight. "This boy you speak of—this St. Marr—how came he to be wearing this?"

"His mother was Princess Lakshmi—a daughter of a hill prince. Captain St. Marr married her, but she died when Niall was a baby. The amulet was hers."

"A half-breed, then." Rayn's shrug was eloquent.

"Don't call him that!" she flared. "He was my best friend."

"Sir Edward Ashland's daughter and an Anglo-Indian boy?" he jeered. "Impossible. You English are more caste conscious than we are. Your parents would never have allowed it."

Old hurts roughened her voice as she explained, "There were no other children in Sri Nevi. I played with my nurse's little boy, Adham Khan, and the gardener's daughter, Sita. But Niall was like a—like an older brother."

Rayn didn't comment. Almost forgetting to whom she was speaking, Merial added, "He didn't make me feel as though I were a nuisance. Sometimes he called me 'Highness' and made me laugh. He taught me to ride. And—and on that day when the *budmarshes* from Sri Nevi drove us into the hills, he stayed behind with his father. I begged him to come with us, but he wouldn't, and when we drove away I heard his voice calling out his father's battle cry. I've heard it in my dreams all these years."

She wanted to say more, but her tears wouldn't let her. The old wounds were bleeding again. "I'll protect you, Meri," he had said, "my life for yours." And protecting her, he had died.

She wept silently without attempting to cover her face or wipe away the tears that streamed down her cheeks. She heard Rayn say something under his breath, and then he put his arms around her stiff shoulders. "Let the tears come," he told her.

Dimly Merial registered the fact that Rayn was drawing her into his arms. Thoughtless except for her grief, she leaned her cheek against his broad shoulder and sobbed out her heart.

He held her exactly as one might hold a weeping child. Smoothing back the dark curls that has escaped the chignon at the nape of her neck, he ran his big hand over her back, soothing, gentling, stroking until the rigidity left her shoulders, and she relaxed against him. "It's all right" he murmured, and hearing the croon of his deep voice, Merial felt an inexplicable sense of comfort. Unthinkingly she drew closer to him as she wept for the man he had slain.

The irony of this fact didn't escape Rayn. The expression on his face wasn't pleasant, and there was a twist to his mouth as though he mocked himself. As he felt Merial's slender body heave with sobs, he wondered if she'd allowed herself to cry before this. After all, the English demanded a stiff upper lip. She had probably stayed true to that code and taken what life offered—and from what she had told him, life had given Ashland's daughter very little.

Grimly Rayn damned her useless father, who had cared so little for his daughter that her only comfort had been this dead, half-caste boy. Then his eyes hardened as he recalled how Niall St. Marr had died.

Her sobs had ended, but she was still shaken by tremors of grief. Almost as much to himself as to her he said, "Peace, now. It's over. Let the dead bury the dead."

She lifted her head to look at him. Her eyelashes were smudged with tears, and the look in her eyes brought him inexplicable hurt. "Let there be peace between us," he said in a low voice.

"But Niall is dead, and—"

"I said peace." More to stop her words than for any other reason, he bent his mouth to hers in the ritual kiss of peace.

It was no more than a brush of lips against lips, and Merial didn't flinch away. Instead, she raised her face to his.

She heard the intake of Rayn's breath a moment before his mouth sought hers again. But if his first kiss had been gentle, the second was not. It jolted Merial like a bolt of lightning, and his mouth sought hers with an intensity that drove all logic and sense away.

Everything in the moon-silvered world seemed to stop. Merial could hear nothing but the pounding of her own heart and Rayn's ragged breathing. When she felt his tongue-tip circling her lips, they parted involuntarily under his.

The bold stroke of his tongue awakened memories, stirred the embers of a shameful fire into life. Emptied by grief, she was now flooded by sensations and feelings that she couldn't withstand. Nothing mattered, nothing existed but Rayn's arms and his mind-drugging kisses.

Rayn felt the yielding of Merial's soft body, and passion blazed through him until his bones and nerve ends seemed on fire. Desire hammered white-hot through his loins, dazing him, driving every other consideration from his mind. He began to caress her hair, her slender throat, the curve of her breast, then drew his lips away from hers to press his mouth against her still-clothed breasts.

"Mira," he murmured. "My Mira."

The new name he had given her fitted the mood evoked by the night. Merial Ashland didn't exist anymore. She was Mira, a creature made for this rose-scented darkness. Rayn was the wind, the fire, the maelstrom into which she was falling, and Merial—*Mira*—wanted to fall.

His mouth left her breast to seek her lips again, drinking from her mouth, breathing her breath, consuming her. Merial felt herself disintegrating, dissolving into him. She no longer knew where Rayn began and Merial ended.

In the drum of his white-hot blood, Rayn sensed her surrender. Still kissing her, he went down on one knee and drew her down with him onto the cool, mossy ground. Faint moonlight silvered her loosened hair, dazzled gems into her eyes. The English rose had disappeared, and instead there remained this pagan goddess who opened to him like a moonflower to the night.

With a deft movement he tugged her blouse from her skirt and pushed aside the linen shift that shielded her breasts. She felt the cool night air against her taut nipples before his mouth brought warmth. She cried out softly at pleasure so exquisite it was almost pain.

"My beloved has roses wreathed in her black hair." His whisper against her breast, the stroke of his tongue against the taut peaks, his hands caressing, teasing, tormenting with incredible pleasure. Merial felt as though her soul was being sucked out of her.

Now his lips moved away but only to trail a path of kisses over her smooth abdomen. "Where is my beloved tonight?"

She was here, in his arms. She sighed his name before he found her mouth again, and his kiss scalded her with its passion. In contrast his hands were gentle as they caressed her breasts, then dipped to explore the rounded curve of her hip. Meanwhile, her own hands were busy as they smoothed the thick darkness of his hair, learned the hard musculature of neck and shoulders and back.

Now his hands roved lower, tugging up her skirts to caress her legs and knees and the warmth between her thighs. At his touch the spiderwebs of pleasure that were spiraling through Merial's blood coalesced into desire that singed her with its intensity.

"Please—"

The English word was wrenched from her. Incongruous, fitting neither the place nor the sensations that were sweeping them both, the word reached down into the far place to which Rayn's conscious mind had retreated. It made him recall that the magical woman in his arms was Edward Ashland's daughter.

And the proud memsahib was his for the taking. Beyond the desire he'd felt for this woman from almost the first moment of their meeting, making love to Merial Ashland would be exquisite revenge—

Merial felt his arms tighten almost painfully about her before they let her go. Instinctively she protested this release by clasping her own arms about his neck and felt him shiver as though an electric current had jolted him.

With a swift, fluid movement Rayn regained his feet. He caught her by the arms and raised her so that she was facing him. She stumbled and would have fallen, but he steadied her.

"Regretfully, there is no time for dalliance," Merial heard him say. "Our ways part tomorrow."

His meaning penetrated at last. In return for letting them go, the Tiger had exacted a cruel price. Like a cat playing with a mouse, he had broken her to his will and then contemptuously had set her free.

Though Merial could still feel the fire of Rayn's lips on hers, and the imprint of his hard body seemed burned into hers, she felt chilled. Her fingers felt numb and useless as she struggled to pull her clothes together.

There was the sound of rustling in the underbrush near them followed by a discreet cough. "Lord," Deen's voice said urgently, "forgive this intrusion, but there's been word from the sentries. A contingent from Baranpur is riding toward us. A hundred of the *Kotwal* Ibrahim's police."

"Now why would Ibrahim Ali Shah be riding out to meet me at this time of night?" Merial saw a look pass between the two men. "Take half our men and go to meet our esteemed chief of police," Rayn ordered. "The others are to arm and wait."

Why should he take such precautions if these men were from his own kingdom? As though he'd read Merial's mind, Rayn said, "It's always wise to expect the unexpected."

His voice was grim, and as he turned to follow his captain of lancers, a sliver of moonlight glinted against the moonstone at his throat.

··*Five*··

MERIAL FOUND THE camp transformed. Gone was the free-and-easy camaraderie between officers and men as Rayn's *bhaldars* readied themselves for possible trouble. Deen and his men had already left, and the remainder stood at attention before Captain Rassul.

"Go back to your tent and stay out of sight," Rayn commanded Merial.

As she turned to obey, there came the sound of pounding hooves, and a lancer came galloping into the camp.

"I bring word from Rassul and his sentries, lord. Minister Panwa's with Ibrahim."

"Panwa!" Rayn exclaimed. "This time of night should find the honored lord in bed with his latest woman. Unless—" He broke off to add, "Welcome His Excellency and the *kotwal,* Ghazni, but tell Deen to stay alert."

As the man saluted and rode away, Merial wondered, "Who is Minister Panwa?"

"Panwa Puar is a distant cousin and one of the rana's youngest ministers. His late father was Bhupinder Puar, one of the greatest statesmen in Baranpur's history." He frowned and added, "I thought I told you to go to your tent and to stay out of sight. Don't show yourself for any reason."

The night wind brought voices, sure sign that the party from Baranpur was near. Hurriedly Merial did as she'd been ordered and stood holding the tent flap a little open. From this position she could see but not be seen.

Before long, many riders trotted their horses into the clearing. Merial couldn't see their faces in the darkness, but the firelight glinted on their weapons. Two men, one tall and muscular, the other a huge man built like a bull, trotted their horses forward.

"Greetings, Shield of the Kingdom," the first rider said in a languid, somewhat affected voice. "We bring you the greetings of the glorious Khem-Rana."

Rayn asked, "Is all well with my father?"

"It is well, my friend."

Tension didn't leave Rayn's broad shoulders as he said, "You are welcome, Panwa." A pause. "And you, *Kotwal.* "

The bull-like chief of police said in a truculent voice, "I've come for the prisoners, Highness."

"What prisoners?"

Merial, listening in renewed terror, heard the chill note in Rayn's voice. So did Panwa Puar, who shrugged his slim shoulders.

"The good Ibrahim is so subtle," he said with a sigh. "He means the *Angrezi* you captured on the border, my friend. In these unsettled times news travels on swift feet, and when the rana heard about the *Angrezi* devils, he became excited and sent me to fetch them to Baranpur at once. You know he abominates the cursed *Angrezi* even more than you do, my prince."

Merial's heart was pounding against her rib cage. *Deny it,* she pleaded silently with Rayn, but he merely shrugged his broad shoulders.

"Is that all? You might as well have saved yourself a long ride by moonlight. My prisoners and I would have reached Baranpur by tomorrow."

And he said he was going to let them go. Merial turned to look at her sleeping father and knew that there was no escape. There was no way that this sick man could hope to outrun armed, mounted men.

She watched despairingly as the minister flipped his reins to one of Rayn's men, then dismounted. In the flickering torchlight Merial saw that he had a long, handsome, aristocratic face and a precisely groomed mustache. He fingered this as he drawled, "It's good to see you again, Prince of a Thousand Victories. News of your latest exploits against the Afridi is being sung by the women in the marketplace. Naturally they're all in love with you. You can have any woman in Baranpur for the asking."

Rayn laughed. "Unless you see her first."

The two men embraced, and the police chief shifted his bulk in the saddle. "Those prisoners," he reminded Rayn, "are a great concern to the rana. As chief of the King of Kings' police, I came along so that Your Highness needn't burden yourself further."

"That was unnecessary." Nothing could have been more courteous than Rayn's words, but Merial caught the undertone that could mean distrust or contempt. "I will personally hand the prisoners over to my father. You've made the long ride for nothing, Ibrahim Ali Shah."

In the silence that followed, Merial held her breath. Perhaps he would let them escape yet. Perhaps tonight, while the others slept—but Panwa was shaking his head.

"So I told the rana, but he wouldn't listen. He sends word that he wants the prisoners tonight." He fingered his mustache again. "Word is that the English woman's a beauty with eyes like mountain lakes. If our arrival interrupted your pleasure with her, I'm sorry, Highness.''

Rayn laughed, and that short, male bark sickened Merial. Her face flamed with disgust, which was mostly aimed at herself. She had allowed the Tiger of Baranpur to take her in his arms and use her shamelessly. Perhaps he had never meant to let them go and had simply been amusing himself. "Oh, damn him," she whispered.

"Merial—is that you?"

Slowly Merial walked to her father's side. There, sinking down on a low stool by his bed, she took his hand and held it wordlessly. Sir Edward looked so thin and white in the sputtering lamplight. He hadn't been shaved in days, and gray-white stubble covered his usually smooth cheeks. His mustache and beard were in disarray. Inconsequentially, Merial wished she could make him look better when they were led in front of the English-hating rana. Even if Khem Raoshad hated the English, he should give Sir Edward Ashland the respect a British aristocrat deserved.

There would be no escape now. They would be paraded into Baranpur. Mocked and jeered at, they would be taken before the rana for sentence. Angrily Merial derided herself for ever having believed Rayn's word.

She started as Big Fanji lifted the tent flap and pushed his face inside. "Prepare to ride to Baranpur," he bawled.

"Now, in the dead of night?"

"The rana wants you in Baranpur, so the prince has ordered we're all to go." Fanji shrugged with easy sympathy. "If Ibrahim had waited an hour or two, you'd have been safely away. That's life, eh?"

So Rayn *had* meant what he said about letting them go. The knowledge didn't comfort Merial as, dully, she began to ready her father for another journey, washing his face and hands and trying to smooth back his hair. Both his clothes and hers were beyond repair, and she had no comb. How the rana would laugh when he saw the hated English people, she thought bitterly.

"You can still get away," Sir Edward urged. "Slip out the back of the tent and hide. You've got to get to Perce and tell him—"

"So these are the prisoners we heard so much about."

The affected drawl belonged to Panwa Puar, but it was the man standing behind the slender minister that held Merial's gaze. The *Kotwal* Ibrahim was a hulking presence, almost as big as Fanji. Unlike Fanji, however, this man's bulk was not made of muscle but of fat. Narrow dark eyes set in a square, many-chinned face, darted from Sir Edward to his daughter.

"These are the prisoners." Rayn had also entered the tent. His eyes met Merial's briefly, and she saw a flicker of regret in them before he added, "As you see, the man is of little worth."

"You can't say the same about the woman." At close hand Minister Panwa was even more handsome than Merial had thought. A man in his late twenties, he wore his travel cloak with a flair, and his longish dark hair was carefully coiffured under a cap emblazoned with gems. As he stepped closer, she was enveloped in musky perfume. Even so, Merial had the sense that this was no effete dandy but a vigorous, intelligent man.

"Not bad," he said, "but too slender a bud to tempt the rana—or me." The *kotwal* grunted, and Merial saw his eyes flick over her breasts and body. Nauseated, she watched Ibrahim lick his thick lips.

"We are ready to ride," Rayn said abruptly. He held the tent flap open for the *kotwal,* who stamped out immediately, but Panwa remained behind to speak quietly to

Rayn. "I'm sorry about Ibrahim, Highness. I tried my best to leave him behind, but—" He shrugged expressive shoulders.

Rayn glanced at Sir Edward and then at Merial. His face seemed wiped clean of expression as he ordered, "Make sure you strap your father down well. It won't be easy riding downhill on a litter."

They left immediately. From her place beside her father's litter, Merial felt every jolt that the litter took on the long, downward-sloping road. And yet, as dawn turned the sky to opal colors, she had to admit that the valley into which they were descending was beautiful. Wild roses grew everywhere and perfumed the air. Birds sang in wild cherry trees and sky-blue butterflies danced over terraced farms of tea and fields of golden saffron.

The people who tended these farms came running to shout greetings. One burly farmer, swinging a six-foot pole, hailed Rayn as *Annadata.*

This apparently didn't sit well with Ibrahim. "Only the ruler of the land should be called the 'giver of food,' " he growled.

"When I am on the rana's business, I stand in his stead." Rayn's voice was calm, but there was steel under its quiet. "I'm sure you remember that, Ibrahim."

The crowds increased as they descended into the valley itself and followed a broad, well-kept road. Baju, who had insisted on riding behind with the Ashlands, explained that the road led to Rasgani, the capital city of Baranpur.

After they had ridden some time, they came to the bank of a river. Merial saw with surprise that it flowed directly across the road, intersecting it and forming a natural barrier. "The Azara has its origins in the land of Kashmir," Baju explained. Then he added proudly, "But Baranpur

is even more of a jewel than Kashmir itself. And Rasgani
is not a city but a pearl."

The pearl was well guarded. As they waited for a drawbridge to be lowered over the river, Merial could see heavy
fortifications in the low hills immediately surrounding the
city. Baranpur was prepared for war—perhaps even war
with as formidable an adversary as England herself.

This realization was reinforced as they approached the
city gates. Here a division of mounted men, clad in orange
uniforms and silver turbans, had mustered to meet their
prince and commander. A gray-mustached, much-
decorated officer, whom Rayn addressed as General Jaga,
rode forward to salute.

"The army of the great Khem-Rana, King of Kings,
have awaited their prince's return," the general announced formally.

The militia weren't the only ones who had been waiting.
At the outskirts of the city a band of musicians were await-
ing their prince. Wailing Indian music accompanied them
into the city gates as they rode into a city of fair white
houses surrounded by gardens. Above the roofs of these
houses rose Hindu temples dedicated to Shiva and Vishnu
and a pagodalike edifice which Baju explained was the
mosque where Rasgani's Muslim population went to pray.
"All faiths and all people are welcome here," he added.

But not *Angrezi*. The crowds that gathered along the
roadway might cheer the prince, but they were definitely
hostile toward his prisoners. "See the proud *Angrezi*—oh,
see!" a woman shrilled.

There was the sound of a man's voice cursing, and a
rock flew through the air and caught Merial a glancing
blow on the arm. Another smashed against the side of Sir
Edward's litter. "Stop that!" Baju shouted, but his voice
was lost in a chorus of angry voices.

English murderers—prince killers—unbelieving dogs!
Accompanying the words were more stones. Merial drew
her horse closer to Sir Edward as a ring of dark, threatening faces surrounded them and pressed closer.

"Enough!"

Rayn's roar sliced through the noise. Merial hadn't seen
him ride up, but he was beside her now, and before his
stern gaze the threatening crowd melted away. "These are
my prisoners," he continued. "If one hair of their heads
is hurt, you'll answer to me."

Rassul, Deen, and Big Fanji had followed their prince
and now rode forward toward the crowd, but the people
of Rasgani were already on their knees. Rayn turned to
Merial asking, "Are you hurt?"

She tried not to show how afraid she was. "No," she
replied. "Their aim was very bad."

But through the tear in her sleeve he could see the dark
welt on her arm. Rayn's dark brows drew together. "You
will ride with me," he announced.

He caught the reins of her horse and sent his own at
a trot back to the head of his party. Panwa raised his well-
plucked brows, and the chief of police demanded, "You
are offering a mark of royal favor to an *Angrezi?*"

Rayn replied curtly, "Instead of daring to question me,
attend to security. This incident would not have happened
if your police were deployed properly."

Ibrahim's face turned a dark magenta. He saluted almost violently and turned to bark orders at his men, but
the look he gave Merial was so malevolent that it terrified
her. She kept her eyes directly in front of her and tried
not to think of what awaited them at the end of this ride.

She could only hope that her father, also, was protected
by the prince's order. Riding so close to the Tiger, she was
again aware of his physical presence. Panwa, though tall

and strongly built, appeared a mere stripling in comparison, and the hulking *kotwal* merely looked deformed. With his broad shoulders and arrogant carriage, Rayn seemed to tower over all men.

She tried to quieten her nerves by looking about her and saw that they were now riding beside the lake she had seen from the mountain peak. Its aquamarine waters were no less beautiful, but from the heights she had not seen the many houseboats that clustered along its shores. Men and women called greetings from these houseboats, which were laden with flowers, fruit, and other merchandise. Then, suddenly, the crowds fell away and she realized that they were nearing the rana's palace.

The palace had high stone walls and a stone gate emblazoned with the emblem of the sun from which Khem Raoshad was said to have descended. The gates stood wide open to receive the prince and his escort, which rode into an enormous courtyard. Merial saw a sea of color—the orange and silver uniforms of military men, the gray and olive worn by Ibrahim's police, and the white and silver affected by the rana's personal palace guards. Beyond all of these people she could catch a glimpse of lush gardens which opened on the lake.

The palace itself was built of palest rose marble, its turrets and minarets capped with silver. Its huge doors to the palace were made of silver and blazed in the sun.

"The 'Silver Palace' meets with your approval?" Panwa was asking. When Merial nodded, he smiled. "I see that you understand our language. Do you speak it?"

"She speaks well enough for an *Angrezi*," Rayn answered for her.

"What is your name, then, my rose?" Panwa persisted. Merial opened her mouth to answer and intercepted

Rayn's warning look. He was warning her of what? Of Panwa Puar? No—of giving her name.

"My—my name is Mira," she stammered. "Mira Larkwell."

Larkwell had been her mother's maiden name and was the only one that came to mind. It had stumbled over her tongue, but Panwa evidently thought that had been caused by her unfamiliarity with Hindustani and simply nodded. The *kotwal,* however, turned his narrow-eyed gaze on her.

"An *Angrezi* who speaks the language could prove interesting," he grunted.

The prince's party had now ridden almost up to the marble steps that led to the palace. Dismounting, Rayn extended a hand to Merial.

"It's time to get down."

He had saved her life on the Bridge of Winds. He had kept her from being stoned. But there was nothing, no help at all in his face now as he lifted her down.

Even so, she dared to ask a question. "What is going to happen to us?"

"That depends on the rana. Go back to your father."

Ordering Fanji to guard the prisoners, Rayn walked up the steps past salaaming guards. Then, followed by his *bhaldar* captains, Panwa, and the chief of police, he strode through the silver doors of the palace.

There was nothing to do but wait. Half an hour or so later one of the palace guards emerged from the great silver door and called, "You are to bring in the *Angrezi* prisoners."

Fanji gave a little grunt and said not unkindly, "It's time to go, girl."

Merial found that her legs were shaking under her, but when Sir Edward looked up at her, she managed a smile. "We are going into the Tiger's den, Father."

Two other *bhaldars* caught up Sir Edward's litter as Big Fanji escorted Merial up the marble stairs. Walking, she felt as though a thousand unseen eyes were watching them. A sense of unreality filled her as they stepped through the silver door.

"We're going to the Hall of Audience," Fanji rumbled. "When you are in the rana's presence, get down on your knees and salaam to the floor. The King of Kings likes that sort of thing. It may help you, girl."

Merial translated this for her father, who muttered, "An Englishman doesn't bend the knee except to his queen."

Before she could argue, they entered the vast hall of the rana's palace. The hall was made of blue-veined marble, and the ceilings had golden chips in it as though to mirror the sky. In the central arch was the blazing symbol of the sun. The walls were painted with murals of gods, angels, and demons.

"This way," Fanji prompted.

The hallway stopped at a door inlaid with ivory, gold, and red tile. The palace guards at each side of this door snapped to attention and swung open the door. Fanji gestured that they were to go in, and Merial stepped into a huge, oblong room.

On both sides of the Hall of Audience stood rows of men. Most wore flowing white robes and seemed to be statesmen or *diwans*—ministers of the state, but there were also senior officers in military uniform who turned their fierce, dark faces to stare curiously at the English prisoners.

Merial, hesitating at the very edge of the audience hall, saw that the men present made a living pathway to a golden dais. Here, under an arch of gold encrusted with gems, was a *gaddi* or royal seat made up of saffron and gold cushions. On this throne sat the rana.

"Prostrate yourselves," Fanji hissed.

Merial knelt and bowed her head almost to the floor. She remained there until the man on the throne called, "The prisoners may approach me."

It was a harsh, hard voice, and the face of the man who had spoken was harsh as well. Under a white turban crested with a blazing ruby, his face was seamed, lined, and narrow. His lips, framed by a white mustache and beard, were thin, and on either side of a scimitar of nose were large, hooded, brooding eyes. They regarded the Ashlands with unblinking venom.

"So," he said, "here are the rats who walked into my trap."

Merial had never heard such gloating in a human voice. It chilled her blood. She didn't want to look at the rana again, but her eyes were drawn back to him as though hypnotized. As she did so, she heard Rayn say, "These are the prisoners, my lord father."

The Tiger was seated on a silver cushion at the rana's right hand. He was still dressed in his travel-stained clothes, but a golden chain denoting royalty had been hung about his neck. Standing behind their lord were Deen and Rassul, and Panwa and Ibrahim had taken positions close by.

Rayn continued, "As you see, they are hardly worthy of your notice. The man is sick and will probably die."

"But there is the woman," Khem-Rana pointed out. Contemptuously he added, "The English will do much for the sake of their women."

It took every ounce of Merial's courage not to scream when she saw Ibrahim turn and stare at her from his place near the rana. The chief of police smiled a little as Rayn said, "She's not worth very much."

He looked directly at her as he spoke, and she thought she saw, in the depths of those golden eyes, a warning. Calmly he continued, "From what I can make out, these *Angrezi* are not wealthy or well connected. Few would give a *pice* to save their worthless hides. The only reason I took them captive was because they stumbled into my way. I was about to send them off when Panwa and Ibrahim reached my camp."

The rana played with a jewel that hung about his neck. "What is your name?" he snarled at Merial.

In a low voice she managed, "Mira Larkwell, my lord rana."

"And the man's? Let him crawl to me on his knees."

The *bhaldars* had lowered the litter to the floor. Hearing the rana's command, Sir Edward tried to get up but fell forward on his hands and knees.

"That's it, dog. On your knees," the rana jeered.

Sir Edward may not have understood the words, but he heard the laughter. His pale face flushed and he snapped, "No wog is going to talk to me that way."

The words were hardly out of his mouth when one of the palace guardsmen sprang forward and clubbed him down. Merial screamed faintly as her father pitched unconscious onto the marble floor. She would have risen to go to him if Fanji's big paw hadn't clamped down on her shoulder.

"Stay where you are."

Calmly Rayn remarked, "The man is her father. His name is Edward Larkwell and he's some minor servant of the English government. He's of no consequence, unfortunately."

Why was he lying? Merial's heart knocked against her

ribs in sudden hope. If Rayn didn't reveal these things to his father, perhaps it meant that he was trying to help her.

"Panwa, what say you?" the rana demanded.

Panwa took a step closer to the royal dais and bowed deeply. "The prince is a superb judge of men, King of Kings. If he says that the prisoner is worthless, he is."

It wasn't the answer that the old tyrant wanted. He scowled at Panwa before turning to the chief of police. "Ibrahim Ali Shah, what is your counsel?"

"I would hold them for ransom, King of Kings."

The rana shot a glance of triumph at his son. "Good. That is my plan exactly. Someone will pay ransom for these dogs of *Angrezi*, though they are trespassers, criminals." His hooded eyes glowed with a fanatical light. "Put them in the dungeon and guard them well. If no one will pay their ransom, the royal elephant will crush the man's head. The woman, however, will be useful in other capacities."

Ibrahim turned his head and looked gloatingly at Merial. Mutely she shook her head as though to dispel a nightmare, and as she did so, she heard Rayn laugh.

"My father, you are a fount of wisdom. You see through my soul and read my intentions. That is exactly what I had intended."

"What do you mean, my son?"

Lithely the prince rose to his feet and sauntered toward Merial. "Indeed, she would provide a man with sport." He cupped her chin in one hand, adding, "I'd enjoy breaking and riding her."

Merial tried to shake her head loose, but she couldn't break free of Rayn's grip. "Indeed, King of Kings," Panwa drawled, "it may be that the prince needs some other exercise besides fighting."

The old tyrant gave a short bark of laughter. "You

speak like the lecherous young fop you are. But you are right, Panwa. If you want her, Narayn, the woman is yours, but do not become too enamored of her body. She is *Angrezi*—my enemy and yours."

"In bed all women are alike," Rayn said. He smiled down at Merial's horrified face, then dropped his hand and turned his back on her. "With your permission, my father, I will have her taken to my palace. As for the man, I have a suggestion. A dead man brings no ransom. Let my *hakim* watch over him at the hospital. Once Lark-well's returned to health, he will bring a better price."

The rana nodded, but without much enthusiasm. "What you say makes sense."

As she listened, Merial felt herself retreating further into the unreality of nightmare. She knew she should be relieved that her father was being reprieved from certain death, but all she could feel was a dull horror.

"Bow deeply to the rana," Fanji rumbled. "You're dismissed." Merial bowed and the lancer lieutenant added, "Now to the prince, your master."

She would not bow to him. Not if he killed her, now, here, she would not bow her head to him. Merial flung up her head and glared across the room at Rayn. Common sense, fear, even the instincts of self-preservation deserted her. Forgetting where she was and the danger in which she stood, she got to her feet and faced him directly.

"Damn you," she said in English. "I'll never belong to you. If you put one hand on me, I'll kill you. Oh, damn you to hell—"

Their eyes met, clashing liked naked sword blades. Then, unexpectedly, Rayn grinned.

"Cover her face so that other men don't see her beauty," he commented. "Taming this English she-wolf is going to be entertaining."

*   *   *

Later Merial wondered how she'd managed to leave the rana's presence. Her knees were buckling, and her body felt numb. Once outside the palace doors sanity returned. She was even able to give an explanation to the anxious Baju, who patted her arm.

"I will take good care of your father. You saved my life, and I will not forget that. And you will be safe, too. Prince Rayn protects what is his."

She belonged to the Tiger. She was his booty, his plunder, his spoils of war. Merial felt a sickening dizziness as she recalled his words.

Baju seemed to read her mind. "Better the prince, my daughter, than such as the *kotwal*." Then he added philosophically, "Such is the lot of women. Even the great lawgiver, Manu, decreed that a woman should never be allowed free thought or action."

Sir Edward had groaned back to consciousness, and Merial tried to explain what had happened. She wasn't sure whether he understood what she said, but when Deen came to fetch her, Sir Edward clutched her wrist and whispered fiercely, "If that scoundrel Narayn dares to put his filthy hands on you, Merial, death is better than dishonor. Remember who you are."

Now that she was their lord's woman, the *bhaldars* treated her with more care. A palanquin had been called for her, and she apprehensively sank into its soft cushions. Silken curtains were lowered about the royal litter, which was then carried swiftly away.

"Where are we going?" Merial asked Deen, who, together with Big Fanji, was escorting her.

"To the Bagh Mahal," was his reply. "The Tiger's palace."

After the events of the last hour, it should have been

pure comfort to lie against the comfortable cushions of the palanquin, but Merial was past feeling. She hardly noticed as the bearers carried her through the busy capital city, and she stared with all-but-unseeing eyes at a sunlit fountain in the midst of the city square. Here women were filling their water jugs and gossiping, and one of them burst into a lively love song.

"Aha," Merial heard one of the other women shrill, "Sushilla is happy today. Her new husband must be a bear in bed."

Death, Sir Edward had said, was better than dishonor, but Merial knew that this was too simple. Such words might sound fine in English drawing rooms, but out here in Baranpur, everything was different. If she killed herself, Sir Edward would also be put to death. She knew that as surely as she knew the beat of her own heart. She had read his sentence in the rana's cold eyes. Only Rayn's interest in her had kept him alive.

"I must be a realist," Merial told herself. "We must both survive. And perhaps Mr. Perce will pay the ransom. Surely the English will not leave us to die here."

But her hopes sank again when they came to the Tiger's palace. It fronted the road on one side and on the other the lake, and its tall bronze minaret rose like a fist into the sky. Deen called an order, and the huge iron gates were flung open.

When Deen explained the situation to the black-and-gold-clad guards who had opened the gate, the men salaamed reverently and stood aside. Deen helped Merial out of the litter and escorted her through the gates and up a flight of marble stairs to the doorway of the large dwelling. Inside was a great hall where a fountain splashed cool water over marble stones interspersed with flowers. A staircase, carpeted with Turkish rugs, spiraled up to one side, and as Merial entered the palace, an elderly woman came down the stairs. The silver bracelets on her wrists and ankles jingled as she bowed low to Merial. "A messenger was sent on ahead," she said. "Your quarters are ready for you, Sahiba. My name is Geeta, and I will be your handmaid."

"Our lord will be here in an hour or so. See that she is ready for him." Deen gave the elderly woman her instructions, then turned a lopsided grin on Merial. "Don't look so frightened, Mira-Bai. Our lord's a kind man."

A kind Tiger— Merial's careful logic crumbled. She almost begged Deen and Fanji not to leave her, but the woman named Geeta bowed and said, "Sahiba, food has been prepared. But first, perhaps, you would wish to bathe?"

A bath. A real bath. Merial's laugh contained a sob. "I would descend into hell for a bath, Geeta."

Swiftly and silently the woman led the way up the carpeted stairs. On the second floor Merial could hear the sound of a zither being played. How many of Rayn's other women lived in his palace? she wondered. Geeta opened a door and stepped aside to let her pass.

The room was spacious and furnished comfortably in the fashion of the East. There were rich hangings on the walls, a couch made up of plump cushions, tables of ebony inlaid with ivory. Open windows let in the fresh air from the lake. This chamber led to two others, one a sleeping chamber with a large bed hung with gold cloth. After a swift glance Merial ignored this room and turned to the other, a large chamber tiled in marble and dominated by a sunken marble pool. This pool was filled with steaming, clear water.

"The bath has been drawn for you, Mira-Bai," Geeta said. "I will now help you undress."

As her travel-stained, fire-singed clothes were stripped away, Merial felt a strange sense of release. Gratefully she stepped into the sunken pool of water. For a moment the heat of the water nearly scalded her, but her body adjusted quickly to its warmth. She sank deep into the pool, letting the water cover even her head.

Dismissing Geeta, Merial washed herself and her hair in the perfumed soap that the woman had left behind. Then, once more, she luxuriated in the water. In spite of her knowledge of what was to come, the hot water soothed and comforted her, and as she relaxed Merial felt her strength and courage seeping back. "While there's life, there's hope," she exhorted herself.

She wasn't going to give up, and she wouldn't give in. She would find a way to escape, somehow. Lost in these comforting thoughts, Merial didn't open her eyes when she heard the door to the marble chamber open. Instead, she sighed, "Geeta, this is heaven."

"A very un-English idea of Paradise," Rayn commented.

··*Six*··

HE WAS STANDING with his back to the door, his arms folded across his chest. He had changed into jodhpurs, which emphasized the hard muscle of thigh and leg, and a brocade coat or achkan that fitted his broad-shouldered torso like a glove. A silver cap crowned his dark hair and a gem-encrusted sword was at his belt.

Fury and outrage dissolved into terror as she realized why he was there and exactly what she was to him. Merial slid backward until her bare back contacted the marble side of the pool. Then, drawing her knees up to her chest, she shook her dark hair around her like a cloak.

Rayn watched the rosy color in her cheeks ebb away. She was like a statue carved out of mother-of-pearl. Only the tumble of her jet-black hair seemed to have any life.

She flinched as he began to walk toward her, but he only seated himself on a carved ivory couch beside the pool and stretched out his long booted legs.

"It's fortunate for you that the rana wants to hold you for ransom," he began in a conversational tone. "Your father would fetch little on the slave block, but any man looking at you now would pay a worthwhile sum for you."

Slender, but beautiful rounded limbs, a proud swell of breasts breaking the water's surface, the clean, young lines of her rounded hips,—Rayn's appraisal was interrupted by a stab of desire so strong it astonished him.

Beautiful women had always vied for his favors, and he'd enjoyed them at will. Merial Ashland was no different from those nubile maidens. That she was an *Angrezi* and his by conquest should add flavor to the act of love.

All he needed to do was to lift her from the pool and carry her to the bed in the next room. Or he could have her here on the couch. When he thought of drawing the rosy crowns of her breasts into his mouth, Rayn's passion rose to a white heat.

She almost cried out as he got to his feet. The fluid, cat-like movement terrified her as much as the expression in his eyes. In an instinctive need to escape, she rose quickly and scrambled out of the pool, but before she could reach one of the towels that Geeta had left for her, he caught her by the wrists.

"I beg you, no," she whispered.

Veiling her closed eyes, dark eyelashes fluttered like terrified butterflies. A blue vein of pulse was beating wildly at her throat.

"Such maidenly protests aren't necessary," Rayn mocked. "You do recall you belong to me."

Merial's terrorized thoughts went to Sir Edward, also helpless and sick and somewhere in the Tiger's city. She shivered violently and suddenly went still.

Death is better than dishonor—but she knew that she hadn't the courage to die. She had no honor, no resolution, and nothing but fear and shame before her. A moan was wrenched from her as, still grasping her wrists, he drew her closer to him.

She could hear his even breathing as he let go of her

wrists and ran his hands along the line of her shoulders and down her arms. Merial felt true despair, for under the icy crust of her fear, desire was still alive. His touch evoked a moonlit glade in the mountains. She could taste his kiss. She could feel the remembered heat of his mouth on her breast.

Sweet God, she thought, what's wrong with me?

He stroked her arms again, then ran his hands over the satin of her back, roved lower to lightly cup them around her rounded bottom. He drew her gently toward him, and she swayed toward him as though bewitched.

She had started to shiver again, but Rayn sensed that these tremors were not caused by fear. Her lashes still veiled the expression in her eyes, but her lips were soft with an invitation no man could resist.

He wanted her. He wanted to tear off his stiff court clothes and lower her to the couch by the side of the pool, wanted to feel the cool wet silk of her hair caress his heated, naked body. He wanted to part her long, lovely legs and slake his throbbing need in her honeyed heat. She was pearl and jet and coral—the gods themselves could not have created more perfection.

And surely the gods, who enjoyed the act of love more than mere mortals, would blast him if he turned his back on taking his pleasure with this *Angrezi* rose—Rayn's thoughts were becoming clouded, hazy. The decision he'd made about Edward Ashland and his daughter didn't seem important anymore. He forgot everything, everyone, as he bent his lips to hers.

The savage, single-minded intensity of his kiss seared through Merial like flame. Her naked, wet body was no longer cold but burning. A sob was wrenched from her as, without power or volition, her mouth opened to the invasion of his tongue.

That hopeless sound reached through the haze of passion and touched some part of Rayn's mind that he didn't want to acknowledge. Merial felt the powerful body tense against her as the chill wind of reason cooled his passion. Her eyes snapped open as he dropped his arms from around her, picked up a towel, and tossed it around her shoulders.

Wrapping it tightly around her, she retreated several steps. He didn't try to stop her. "The rana has called a counsel with his generals and senior ministers. I'm on my way to the Silver Palace now." She eyed him warily, and he added, "I'll send your woman to you."

He was going away. He wasn't going to—to—Merial felt a relief so profound that she felt mute and stupid. "You will be safe here," he was going on. "Tomorrow you may visit your father at Baju's hospital."

The frightening look had left his eyes, but she knew that under the veneer of polish and calm, there was something untamed, something primal and nameless that could consume her with its heat. The Tiger was still dangerous. "You—you will really allow me to see him?" she stammered.

"I'm placing a palanquin at your disposal. After all, I want Edward Ashland to recover as soon as possible, and he'll heal better knowing his daughter is, ah, safe."

Her nerves snapped under the tension of conflicting emotions. "You mean that dead men don't bring ransoms," she flared.

She flinched when he raised his hand, but he only reached out to smooth a tendril of hair away from her face. His fingers grazed her cheek in a touch that was almost but not quite a caress.

"Sleep well, Mira," the Tiger purred. "I hope your dreams are pleasant ones."

*   *   *

Merial woke to find the sun streaming through the gauze hangings that surrounded her bed. The sun was coming from an easterly window, and the breezes that filled her chamber carried the scent of flowers. Outside, birdsong mingled with the splashing of waters.

"Did you sleep well, Mira-Bai?" Geeta had entered on soundless feet and was smiling down at her. She parted the gauze curtains to add, "It is a fine morning."

Golden sun winked on Geeta's nose ring, and her bracelets and anklets tinkled cheerfully. When she moved, there was a scent of sandalwood that recalled Jassmina.

Perhaps it was the memory—or the first real rest she had had in days—that made Merial feel cheerful. She sat up and stretched, and Geeta smiled.

"Assuredly you have slept. You dreamed through the afternoon and night and into the middle of this day. Prince Rayn left orders that on no account were you to be wakened, so even the peacocks in the gardens have held their tongues."

The mention of the Tiger destroyed all illusions of peace. She got up quickly from the low, soft bed and went to the window which overlooked a garden. Here peacocks strutted amongst beds of lilies and roses.

She hadn't expected the Tiger's den to be a place of such beauty. As if reading her mind, Geeta explained, "The prince, alas, has no love for flowers or gardens. Like most men, his mind is set on war and statecraft. Perhaps when he has taken a wife, she will oversee his household. Meanwhile, Rukmiri-Bai oversees us all."

"Lady" Rukmiri was probably one of Rayn's women. Merial was vaguely surprised that he hadn't married early, according to the customs of the East. But perhaps he was too busy killing Englishmen to think of marriage.

Merial swiftly brushed that thought aside and attended to Geeta, who was saying, "Rukmiri-Bai has her own house, which is adjacent to the Bagh Mahal. She is, alas, childless, and it is said that her gardens take the place of the children she never had." Geeta paused in her gossip to add, "After you bathe and break your fast, she has requested that you visit her."

"But the prince said I might visit my father," Merial demurred.

"First you must see Rukmiri-Bai," Geeta said firmly, and Merial understood that the request was really a command. The Tiger's chief concubine wanted to view the newest addition to her lord's harem.

While Geeta fussed about her, Merial wondered why Rayn hadn't pressed his royal advantage last night. Perhaps it was because he had been summoned to the minister's counsel. But if so, why hadn't he awakened her when he returned?

A shadow seemed suddenly to fall across the sunlit room. "When is the prince expected to return?" she asked nervously.

But Geeta replied that Prince Rayn had many duties and might not return to the Bagh Mahal all day. That sounded hopeful, and Merial found she was hungry. As she ate the fruit and steamed rice cakes Geeta served, the servant continued a stream of chatter on the subject of her beloved Prince Rayn.

"He is not called the Shield of the Kingdom for nothing," Geeta explained. "He is commander of Khem-Rana's armies and keeps our borders secure from Afridi raiders and *Angrezi* alike. Ibrahim Ali Shah and his police guard the internal security of Baranpur, but the prince has a task that few men could accomplish."

"He has his *bhaldars,*" Merial pointed out.

"Indeed, and each of those fifty men is an army in himself. The lancers would gladly be cut to pieces for their lord." Geeta wagged her head wisely. "He saved his younger captain, Deen Sardar, from death, and he has raised each of his four lieutenants to honor when others did not see their merit. Fanji, for instance, was a wrestler, and it's rumored that Chetak was a *dacoit*—bandit—before my lord vanquished him."

Merial recalled the quiet captain who had given her water. "What of Rassul?" she asked.

"Rassul Kahn has been with the prince the longest. They fought together when Prince Rayn was younger. He's a fearsome man in battle but loves his wife and children dearly. He enjoys peace as well as war, and the other *bhaldars* respect him and often go to him for advice." Geeta shook her head, adding, "But I must not waste your time, Mira-Bai. You must choose your day's attire."

Merial wondered whether the rainbow of saris that Geeta spread before her had been worn by Rayn's other women. She chose indifferently, and Geeta clucked her tongue. "No, Sahiba," she scolded. "These faded colors are not for such as you. Let me choose for you."

She dressed Merial in a short turquoise-blue blouse which emphasized the swell of her breasts and exposed the cream-white of her midriff, then draped over this a silver and turquoise sari of finest silk. The effect was disturbingly sensual, but Geeta would not hear of Merial changing.

"A woman is meant to be beautiful," she said as she brushed and coiled Merial's dark hair. "It may surprise you, but here in Rasgani we do not keep strict *purdah,* and women may come and go as they please without the *bourka*. Some, of course, still veil themselves so that men may not see their beauty and attack their virtue."

The only one likely to attack her virtue was the Tiger, Merial thought. No, not the Tiger—Prince Rayn Raoshad, who held her life and the life of her father in his hands. She reminded herself of this fact as Geeta led her out of the Bagh Mahal and into the garden.

In spite of the fact that this was an early afternoon at the end of May, it was pleasantly cool in the garden. The plains must be sweltering and Sri Nevi would be hazy with heat, but this valley kingdom was cooled by breezes that swept down from the mountains. Merial looked appreciatively about her. Beds of humble marigolds mingled with lilies and roses and lined the garden path toward Rukmiri-Bai's house.

This house was only some three hundred yards from the Bagh Mahal—how convenient for the Tiger, Merial thought wryly—and though not large was built along gracious lines. Surrounding it were fountains, fruit trees, and exotic flowers. Orchids that Merial had never before seen grew from the bark of trees, and vines bearing magnificent blossoms almost covered the walls of the house. They also hung over the veranda, where a lady in a salmon-colored sari was reading.

As Geeta placed palm to palm and bent reverently to the ground, the lady raised her head and turned toward them. Merial was astounded to see that Rukmiri-Bai was a tall, middle-aged lady with a hawk-nosed face that reminded her of Khem-Rana.

Then she smiled, and her face softened into friendliness. "So," she exclaimed in a deep contralto voice, "you are the *Angrezi* female that the servants have been buzzing about! Let me look at you, Mira Larkwell."

Again Merial placed her palms together, raised them high over her head, and bent to the ground. When she gave greeting in Hindustani, the older lady nodded thoughtfully. "I can see why my nephew was intrigued by you."

A monkey, chattering and making faces, flung itself from one of the climbing vines and plopped into Rukmiri-Bai's lap. Calmly, as if such things occurred all the time, she began to stroke the animal. "I hear that Prince Rayn visited you yesterday afternoon but stayed only a few minutes," she continued. "You have much to explain to me, Mira Larkwell."

Merial felt her cheeks burn as she murmured, "What does Your Highness want to know?"

"First, remove that shawl and sit down." Merial approached the cushions to which Rukmiri-Bai pointed and picked up the shawl that lay upon it. The shawl was made of wool but was as soft as silk.

"It's our wool," Rukmiri-Bai said proudly. "It comes from sheep bred especially to produce the finest fleece. Rayn has encouraged the hill people in our northern cities to breed the sheep and spin the wool, and we already trade with Kashmir and parts of India. Unfortunately, we will never be able to trade with the *Angrezi* while my brother is rana. Perhaps when Rayn succeeds to the Silver Throne, there will be a change in policy."

Rukmiri selected a banana from a bowl of fruit beside her and began to feed the monkey. "There are," she went on, "few people as capable to rule this princedom as Prince Rayn. I tell you this so that you will know the man who is your master. It will be easier for you to please him if you understand him." When Merial didn't reply, the elder woman said sharply, "You're no longer in your country. Our ways are different. You belong to Prince Rayn, the rana's adopted heir."

"His *adopted* heir?"

Rukmiri-Bai nodded. "My brother's only child, Prince

Bikaner, was killed hunting near the southwestern border. A drunken *Angrezi* mistook him for a marauding Afridi and shot him. My brother had no love of your people before this, but when his son was murdered, his dislike turned to hatred, he wanted you all destroyed."

Rukmiri-Bai removed the monkey from her lap and bent forward to explain. "My brother had three wives and many concubines, but he had only daughters who died in infancy. His nephews died when they were young—all, alas, including my own son."

There was a short pause during which Merial asked, "Then who is Prince Rayn?"

According to Rukmiri-Bai, Narayn was the orphaned son of a noble Kashmiri family. He had come to Rasgani when he was a youth and had been raised as a warrior.

"So fearless was he in battle that all our enemies feared him," Rukmiri-Bai recounted. "He became a commander in my brother's armies, then rose to the rank of general. When he saved Khem-Rana's life in battle, my brother made him supreme commander of the armies and adopted him as his heir."

Intrigued in spite of herself, Merial said, "I've heard that royal families often adopt heirs, but I thought that they chose a child from their own families."

"My brother broke with tradition. There were many who spoke against the adoption. Ibrahim suggested that Panwa Puar, who is a distant cousin by marriage to the house of Raoshad, might be more suited to be the crown prince. But Panwa's late father, the great Bhupinder Puar, counseled otherwise. He said that the kingdom needed a warrior prince who had the wisdom to rule in peace as well as in war."

Rukmiri-Bai paused and turned her intelligent dark eyes on Merial. "Rayn is not my blood nephew, but he has been kind to me. He gave me this house and pretends he needs me to watch over his household so that I may have a purpose in my life. He is dear to me."

Merial wasn't sure whether this was a statement or a warning of some kind. She listened in silence as Rukmiri-Bai continued. "Here a woman without family has no protection. Be grateful that you belong to Rayn and not to a cruel or abusive master. When he tires of you—and men, alas, tire of women—he will assuredly reward you as he has rewarded the other women who have fleetingly caught his eye. Remember this, and I also will protect you as much as I can."

Merial was thoughtful when Geeta ushered her out of the princess's presence and conducted her to a door that fronted the street. Here a palanquin, attended by bearers wearing the black and gold of Prince Rayn's household, as well as two armed and mounted *bhaldars,* were waiting to take her to visit Sir Edward.

Yesterday she had been too apprehensive to pay close attention to her surroundings. Today she could admire the city. As Geeta had said, many women here did not wear the tentlike *bourka* and were casual about their veils. Dressed in bright colors, they went freely about their business, gathered about the central fountain near the palace, and laughed, gossiped, or chaffered with the vendors in the marketplace. Brown, naked children tumbled like small seals in the lake. An old man sat in a doorway smoking a waterpipe, while his daughter-in-law scrubbed the white steps of the house. A small, dark-faced flower vendor, carrying a tub of scarlet gladioli, passed by, and a monkey man, his monkey riding on his shoulder, beat his drum.

With something of a shock, Merial noticed that there were no beggars in the city. In Calcutta, in Delhi—even in London—there were poor, sick, or hungry people, but here in Rasgani everyone seemed well fed and busy. The scents of the city were not of heat and dirt but mingled incense, cooking, and the fragrance of fresh flowers.

When her palanquin finally stopped at a large, square building made of stone, surrounded by a flower garden, Merial was surprised again. She hadn't expected the unpretentious Baju to live in such a palatial home. "Does this building belong to the *hakim* Baju?" she asked one of the guards who rode beside her.

The guard nodded, then shouted to a white-clad orderly who had poked his head out of the door of the house. The man came running. "Do you bring another sufferer to the *hakim*'s hospital?" he asked.

Merial explained, and the orderly bade her enter. As she did so, she was even more astonished. She'd seen the English-administered hospital in Delhi and a native doctor's so-called hospital in Armitsar, but this was a far cry from either. The walkway and the veranda of the stone house were spotless, and once inside the orderly led her down a pristine corridor. On each side of the hallway were large rooms with many beds, and a smaller chamber, bright with sunshine, where Sir Edward lay.

Sir Edward looked much better, but when he saw Merial, he frowned. "My God, girl. Anyone seeing you would say you had gone native."

"My English clothes were in rags," she reminded him. She leaned to kissed his cheek, adding, "You are looking well, Father. I'm grateful to see you're being well treated."

Sir Edward snorted. "I don't trust these wogs—they're likely fattening me up for the kill. How have you fared, Merial?"

The casual question didn't mask his anxiety. "I'm all right," she told him.

"That fellow—the prince—he hasn't—" She shook her head, and he looked greatly relieved. "So they've come to their senses. Even the rana, curse him, knows that if they touched you, English armies would tear this place apart."

Just then Baju came into the room. He beamed when he saw Merial and exclaimed, "But for your eyes you could be a daughter of our people! Our clothing becomes you."

He added that he was pleased with Sir Edward's progress. "He is past the worst of his fever and will gain in strength as the days pass. In a few days he could be released."

"Released to be imprisoned in the rana's dungeons?" Merial asked bluntly.

The old doctor considered this. "No, you are right. I will not give the order for his release, for in the rana's dungeons he will only be sick again. Don't fear. He will be safe here."

Tears of relief filled Merial's eyes. She caught Baju's hand in both hands and whispered, "I can't thank you enough."

"You saved this old life, remember?" Baju smiled benevolently as he added, "Prince Rayn has agreed that you may come here as often as you like, so do not worry about that."

The *hakim* had an old chess board, and Merial spent the afternoon playing chess with her father. He fell asleep after a few hours, and while he dozed she walked out into the corridor to stretch her legs. As she did so, she heard a child begin to scream.

Drawn by the terrified sound, Merial ran down the corridor. In one of the large rooms she saw that a little girl had wedged herself under the bed. An orderly was trying to get her to come out, but in spite of the fact that blood was soaking through the dirty rag that had been wrapped about one skinny brown leg, she remained where she was.

Merial stopped in the doorway to ask what was the matter, and the orderly replied impatiently over his shoulder, "This child of a nameless father has cut herself badly. A servant brought her to the hospital since her mother was not about. She is but a baby and fears strangers."

"I'm not a baby," the child wailed, "and my father has a name. He's Karan Vedi. He's a g-gardener at the B-bagh Mahal."

"Then come out from under that bed and stop making trouble," the harassed orderly urged.

Merial went into the room and knelt down beside the harassed man. "What is your name, little sister?" she asked.

The child stared at the pretty lady with the oddly colored eyes. "Nirmale," she breathed.

"I see that you are playing a hiding game." Merial reached out and gently took the child's small brown hand in hers. "Later we can play together. But now, Nirmale, you must let this elder brother take your hurt away."

Baju came into the room just as Merial had managed to coax the child out from under the bed. "That's it," he approved. "Keep talking to her while I tend to her wound."

Merial took the little girl in her arms and began a nursery rhyme Jassmina had sung to her as Baju sutured the ugly cut. The doctor was wrapping the wound in clean bandages when the child's mother burst into the room. She stopped and made the sign against the evil eye. "What is *she* doing to my child?" she shrilled angrily.

The woman's hostility was like a physical blow. Merial left the sickroom and, too upset to return to Sir Edward's side, went out into the small garden that fronted the hospital. She had longed for India, and yet there was no place for her here. "I don't belong here," she told herself sadly.

Her thoughts were interrupted by the sound of hoofbeats, and, looking up, she saw that Rayn, accompanied by his captain of lancers, Deen, was riding down the road toward the hospital. Involuntarily she caught her breath, and as if aware of that small sigh of sound, he looked directly at her. Their eyes locked with an intensity that left her shaken. He turned to speak to Deen, who grinned, saluted, and rode swiftly away.

Merial's heart had begun to pound irrationally. As though the hospital were some sort of sanctuary, she turned and began to walk toward it, but Rayn caught up to her before she reached the door.

"My aunt told me that you had left for the hospital in the early afternoon," he said.

She protested, "It was you who told me I might visit my father."

"You've had your visit. Now it's nearly sunset, time you returned to the Bagh Mahal."

If she angered him, he might rescind his permission to visit the hospital. "May I say my good-bye to my father?" she asked.

Her words were suitably humble, but her tone was defiant. Rayn's dark eyebrows rose quizzically as he considered her. "You can see him tomorrow if you wish. Just now there's something we need to discuss."

Did he mean for her to ride with him on his horse? He did. Merial took a deep breath to suppress her rising panic. Then, squaring her slim shoulders, she took his proffered hand, set her small foot on his booted one, and was lifted to sit pillion behind him.

She did her best to keep her distance from him as his cream-white stallion trotted forward, but the animal's movements threw her against him. The contact was disturbing, and even more disturbing was the knowledge that he had said he would return to the Bagh Mahal with her. He had let her alone last night, but today was another story.

Merial bit her lip, hard, to choke off such thoughts. She must not try to anticipate future horrors. She tried instead to concentrate on the road and realized they were leaving the main thoroughfare and approaching the lake.

"We'll travel by water," Rayn explained.

As he spoke they came to the edge of the lake. Here Deen was waiting near a boat. The old boatman bent to touch the dust at Rayn's feet. "I am blessed by your protection, Shield of the Kingdom!" he cried. "It's a beautiful evening."

"That it is." Rayn nodded dismissively to Deen. "You can return to the Bagh Mahal. I don't need you now."

Deen's scarred face twisted into a grin. "I trust the fires of the, ah, sunset will not scorch you, lord."

"Damn your impudence." But Rayn was smiling, too, as he dismounted, lifted Merial from the saddle, and led her to the boat. "Ladies first, I believe you English say."

"You *speak English?*"

"Learning an enemy's language is good battle strategy," he replied easily.

Had Rayn understood every insult Sir Edward had hurled at him? That horrible thought silenced Merial as he swept aside the curtains and handed her on board the vessel.

The boat was large and luxurious. Curtains of pale gold silk gave privacy to the midsection of the vessel, where there was a couch of satin cushions, a table laden with fruit and sherbet. Rayn led her to the couch, and as she sank gingerly into the cushions, the boat glided onto the lake.

Just how much of Sir Edward's insults had Rayn understood? As he took his seat next to her, Merial decided to try an experiment. "So you could understand us all the time," she said in English.

"Of course. Only a fool underestimates his enemies."

There was no trace of accent in his English, but after a moment he went on in Hindustani. "I prefer my mother tongue, however, so you will indulge me in that—and in other things."

Involuntarily Merial glanced at him. The hard planes of his face were in shadow as he continued. "I'm sure you remember the terms on which you were spared from the slave block. Repeat them to me now."

The purr with which the words ended sent a shiver through Merial. It was not entirely a shiver of fear. She had the sense that familiar dark fires were stirring deep within her, waiting to ignite at a word or touch.

Shame made her angry and she snapped, "Very well, then. Your father, the rana, wanted to put us in prison to hold us for ransom. You said that Sir Edward should be taken to the hospital and that I"—in spite of herself her voice broke as she finished—"that I should be given to you."

Only the splash of the oars broke the silence that fell between them. Merial caught her breath as he leaned toward her, but it was only to lift the curtains on her side of the boat.

She wasn't prepared for the scene that met her eyes. The sun was beginning to set, and the lake, strewn with water lilies, was burning with color. Streams of gold and crimson and faintest mauve filled the sky. Birds called as they sped homeward, and an evening breeze brushed her cheek like a lover's hand.

Rayn was asking softly, "Does a properly brought up English lady know what it means to belong to a man?"

He leaned forward as he spoke, and his body almost touched hers. Merial caught her breath and found her lungs invaded with the scents of leather and the outdoors —*his* scent.

"To belong to a man," Rayn was saying, "is to give yourself entirely into his hands. Your soul and your spirit. Your heart and your body. He becomes your God, and you won't exist without him."

He didn't touch her. He didn't have to. His voice was one long caress. The dark fires within Merial were turning amidst the embers, smoldering into shameful life. Under the tight turquoise blouse her breasts seemed to await a lover's caress.

She wanted to do something to break the spell he'd woven around her, but she couldn't. Like a moth hypnotized by flame, she listened spellbound as he went on. "And in turn the man must protect and cherish his woman."

His lips were very near. They almost but not quite brushed hers. Merial felt as though she were once more on the Bridge of Winds and as if she were plunging from a great height. In the dizzy tumult of her senses she registered the fact that she *wanted* to fall.

"I pity the man to whom you belong, Mira," Rayn murmured. "He'll think he owns you, but he will become your slave."

A heron flew by the boat with a beat of white wings. The sound added another dimension to the sorcery of Rayn's words and emphasized the fact that they were alone except for the water and the birds and the sun.

That sun was setting. Red, passionate, the ball of flame was dipping into the water. Merial could almost hear the fires of the sun hiss silent in the cool of the lake. Crimson, gold, orange—the water blazed with heat.

He spoke quietly, almost against her cheek. "This is what I wanted to show you, Mira. Like a woman, Baranpur is beautiful and must be cherished and protected from your people."

At the unexpected words she turned sharply. Instead of desire, there was icy determination in his hard topaz gaze. "I don't understand," she stammered.

His voice was unexpectedly grim. "When I asked the rana for you, it wasn't your body I wanted but your safety." She began to speak, but he interrupted. "If your father dies, it would be an excuse for Perce to declare war on us."

"No one asked you to take us prisoner," she flashed.

"Indeed, nobody did. I acted unwisely—a sin that arose from anger. I shouldn't have lost my temper, no matter what the provocation."

"Provocation! We did nothing . . ." But her words died away as he reached out and cupped her chin in his big hand.

"What I'm trying to say, my thorny English rose, is that just as your father must come to no harm, so you must remain pure and virtuous. I don't want to go to war just because you've been raped."

Was he telling the truth? She wasn't sure. She could never be sure of the Tiger or of herself when he was near her. She feared this man as she had feared none other, and yet she was drawn to him by tangled emotions she could neither understand nor accept.

His white teeth flashed in a smile. "Disappointed?"

She slapped him—tried to, anyway—but he intercepted

the blow, caught her hand easily and held it in his iron grip.

"Much as I regret the pleasure I would doubtless find in your bed, I must resist the temptation," Rayn purred. He lifted her hand and raised it to his lips as he added ironically, "I'm a true patriot, Mira, and Baranpur means everything to me. For the moment you're safe from me."

··*Seven*··

"BE STILL FOR one more moment, Nirmale," Merial urged the squirming child in her lap. "We'll soon be done."

"But will my leg be well enough for me to go to the Festival of the Rains?" the child wanted to know. "Mira-Bai, I want so much to see Prince Rayn and his *bhaldars* and Khem-Rana on the elephant."

Deftly Merial secured the bandage. "Now you are ready for a hundred festivals."

The gardener's daughter tried a few hesitant steps, then returned to throw her arms around Merial's neck. "Thank you, Mira-Bai."

She skipped away. Watching from her seat on the grass under the frangipani tree, Merial wondered at the child's energy. She herself had none on this hot, humid, late-May day. She knew she ought to go back to the house and ready herself for her daily visit to Baju's hospital, but she remained where she was. It was cooler here in the garden than anywhere else in the Bagh Mahal even though the sweet scent of the white frangipani blossoms was cloying.

She didn't hear Rayn coming down the garden path until he remarked, "The monsoon rains are on their way."

Merial glanced up at the overcast sky and remembered the seasonal rains that had almost drowned Sri Nevi from June to October. "I didn't know it could get so hot here in the valley," she said with a sigh.

Rayn looked down into her upturned face and thought that with her eyes crinkled against the refracted sunlight, she looked very young. She'd sounded young, too, when he'd heard her laughing with his gardener's child.

"It's going to storm," he told her. "I don't want you to go to the hospital today."

She got to her feet at once protesting, "But I'm needed there. There's a little boy at the hospital—he's got the most horrible skin ulcers and won't allow anyone but me to treat him. Besides, my father will be worried if he doesn't see me."

"By all accounts he's well enough to leave the hospital." Rayn had spoken coldly. "Baju doesn't think so," Merial retorted.

She had spoken almost defiantly, but her eyes were frightened. Rayn was reminded of a dove trying to defend itself against a hawk's attack.

"I've heard of the work you've done at the hospital," he said in a milder tone.

He'd heard because his aunt had filled his ears with Mira's accomplishments. In a short while she'd not only learned a great deal about the Ayurvedic medicine that Baju practiced, but was now one of his most devoted assistants. It irritated Rayn that in the past two weeks Rukmiri-Bai had become Mira's champion. She had told her adopted nephew roundly that though he might consider Mira a mere plaything, there was more to the *Angrezi* girl than met the eye. See, for instance, how the domestic staff loved her—and one could never fool servants.

It was unquestionably true. The gardener and his family had become devotees, and Nirmale followed her like a small shadow. Even the lancers had begun to accept Mira ever since she'd cured Rassul's oldest son's cough with an infusion of wild-pepper tree, thus earning the gratitude of the *bhaldar* and his gentle wife. Chetak, Big Fanji, and even the impudent young Deen had consulted "the *Angrezi hakim*" on occasion.

But while Mira endeared herself, Sir Edward tipped the scales on the other side. As his health returned, he became even more demanding of Baju and his orderlies. If the roles had been reversed, Rayn knew, Edward Ashland would have wasted little sleep over his daughter's welfare.

"Forget about your father for once," he commanded. "You're not to leave the Bagh Mahal today."

His high-handedness rankled her. Besides, Merial noted that the prince was dressed in court clothes—an achkan embroidered with gold thread, white jodhpurs, and the half-turban that only royalty could wear.

"*You* are going out," she pointed out.

"That's different," was all he said, but the speculative expression in his eyes unnerved her. Since their talk on the lake that evening two weeks ago, he had not laid a hand on her or even been alone with her, but Merial could sense him watching her sometimes with that same disconcerting look.

She said, "What could there be to fear when the whole city is preparing for the Festival of the Rains? Nirmale can talk of nothing else but the military parade and Khem-Rana riding on his elephant." When Rayn didn't respond she added, "I know that it may rain, but a little rain won't hurt me."

"It doesn't just rain in Baranpur." When she renewed her protest, he covered her mouth with his hand. "Enough. Just do as I say."

The fingers against her lips were proprietary. Merial jerked her head away. "And if I don't?"

"You will," he said.

Naturally he'd assume that the world rotated according to his every wish. Merial watched Rayn stride away and felt a childish desire to stamp and scream.

"I don't care what you think—I don't belong to you!" she cried, but he was out of earshot. "Damn you," she continued, "you said I might go to the hospital—and go I will."

Too furious to weigh the consequences of her disobedience, she returned to the palace and summoned her palanquin. Until now she had been too afraid to be angry, but two week's rest and the relative peace she had found at the Bagh Mahal had given her time to realize all the crimes committed against her and her father. Prince Rayn had kidnapped the Ashlands, dragged his innocent captives to his country, and placed them in terrible peril. If he now repented and tried to protect them, it was only because he was afraid of getting into a war with England.

"He'll not order me around as though I'm his slave," Merial swore.

She continued to fume as she entered her palanquin, but even so she did not miss the strong wind that was blowing down from the hills. The *bhaldar* assigned to guard her today cast an anxious look toward the mountains and asked, "Are you sure you wish to journey forth, Mira-Bai?"

"I'm sure." But Merial began to have doubts as the winds grew more fierce and women began to call their children in from play. As they passed the central fountain, she saw other women, their clothing whipping about in the wind, hastening to fill their jars.

Even the little flower seller who was always by the fountain was packing up his wares. When he recognized the distinctive black-and-gold palanquin, he came hurrying toward Merial.

"For you, Sahiba." He grinned as he thrust a large bouquet of scarlet roses into Merial's hands. To her surprised thanks he replied, "No, it is I, Ahmed Ibin Amin, who must thank the sahiba. You helped my little Ameera when she was taken to the *hakim* for a fever." He bowed as he added, "May God, the merciful and compassionate, guard you from harm."

The tight knot of anger caused by Rayn's treatment dissolved as she drew in the roses' fragrance. Then Ahmed Ibin Amin added, "And may He protect Prince Rayn, who is your master and mine."

"Is he indeed?" Sharply Merial signaled her bearers to move on. But before the men could obey, there was a flash of light. She thought that it had begun to thunder until she heard the dull *thunk* of something hitting the cushions beside her. Looking down she saw the haft of a dagger protruding from the silk.

There was a shout of warning from her guards, and simultaneously one of her bearers screamed. The palanquin was jolted to the ground and its curtains ripped aside to reveal a dark face twisted with hate.

"English bitch," a harsh voice grated, "you're going to die."

Acting instinctively, Merial rolled to the other side of the palanquin and, tearing open the door, rolled outside. But as she did so, a man wielding a tulwar came rushing at her.

"Run, run, Mira-Bai!" the little flower seller shouted.

He swung his flower basket at the man with the tulwar, but was instantly bowled aside.

"Run, Sahiba!" shrilled Ahmed.

Merial began to run across the deserted square. It wasn't easy to run in a sari, and a wicked gust of wind caught her and spun her around. The stones of the square were wet with spume from the fountain, and the flat-soled slippers she wore couldn't get a purchase on the slippery ground. She could hear footsteps drumming behind her and turning saw that her pursuer was almost upon her.

"Prince killer, this day you'll be in hell."

Dodging his first blow, she ran around the fountain, but another gust of wind caught her and sent her spinning backward into her attacker's arms. She heard his satisfied grunt and tried to twist loose, but slipped on the wet stones and fell to her knees. She cried out—once—as something foul was twisted around her throat.

That was when the rain came. Not any kind of rain she was used to, but a solid waterfall. The force of it almost stunned her, and the murderous pressure around her throat slackened. With an effort she pulled clear and scrambled to her knees.

She began to run again but hadn't taken three steps before steely arms seized her. She cried out and battered her fists on a solid chest until she heard Rayn say, "Get behind me and don't move."

He shoved her roughly behind him, and she felt, rather than saw, his sword arm rise and fall. Then there was a howl of pain that was muffled by the roar of falling rain.

"Is he dead?" she stammered.

Unceremoniously Rayn kicked the still form at his feet. "Didn't I tell you not to leave the Bagh Mahal?"

Merial's legs had gone rubbery, and she had to swallow

the lump in her throat. "I didn't realize—I never thought—you don't own me. . . ." Her whisper died away.

There was a chuckle, and another voice spoke out of the rain-induced dark. "Women can be trickier than Shaitan himself," Panwa's voice drawled, "and they never listen to a man. You're a wise man never to have married, my prince."

Ignoring this, Rayn demanded, "How many dead?"

Rassul's measured voice replied out of the murk. "We killed two, but the others took to their heels. Chetak and Fanji are in pursuit. We have lost one of our comrades, lord, and also a bearer."

Rayn caught hold of Merial's wrist and dragged her back to her downed palanquin. Three dark shapes lay on the ground, and Rassul knelt beside them. "It's Hari, lord," Rassul said. "He took a knife-thrust in the heart and died quickly."

"He died because you couldn't obey orders." The Tiger's snarl followed Merial as she, too, knelt and tried for a pulse. There was none. The bearer, too, was dead. As she turned to the third man, a flash of lightning illumined a lean, hawk-nosed face and glazed eyes that still held hate and fury. Beside this man lay a sodden handkerchief with knotted ends.

Rassul silently picked it up and handed it to his prince, who snapped, *"Thug."* His voice hardened as he added, "Take the *bhaldars* and fan out through the city. I want a prisoner I can question. No, stay—I need an escort to take this *lady* back to the Bagh Mahal."

The ominous note in Rayn's voice sent ice up Merial's spine. But Panwa said, "That's not necessary, my prince. I myself will take Mira-Bai to your home."

"I don't need—" But Merial was interrupted by Rayn's roar.

"Damn it, you'll do as you're told!"

Merial flinched. Panwa said peaceably, "Your *bhaldars* will find the villains who dared attack your woman. Go, my prince, to the Silver Palace. The rana requires your presence immediately."

"I'm in your debt." Without so much as a glance in Merial's direction, Rayn strode away.

"I have never seen Prince Rayn so angry," Panwa commented. "You must mean a great deal to him to enrage him so."

She said bitterly, "I'm his property."

"Is that why you called out his name when you thought you were going to die? Come, Mira-Bai, we must obey our prince."

He called out an order, and men of his household followed. Shaken, Merial mounted her steed. She had no recollection of having called out for Rayn, but then, she couldn't remember very much of the last ten minutes.

"We must ride swiftly," Panwa urged. "The storm will worsen, and the thugs may still be about."

She'd heard of the murderous ones who worshipped Kali, goddess of destruction, and offered ritual sacrifices of blood to their dreadful goddess. "The brotherhood was strong before the uprising that you *Angrezi* call the Mutiny," Panwa told her as they spurred their horses, "but they were forced underground when you established control of this country. Lately they have grown strong again. Though outlawed in Baranpur, they have many sympathizers who want to destroy the *Angrezi* and Perce's railroad."

"Why should they be outlawed?" she asked, bewildered. "Doesn't the Ti—doesn't the prince also want to destroy the railroad and my countrymen?"

"His methods aren't extreme enough to please the

thugs. Prince Rayn is no assassin." Panwa's voice lost its drawl and became earnest. "You have to understand that you can't reason with a man like Perce. Force is all he understands. But the prince truly wants peace, not war."

"And you?"

"I, too, wish peace and so did my late father before me," Panwa agreed gravely.

There was a short silence after which Panwa resumed, "These fanatic thugs believe that *Angrezi* blood will get them into paradise. They think that if they offer their goddess enough sacrifices, she herself will help destroy the enemy. They'll stop at nothing to persuade Khem-Rana to make war on your country."

As he spoke, a flash of lightning stabbed downward and was followed almost immediately by a peal of thunder. Merial's horse reared and neighed fearfully.

"We must hurry," Panwa urged. "Come. I know a shorter way."

The storm had worsened by the time they left the main road to follow a narrow path that edged the lake. Though it was noonday, it was almost as dark as night, and the rain and wind made it impossible to see. Already it had started to flood, and in some places the horses sank up to their hocks in water.

Now the wind seemed to change direction. Instead of riding into the wind, it seemed as though they were now being pushed along as though by invisible hands. The lightning and thunder moved closer.

"We are nearly there," Panwa encouraged.

Lightning flashed, and in that eerie green glow of light, Merial saw a man—no, several men—on horseback spurring toward them along the lip of the lake. Dark turbans, dark tunics, upraised curved swords—she saw it all in a blink-flash of horrified time, saw their wild eyes and open mouths.

"Kali—Kali—dreadful goddess of power—devour, cut, destroy our enemies," their leader chanted. "Kill the *Angrezi* bitch now!"

As he spoke, Merial felt the air change. The hairs at the back of her neck seemed to rise, and there was a metallic taste in her mouth.

Suddenly the world exploded into light. Merial screamed as the thug leader's sword blazed with an eerie green glow. It flowed down the metal blade until he seemed framed in electric flame. A blast of thunder that shook the earth drowned out his agonized death-cry.

Panwa grasped Merial's bridle, spurred the horses, and rode through the mass of terrified, disorganized assassins. No one stopped them, but Merial, glancing over her shoulder, saw that the thugs had dismounted and were staring down at the charred remains of their leader.

Panwa spoke grimly. "They should be pleased. A blood-sacrifice selected by the gods themselves—what could be more appropriate?"

They reached the Bagh Mahal some ten minutes later. As soon as she was safe, Panwa left Merial.

"I must hasten to report this new attack on your life," he said. "If Prince Rayn's *bhaldars* are unsuccessful, Ibrahim Ali Shah must ferret the villains out. Baranpur's chief of police is a man of deep intrigues and secret connections."

Merial could do no more than stammer her thanks. Death and blood and the terrible scene she'd just witnessed had brought on a kind of shock, and she'd started to shiver so violently that her teeth literally chattered together.

Geeta summoned the princess, and Rukmiri-Bai ordered Merial into the hottest bath she could stand. The heated water wouldn't stop her tremors. Merial could still see the look on the thug leader's face when the lightning struck him.

"Those who mock the gods are destroyed by them," was all Rukmiri-Bai said. She gave Merial a brew of poppies mixed with honey. "Drink this now and you will sleep and find your strength again."

And she slept. Sliding miles deep into darkness, she wandered in dreams that had no beginning, no meaning, no end. She seemed to be running through the woods again, looking for help for her sick father. Then she was on horseback, clinging to Rayn. And then again she stood on the edge of the Bridge of Winds and a thug was menacing her with his sword. "Jump, *Angrezi* bitch," he rasped at her, and she took a step backward into void. Merial screamed and screamed as she fell. . . .

"It's all right, Mira. You're with me—you're safe."

At first she thought that he was a part of her nightmare. She clung to him, sobbing incoherently, and he held her and smoothed back her rumpled hair and rocked her like a child. Then he said, "You're at the Bagh Mahal, in your own bed. Nothing's going to hurt you."

He wasn't a part of her nightmare or a figment of her imagination. The bare chest against which she was pressed was solid. Confused and bewildered, she drew back a little and saw that, as he'd said, she was on her bed. Her silk nightgown was soaked through with perspiration, and her loose hair was damp as well.

"I ache everywhere," she murmured, "and my head feels like lead."

He loosened his hold on her and took a goblet from her bedside. "Drink this."

She drank the cool water thirstily, and some of her muzziness lifted.

"How long have I slept?"

"Through the day and half the night," he replied. "It's only a few hours to dawn."

Merial glanced at the sky that showed through the arched, latticed windows of her chamber. Rain was still falling heavily, but the lightning flashes that lit the sky were sullen and far away. Had he sat beside her all this time? she wondered, but her throbbing head made it hard to think.

For the first time she looked at him fully and noted that Rayn, too, was dressed for sleep. A wine-colored *longhi,* or length of cloth knotted around his lean waist, was his only garment. The light of a single lamp played over the muscled shadows of his bare chest, picking out the curly darkness of his chest-hair. At his throat Niall's amulet glowed as with inner fire.

"The meeting with the rana took longer than was expected," he explained. "I was going to my rooms when I heard you cry out in your sleep."

She shivered convulsively. "I dreamt of him—that man who was struck by lightning. I never saw a man die like that. It was horrible. . . ."

He didn't tell her not to think of it. Instead, he poured more water into her goblet. As she drank, some part of Merial's slowly clearing mind warned her that she still stood in danger. Prince Rayn had been furious with her when they parted earlier.

"I'm sorry," she said in a low voice. "I was wrong to go out today. I know I'm responsible for the deaths of your men—"

She broke off as he reached out to cup her cheek in his palm. The touch seemed to travel through skin and flesh and bone to her heart. She wanted to draw away from him and couldn't.

"I should have brought you back to the palace myself instead of leaving it to Panwa."

She wished that he hadn't touched her. The caress of his fingers seemed to reach deep inside her to a place she didn't want to explore. She was grateful when he let go of her and got restlessly to his feet.

"I underestimated the thugs, but I'll not make that mistake again." After a pause he added, "My father has ordered Ibrahim to comb the city for them, and my *bhaldars* are searching as far as the border. They'll find one of the brotherhood for me, and when they do—"

Something in his voice brought back the cold, hating eyes, the rasping voice of the man who had tried to knife her in her palanquin. Merial caught a painful breath, and he said, "You're chilled and tired. Rest, now, and we'll talk in the morning."

He came back to her bed and stood looking at her for a moment, then bent to kiss her on the lips. It was a gentle kiss, light and passionless, almost a kiss of atonement for all that she had suffered. Yet when his mouth touched hers, Merial felt as though an electric current were passing between them. Once more she seemed to be lost in the storm, feeling every cell and fiber of her body come to aching readiness.

She looked up and her world dissolved in the golden depths of his eyes. She whispered, "Don't leave me."

Almost convulsively his arms closed about her. He sank down on the low bed beside her and held her tightly, so tightly that she could feel the prickle of his chest-hair through the thin silk which was her only covering. His lips formed fierce words against her ear. "By all the gods,

I was afraid that I'd lost you. I wouldn't have forgiven myself."

Only half aware of what she did, she twisted her face so that their lips could meet. He kissed her with a ferocity that seared through her until it found her heart. Responding to the madness his mouth invoked, she clung to him as if he were the only safety left in the world.

"Mira," he said against her lips. "My Mira." He smoothed the damp tangle of her hair, then ran his fingers along the curve of her jaw, her throat. As if in tune to this same music, her hands roved over his shoulders, smoothing down the muscular slope of his back, the rugged fortress of his chest, hard belly, and strongly muscled thighs.

Her hands were like fiery butterflies. They ignited his body with a passion as strong as the storm that had raged today. Before the tempest of his emotions, Rayn's careful reasoning fell away.

With a swift, fluid motion he caught her nightdress and lifted it over her head, then held her to him a moment before lowering her back against the sheets. She moaned with pleasure as his dark head bent to take first one and then the other of her nipples in his mouth, drawing deep of their honey.

"Rayn—"

He heard the exhalation of her breath as she spoke, and with it came the memory of how she'd cried out his name today. The realization of what would have happened if he hadn't been near shook him, and for a moment he could think clearly again.

She felt him pull away from her and reached out to draw him back to her once more. But instead of obeying her wordless request, he gritted, "On the lake that day I swore that I wouldn't touch you."

Merial knew that it wasn't Rukmiri-Bai's drug that

made her limbs feel weak or her heart beat wildly. It was what she knew in her heart of hearts: that the promise made on the lake that day had been fated to be broken.

As though he were speaking to himself, Rayn went on, "There was good reason for my decision. Nothing's changed."

But he was wrong. Today she'd thought she was going to die, and everything had changed irrevocably. She was no longer Merial Ashland but Rayn's Mira, and she wanted him. Since the moment she had faced him in the deserted hills, she'd wanted him.

"This was meant to happen," she whispered.

Her words found echo in the knowledge he'd tried to hide from himself. Rayn swore softly, but the curse was smothered against her lips.

His mouth claimed hers as though by right. And as though by fealty bound to him, Merial's head tipped back to allow him greater pleasure. His tongue curved about the periphery of her lips, and her lips parted to its bold stroke. The dark fires that had been slumbering within her woke and shivered through her veins as his hand traced a sensuous pathway between her breasts, circling the mounds until at last they teased her nipples.

Now his lips followed the pathway his hands had taken, and she felt as though he was sucking her soul from within her. Waves of pleasure so intense that they were like fire rippled through her, and she sighed his name. Then his mouth left her breast to seek her lips again, and his hand moved down to smooth the silk of her inner thighs until he came to their joining.

Against his lips Merial cried out at the agony of pleasure that lanced through her. When his touch stopped, she instinctively lifted her hips to seek it again. She wanted his touch—she wanted him.

"I promised that I would send you back to Sri Nevi, but that wasn't the way it was meant to be. You are mine and have always been and always will." Rayn's hushed voice was another caress, as soft as music, as deep as darkest night. "Our lives are linked together, Mira, linked before time. We have been together forever, before we were even born."

He had told her once what it meant to belong to a man. Now she knew. "Rayn—" Her voice broke on his name and tore away his last resistance. Not gods or demons could prevent him from loving her. It was destiny—his and hers. There was no escaping it.

He twisted free of the cloth around his hips and lay down beside her on the low bed. The soft pillows shifted to his weight, and she reached for him, murmuring inarticulately against the lips that sought hers. But as he drew her hard against him, she felt Niall's amulet between them.

Rayn registered the tension shivering through her. Without letting her go, he drew the chain from around his head and dropped it to the floor. She heard the sound it made as it fell—soft, gentle, sad.

Niall, forgive me, she thought.

Then all thought ceased. Rayn showered kisses on her lips, her throat, then bent to her breasts again, the satin of her belly, and lower to her inner thighs.

His lips and tongue brought unbearable joy. Fire consumed her, maddening her with desire. Instinctively her hips began to move and thrust, and her thighs parted to receive the hard, sleek gift of his love.

Rayn wanted to be patient, to ease himself gently into her so that her virginal body could accommodate itself gradually to the fullness of his manhood. But when he entered her, she pressed against him, twisting and rising so that they were fused together. He could hear her cries mingling with his as she sheathed him, moved with him, sought to take him deeper yet until he reared and plunged in her satin heat.

She was dying, Merial knew. Had to be. Pain and pleasure mingled in her until she could not bear it. She was being riven apart, consumed. She heard Rayn's shout of triumph and her own cries as they shattered into light that was beyond sense, beyond feeling, beyond conscious thought.

··*Eight*··

LIKE A LEAF floating earthward after a storm, Merial came back into herself. Her scattered senses and her body seemed to be hers again. She sighed, stretched, and opened her eyes to velvet darkness.

Yet not quite darkness. The rain had ceased and a quarter moon peered unsurely through the arched windows of her chamber. Its tentative light touched the strong-muscled body next to hers. Still half asleep, she turned instinctively toward Rayn and felt his arms close protectively about her.

"So I wasn't dreaming," she wondered aloud.

Rayn had awakened first, and his thoughts as he watched Merial sleep had been troubled. Now, as she opened her eyes and looked full at him, the confusion left him and the tightness around his heart eased. He had been right when he told her that she had always been his. Since the moment of their first meeting they had belonged to each other.

"Who can protest the will of the gods?" he wondered aloud.

He stroked the love-tangles from her hair, which curled

lovingly about his fingers. Her back was silky, but the skin between her thighs felt more like satin.

Rayn wondered again at the renewed force of his desire and reminded himself that in spite of her eager lovemaking, Mira had been a virgin. He tried to draw away from her, but that was the last thing she wanted.

What she wanted was him. She needed his hands and mouth that could play her body like an instrument. She yearned for the weight of his body on hers, the hundred small rituals of loving—all unknown until last night but now as much a part of her as the beat of her heart—that culminated in the one shattering act of love. She slid her arms around his neck, raising her mouth to his.

"Beloved." Her lips knew his, now, knew the lazy stroke of his tongue around the periphery of her much-kissed mouth. "It is near dawn," he continued. "I watched you sleeping this past hour. I wanted to wake you, but you looked too peaceful."

As he spoke, his fingers were tracing sensuous patterns along her back and buttocks and breasts. Lightly, tantalizingly, they grazed her nipples, and she purred, "I don't feel peaceful now."

He smiled as he continued to caress her. "You're more lovely than the lake at sunset."

It was a fitting comparison. Mira could be as serene as the cloud-reflecting lake, but the currents within her ran deep. They could carry a swimmer far—to undreamt of paradise or to destruction.

Rayn didn't care for the direction his thoughts were taking. He kissed her once again and this time swung out of her arms to sit up on the edge of the low bed. This time Merial didn't protest. His unspoken unease had communicated itself to her, and all the thoughts that she did not want to face came crowding into her mind.

To still these thoughts, she asked a question. "You said last night that we'd always belonged together. Do you believe in reincarnation?"

"The priests say that we live many lives and that all is predestined." Rayn caught up the moonstone amulet from the floor and slipped it over his head. Merial noticed the old battle scars which gleamed whitely on his powerful back, and she felt even more troubled.

"Then Niall's death, too, was . . . meant to happen?" she asked unhappily.

He shrugged. "It was his fate to die."

"But there must be such a thing as free choice!" she cried. "Otherwise, we'd be nothing but blind, mute slaves."

He turned to face her then. "I'm not one for gods and priests," he replied, "but I believe our destiny is written before we are born. Within a certain framework, though, we can shape the progress of our lives. It was written that your friend die in battle, but *he* chose to die protecting you. It was written that I conquer him, but I could have brought him to Baranpur to live out his life as a slave. Would that have been better?"

Merial tried to picture Niall. The long-ago memories were hazy, and the living, vital image of Rayn interposed itself between her and what she remembered of Niall's face. But when she thought of St. Marr as a slave, she knew how wrong that would have been. "He'd have rather died," she whispered.

Rayn said quietly, "I think so, too. He had a clean death in fair fight. There are worse ways to die, Mira. So, his destiny—and mine—was accomplished."

"Then it's also fated that you hate English people?"

Rayn couldn't answer that question without causing her pain, but he knew that certain facts weren't changed. Last night notwithstanding, he was still crown prince of Baranpur, and she was Edward Ashland's daughter. For one moment hatred for Ashland's kind flooded through Rayn, but when he looked into Mira's eyes, his anger died.

With a smothered curse, he reached across the tumbled bed and crushed her to him. He could feel her tense against him for a moment, but then she yielded to the fierce pressure of his arms.

"To hell with fate and the gods," he grated.

Questions and doubts drifted away like shadows across the moon as their lips met, and Rayn whispered, "I knew you were my woman long ago. Knew it when you first looked into my eyes. This is *my* choice."

Was he speaking to her or to quieten some protesting voice within him? Rayn didn't know. He only knew that her mouth was sweet and that her breasts were pressed against him so that her taut nipples caressed his chest. "My choice," he repeated, and lowered her to the rumpled pillows.

Merial knew that she, too, had chosen this moment. From that evening when Rayn had kissed her in his tent, she'd known what her choice would be. She shivered with desire for him.

Rayn registered that tremor in his own heart. Together with his want of her was a desire to protect the woman in his arms. He wanted to hold her gently, tenderly, to keep her safe. He wanted to worship her lovely body as much as he needed to possess it.

With a slowness that belied his mounting passion, he trailed kisses from her lips to her throat, down the velvet valley between her breasts. Merial sighed her pleasure and impatience as his mouth and tongue curved slowly around the base of the firm mounds. She murmured his name and moved enticingly against him, but he wouldn't be hurried.

His lips trailed slow caresses upward until with tantalizing slowness, she felt moist warmth engulf her nipples. A moan was wrenched from her as he sucked first one and then the other of those aching peaks.

The ripples of pleasure within her became a molten torrent as Rayn's tongue and lips played delicately with her nipples. Meanwhile, his hands roved over her, relearning the now-familiar delicacy of her waist and belly, her inner thighs. When they parted under his eager insistence, he found again the honey of her desire for him.

Merial felt as though her entire being was opening to her lover, welcoming him. When his lips left her breasts to follow the course of his hands, her breathing became shallow gasps. Her knees, her inner thighs—Merial cried out as his fiery kisses worshipped the center of her woman's being.

And yet he would not love her. Not even though her hips arched up, mimicking the dance of love. He caressed and kissed her until she was on fire, until she caught his dark curls in her fingers, tugging him to her. "Rayn," she pleaded, "do you want me to die for wanting you?"

He came back to her with the swift litheness of a young tiger. His golden eyes smiled down into hers. "By all the gods, Mira, this is *our* choice."

Their choice that the act of love between them would burn them like fire. Their choice that she should cry out his name as he entered her, wrapping her legs around him to bind him closer to her as she took him deep. Their choice that she should stroke his strong neck and back, that he should bend his mouth to her breasts as though he wanted to draw her wild honey into himself.

And as they climbed higher and higher toward the sun,

Merial heard the cry burst from her. "I love you. God help me, I love—"

Together they shattered into light.

At dawn Rayn's lancers returned. Grim-faced and weary, they brought no prisoners with them. Rayn met them in the courtyard, and Merial could hear no more than a few snatches of Rassul's report, but Deen's glum face confirmed that the news wasn't good. What she caught of his words—"Those sons of whores seemed to disappear into nothing as though they were in league with Shaitan himself"—confirmed the bad news.

Almost immediately afterward, Rayn left the Bagh Mahal. "Today Rasgani begins the Festival of the Rains. It'll go on for days, as you know," he told Merial. "I'm going to remain at the palace all day, and I won't be returning to the Bagh Mahal tonight."

The disappointment she felt was gentled as she saw its reflection in his eyes. "I don't have to tell you how easy it would be for assassins to mingle with the crowds. Stay in the palace today."

"An order?" she challenged softly, and he smiled and kissed her.

"A request. For my sake if not for yours, you must be safe."

Merial spent the morning in Rukmiri-Bai's drowned garden, helping the princess, who would not trust her gardeners near her precious roses. "To me, flowers are like people. In fact, they are better, for they are straightforward and honest and don't seek to hurt each other or take what doesn't belong to them."

When Merial agreed, the princess shot her a shrewd look. "You seem to have recovered from your ordeal with the thugs, Mira. You're blooming like one of my roses this morning."

Merial felt heat flood her cheeks, and the princess chuckled. "My dear, I'm an old lady and have seen a great deal of life. I'm delighted that my adopted nephew has found someone who gladdens his heart. Being too concerned with war and statecraft makes for a lonely man."

Merial remembered her own backwash of loneliness when she'd watched Rayn riding away this morning. When she thought of him now, her body ached with newfound want.

"Rayn isn't an ordinary man," Rukmiri-Bai was saying. "He will be rana of Baranpur someday."

The truth of those words brought another kind of ache to Merial's heart. Though Rayn's love had filled a part of her heart that had long been empty, the boundaries of that love were far from clear.

Rayn was still the Tiger of Baranpur, the enemy of all *Angrezi.* Merial's hands slowed as she rescued a toppled rosebush. In his arms last night she had felt all their differences unimportant, but they hadn't gone away. She thought of what her father would think if he knew. In Edward's eyes she would be contemptible, beyond the pale of decent society.

Merial was glad that the gardening took so much of her time and energy. While she was working, she didn't have to think, and that night she was tired enough to sleep soundly. But dawn brought the sound of drums and horns as Rasgani began to celebrate the festival honoring Shiva and his consort, Parvati.

Predictably, Geeta was full of information about the Festival of the Rains. Over breakfast she explained that every year after the first rains the rana rode on the royal elephant to bless the lake and all the waters. She added that Prince Rayn and his *bhaldars* would be featured in a military parade in honor of the rana.

"Rukmiri-Bai has ordered her palanquin to observe the festivities," Geeta chattered. "You'll go to watch, also, won't you, Sahiba?"

Mindful of Rayn's warnings, Merial remained at the Bagh Mahal and was checking the roses in the garden when she heard a man's footstep behind her.

Rayn—but the joyous welcome died unspoken on Merial's lips. The man sauntering across the gardens toward her was Panwa Puar.

She went to meet the young minister at once and placing palm against palm bowed deeply from the waist. "My lord, I thank you for saving my life yesterday," Merial said.

Fitful sunlight glinted on a ruby in Panwa's turban and the gold brocade of his elegant tunic as he sketched a salaam. "You forget that the gods themselves intervened to save so beautiful a woman."

In spite of his languid drawl she sensed that he was troubled about something. "The prince is not here," she began.

"I know. I have but now left him at the Silver Palace. It's you I came to see."

Surprised, she gestured toward the Bagh Mahal, but he shook his head. "Walls have eyes and ears. Let us walk in the garden instead, although I am much afraid that the grass will ruin my shoes."

The distaste with which he looked down at the sopping grass would have been comical if Merial hadn't noted a heightened tension in Panwa.

"Is something wrong?" she asked apprehensively.

"Edward Ashland has been arrested and is being questioned by the police," was his abrupt reply.

The horror of what he'd said was compounded by the casual way in which he spoke her real name. It took all her self control to say, "Our name is Larkwell, my lord."

"It's not necessary to continue the masquerade," the minister said impatiently. "If I were not your friend, would I be here to warn you? Ibrahim's men arrested one of the thugs this morning, and under torture he confessed to attacking you because you were the daughter of Perce's underling."

Merial felt sick. "What is the *kotwal* doing to my father?"

"Ibrahim Ali Shah isn't known for his humanity."

The knot that had formed in her stomach rose into her throat, but she swallowed back the bile and resolutely asked, "What can I do?"

"The less you do the better." Panwa frowned as he added, "The border sentries report that Perce has changed his plans for the railroad. It has veered east and now actually touches our border. Khem-Rana's rage was unequaled when he heard that your father worked for Perce."

Merial thought of her father in the dungeons attached to the Silver Palace. All her fears, lulled by these weeks of quiet at the Bagh Mahal, flooded her mind. Her voice shook as she cried, "I must go to him!"

Panwa said sternly, "Not only would that be impossible, but it would also be unwise. So far the rana hasn't ordered your arrest, and since you belong to Prince Rayn, even Ibrahim will not dare to lay a hand on you. But it would be suicide to go to the Silver Palace now. I've come to caution you to stay in the Bagh Mahal all day."

She caught her trembling lower lip in her teeth and bit down hard. "Thank you, my lord," she managed to say.

Mingling with the languid look he gave her, there was

a gleam of real sympathy. "I'm devoted to Prince Rayn. Ever since he arrived in Baranpur, he was loved by my late father, and I regard him as an honored brother. I know he values you and would want you safe."

He drew a ring fashioned of onyx and diamonds from his finger and put it into her hand. "I must take my place in the parade of ministers that will escort the rana in his sacred mission, but first take this. It's been in my family for generations and is said to have been fashioned by one of the jinn. It supposedly can open locked doors." Panwa's lips quirked in an ironic smile, but he immediately became grave again as he added, "Anyone will recognize the ring as mine. If danger threatens you, show it and say that you are under my protection."

Before she could thank him, he was walking away across the garden. Merial clutched Panwa's ring tightly as she watched him go, but the hard metal gave her no sense of security as she thought of her father. "Rayn will help him," she whispered aloud.

But realistically she had to ask herself if that was true. Despite his love for her, Rayn had nothing but contempt for Sir Edward. And even if he wanted to help, how could he? To do so was to admit that he'd lied to the rana about his prisoners' identity.

Sir Edward's only chance was to get out of Baranpur. Merial looked down at Panwa's ring, the one with the power to open locked doors, and an idea took shape in her mind. There was one way in which Sir Edward could escape.

Before she had time to examine her idea, she heard Nirmale calling her. "You must be careful in the garden, Mira-Bai," the gardener's daughter warned. "You will get wet. My father is soaked to the skin, and my mother has sent these clothes for him to change into."

Nirmale was carrying a coarse dark cotton tunic and work trousers over her arm. Seeing them made everything fall into place for Merial. Her plan was so simple that it might work.

Merial smiled at the little girl. "I'm already very wet, so I will take those clothes to your father for you." Nirmale protested, and Merial added craftily, "If that bandage on your leg becomes wet, you may not be able to go to the festival today."

When Nirmale handed over the clothes, Merial walked swiftly back to the Bagh Mahal and summoned Geeta. "I've decided to go and watch the festival after all," she lied. "His Excellency Panwa Puar came to tell me that the prince is expecting me."

Geeta grinned. "I'll give the order for your palanquin at once. You'll be just in time to see His Highness in the military parade."

"No palanquin—the thugs might recognize it," Merial pointed out. "Have a groom saddle a horse, and bring a *bourka* to my room so that I may cover myself."

As soon as the servant had gone, Merial hastened toward her rooms. Then another thought occurred to her. When walking into danger, it was better to be armed.

Resolutely she took the turn in the corridor that led to the prince's quarters. To the manservant who opened the door of the prince's suite she said, "His Highness has ordered me to meet him and bring him some articles of clothing. Take me to his clothing room at once."

The manservant goggled his astonishment but did not dare to argue with Merial's haughty tone. Backing away from the door, he left Merial to look about her. She had never been in Rayn's rooms before, and she was surprised at the simplicity in which this crown prince lived. The walls and ceilings of his rooms were made of beautifully carved wood, and the marble floor was so polished that she could see her own reflection in it. But there were no carpets, no wall hangings, and his bed had no curtains about it. The rest of the furniture was simple and functional. There was no hint of warmth or ostentation—no hint of the prince's personality anywhere.

She didn't have time to think of such things now. In his dressing room she looked over rows of rich court clothes and military uniforms as well as functional travel garb, and kaftans such as he'd worn in his tent that first night.

The manservant was watching her, so Merial chose a silken sash. Then swiftly she palmed a slender throwing knife that lay on the table amongst other weapons.

She was trembling violently by the time she reached her own rooms so that it took her several minutes to remove her sari and dress herself in the gardener's clothes. Fortunately, Nirmale's father wasn't a big man. Merial belted the trousers tightly about her waist with Rayn's sash, then used a length of plain white cotton to arrange a turban around her head. This done she looked at herself long and hard in her mirror. If she kept her head down, she *might* be taken for a serving lad.

She hoped that the guards would be too engrossed in the festival to pay much attention to her. Maybe they wouldn't notice her odd-colored eyes. Merial reached for the *bourka* that Geeta had laid on the bed and noted with gratitude that the tentlike garment hid her completely.

She went downstairs and into the courtyard, where a groom awaited with two horses. The one he'd saddled for her was a beautiful mare, almost snow white but with a dark star on her forehead. "The prince would want you to ride Amrah, Mira-Bai," the groom explained. "She's Kumari bred."

She hadn't counted on the groom's coming with her. Merial didn't dare rouse suspicion by ordering him to stay behind but knew she could never carry out her plan with him hovering about. She compromised by saying, "You will escort me to the Silver Palace. There you will wait for me while I join the prince." She lowered her voice to a confiding tone. "Prince Rayn wishes my arrival to remain a secret."

Once outside the gate she was swept into the celebration that was in progress. Baranpur's citizens had been flocking into Rasgani for a whole day. Dressed in their best costumes, they chaffered and laughed and listened to the *fu-fu* bands, watched dancers and acrobats, and awaited the appearance of royalty.

No one noticed the figure shrouded in the *bourka* and her attending groom, and none paid any heed when Merial stopped some distance from the rana's palace. "Wait here," she ordered her groom.

Just then there was the sound of a drum banging, a trumpet's blast, and a roar from the assembled crowd as General Jaga led the pick of Baranpur's infantry out of the palace gates. The infantry marched past in a flurry of flags and was followed immediately by a phalanx of palace guards, resplendent in their white uniforms and silver turbans. Next came chief ministers on their horses, and Ibrahim Ali Shah and several dozen of his police. Seeing that bulky, menacing figure, Merial slipped down from her horse and stood clutching her *bourka* more closely about her.

"There he comes!" a woman shrilled.

A powerful black-and-gold clad figure astride a creamwhite stallion now cantered through the Sun Gate followed by his two captains, also dressed in gold and black, their backs as straight as their tall golden lances. Behind

Rassul and Deen came the *bhaldars* and after them Baran-pur's cavalry, mounted on horse and camel.

"Look, see, the Tiger comes," the people roared. Mothers lifted their children for a better look, flushed young men shouted themselves hoarse as their idol swept by. One fierce-looking, mustachioed old man near Merial drew himself up to ramrod straightness and saluted. Merial saw tears in his eyes.

The crowd was just settling down when the rana appeared. Sitting in a golden *howdah* that was perched atop a black bull elephant, Rana Khem Raoshad rode through the Sun Gate and made his royal progress toward the lake. As his people yelled themselves hoarse, palace guardsmen scattered money to the crowd.

Amidst the confusion, Merial removed her *bourka*. She hid it and, mounting her horse again, rode up to Sun Gate.

The guards at the gate were busy watching the parade and hardly glanced at Merial. Pitching her voice as low as she could, she said, "I have a message for His Excellency Panwa Puar. I'm to deliver it to the guards who attend the *Angrezi* prisoner."

She showed Panwa's ring and held her breath until one of the guards nodded. "It's the minister's ring, all right," he said. "Go ahead, lad."

Outwardly calm, Merial rode into the courtyard. So far so fair—but her heart was thumping wildly under her borrowed clothes. Her eyes lowered so that no one could see her light eyes, she rode through the darkened courtyard.

She remembered everything about that single visit. She relived the same sense of menace that hung about the place as, drawing in one deep breath for courage, Merial trotted her horse toward the dungeons' outer door.

The dungeons had been built under the Silver Palace, but for convenience's sake there was an outer door that led down to the depths. This heavy, iron-studded door to the dungeons was guarded by palace guards and several hard-faced policemen in gray and olive uniforms. As Merial dismounted, one of these policemen challenged her.

"Where the hell do you think you're going?"

She spoke her piece again, but it wasn't going to work as easily. "I don't recognize you as one of the minister's servants," the policeman who'd spoken demurred. "Stand closer so that I can see your face."

She raised her hand with the ring on it and let the diamonds glitter in the afternoon sunlight. "My identity, like my errand, is secret," she said in her gruffest voice. "I must speak with the prisoner."

"Maybe the *Angrezi* has a thing for pretty boys," another policeman snickered. "Might as well let him have his fun while he can, Mustafa."

The man who'd challenged Merial scowled. "It's no laughing matter. That *Angrezi* must be Shaitan himself, the way the *kotwal* is acting. I can't let you see him without written authorization, boy."

Desperation gave her courage. "Very well. I'll return to His Excellency the minister and tell him you turned him away." She paused. "Your name is Mustafa, isn't it?"

She turned her back on him and walked back to her horse, but before she could mount, the man called Mustafa gave in. "All right—you can see him. But I'll take you down and I'll wait for you."

He opened the iron door and stepped through it, and, heart thumping, Merial followed him into the rana's dungeon. The heavy door slammed shut behind her, and she started. "Don't like the sound, eh, pretty boy?" Mustafa jeered. "For some it's the last thing they hear on earth."

It hurt to breathe as she followed the guard down a

dank corridor. A clamor of voices, entreating, protesting, cursing, rose from prisoners crammed into cells that smelled of mold and human waste. Merial's escort ignored both the laments and the curses and conducted her down a flight of stone stairs and then another.

How was she ever going to get Sir Edward out of here alive? Down and down they descended until there was almost complete blackness. Merial's stomach was churning with apprehension by the time they stopped before a door. Inside it was as black as pitch, but she could hear someone stirring within.

"Go ahead." The policeman swung the iron door open and motioned Merial inside. "I'll wait for you here."

Pretending a coolness she didn't feel, she shook her head. "My lord Panwa's orders were that I speak to the prisoner without being observed or overheard." As the policeman hesitated, Merial added, "That is unless you want to take responsibility of hearing something that doesn't concern you. Something that could be—dangerous to you."

He frowned at that, and she knew she'd reached him. Lowering her voice, she added, "Mustafa, we're both servants to our masters' will, eh? We do what we're told to do. I don't want to see you get in trouble because you were too curious."

That got to him. "I'll wait at the top of these stairs," he snapped. "When you're finished, call me."

Legs shaking, Merial walked into the cell. She could see nothing, but again she heard that pitiful rustling, and now a hoarse voice spoke in English.

"Who's there?"

Straining her eyes, she made out a huddled shape sitting in a corner of the dungeon. She started toward him, and he shrank back, snarling, "Get away from me, you filthy savage—"

For the waiting policeman's benefit, Merial pitched her voice loud. "*Angrezi* dog, you smell like a dead pig." Then, lowering her voice, she whispered, "Father, I've come to help you."

"Merial?" Sir Edward gasped. He reached out to catch her wrist, and she heard the clank of chains. "Have they arrested you, too?"

She shook her head, no. "Have they hurt you, Father?"

Her answer was a harsh sob. "That bastard, Ibrahim— he'll rue the day. When the English rescue me, I'll see him hanged. Yes, and the rest of his henchmen."

"Father, *please,*" Merial whispered.

"It's all right, Merial. You mustn't be afraid. We're English and far superior to this scum. Death is better than dishonor any day."

He was quoting that old saw as if it were some kind of charm. He didn't realize that death was the least of what he had to fear. "You must leave now," she told him. "There's not much time. You have to take my clothes and pretend to be me. There's a horse outside—"

As she detailed her plan, the hand that was holding hers tightened. "You're a good girl, Merial, but you can't take my place."

An ache of tenderness warred with her desperation. "Yes, I can. You must go quickly. I don't know how long the guard will stay out of earshot." When he still refused, she added with a certainty she didn't feel, "I have nothing to fear. I belong to Prince Rayn, remember? Not even the rana will dare to hurt me."

"If he finds out you helped me escape, the Tiger will kill you himself. Besides, the bastards have made sure I won't try to escape." Sir Edward took her hand and guided it until she felt the steel shackles on his wrists. "They're connected to an iron ring in the wall," he explained.

She'd been a fool to think that Sir Edward wouldn't be chained. Merial groaned in her desolation, and he put his arm around her in a rare gesture of affection. "You're a brave girl. You must be brave enough to get out of this hell-damned country and find Perce. Get him to send the Sri Nevi garrison."

There was no other way and both of them knew it. Merial wanted to burst into wails of grief, but she forced herself to speak quietly. "I'll try, Father," she whispered. "I'll do my best." For a moment they embraced, and she pressed her face against his stubbled cheek. Then she remembered the knife she carried. "Take this," she told him. "In case they—in case you want . . ." Her words died away in tears she couldn't check.

Sir Edward eagerly took the knife. "I'll know what to do with this. Now, get going. That wog will suspect something if you stay too long." He paused, then added, "Be careful, daughter."

She swallowed her tears and raised her voice to angry Hindustani. "*Angrezi* dog. Not even for love of my lord Panwa can I remain in your filthy presence a moment longer."

Mustafa came and let her out. He was obviously bursting with curiosity about her supposed message to the prisoner, but he didn't question her as she followed him back upstairs through the stinking, noisy corridor. This time the policeman drew his sword and rattled it against the sides of the cell bars.

"Silence, you dogs!" he shouted. To Merial he added, "They're mostly Afghan prisoners—they'll be questioned and then put to death. Of course, the *Angrezi* dog's case is special. For *him* the torturer is preparing refined torments."

She thought of the knife that Sir Edward had. If nothing else, it would bring him release from life. She thought, I've as good as told my father to kill himself, and felt as though she were going insane.

Out in the courtyard she mounted her horse and rode back toward the gate. The populace had followed their rana to the lakeside, and the street leading out of Rasgani was all but deserted. Merial turned her horse's head away from the city and the Bagh Mahal. Then, head bent low, she began to ride.

If she rode through the night and the next day, she might perhaps reach Baranpur's border while Sir Edward was still alive. And Rayn—the thought of him brought deepest pain, for what she'd feared had happened. The boundaries that surrounded Rayn and Merial were no longer blurred but fixed, and they were once more enemies eyeing each other across a chasm of hatreds and loyalties.

The tears that she had held back so long blinded her, and she wiped them impatiently away with the back of her hand. There was no time for looking back.

Panwa's ring got her across the drawbridge that spanned the Azara, and the surefooted Kumari mare seemed to know its way up the steep road that led out of the valley. By the time the swift Indian twilight had fallen, Baranpur was miles behind. Merial had nearly reached the top of the valley road when she heard voices.

Instantly she reined in her mare. She could make out several dark shapes ahead, and one of them said, "What are our orders, Yuir Singh?"

"Simply that we wait," a harsh voice replied.

Merial started so hard that she nearly cried out. That

distinctive voice belonged to the thug who had tried to drag her out of her palanquin yesterday.

There was a growl of dissatisfaction, and the first speaker argued, "I say that we must move, and quickly, too. The prince and his *bhaldars* are busy with the festival. What better time to strike for Mother Kali?"

Were there four blurred shadows or five? Merial couldn't see anything in the darkness. She strained to hear as the thug leader, the one called Yuir Singh, said, "We take our orders and do as we're told. Our orders are to wait. We have waited for many years for this moment, and Ma Kali will not mind waiting a little longer to taste blood."

"*Jai ma Kali,*" several voices intoned reverently. "Glory to Mother Kali."

As the chant rose higher, Merial felt herself seized from behind. So quickly did it happen that she was tumbled out of her saddle and on the ground before she could draw breath. A scream was forced back into her throat, and dark spots danced before her eyes. She could hardly breathe, she was suffocating, dying—

"Make one sound and you'll die right now," said the hard whisper in her ear.

Ahead of her, the shadowed thugs were still talking. Apparently, they were planning some future meeting, but Merial no longer listened. She was being pressed down into the ground with her captor's knee in the small of her back. One iron hand covered her mouth, and an arm was wrapped around her neck. The slightest movement on either of their parts would snap her neck.

"Be still," her captor commanded.

There were rustles up ahead and then hoofbeats as the thugs rode away. Merial could hear the swish of underbrush, the crunch of twigs under their feet as they slipped into the darkness.

"I am going to take my hand away," the man holding her said. "If you stay quiet and answer my questions properly, I *may* let you live."

The stifling hand was removed, and Merial drew a sobbing breath. "Who are you to lay hands on me? I am here on official business for His Excellency Lord Panwa—"

"Shaitan!"

Her words ended in a gasp as her captor twisted her around so that she stared up into a hard-planed, square-jawed face that even the darkness could not disguise.

It was Rayn.

··*Nine*··

"WHAT IN HELL'S name are you doing here?" Rayn demanded.

All she could think of to say was, "Ibrahim has imprisoned my father."

Even in the darkness she could see the glitter of his eyes. "They arrested him last night."

"You *knew?*"

All the time she had lain in his arms, Sir Edward had been in that terrible dungeon. And she had given herself to Rayn, believing his words about destiny and love. She cried, "I'll never forgive you for not telling me."

"You were riding for Sri Nevi," he challenged, and she knew that they were enemies again.

She flared, "Did you expect me to do nothing while Ibrahim tortured my father?"

She was interrupted by Deen's tense voice. "Riders, lord. Ibrahim's men—at least fifty of them."

He said grimly, "Naturally. They followed her." He whistled softly, and dark forms materialized out of the dense forest.

"We're all here, lord," Deen said, "except for Chetak, Ashok, and Chander, who are following the thugs."

"Mount up," Rayn ordered. He caught Merial about the waist and almost threw her onto her mare's back.

She glared down at him. "So you're going to hand me over to Ibrahim?"

Without answering, he mounted his stallion, and in orderly silence his *bhaldars* ranged themselves at his back.

Some minutes later the vanguard of Ibrahim's police came cantering up the path. They halted when they saw the wall of waiting men, and steel rang as swords were drawn.

"Who's there?" Ibrahim's voice challenged.

"Who dares to ask?" Rayn's roar filled the woods.

"It's him—it's the Tiger, the prince." A shocked ripple ran through the phalanx of men. It died down as the bulky Ibrahim trotted his horse forward.

"Highness!" he exclaimed. "I thought you were taking part in the festivities. I didn't expect to meet you on this mountain road."

"Nor I you," Rayn retorted.

Ibrahim eyed the prince warily. "I regret to report, Highness, that the *Angrezi* woman has escaped."

"Indeed? But I've never yet needed help to retrieve my own property."

Rayn's voice was icy, and the policemen shifted uneasily in their saddles. Ibrahim continued. "The—*your* woman infiltrated the prison and gave her father a knife. Then she fled toward the border. We're pursuing her, Highness."

Merial's heart sank as Ibrahim leaned forward to hand Rayn the little knife she'd stolen. In an emotionless voice Rayn asked, "Has Ashland escaped?"

Ibrahim's teeth flashed in a smile. "Not he. We have

him safe, and, after some persuasion, he told us what had happened." Contemptuously he added, "A few moments on the rack, and he wept like a virgin on her wedding night."

Rayn could feel Merial stiffen beside him as he said, "I won't detain you, *Kotwal.* Go with the blessing of the gods."

As Ibrahim saluted, his eye lit on Merial's white mare. "A Kumari horse," he muttered. "The guards at the gate said—" He broke off, and Merial saw him raise his head, like a hound that had caught the scent.

So, Rayn thought, the game could no longer be evaded. He felt a rush of conflicting emotions—hurt that she hadn't trusted him enough to let him arrange matters, fury that she'd been ready to betray him and their love in order to save her precious father.

With a calm he was far from feeling, he said, "The ways of the gods are strange, Ibrahim. While we were tracking those thugs, this pretty bird flew into my hands. I am taking her back to the Bagh Mahal."

Baranpur's chief of police argued, "Highness, this is a matter of security. As the rana's chief of police, I must insist that the woman be handed over to me."

"You *insist?*"

Rayn's voice was silky, but the menace in it raised the hair on Merial's neck. The *kotwal's* followers looked scared as Rayn continued, "You forget yourself."

But Ibrahim didn't back down. "I am in charge of Baranpur's security," he maintained. "I claim the woman as my prisoner."

"Don't you think I know what to do with runaway slaves? She's my property. She abused my trust. The knife she left with her father was my knife. I am taking her back to the Bagh Mahal where her punishment will be meted out—by me."

Deen, his young face hard, let his hand fall on his rifle. Beside him, Rassul did likewise. "I cannot agree with you, Shield of the Kingdom," Ibrahim muttered.

"Your agreement is not required," Rayn snapped back. "Merely your compliance. By rights you should be following the thugs as my lieutenant, Chetak, is doing. The capture of their leaders is something we all desire."

Ibrahim didn't like it, but he didn't dare argue further. He bowed his head, but Merial could see the way his fists tightened on his reins.

"Very well, Highness," he said. "But I urge you not to kill the *Angrezi* woman in your anger. The rana will surely wish to question her as well as her father."

So Sir Edward was still alive—Merial had barely time to register this thought before Rayn caught her horse's bridle and urged his white stallion forward. The policemen hastily made way for him, bowing reverently as their prince and his lancers swept past.

"What will they do to my father?" Merial managed to ask.

"A runaway slave is usually beaten to death. The question, my English rose, is what I am going to do with you."

It wasn't the prospect of punishment or pain that hurt as much as the jeer in his voice. "Another of your just laws?" she cried.

"You betrayed me, Mira."

There was no use pointing out that in hiding her father's imprisonment from her he'd betrayed her, also. Merial wondered bitterly whether Rayn had been mocking her all along, whether his lovemaking the other night had been some sick idea of revenge. The urge to scream questions at him was so strong that she could keep silent only by gnawing her lips until they bled.

She was exhausted by the time they reached the city. Here Rayn handed her reins to Rassul. "Take her to the Bagh Mahal," he ordered. "Guard her door until I return." The *bhaldar* captain hesitated. "What is it?" Rayn asked impatiently.

"Lord, it was her father that she tried to free," Rassul said. His eyes were troubled as he added, "I do not presume to question you, but between parent and child there is great love. And love is often blind."

Rayn's eyes blazed. "You forget that this woman betrayed my trust," he said angrily. "You've become a sentimental fool." He added to Deen, "Go in his stead."

Looking unusually subdued, Deen saluted and led Merial toward the Tiger's palace. They rode in total silence, and, when the astonished gateman opened to them, Deen escorted her to her suite of rooms. "Shut your door after you, Mira-Bai," he then said, "and wait for the prince."

"You mean, wait for my punishment," she corrected.

The young captain scowled. "If that's his will."

"And his will is your law," Merial couldn't help crying.

Deen touched the scar on his cheek. "Afridi raiders slaughtered my family when I was a boy. They'd have killed me, too, had not the prince saved me and let me enter his service. He is my lord and my master and commands my sword and my life. Anyone who betrays him is my sworn enemy."

Meaning that she was his enemy as well. She said quietly, "I never meant him harm, Deen. This I swear to you."

He looked unhappy but resolutely took his place before the door of her rooms. No one was allowed near. She could hear Rukmiri-Bai demanding to know what was going on and Geeta's protests, but Deen kept everyone away. In the silence that finally fell over the Bagh Mahal, Merial took a seat by the window and waited. She seemed to wait for a very long time, and she was very tired. In spite of herself, her eyes closed.

She was jerked out of her troubled doze by footsteps on the stairs. There was a terse command at the door, and a moment later Rayn strode into the inner room where she waited. Merial nearly cried out as she saw the look in his eyes.

It wasn't Rayn standing there—it was the Tiger, who had a riding whip curled tight around one fist. His eyes were steely, and there was menace in his voice as he ordered, "Get up."

Automatically she got to her feet, and he seized her by the shoulders. "Damn your treacherous English soul to hell," Rayn snarled. "Do you know what you've done?"

Each word was hurled at her like a weapon. "I suppose you're going to beat me!" she cried.

"A beating will seem tame compared to what's facing you. If Ibrahim has his way, you and your father will be tortured and killed. Our esteemed chief of police wants the rana to send your mangled remains to Perce as a warning."

A cry of horror was wrung from her.

"When your father was arrested by Ibrahim's men," Rayn continued grimly, "I met with Panwa, General Jaga, and several other ministers and senior officers. We agreed to wait until Khem-Rana's anger had cooled and then counsel prudence. I didn't tell you about your father's imprisonment because I feared you'd do something foolish."

No longer able to meet his eyes, she protested, "I was

desperate. You weren't here when Minister Panwa came to warn me."

He let go of her so suddenly that she stumbled. "Panwa wanted to make sure you didn't act rashly. Ironically, his precaution has precipitated a crisis." His voice rose as he added, "What you've done will cause the destruction of Baranpur."

He was thinking of his country—not of her. Irrational though it was, that truth hurt. "Whatever happens to you," Rayn continued, "you've brought on yourself."

"I had to try to save him."

His eyes narrowed, and he raised his hand as if to strike her. Involuntarily she flinched back, and the borrowed tunic slipped off her shoulder revealing against her white arm the mark of his bruising fingers.

"Damn you!" Rayn roared.

Merial cried out as she was pulled forward into his arms and crushed in a merciless embrace. She could feel the imprint of him against her as he bent his head to hers.

There was no tenderness in his mouth. It meant to punish, to degrade her. She felt the heat of his anger as well as his passion, and the pressure of his arms hurt. Merial struggled but couldn't free herself from his inexorable grasp.

Then, as swiftly as it had begun, the savage kiss changed. Rayn's mouth gentled against hers, and his arms eased their cruel grip. Involuntarily her lips parted to his nudging tongue and felt its remembered, deep stroking.

Reality fled away. Merial forgot where she was and even who she was. She forgot her fears for her father. All that mattered was that Rayn was holding her again and kissing her with love. She felt her body respond to that love as a flower to sunlight.

"Rayn—"

He felt his name tremble against his lips, and all his tangled emotions coalesced into a need to possess this woman. He could feel her shiver with desire as his mouth left hers to journey down her shoulder, to find the cruel mark of his fingers, lower, then, to her breast.

Merial murmured her pleasure as his mouth found and covered the taut peaks of her breasts. Her ruined tunic fell to the floor. Rayn untied the cloth at her waist, and the borrowed trousers sighed down to join the tunic. His hands slid under the silk of her undergarments, cupping her buttocks and drawing her against him. Through the fragile silk she could feel the strength of his desire. Then the silk, too, fell to the floor.

"May all the gods damn you, Mira."

The curse was almost a prayer. She registered it in her deepest self as his mouth came back to find hers. He swung her up into his arms and carried her to the bed, then swiftly shed his clothing and lay down beside her. Next moment his body covered hers.

Tonight there was no slow seduction. There was hardly any love. Rayn's need for Merial was as elemental as hers for him. Her body opened to him and drew him deep, sheathing his passion, his fury, his longing, his hatred, and his love. The fierce dance of their mating was almost like combat.

He made no effort to prop himself up on his elbows, and his body lay heavy on hers. She welcomed the crush of it. In the maelstrom of her emotions, Merial wanted to get closer, to press her hipbones into his, meld with him, absorb into herself everything about him. The prickle of his chest-fur against her kissed-tender breasts, his heat, his strength, the scent and taste of his skin. She needed him. She wanted him. The dark fires snarled and whirled within her, whipping her senses into madness.

As her slender body bucked and shuddered under him, Rayn tried to cling to sanity. Her cries were in his ears, her honeyed warmth held him prisoner, tortured him with ecstasy—but he could never forgive her—she was his enemy—she was his love.

Rayn no longer knew what he thought or felt. He wanted to devour Mira, to absorb her into his skin and bones, to consume her completely. He began to move more swiftly within her, and she matched his movements until their bodies pounded the softness of the bed. Their gasps became cries.

Clashing, warring, loving, they clung together, tasted each other, breathed with each other's tormented breath until they shattered and fell together into the incandescent darkness.

Into peace.

There was the sound of hoofbeats outside in the courtyard, hammering on the gate, a voice shouting. Merial came awake with a start to hear footsteps running up the stairs.

She drew the coverlets about her and sat up as Rayn snatched up a length of cloth. Knotting it around his lean waist, he went out into the outer room. "Report," Merial could hear him command.

Deen's voice replied, "Lord, the rana has summoned an emergency counsel of all his ministers, barons, and generals. You are to go to the Silver Palace at once—and you're to bring Mira-Bai. Ibrahim's sent some of his men to escort you, but Rassul sent Fanji and a dozen *bhaldars* to give you warning."

"Good," Rayn said. As he lowered his voice to issue further orders, Merial went to the large sandalwood chest where her saris were kept.

"No. You'll wear this tonight." Rayn had returned to her side and was selecting indigo trousers and a matching tunic made of tough raw silk.

As she took the clothes from him she asked, "Does this summons mean that—that Ibrahim has convinced the rana to kill my father and me?"

"We'll soon see." He took a gauze veil from the chest and tossed it to her. "Tonight you must veil yourself and appear humble and contrite. Say nothing, do nothing to anger the rana. If the gods are kind, he'll listen to us and not to Ibrahim."

They stared at each other across the chasm of their loyalties. Then—"Courage," he said in English.

He turned away and began to dress. In a sense of unreality, she also dressed. Her mind was tumbling back across time to a night long ago when she had been awakened by a tearful Jassmina and bundled into her clothes. That night, like this, had echoed with male voices and the heavy tread of feet and had smelled of sandalwood and fear.

There were more hoofbeats outside, the gateman's challenge. Merial went to the window in time to see a dozen mounted men riding into the courtyard of the Bagh Mahal. Sleepy, frightened servants brought lamps that shone on Ibrahim's police, all mounted and armed.

"Lighten our darkness, we beseech Thee, O Lord, and by Thy great mercy deliver us from all perils and dangers of this night—" The words from another world came automatically to Merial's mind but broke off as Rayn's lancers, led by Deen and Big Fanji, strode out of the Bagh Mahal and ranged themselves on the steps.

Deen stepped forward and challenged, "What is your business at this inauspicious hour?"

"By order of the King of Kings, Khem-Rana of Baranpur, we have been sent to summon the crown prince,

Prince Rayn, to a council of war," was the formal reply. "Also, it is the will of the rana that the *Angrezi* woman known as Mira accompany the prince. The *kotwal* has sent us as escort in these unsettled times."

A hand fell on Merial's shoulder. "Are you ready?" Rayn asked.

She nodded and squared her slender shoulders. The dark raw silk tunic and trousers made her appear very slight and young. She had plaited her dark hair into a long braid that she had coiled into a knot at the back of her head, and her fragility cried out for protection. Rayn wanted to put his arms around her and reassure her, but there was no time for tenderness.

He led the way down the stairs to where Geeta and the frightened servants were clustered. "May the gods watch over you, Sahiba," Geeta whispered.

With an effort, Merial mustered a smile of thanks. "Tell Rukmiri-Bai that I regret not being able to thank her for her kindness."

Head high, she followed Rayn out onto the steps. He perfunctorily returned the salute given him and handed Merial onto the back of her waiting Kumari mare. Then he and his *bhaldars* mounted, also.

Dawn was still far off, but a rooster was crowing as they rode toward the Silver Palace. There was no moon, but the great palace glowed with a hundred lanterns. Double the usual guard stood at attention at the great Sun Gate, and the courtyard was alive with soldiers.

Rassul was standing at attention at the foot of the steps beneath the silver door. "The council has convened, lord," he informed Rayn. "Minister Panwa requested that the rana wait for you, but he was overruled."

"By Ibrahim, no doubt." Rayn lifted Merial down, and Fanji stepped forward to guard her. The other lancers fell in behind their lord as he strode through the silver doors toward the Hall of Audience.

Lamplight shimmered off the crimson and gold enamel that ornamented the walls of the hall. It glinted over the golden emblem of the sun, set in the ceiling. As Rayn performed a ceremonial bow, Merial sent one swift glance around the crowded hall. In that fleeting moment she registered the fact that today Ibrahim was standing very close to the rana, even closer than Panwa Puar. There was no sign of Sir Edward anywhere.

She sank to her knees and bowed her head to the floor. There was a moment's pause during which she could feel the rana's cold gaze. Then Khem-Rana snapped, "Let the prisoner be brought forward."

A side door swung open, and Sir Edward was dragged into the hall by two burly policemen. His hair was disordered, his clothes filthy, and two days' beard stubbled his pale cheeks. Merial could barely restrain a cry as Ibrahim's henchmen forced their prisoner to his knees.

Rayn could feel Merial's agony. If she called attention to herself, he couldn't save her. He prayed that she'd have the sense to remain silent.

"So, *Angrezi,*" the rana was jeering, "you are a person of great importance. You were going to Sri Nevi to help that dog, Perce, build his railroad."

Sir Edward's reply was so low that no one except Khem-Rana could hear. His face twisted, his hand clenched, he leaned forward in his golden chair and snarled, "So you admit your crimes. But you will do better than that. You will tell me Perce's plans for that accursed railroad."

This time Sir Edward's voice was stronger. In his halting Hindustani he said, "I don't know his plans."

"You don't *know,* you filth? Well, your tongue can soon

be loosened. Ibrahim, get me the truth from this son of an *Angrezi* whore."

Ibrahim suggested, "King of Kings, the *Angrezi's* tongue might be loosened more quickly if his daughter were placed on the rack. The sight of her white body being torn and twisted may make him remember what he says he has forgotten."

Merial's skin crawled as the rana's attention shifted to her, but before Khem Raoshad could speak, Rayn said, "The woman knows nothing."

Ibrahim actually laughed aloud. "It's hard to believe, Highness. She infiltrated the dungeons and took a knife to the prisoner."

"If an *Angrezi* woman with eyes the color of a mountain lake can get past your police so easily, it says little for your security," Rayn retorted. "Be careful when you talk about torturing my property, Ibrahim."

Panwa cleared his throat and said suavely, "With permission, King of Kings, we are getting away from the most important matter at hand. We must consider how best to deal with Perce's railroad without inviting war and destruction."

The rana's laugh wasn't pleasant. "I do not fear war. We will send the *Angrezi* the mutilated bodies of these two as a warning of what may happen if Perce persists in encroaching upon our borders."

Most of the ministers and officers exchanged uneasy glances, and even the grizzled General Jaga frowned. Rayn interposed, "No one hates the *Angrezi* more than I do. You know, King of Kings, how I have fought them for years. But we are not strong enough or large enough to fight England."

"You dare to disagree with me?"

Without flinching, Rayn met the furious monarch's

eyes. "I dare because I am your devoted subject. I have been wounded many times over in your service. My sword is yours. My life is yours." Holding his adopted father's eyes with his, Rayn strode forward along the marble floor, halting at the steps leading up to the royal dias. "I have never spoken anything but truth to you, and I speak it now. If you kill these prisoners, you will plunge Baranpur into a war from which it will never recover."

A murmur of agreement echoed around the room, and General Jaga said bluntly, "The prince is right. The *Angrezi* have armies that make ours look insignificant. They can destroy us at their pleasure, King of Kings."

The rana slammed his jeweled hand down on his knee. "You speak like an old woman, Jaga!" he shouted. "If we fight the *Angrezi,* other kingdoms will come to our aid. Our ally, the rajah of Kumar, will send us more of the precious white horses."

"What use are horses against cannon?" Rayn argued.

"I would rather die with a sword in my hand than suffer my borders to be violated by Hamilton Perce." The rana spat the name with purest venom. "Ibrahim counsels war."

"Ibrahim's a fool," Rayn snorted.

The chief of police stiffened. "I ask you, *Highness,* why you shelter the daughter of a criminal *Angrezi.*"

"Don't dare take that tone with me," Rayn shot back, "or you'll feel six inches of steel in your fat belly. You're advising my father to take a course that would destroy our country."

As the two men glared at each other, the rana shouted, "Be silent! This is no time for fighting amongst ourselves. My son, your loyalty to me is beyond question, this I know. Otherwise, I would not allow such talk from you."

"Then listen to me, King of Kings, for there are other

ways to humble Perce." Rayn made a gesture of contempt toward Sir Edward as he added, "Sell him on the auction block."

There was a little ripple of surprise and Ibrahim's eyes narrowed. "The woman, too?"

With a swift, almost feral movement, Rayn strode back to where Merial knelt. He caught her veil and tossed it aside. Then, cupping her chin in his hand, he turned it to the light. She tried to tear her head away, but his grip was too strong. "She's fair to look upon, and any man would enjoy bedding her. Why not take pleasure from her body instead of breaking it on the rack?"

Ibrahim ran his tongue over his thick lips. "But," he protested hoarsely, "she is your woman."

"I'll not have a treacherous bitch about me. Edward Ashland is a coward and beyond contempt." Every word seemed to bury itself deep in Merial's heart as Rayn turned back to the rana. "Sending these two to the auction block would be an insult to the proud *Angrezi.*"

His voice carried utmost conviction. The expression in his eyes was the same as that when he had accused her of being first and foremost Edward Ashland's daughter. Rayn continued, "Killing is too good for *Angrezi* dogs. This way is better."

Panwa was quick to heap coals on the fire. "The prince is a master of subtlety, King of Kings!" he exclaimed. "This method of punishing the prisoners will achieve all things. The *Angrezi* will not know for sure that their countrymen are slaves. There will be rumors, of course— enough rumors to make them fume, but no proof. The *Angrezi* are too fond of law and order," he added mockingly, "to fight a war on hearsay."

"And while their generals think of what to do, we will conduct border raids on Hamilton Perce," Rayn added.

"In the end he will abandon the railway. If he does not, then we can still send him the mutilated body of the *Angrezi* slaves."

The rana nodded slowly. "It is a good plan," he conceded. "What think you, Ibrahim?"

The police chief's narrow eyes were devouring Merial's face. They dropped to her breasts, and Merial felt as though snails were sliming across her body. "I'm not sure I agree with the prince," Ibrahim said at last. "It's better to kill the man, at least."

His objections were drowned out as most of the ministers and generals raised their voices to agree with their prince. Many of them stared openly at Merial, and she could see the lust in their eyes. With shaking hands she pulled the veil back over her face as the rana decreed, "Let it be done. Take the English dog back to his cell and send his daughter with him. In the morning dispose of them on the slave block."

Sir Edward hadn't been able to follow much of what was said, but when the rana spoke, reality at last seemed to penetrate. "Savage, heathen bastards!" he cried. "Leave us alone if you know what's good for you."

He had spoken in English, but his meaning was unmistakable. Ibrahim's policemen clubbed him down, and as he fell half senseless to the marble tiles, they continued to beat him.

"Please, I beg you, stop—" Merial started to get up to go to him, but Fanji held her down with one big paw.

"Stay still, girl."

"Stop that," Rayn said impatiently. "The creature is useless already. Why decrease his small value?"

The policemen ceased beating Sir Edward, but Merial's horror remained. She stared at Rayn and saw not the man in whose arms she had lain a few scant hours ago but the Tiger of Baranpur.

"You coward," she snarled at him in English. "You're nothing but a—a ruffian. All that talk of love and—how I wish I could kill you myself."

For a moment their eyes met, and she thought she saw something shift in his golden gaze. Then he smiled.

"She may have the face and body of an angel, but she's a hellcat," he said. "I warn whoever buys her that he'll have his hands full."

She tried to reach him, to claw at him, but Fanji hauled her back and delivered her to Ibrahim's henchmen. The last sound Merial heard as they hustled her out of the Hall of Audience was the Tiger's laughter.

··Ten··

SIR EDWARD GROANED with pain as he and his daughter were dragged down to the dungeons. Merial cursed the men who were manhandling her father, and one of them jeered, "You won't sound so brave tomorrow. I wish I had the money to buy you, she-demon. You'd be fun to tame."

"No chance of that. Did you see the way the *kotwal* was looking at her?" Another policeman sniggered. "I'll wager you a *pice* that he'll have her clothes off before he gets her home. He's got strange tastes, they say."

The men roared with laughter, and Merial spat at them like a wild animal. Back in the hall she'd have gladly clawed out Rayn's eyes. How could he have done those things, said those things, when only a few hours ago he'd acted as though he cared about her?

Pushing and shoving their captives along, Ibrahim's men descended to the lowest level of the dungeons. Here even torches brought little light. There was a scrape of metal, a door swung open, and a brutal push sent Merial tumbling into the darkness beyond. She landed painfully on her knees, and under her hands felt dank stone. Then Sir Edward was flung against her.

"Damn those heathen savages," he cursed bitterly. "Merial, did I understand that we're to be sold as slaves?"

She wanted to put her head down on his shoulder and cry, but he sounded so terrified that she reached out in the dark for his hand.

"It's not tomorrow yet," she managed to gulp. "Where there's life, there's hope."

He seized on that trite saying. "You're right, we mustn't despair. We'll be rescued, Merial. You'll see."

He was still clinging to that pitiful fantasy. Merial thought of Rayn's lancers picking off the vanguard of any army foolish enough to try and cross the Bridge of Winds. No one was going to help them.

"I never meant to put myself into their power again," Sir Edward was groaning. "When the bastards came back to get me, I meant to kill myself. But I wasn't quick enough. They disarmed me and dragged me to a horrible room and put me on the rack, and that fat villain, Ibrahim, stood there laughing, watching me."

He drew a sobbing breath. "I honestly didn't know anything—Perce never told me his plans for the railroad. I tried to tell them that, but they wouldn't believe me."

Merial put her arms around her father and tried not to cry. "Don't think about it. We're together now. And—and it will come out all right. It's bound to come out all right."

How long they sat like that, she did not know. Worn out, Sir Edward dozed off on his daughter's shoulder. She didn't want to move for fear of waking him, so she made herself as comfortable as she could and stared into the dark. It was very still except for the intermittent sound of mice scuffling in the straw. Merial knew she also should rest while she could, but in spite of fatigue, sleep stayed a million miles away. Merial felt as though she were pinioned between the past and the future. Between Rayn's deceit and that hot, cruel look in Ibrahim's eyes.

"If he touches me, I'll kill myself," she swore.

Footsteps echoed through the dark stillness, and she tensed as lamplight gleamed into the cell. Sir Edward awoke and clung to his daughter moaning, "I can't stand any more torture. Merial, don't let them take me."

"Be still." On the heels of Rayn's whisper was the sound of the key turned in the lock. "Get out quickly. *Move!*"

When shock kept Merial rooted to the floor, he strode inside to drag her to her feet. She resisted and he snarled, "Do I have to knock you unconscious and carry you out?"

"Where do you want us to go—why are you here?" she stammered.

"To get you out of Baranpur," was the grim reply.

"Why should you help us?" Sir Edward quavered. "You're a murdering savage like the rest of them."

"Then stay here." Gripping Merial's wrist, Rayn practically hauled her out of the cell. Sir Edward followed, still protesting.

"Where are you going?" he demanded fearfully.

As he spoke, they came flush up against a stone wall. It looked solid and immovable, but Rayn reached for an iron ring that was set in the floor. He pulled back, and, with a shuddering, grating sound, the wall swung open.

"There's a passage under the dungeon," Rayn said. He turned to Merial. "Ladies first, as you English say." She hesitated and he jibed, "Unless you'd rather live a short and vastly unpleasant life as a member of Ibrahim's harem."

Merial directed a hating glance at him and took a step forward. "Follow her," Rayn ordered Sir Edward.

Did he mean to push them into some hole and wall

them in? Merial's heart pounded as she stepped down into a darkness so profound that it made the dungeon seem a place of light. By the feeble flicker of Rayn's lamp, she could see that they were in a narrow tunnel carved out of earth. Its ceiling was so low that they had to stoop almost double, and the earth smelled sour and moldy.

"This passageway was built by my father's grandfather." Rayn's deep voice seemed louder in the enclosed place. "It leads out of the palace. In case of siege the old rana had a way of getting out."

"Where does it lead?" Sir Edward asked. "I'm not going farther until you tell us . . ."

His words trailed off as the rock door behind them grated shut. There was no going back. Merial took a step forward and nearly screamed as she almost trod on something soft and squealing.

"Don't pay any attention to the rats," Rayn told her. "They're more afraid of you than you are of them."

Merial could hear her father swear bitterly. As she stumbled forward, Rayn continued. "The old rana told no one about this tunnel except for his heir. He in turn told his son, and so on down until I came by the knowledge."

Bending low, Merial walked forward until she came to a place where earth had fallen from the ceiling. The way was almost blocked, but Rayn said, "Go on. We can squeeze through."

Merial hesitated, paralyzed by the fear of being buried alive in this terrible place. "I can't do it," she gulped.

"You're the one who wanted to kill me back at the hall, remember?"

She wished she had a knife to hand, a pistol, anything, but she was unarmed and helpless and had to do his bidding. She hated him, loathed him. She wished he were dead.

"That's the spirit," Rayn approved as Merial pushed and squeezed through the earthen barricade. "Now you, my fine English lord, unless you want my dagger in your guts."

"I hope the English soldiers catch you and hang you," Merial panted.

He jeered, "My bloodthirsty rose."

She drew breath in order to respond to his taunting and instead of fetid tunnel air caught a whiff of freshness. Straining her eyes, Merial could now see a faint light against the darkness. The passageway narrowed still more, and as she went down on hands and knees, she heard the sound of running water.

"Be careful—the passage opens into the Azara," Rayn warned.

A tangle of vines caught at Merial's hair, and then she was out of the tunnel and on the bank of the river. She breathed deeply, gratefully, of the blessed, clean night air as Sir Edward and Rayn joined her on the bank.

Rayn whistled, and there was the sound of oars plashing water. A shadowy boat materialized on the water, poled by a solitary figure. "Your report," Rayn commanded.

"Ibrahim's police were watching the river at the usual checkpoint," Deen's voice replied, "but Fanji drew them off. Rassul has led the other *bhaldars* out of the city as you commanded. Ibrahim thinks that you're with them, lord, and riding for the troubled Afghan border."

"With the *Angrezi* rats safely in his dungeon, Ibrahim no doubt feels that he can relax." Rayn motioned Sir Edward down into the boat, then turned to help Merial. As she stepped on board the rocking craft, she slipped on the wet earth and fell forward against him. For a moment he held her tightly, and in that heart's beat of time she felt her treacherous body's response to him. Then he lifted her into the boat and picked up a pole.

Together with Deen, Rayn began to pole the boat downriver. Sir Edward cleared his throat to say in his deplorable Hindustani, "You're a wise man, Prince. By helping us you'll earn the gratitude of the English crown."

"Keep your friendship and gratitude," Rayn retorted in English, and Merial saw her father stiffen in astonishment. "In fact, you can give Perce a message. If he doesn't divert his railroads from our border, the destruction that follows will be on his head."

River mist rose about them. In that shrouded darkness Merial could hear the sigh of wind. She shivered and drew up her knees to her chest as Rayn continued, "I'm getting you out of Baranpur for my country's sake. I wouldn't have turned a hand to save you otherwise, *Sir* Edward Ashland."

Merial felt as though she'd been slapped. Though she realized now that Rayn had been acting back at the Hall of Audience, his loathing for her father was very real, and she felt included in the Tiger's scorn.

After a moment Rayn went on, "You had better rest, both of you. Tomorrow we will ride for the border, and we won't stop except to water the horses. If either of you can't keep up, you'll be left behind."

As Sir Edward subsided, Merial realized she'd come to the end of her strength. Resting her cheek on her knees, she closed her eyes, but sleep would not come. Against her closed lids burned images—Khem Raoshad crying out for war, Ibrahim's lustful eyes, the shadowed voices of the thugs demanding English blood. She had loved India all her life and with all her heart, but it wanted no part of her. Nor did Rayn. She was an *Angrezi* and his enemy, and if it weren't for his country's safety, he would have let the Ashlands rot.

Dreary thoughts accompanied her into sleep, and when she awoke, the boat was bucking fitfully. Looking about her, Merial saw that dawn was brightening the east and that the river had widened. Wild currents now turned and twisted their boat, and foam boiled by them. Sir Edward was sleeping exhaustedly, but at the prow of the boat, Rayn poled the boat with seemingly tireless concentration.

Deen was chanting a hymn to Ushas, goddess of dawn. Merial lay listening to the music of his clear, tenor voice until the boat rocked again. This time the impact was so violent that Merial fell to the bottom of the boat. She sat up and pushed the dark hair from her eyes.

"Where are we?" she wondered.

Without turning Rayn replied, "We're approaching the Falls of Ravanna."

Ravanna was the name of a multi-armed demon king, one of many Hindu devils. The boat shuddered strongly as Merial asked, "Isn't that dangerous?"

"We won't go over the falls, but our boat will. By now your flight will have been discovered, and Ibrahim will have sent his men after you. They'll be watching the river as well as the roads, and when they discover the empty boat, they'll think you were lost in the falls and stop the pursuit—or at least, I hope so. Are you afraid?"

"Of course I am." Her frankness made him smile in spite of himself, and he turned at last to look at her. Dawnlight caught the blue glints in her black hair, and her turquoise eyes were apprehensive. In spite of himself, Rayn felt an almost uncontrollable urge to reassure her.

But her next words banished such feelings. "It must amuse you to see us like this," Merial said bitterly. "You must enjoy humiliating us as you did in the Hall of Audience. I hate being in your debt."

"You wouldn't have enjoyed being sold to Ibrahim." He turned back to the river again. "Best wake your father," he added. "Don't you hear the falls?"

She did. The sound was like an echo, a dull, grating noise which became stronger and stronger yet until it was a full-throated roar. The waters around the boat became more and more turbulent, and the craft was tossed on the white water. Sir Edward clung to the sides of the boat and stared about him with wide eyes.

"I can't swim," he spluttered. "Are you trying to drown us?"

Neither of the other men paid any attention to the Englishman's complaints and curses, and Merial saved her breath in order to cling to the side of the boat. With powerful strokes Rayn and his captain of lancers began to pole for shore. It was difficult going, for by now they were caught in the strong current of the falls. The roaring became louder.

"We're going over!" Merial cried.

"There's nothing to fear." There was something in Rayn's voice that laughed at death, a note that stirred some dim, half-forgotten memory in Merial's mind. But before she could analyze it, Sir Edward clutched at her arm.

"My God—look!"

Barely a hundred yards away, the river seemed to stop. Beyond them lay mist and roaring sound, behind and around them boiled foaming white water. It was the edge of the world.

Merial screamed as a wave crashed over the occupants of the boat. She clung to Sir Edward and shut her eyes. Any moment now they'd be over the falls. But instead, she heard the grate of the boat's bottom touching sand. Next moment Rayn had picked her up in his arms and was carrying her onto the riverbank.

"Why are you afraid?"

His eyes laughed into hers, and his grin made him look much younger. Again she was reminded of some*thing*— and then that unnamed memory coalesced with more powerful, recent images. She could feel the beat of his heart against hers, feel his breath brush her cheek. In spite of everything that Rayn had said and done, Merial felt a desperate need to lay that cheek against his.

Then she heard Sir Edward cursing behind her, and the moment passed. Glancing over her shoulder, she saw that Deen had slung the Englishman over his shoulder like a sack of grain. He dumped Sir Edward unceremoniously on the ground and reached for rifles and saddlebags from the bottom of the boat before pushing the boat free. Immediately it slid back to mid-river and was caught by the current. Merial shivered as she watched the small craft being dragged toward the falls.

"That was well done." Setting Merial down, Rayn picked up a rifle and, throwing his saddlebags over one broad shoulder, started to walk down the riverbank which followed the path of the falls. In this place of spume and mist the sound of the falls was like a continuous boom of thunder. Merial looked back over her shoulder and saw the Falls of Ravanna rising a hundred feet above them.

"Sweet God," she breathed. "We nearly went over that!"

Rayn shrugged. "There was little danger of that happening," he said. "But we had to get close enough to make certain that the boat would go over the falls."

Merial shivered. "We could have been killed," she accused.

"We all have to die sometime," he reminded her. "Save your breath and energy for walking, now."

A half hour's walk later the river quietened again, and they began to see signs of life. A few women in bright-colored saris were washing by the river, while their sun-browned children swam nearby. A few moments later a youth with a fishing pole came walking up to the river-bank. He took one look at Rayn and dropped on his knees.

"Shield of the Kingdom!" he exclaimed.

Rayn said, "Fetch your father for me, Yusuf."

The youth salaamed and went hurrying off, and moments later a portly individual came puffing to the bank. He went down on his knees and touched the dust at Rayn's feet, crying, "Heaven Born, you honor us by visiting my poor village. In what way may I serve you?"

Rayn requested four horses and provisions for two days' ride. "And you have neither seen nor heard of us," he added.

"I am deaf and blind, Great One."

As the portly headman bustled away, Merial remarked, "He doesn't seem surprised to see you."

"The Azara has been useful to me in the past," Rayn replied. "These villagers are loyal subjects and value my protection. They'll truly forget they saw us."

The Tiger seemed to have an answer for everything. "But how will you explain to your father that you helped us escape?"

His eyebrow quirked up. "Concern for my well-being? Well, you needn't fear for me. Two of my lancers created a disturbance near the dungeons by pretending to be drunk, and no one saw me go down into the dungeons." Rayn's voice turned ironical as he added, "It's assumed I'm riding toward the Afghan border with Rassul. I'll meet him and my lancers there, and we'll all return to Baranpur together. Of course the rana will be furious that you've escaped, but Panwa will calm him."

In a remarkably short time horses were brought to the riverbank. Rayn lifted Merial into the saddle, then warned, "We'll have to move hard and fast. There's danger until we reach the border. Can you and your father keep up?"

"We'll have to," she said and paused to look down at him. The sun had dried his hair into curls that framed his hard-planed face. Sun spilled into his narrowed eyes, turning them to a warm topaz. Merial's heart contracted. Even now, even after everything, she thought despairingly, all she wanted was for him to take her in his arms.

They rode single file. Merial followed Rayn, and Sir Edward came after her. Deen brought up the rear as they rode in a silence interspersed by the buzzing sound of insects, the croak of frogs, and the plash of the water. After an hour of riding they suddenly swung inland and began to climb up a steep mountain trail.

Up and up they climbed, and when the afternoon sun was falling westward, they were still climbing. By the sun's reckoning, Merial estimated that they were going in a southwesterly direction, but had no idea where they were.

Near sunset they encountered mounted men who wore the gray and olive of Ibrahim's police. Backed into the concealing forest by the side of the road, they watched the men pass, and Rayn said, "Ibrahim is watching this road. We'll go another way."

Darkness fell, and it began to rain. Merial made no complaint, but she was sodden and utterly weary by the time Rayn decreed, "You'll ride with me."

Even if she'd wanted to protest, she didn't have the energy. In exhausted silence she felt herself lifted down from the saddle and set up on his stallion. He mounted behind her and told her, "Lean back against me and go to sleep. We won't reach the border until dawn."

"My father," she mumbled, but her protest was stilled by utter exhaustion. Merial leaned back against Rayn's familiar, unyielding warmth and plunged into a dreamless sleep.

She awoke to more darkness and the sound of water dripping from the trees. While she'd slept the rain had ended and the countryside had changed. They had ceased to climb and were now traversing a thickly forested plateau. Merial could hear Rayn's quiet breathing and Sir Edward muttering querulously, complaining of his hurts and making threats against Khem Raoshad and his son.

"How do you feel?"

Rayn had formed his words against her cheek, and she realized that she had pillowed her face against his chest. She drew herself up and away from him as she asked, "Where are we?"

"Near the border," was the reply.

He called a halt to water the horses, but when he handed her down, Merial found she could hardly bear to stand. As she hobbled about to loosen her cramped muscles, Sir Edward limped up to her.

"I'm half dead," he complained bitterly. "That bastard Narayn is enjoying this." He hesitated, then added, "Do you think he'll really take us to Sri Nevi?"

"Where else?" Somehow she'd never thought to doubt Rayn's promise. "He doesn't want his country to go to war, Father. That's the only reason he's doing this."

Sir Edward snorted. "His word! The word of a heathen! I forgot how much I hated this filthy country."

He stamped away and Merial saw Rayn standing nearby, silently tending to his stallion. Though he'd doubtless heard all of Sir Edward's comments, he only said, "There's no time to rest. We're near the border and must push on."

They mounted up immediately and rode on again through the forest that was no longer still but full of the chatter of wakening birds. "They smell the dawn," Deen commented.

As he spoke, the forest thinned, and they could see a plain that led up to a low range of hills. Along the crest of the hills the sky was turning a lighter gray.

"Is that the border?" Merial asked eagerly, and Sir Edward spurred forward only to have his way blocked by Rayn.

"You'll move only on my order," he said sternly. "We're still in Baranpur, and I'm not anxious to run into our sentries. I'd be hard put to explain why I'm helping you escape."

"By Yama, King of Death—look, lord."

Deen was pointing to a huge felled tree. As they rode to take a closer look, Rayn's stallion snorted at the smell of burned charcoal and fresh-cut wood.

"Gods above," Rayn swore.

By the light of the approaching dawn, Merial could see that many other trees had been cut down. The earth was scarred by huge charred areas where the trees had been apparently burned. Seeing the gashes in the trunks of another giant tree, she felt a sudden sadness. These giants had stood for hundreds of years, yet they'd been felled in a few short minutes.

"Perce has crossed into our country."

Rayn's voice was tight with anger as he spurred forward. The Ashlands and Deen followed in a tense silence that lasted as the red rim of the sun began to push over the top of the hills. The oppressive stillness began to fray Merial's already taut nerves.

"How far must we go?" she demanded.

"This afternoon you'll drink tea with the English mem-sahibs," Rayn flung over his shoulder. "I'll be rid of the both of you at last."

He pointed to a rise not far away. "Over that rise lies Sri Nevi. This is where we part company."

Was she supposed to thank him? If it hadn't been for his taking them prisoner, the Ashlands would be in Sri Nevi this long time. Then Sir Edward coughed, and she remembered that if Rayn hadn't intervened to save them time and again, Sir Edward would probably be dead by now.

But before she could voice her thanks, she realized that they'd ridden out of the forest and into a scene of utter desolation. Felled trees were lying everywhere. Bushes had been uprooted, and land had been fired and razed. Dark scars crisscrossed the countryside. The destruction to the lush, green land was like rape.

Just then Deen warned, "Lord, Afridi riders are coming."

Merial saw a dozen riders burst out of another part of the forest as Rayn caught up his musket at his saddle. The new-risen sun shone on his sword as he unsheathed it. As more mounted men appeared over the crest of a nearby hillock, Deen hefted his rifle.

"Well, Ashland," Rayn remarked, "let's see how well you can ride. Sri Nevi lies some miles to the northwest."

Sir Edward needed no urging. Spurring his horse, he shot away toward the rise that marked the border. Merial began to follow, then hesitated and looked back.

Rayn and Deen had gone back to back as they prepared to meet the Afghans' onslaught. Rayn's face seemed stripped of all softness. His eyes reflected the red sunrise and held the cold, intent look of a man who was used to facing death.

Obeying an impulse she couldn't control, she stopped her horse and wheeled it about. "You can outrun them if you turn back to Baranpur!" she cried. "Go now—why should you throw your lives away?"

He didn't look at her, but as she gave her involuntary cry of protest, Rayn saw his woman clearly. He saw her the way he carried her—had always carried her—in his heart.

Involuntarily his voice softened. "Go quickly and don't look back. Stay with your father."

But she sat transfixed again by that elusive shadow-sense that she couldn't identify. It danced on the periphery of her mind, tormenting her because she knew it was there but couldn't grasp it. She had heard those words somewhere before, but where . . .

"Merial, come away at once!"

Sir Edward's shout was interrupted by a crash of musketfire. Two Afghan warriors fell writhing from their saddles, and next moment all hell seemed to break loose. Bending low over her saddle, Merial spurred to where Sir Edward waited.

"Come *along*," he gritted. "Are you mad, staying here? Two men can't hold so many off for long. We don't have much head start before those Afghans start coming after us."

He was right. She needed to go, and quickly. But Merial looked back nevertheless as they galloped away from the noise of battle.

She could see nothing but the mill of mounted men, could hear nothing over the neigh of horses and musket-fire and the clash of steel. She couldn't even see Rayn in that violent tangle. Perhaps he'd already been killed.

·· *Eleven* ··

WITHOUT WAITING TO see whether or not his daughter was following, Sir Edward galloped his horse over the rise. Suddenly he gave a cry of dismay. Early sunlight flashed against muskets and steel bayonets as a squadron of mounted riders rode toward the Ashlands.

"We've ridden into a trap!" Sir Edward shouted. "We've got to turn back—"

"Halt where you are!"

The command had been given in English. "They're soldiers from Sri Nevi!" Merial exclaimed.

Sir Edward spurred forward, waving his hand wildly and yelling, "I'm an Englishman. Don't shoot. I'm English!"

The leader of the approaching soldiers called an order, and two men broke rank. One galloped up to meet Sir Edward while the other cantered up the hillock to where Merial waited.

"My God," he exclaimed, "it's a woman!" He saluted smartly, adding, "Lieutenant Denning, marm. At your service."

Merial could only nod numbly.

"Sir Edward Ashland!" the leader of the English troops was now shouting. "Gad, sir, we thought you were dead. We met years ago—Colonel Malcolm, commander of the Sri Nevi garrison, at your service. We heard that you'd been taken prisoner by that blackguard, the Tiger."

Sir Edward drew himself erect. Though pale from fatigue and dressed in pitiful rags, he was once again the haughty English aristocrat.

"Colonel, my daughter and I have been subjected to unspeakable treatment in Baranpur. It's with difficulty that we have escaped with our lives."

Colonel Malcolm looked incredulous. "You were the *Tiger*'s prisoners and lived to tell of it?"

Again, Sir Edward began his account, but the colonel interrupted reluctantly. "I beg your pardon, but we can't stop. We've got some Afghan raiders to deal with—they come regularly over the border, and these bas—er, these fellows have been giving us the slip for several months."

"I must tell you something of gravest importance first," Sir Edward protested.

But the colonel was no longer listening. "Lieutenant Denning, escort Sir Edward and his daughter to Sri Nevi," he commanded. "Take four men with you as escort."

The young officer who'd ridden up to Merial saluted again and said, "If you'll follow me, marm?"

Sir Edward was still trying to get the colonel's attention when Merial came up to him. "It's not only Afghans you have to fear," he was crying. Then, as the troops rode heedlessly on, he exclaimed, "I've got to ride after him, Merial—tell him that the Tiger's nearby!"

"No." The vehemence of the word surprised them both. "He saved our lives. We owe him our silence at least."

"We owe him nothing!" Sir Edward exploded. "He's a murdering savage."

Merial thought of Rayn's face as she'd last seen it. She said, "If he hadn't stayed behind to fight the Afghans, we might well be dead by now."

Sir Edward looked more cheerful at the thought. "Hopefully, they've killed him. Twenty to two is pretty steep odds."

Lieutenant Denning now approached to suggest that they ride on. "It's not safe so close to the Baranpur border," he explained. "We should start for Sri Nevi at once."

He eyed Merial as he spoke, and she could almost read his thoughts. In her Indian tunic and trousers she looked as though she had committed the social sin of "going native." His reaction might have irritated her at another time, but just now all she could think of was Rayn. Sir Edward was probably right—by now Rayn must surely be dead.

She couldn't bear to think of that hard-muscled, powerful body mutilated by those terrible Afghan swords. Instead, she thought of him full of vital life as he had been on the river. He had laughed at danger then, and the shadowed look in his eyes had been replaced by laughter and light.

Lieutenant Denning had fallen in beside her. "So you met the Tiger," he was saying. "I've heard of him, of course, but I've never met anyone who saw him face to face. How did you escape?"

"He helped us to get away." Merial was not so weary that she missed the look of disbelief that flashed into the young officer's prominent blue eyes. "He didn't do it for us. He didn't want to start a war with England."

And yet he had given his life to protect her. "Go swiftly and don't look back," he had said, and she remembered the tone of his voice. He hadn't spoken as though she were his enemy.

"You can't make me believe that Narayn of Baranpur did anything decent," Lieutenant Denning protested. "You're bamming me—I mean, you're joking, marm. What really did happen?"

"What happened was that we barely escaped with our lives," Sir Edward cut in. As he began a tale that made him the hero of a daring escape, Merial let her weary mind drift. She hardly paid attention to where they were going until they arrived at a river. Here, a partially built bridge extended over the water.

"The railway is going to span the Indus River at this point," Lieutenant Denning explained. "They had to stop construction because of heavy rains. The foundations have to be dug over a hundred feet deep in this area."

The tracks of the railway stopped some distance from the other side of the river, and near-naked Indian workers were busily laying track and working on stone pilings.

"How many workers?" Sir Edward wondered. When told, he mused, "Seven thousand—that's not surprising. Modest, in fact. I heard that forty thousand were used at the Western Ghats."

"About a third of the workers die off periodically and have to be replaced," the lieutenant said. At Merial's horrified exclamation, he added defensively, "You can't help accidents happening when a railroad's being built, marm, and Indians are ignorant and have filthy ways. These apes breed every kind of disease."

"You're talking about human beings, not monkeys," Merial flared, and Sir Edward gave an uncomfortable laugh.

"My daughter was born in this country. She has strange views sometimes. *My* feeling is that you can't trust any one of these beggars. Sly, the lot of them. Would slit your throat as soon as look at you."

Merial thought of Rukmiri-Bai, of wise and compassionate Baju, and the little flower seller who had tried to save her from the thugs. She recalled the Silver Palace, which made Buckingham Palace look tawdry by comparison. Yet Englishmen considered Indian people inferior.

She was silent for the rest of the ride, which took the better part of two hours. The hot sun had climbed into the sky when they came within sight of Sri Nevi, and Merial felt a spurt of joy as she saw the Elephant Gate that led into the city. Ganesh, the benevolent elephant god, grinned down at her as she passed through the stone gates, and she couldn't help smiling back. It was as though he were welcoming her home.

But inside the gates everything had changed. Merial, who had carried the memory of her first home throughout the years, couldn't recognize the place. Smartly uniformed English soldiers stood at the gate, and instead of the muddy street she remembered, there was a broad, well-cared-for road lined with trees. And though she glimpsed some wooden shacks and narrow streets populated by Indian families, these soon gave way to stately homes built to accommodate the English population. A park where Indian nurses walked with their English charges had been built where Sri Nevi's communal well had once stood.

The modest home where Captain St. Marr had lived was gone, and the barracks where the men of the garrison had slept had been transformed. Lieutenant Denning pointed pridefully to the new barracks, adding, "The old barracks is being used as a lockup these days." He indicated a grassy field. "There's the parade ground where we muster. We play cricket and polo here, and there's talk of a hunt club forming. Do you ride to hounds, Sir Edward?"

Merial felt a sense of unreality as they passed the spot

where the commissioner's residence had once stood. It had been a bungalow, which had seemed large to her childish mind but actually must have been quite small and primitive. Now, in the bungalow's place, stood a stately residence surrounded by a high fence.

"Commissioner Perce's residence," the lieutenant said. "I've sent word with news of your arrival on ahead, so he's expecting you."

He called an order to the gateman, who salaamed reverentially as he opened the gate to show a garden sparkling with fountains. These gardens surrounded a villa built in the classical style with wide marble steps leading up to a pillared facade.

An Englishman now stepped out from between these pillars. "Sir Edward!" he exclaimed. "Miss Ashland! Welcome to my humble home. I'm Hamilton Perce."

Unhurriedly he descended the stairs, stopping halfway to smile down at them. He was not tall but lean and muscular, and he walked with a vigorous, springy step. His sun-darkened face was framed with dark hair that had just begun to silver at the temples, and in the lamplight his face was severely handsome.

"You've had a long and difficult journey," he was saying.

Sir Edward nodded. "We fell into the Tiger's hands."

A flicker of emotion passed across Hamilton Perce's face, but then he smiled. "So I was told. I can't tell you how sorry I am that you and your lovely daughter have been subjected to such horrors."

He snapped his fingers and native servants came hurrying down the steps. They bowed almost to the ground, and Perce said, "Yusuf and Hammed will see you to the rooms that have been readied for you. If there's anything you require, you have only to tell them." He added, "This evening 'I am entertaining Lord and Lady Carpe, from London. Lord Carpe has come out to see how my railroad is progressing, and I know he would wish to meet you. If you're not too exhausted, perhaps you would join me for dinner."

"That's very good of you. It will be a pleasure to be in civilized company again." Sir Edward alighted from his horse and handed Merial down. She felt the ache of the long journey in her entire body, but even more she felt uncomfortable. She hadn't said a word to Mr. Perce, but she could feel him watching her as she followed her father up the steps. Perhaps he, like Lieutenant Denning, felt contempt for an Englishwoman in native dress.

She felt as if she'd stepped across the ocean and was in England again. The interior of Hamilton Perce's house was decorated completely in the European style. Rich brocade draped the windows, gilt-framed portraits and English landscapes hung on the wall. As she followed the Indian servants up a curve of stairway, Merial glimpsed marble statues, a stately clock. After weeks of living in the colorful comfort that characterized Eastern dwellings, this house felt stiff and formal.

The rooms assigned to her were no less English. A canopied bed stood in one corner of the room, and overstuffed chairs were grouped under a full-length portrait of Queen Victoria.

The only Indian thing in the room was a pretty young woman dressed in a green sari, who looked at Merial with shocked eyes. The manservant with Merial rebuked her harshly.

"Never mind how she's dressed, Padma. This is the English memsahib that Perce Sahib has been expecting. You're to see to her needs."

In halting English the woman apologized. "My name

is Padma, Miss Sahib. If you want anything, you have only to ask."

She looked stunned when Merial thanked her in Hindustani and requested a bath, but scurried to do her bidding. In a few moments a bath was prepared, and when Merial had emerged from it, Padma was there to wrap her in thick towels and to proffer a silk dressing gown.

"Perce Sahib has said that your luggage was lost," Padma said. "A wardrobe has been selected for your pleasure, and there are many dresses. Before you rest, will Miss Sahib choose which dress she will wear to the dinner tonight?"

Sunlight and the scent of water and flowers and Geeta displaying saris of silk and damask and embroidered gauze—Merial hastily brushed the memory aside.

"It doesn't matter what I wear," she said.

Padma looked shocked. "Please, Miss Sahib, my cousin sewed the dresses and—and Perce Sahib would be very angry indeed." She checked herself nervously to add, "If there is any alteration necessary, my cousin will do the work while you rest."

Merial hadn't missed the scared look in Padma's eyes. She recalled what the shikari, old Walid Mohammed, had said about Hamilton Perce being a hard taskmaster. She held back questions that rose to her lips as Padma displayed a light blue dress of organdy, banded with creamy lace, a low-cut gown the color of sea-foam trimmed with feathers, a cream-colored batiste flecked with embroidered forget-me-nots.

"Does Miss Sahib like any of these?" Padma asked anxiously.

No doubt Padma's cousin would hear of it if the Miss Sahib didn't care for the dresses. Merial selected the organdy and found that the tiny-waisted, bell-skirted gown fitted her perfectly.

"Miss Sahib looks like a queen in this dress. My cousin will be proud. Now you must sleep."

The bed was too soft and seemed to suck her slight body into it. As Padma fussed to lower snowy folds of mosquito netting about her, Merial longed for her comfortable bed at the Bagh Mahal. And for Rayn—A savage pain stabbed through her, and she closed her eyes. She must not think of him, living or dead. He belonged to another world.

For several hours she slept the dreamless sleep of exhaustion. Then, as she began to surface from the depths of sleep, she imagined she was back in time. She was Meri -*baba* again, and this was her familiar bed in her familiar room, and Jassmina was singing a lullaby to her.

"*Nini, baba, nini,*" crooned the familiar voice. "Rest, baby, rest. *Muckan, roti, cheeni*—"

With a start, Merial came awake. It had turned dark, and a woman was sitting next to the bed. She was thin and gray-haired, but even the years and the shadows that filled the room couldn't change the loving expression in her eyes.

"*Jassmina?*" Merial breathed.

The old woman burst into tears as Merial threw her arms around her neck. "Oh, Jassmina," Merial wept, also, "I have missed you so much."

The old nurse rocked Merial in her arms. "You have come home, Meri-*baba.* God, the merciful and compassionate, has returned you to these old arms. But you have returned in no auspicious hour. There is trouble in Sri Nevi, *piara*—my darling. When I heard you had returned, I was torn between joy at seeing you again and fear for you."

"Why afraid?" Merial asked, but Jassmina changed the subject.

"You have grown so beautiful, Meri-*baba*. Those eyes like the sky—that long black hair. *Hai-mai*—how many hearts have you broken?"

Merial kissed the older woman's cheek. It had been brown and smooth when they were last together, and her eyes had been merry. Now the cheek was withered and Jassmina's eyes were full of sorrow.

"I never thought to see you again." Jassmina sighed. "When I think of how we said farewell—*wah,* that was a terrible night. I shall never forget how the priests of the Shaiva Temple incited our people to storm the commissioner sahib's house and how the crowd turned ugly when your father and your mother left Sri Nevi. The priests themselves led the mob that followed after you."

"Why did they do that?" Merial wondered. "What angered them so?"

"It was probably the *dewanee*—madness—that filled India during that terrible time. Surely the mob was mad when they slew the soldiers at the Gujjar Pass." Jassmina lowered her voice. "You know that St. Marr Sahib's son was also killed?"

When Merial nodded silently, Jassmina wiped her eyes with the edge of her sari. "He was a sweet boy and would have made a lovely man. If I knew who his murderer was, I would strangle him with my own hands."

Merial could hear Rayn's deep voice telling her that Niall's death had been fated. An ache of longing so fierce that it was like a physical pain flared within her and then sobbingly ebbed away.

She asked, "How did you find me? Did Perce Sahib send for you?"

"When I heard that the sahib your father was to be the

deputy commissioner of the railroad, I begged Perce Sahib on my knees to let me serve you. He refused at first, thinking me too old for service, but in the end he agreed." Jassmina's lips tightened. "He is a hard man."

"*How* is he hard, Jassmina?" Merial asked.

"He is responsible for many deaths of the workers, because he will not spend the money to pay for adequate safeguards. His own chief engineer, Hugh Sahib, is in disagreement with him." The old woman hesitated before adding, "My people hate and fear Perce Sahib, and because your father works under this man, they may hate you, also. That is why I am afraid for you."

Padma's entering the room to suggest that Miss Sahib dress for dinner cut short the conversation. Jassmina insisted that she arrange Merial's hair, so Padma smilingly stood aside to admire. "Such long, lovely hair!" she exclaimed. "It is as black as midnight and so thick. Surely only a goddess has tresses like these."

Jassmina skillfully braided Merial's hair and arranged it into a crown. Then, with Padma's help, she settled the ball dress around Merial's shoulders. The women then walked about her, admiring her white shoulders, the curve of her breasts, her tiny waist. Their extravagant praises made Merial laugh, and she felt almost lighthearted when she went to join her father.

He was waiting in the hallway by the tall clock. He pulled out his watch, frowned at it. "You took your time, Merial. It won't do to keep Mr. Perce waiting." He then looked at her and nodded approvingly. "At least you look like an English lady and not some native drudge."

She went down the circular stairs on his arm and bowing servants showed the way to a handsome drawing room where a dozen people were talking and laughing amongst themselves. Merial's nostrils were immediately assaulted by heavy European perfume, so different from the Eastern scents of attar of roses and sandalwood. She also had a fleeting impression of bell-skirts and jewels and men in evening dress or military scarlet and black.

"Miss Ashland, your humble servant." Hamilton Perce, elegant in formal dinner clothes, bowed over her hand. "You're so lovely that you take my breath away, ma'am."

His lips on the back of her hand were moist, and his courtesy was mixed with a boldness that was somehow disturbing. Merial curtsied deeply but left it to Sir Edward to express his thanks for his borrowed evening clothes. "They make me feel like a new man," he said.

All talk in the room stopped as Hamilton Perce introduced the Ashlands. Colonel Malcolm's plump, elderly wife, whose graying fringe of curls bobbed alarmingly as she kissed Merial, exclaimed over the change in her.

"For you were a little girl when you went away—and now you have grown into a lovely young woman." She paused. "We have been so worried about you, my dear. You've been through a terrible ordeal."

She introduced Merial to the other women, none of whom Merial knew. There was tight-lipped Mrs. Hugh, wife of Perce's chief engineer; Helen Jarris, a young, sallow-complected woman married to a portly major twice her age; vivacious Lady Alice Carpe in whose husband's honor the dinner was being held. There was also Mrs. Fulks, the high-nosed wife of the colonel's adjutant.

Other introductions followed and blurred in Merial's mind. Army officers and engineers bowed over her hand, but her curtsies and murmured greetings were absent-minded. She could sense that the women in the room were watching her with an avid curiosity that also conveyed a hint of disapproval.

Only plump Mrs. Malcolm seemed wholly relaxed, and

Merial warmed to her. The colonel's lady spoke longingly of her own daughter in England and said that Merial was very much like her Rosa.

"You are the same age, my dear, but my little gel is blond, like me, and quite plump, I fear. That comes with being the mother of two little boys. I wish my grandsons were with me, but India is not a place to raise little children."

"Too much heat, disease, and dirt," drawled Helen Jarris, and the other women nodded critically.

Merial was grateful that she was placed near Mrs. Malcolm at the dinner table. The long formal board awed her, as did the many dishes that were offered by an endless procession of servants. The colonel's lady leaned over to whisper, "Mr. Perce prides himself on setting a fine table. It's said that his dinners would put the viceroy himself to shame."

Before Merial could comment, the high-nosed Mrs. Fulks, who was seated across from Merial, sniffed loudly. "It's always the way, isn't it?" she commented. "When alley cats pretend to be tigers, they growl the loudest."

Mrs. Malcolm looked uneasy and addressed Sir Edward. "We have been dying of curiosity. How did you escape from Baranpur?"

Instantly there was a hush around the table. Sir Edward immediately launched into a much embellished account of their adventures, and his narrative drew shocked exclamations from his audience.

"What I want to know is, what's *he* like?" The laughing interruption came from Lady Carpe. "Is the Tiger as handsome as they say?"

"Good God, Alice!" Lord Carpe exclaimed in a shocked voice. "As if a proper Englishwoman would think of such a thing."

"Now, Barty, don't be so stuffy. I know every woman at this table is dying to ask questions about Prince Rayn." Lady Alice tossed her pretty head and demanded, "What's he like, Miss Ashland?"

Merial thought of that moment when she'd come face to face with Rayn for the first time. "He's a powerful presence," she said.

Helen Jarris, the major's sallow young wife, tittered. "I hear he's over six feet tall."

Tall and broad-shouldered, with golden eyes that could see into her heart—suddenly, Rayn was there, his cool assurance making a mockery of Hamilton Perce and his ostentatious dinner. His image seemed more real to Merial than anyone in the room as she agreed, "He's quite tall."

"Does he live in a palace full of stolen jewels and—and slaves?" Helen Jarris persisted, and Merial saw her lick her sensuous lips. "*Women* slaves, too?"

"We were almost slaves ourselves," Sir Edward interrupted. "The rana wanted to kill us. Later he decided to sell us as slaves. Fortunately, we managed to escape."

Hamilton Perce said smoothly, "The fact that you did says a great deal for you, Sir Edward. You must be an exceptionally brave man."

Sir Edward said modestly, "I wasn't afraid for myself. When I hacked our way out of that prison, I only thought of my daughter's safety." He avoided Merial's shocked gaze as he added, "One thing I'll say for that blackguard, Narayn. He's an adversary to reckon with. I'll tell you that he was furious when he saw that trees have been felled within Baranpur's border."

"I hadn't originally planned to pass so close to Baranpur, but the only other alternative was to blast tunnels through two mountains," Hamilton Perce said. "It was more expedient to do things this way, as I'm sure Lord Carpe would agree."

The English lord nodded, but Anthony Hugh, the chief engineer, said, "Expediency is one name for it, I suppose."

Perce frowned but ignored the interruption. "Prince Rayn will have to get used to the fact that he's living in the nineteenth century," he resumed. "Railroads are the future of India. Baranpur has never signed any treaty with the Crown, so we're under no real compunction to respect his borders."

"That may be unwise, sir." All eyes at the table swiveled to Merial, who said, "Baranpur is ready to go to war to defend itself."

"What, that little country?" Colonel Malcolm scoffed. "What's their standing army, eh? Five hundred men? We'll trounce them soundly if they dare to lift their hand."

Hamilton Perce smiled at Merial. "You seem to have a good opinion of Prince Rayn. He may be a formidable adversary, but he can hardly pit himself against England." He nodded to the engineer, adding, "Mr. Hugh agrees with me when I say that when we're connected with Raulpindi, Sri Nevi will finally enter the nineteenth century."

He sounded so smug that Merial couldn't help protesting, "One doesn't have to destroy the past to reach the future."

Perce's smile became fixed. He was staring at Merial with that bold expression she disliked as he said, "Sometimes it's the only way. Tomorrow, when you are rested, it will be my great pleasure to show you what I've accomplished here."

Next morning, as Merial breakfasted in her room, Padma came in with a note from Commissioner Perce requesting the honor of Miss Ashland's company on a ride around Sri Nevi. Though the request was worded courteously, Merial knew she could not refuse an invitation from her father's superior. Besides, she was anxious to see the changes that the railway had brought to Sri Nevi.

These changes were everywhere. Clad in a turquoise-blue riding costume which, like last night's gown, fit her perfectly, Merial rode down the wide main street beside Hamilton Perce and realized she might as well be in Lucknow or Delhi. Soldiers drilled near the barracks, and one or two English ladies were braving the heat to ride out in their buggies and phaetons. Nearer the Elephant Gate they passed the poorer section, where the Indian people lived.

Merial searched the peoples' faces to see if she could recognize anyone from the days of her childhood. Sullen, hostile faces stared back at her, and once she saw a man shake his fist at Perce's back.

Perce did not seem to notice this hostility. Elegant in a suit of fine gray linen, he looked about proudly. "You'll find that Sri Nevi has become an important point on the map of India," he told Merial. "It will become even more important when we are able to transport troops to and from the border of Afghanistan."

"Is that so important?" Merial wondered.

"Naturally. The Afghans are a volatile people. Colonel Malcolm has his hands full with Afridi raiders who keep coming over the border to steal what they can. England might be at war with Afghanistan at any time, and a railroad originating here near the border would be invaluable." Perce looked smug as he added, "But railroads have been used to help people suffering from famine, too, and there is trade, of course. My railroad will have many uses, dear lady."

She didn't like his familiar tone but tried to suppress

this feeling as she said, "I see miles of railroad track have already been laid. You have progressed very quickly, Mr. Perce."

To her surprise, he frowned. "Not quickly enough, unfortunately. The Great India Peninsular Railway must move more rapidly if all of India is to be linked together. Lord Dalhousie's plans were made long ago and didn't take into account such things as Afghan raiders and Narayn of Baranpur."

He uttered the name with a savagery that made Merial hold her peace. She was silent as they rode some distance away from Sri Nevi and stopped on a hill that overlooked miles of already laid track. A multitude of half-naked figures, dwarfed by distance, toiled on, and Merial realized what a huge undertaking the railroad was. For a moment she was awed by Perce's dream of linking India, and then she thought of Baranpur.

"There are some people in India who don't want any part of your railroad," she said. "Surely their feelings must be considered?"

Perce turned to give her a searching look. "He must have made quite an impression on you."

She said coldly, "I cannot think what you mean."

"I *mean* that a handsome bandit like Prince Rayn has an attraction for nice young ladies." Perce showed his teeth in a mirthless smile as he added, "I notice that you speak Hindustani like a native and that you were dressed in native attire when you first arrived at Sri Nevi. Lieutenant Denning was shocked that an English lady should so far forget herself."

She flared, "Lieutenant Denning can think as he wishes. Please to remember that we were taken captive and in terror of our death. For you to suggest that we were in Baranpur by choice is insulting."

She jerked her horse's head around and began to ride back the way she had come. In a few moments he caught up to her and put a hand on her bridle. Merial's eyes blazed. "Take your hand away from my bridle!" she cried.

To her surprise, he did so. "I must apologize," he said. "You mistook my meaning. Alas, living out here in the wilderness, one forgets polite speech. If I have offended you, I humbly beg your pardon."

This man was her father's superior, she reminded herself. "There is no need," she said stiffly.

"But I must make amends. I beg that you and your father will sup with me tonight." Hamilton Perce smiled as he added, "No tiresome people about as there were last night, I promise. You will come?"

There was no reason why she would want to refuse, Merial told herself as they rode back to Sri Nevi. On the ride home Perce was attentive and courteous to a fault, and she could see that he was doing his best to be charming and considerate.

Yet she felt somber as she dressed for dinner that evening. She and her father were not only staying with the commissioner of railroads, but he owned the very dress she wore. Merial promised herself that as soon as she could afford to do so, she would have Padma's cousin sew her something of her own design. Jassmina, however, had no such reservation and clucked pridefully over the vision Merial made in the light blue gown banded with lace.

"You are lovely, *piara*," she said. "No wonder the sahib is smitten with you."

Merial stiffened. "What did you say?"

Jassmina chuckled. "I have seen men and women regard each other with *that* look before. Perce Sahib is very taken with you."

Merial halted with her hand on the doorknob. "I'm not going down to dinner."

"Indeed you are. It may be," Jassmina added judiciously, "that the sahib lacks a softer hand to rule his life. If he loves you, you may turn his mind to better things."

"But I have no wish to—"

"Do I speak to a babe or to a woman? *Angrezi* women are like their sisters in India. We have no choice in whom we are to marry." Jassmina went on philosophically. "A woman's husband is her god and her king. If she can influence him in any way, that is God's blessing, *piara.*"

"And what of love?" Merial mused.

Jassmina looked at her one-time charge thoughtfully. "Love," she repeated, "sometimes comes after marriage. Did I not come to love my own man—a bear, he was, a lusty bear! We had a son together and many days of happiness. Now he is dead and our son does his duty to me. That is how life goes."

Old, realistic eyes seemed to be looking deep into Merial's heart as Jassmina added, "You must forget love, *baba.* Otherwise, life can break your heart."

The caress of cool lips, the hard press of an arm about her waist. A deep voice calling her name, and laughter that lingered on the warm wind—

Merial rose to her feet and said abruptly, "I'll go down now," she said. "I mustn't keep our kind host waiting, must I?"

Tonight Sir Edward was not waiting to escort her downstairs. Instead, a fawning servant with a five-pronged candelabra lit her way downstairs and guided her to a room off the drawing room. When he opened the door, Merial found herself in a small chamber that overlooked the gardens. Torches made the garden glow with color, and the sound of cool fountains lingered pleasantly on the ear.

"Miss Ashland, how charming you look tonight." Perce came forward to bow over her hand and lead her to a chair near the window. "Your father has not yet come down," he went on, "so we will have time to speak alone."

Not knowing how to respond to this, she seated herself. A silent servant entered with a tray of fine wines, waited for her to select a crystal goblet, then served Perce.

"This is a wine from Champagne shipped out especially for me," Perce explained. "I hope you will like its bouquet."

She smiled at this. "I'm not a connoisseur of wines," she apologized.

"I've cultivated a taste for the good things of life." He paused. "I'm sure you know the story of my humble origins?"

It was said lightly but she heard uncertainty in his voice and remembered Mrs. Fulks's acid remark. Suddenly Merial felt sorry for Hamilton Perce. No matter how much money he made, he would never be "top drawer," would never be accepted by the upper crust of society.

He was saying, "In case you didn't know, my people were tradespeople—from Liverpool. But I've made my money and my mark working on the railroads out here in India. I've even got the former commissioner of Sri Nevi working for me. Here in this country a man who knows what he's doing can live like a king."

The arrogance in his tone was annoying, and she found it hard to hold her tongue as Perce continued, "But all my accomplishments mean nothing, Miss Ashland. My estate, the railroad itself are nothing without the proper woman in my life. Do you follow my meaning, dear lady?"

His face was very near hers. His light gray eyes held

hers with a bold intensity. Involuntarily Merial drew back and said, "I do not believe that this conversation is a proper one."

She was interrupted as the servant opened the door for Sir Edward. Merial felt a surge of relief as her father came into the room exclaiming, "By jove, Mr. Perce, this is quite a room! Almost feels as though we're seated in the outdoors."

As Hamilton Perce rose to greet Sir Edward, Merial saw the flash of displeasure in his light gray eyes. He hadn't wanted to be interrupted. He'd been on the point of some disclosure. It was almost as if—

Merial frowned at the thought. Jassmina's foolishness was infecting her, she thought. Perce couldn't possibly have been about to ask her to marry him.

·· Twelve ··

RETURNING THE SALUTES of ladies taking a turn in their buggies or victorias, Merial trotted her horse down Sri Nevi's broad main street. She bowed to the mounted officers and civilians whom she knew and smiled at *ayahs* who were hurrying their *babas* in to their suppers.

All day she had ached to be alone, and now at last in the cool evening she'd managed to get away. Unaccompanied except for an attending groom, she was finally free from the banalities that made up an English lady's day—the ride between five and seven in the morning, the obligatory luncheon at two, the ritual siesta, and the bray of the military band which heralded the evening.

"It is a horrible life," Merial muttered. "How can any of them stand it?"

Today had been worse than most. The ladies' luncheon she had been forced to attend in honor of the departing Lady Carpe had been full of tension. Mrs. Hugh, whose husband had clashed publicly with Commissioner Perce and who had been reprimanded by Lord Carpe himself, brooded darkly throughout the meal, and the other ladies glanced at her out of the corners of their eyes while pretending interest in the latest fashions in the catalogs sent by steamship from English stores.

It was three weeks since they had arrived, yet Merial still felt like a stranger in Sri Nevi. She and her father continued to live in Hamilton Perce's house. Merial had asked her father to insist on an establishment of his own, but Sir Edward enjoyed the comfort of the grand residence and kept putting her off.

"Let me find my feet here first, Merial," he told his daughter. "Mr. Perce doesn't mind us billeting with him for the moment."

She minded. Merial didn't like the way Perce looked at her. The expression in those pale gray eyes made him look like a cat watching some mouse hole. So far he had not initiated another private talk with her, but it cost her an effort to sit across from him each morning and evening. At mealtimes it was assumed that Merial should play hostess for Perce, pour the tea, listen as he bragged about the progress of "his" railroad. Though he was usually courteous and careful, his smug attitude grated on her nerves.

Fortunately, the commissioner of railroads and his assistant had been busy each day with their duties near the Indus River. Each day Sir Edward complained about worthless native workers who were hindering the completion of the bridge. Last night he'd said that a part of the bridge piling had collapsed, killing fifty workers and injuring another hundred.

"Mrs. Hugh made some remark the other day that too many workers were being hurt," Merial had mused. "Does Mr. Perce take enough safety precautions?"

"Of course he does—Hugh's an alarmist, and it'll serve him right if Lord Carpe recommends his recall to England." But her father's suddenly averted eyes belied his words.

"There goes the daughter of an accursed father!"

Her thoughts interrupted by the harsh male voice, Merial realized that she was riding past the temple dedicated to Shiva. An elderly priest was glaring at her, and when he saw he'd caught her attention, he shook his fist.

"Be off with you!" Merial's groom shouted. "Perce Sahib has horsewhipped men for less."

The priest retreated into the temple, but the hostility of the people who had gathered by the roadside was palpable; their dark eyes expressed volumes of hate. Merial felt sick at heart, and as she approached the city gates, she sent up a little message to the cheerful elephant god who adorned it.

"You're supposed to ease burdens, Lord Ganesh. Can't you do something for these people?" And then in spite of herself, she added, "And please—let me hear something about *him.*"

There'd been no news—none at all—about Rayn. The border had been still, and even though Perce's workers were felling trees within Baranpur, the Tiger did not ride against them. How could this be unless—

Unless Rayn were dead. Unless he was rotting in the rana's dungeon for helping the *Angrezi* prisoners escape.

Merial paused at the Elephant Gate knowing that she should turn back. It was much too late in the day for her to be riding outside the safety of the city gates. Yet she couldn't bear the thought of returning to the artificial world and the stuffy rituals that her people had created here in Sri Nevi.

Spurring her horse, Merial rode through the Elephant Gate and out of Sri Nevi. Then, turning her back to Perce's railroad and attended only by her groom, she cantered in the direction of the faraway rise beyond which lay Baranpur's border.

As she cantered along, the earth took on the violet shades of the twilit sky, and the clumps of pine trees threw elongated shadows. A measure of peace returned to Merial until she realized that she wasn't alone. A rider was riding down the slope of a nearby hillock.

Her heart sank as she recognized the rider as Hamilton Perce. And apparently, he'd seen and recognized her, too, for he now began to canter toward her. Merial bit her lip in dismay. She had no wish to meet the commissioner of railroads, especially out here, alone, in the twilight.

But perhaps he hadn't actually recognized her—perhaps if she made for that thick grove of pines nearby, she could remain hidden till he passed by. Calling an order to her attendant groom, Merial rode toward the pines.

Luck was with her, for some minutes later Perce galloped by her hiding place. Her groom sucked his teeth and remarked, "His Honor seems to be in a hurry, Miss Sahib."

As if he'd overheard, Perce reined in his horse and stopped some twenty yards away. Now she would have to explain why she'd tried to avoid him. But before Merial could think of some convincing lie, she saw that several riders were spurring over the hillock.

"Afghan raiders," Merial's groom groaned. "We must get back to Sri Nevi at once, Miss Sahib. Maybe we can outrun them."

There were a dozen of the Afridi, each man armed to the teeth. Couldn't Perce see them coming? But he simply sat on his horse and waited until they were within a few yards of each other. Then a man who was apparently their leader spurred forward.

"Greetings, Your Honor," he called.

Merial started. Even at this distance she recognized the man's distinctive voice. It was the thug, Yuir Singh.

But the thugs hated the English, didn't they? At once horrified and bewildered, Merial heard Perce say, "Does the plan go forward, Yuir Singh?"

"Assuredly," the thug replied. "As you ordered, many of our brethren have infiltrated the ranks of the railroad workers."

He lowered his voice and Merial couldn't follow his words. Desperate to hear more, she dismounted and handed the reins to her groom.

"Wait here."

The man rolled his eyes in panic. "Miss Sahib, do not go near those evil men," he pleaded. "If they catch you, they will murder us both."

Ignoring him, Merial moved stealthily through the pines. Hidden by the trees, she managed to get within a few yards of the group. Now she could hear Perce say, "Assuredly, many will die. My government won't act to crush Baranpur unless the Indus turns red with blood."

Merial watched Yuir Singh's narrow, fanatical face blaze with enthusiasm. "It will be holy blood, shed for great Kali herself. When do you wish us to set the dynamite charges, Your Honor?"

"Not until I give the command." Perce added, "In a month's time—perhaps earlier—the bridge will be completed. To mark the event there will be a ceremony. Colonel Malcolm and his garrison soldiers will muster at the bridge, and all the sahibs and memsahibs of Sri Nevi will be there to watch the military review. That is when I will give you the signal."

Merial stifled a cry of horror.

Yuir Singh gloated. "We will watch for your signal.

And when it is given—" He smote his palm on his saddle and snarled, *"Narayn tubbah shood ba hur soorat."*

Narayn shall be annihilated—but this meant that Rayn still lived and was a force to be reckoned with! Merial's wave of relief was followed almost immediately by horror as Perce spoke sharply. "Naturally he will be destroyed. As soon as the bridge is blown, Colonel Malcolm will march against Baranpur. Even if the Tiger holds Malcolm off, more soldiers will come from England to crush the house of Raoshad. Then you, my friend and ally, will reign in Baranpur."

Yuir Singh bowed deeply, his hand on his heart. "I am Your Honor's servant," he murmured.

"You will wait for my command to set the charges," Perce ordered.

He wheeled his horse and cantered back toward Sri Nevi. As he rode away, Yuir Singh spat. "You, too, will be annihilated, *Angrezi.* But first you will do Ma Kali's work and destroy the Tiger. Once Prince Rayn is dead, our lord will hold Baranpur in the palm of his hand."

He signaled his men, and they rode off over the hillock and out of sight. Merial stood as though transfixed until her trembling groom crept up to her. "Miss Sahib—we must return back to Sri Nevi. Those *budmarshes* may come back."

During the silent, tense ride back to town, Merial had time to register all she'd heard. Perce was using Yuir Singh to destroy Rayn, and the thugs were using Perce to kill the English. Or, at least, they thought so. Merial knew the commissioner of railroads was no fool. Yuir Singh and his men would more likely find themselves ornamenting the garrison's gallows than ruling Baranpur.

But who was the "lord" of whom Yuir Singh spoke?

Merial thought of Khem-Rana's great council and recalled the look in Ibrahim's eyes.

"Perhaps it is Ibrahim—perhaps not," she muttered.
"Whoever it is, I must warn Rayn."

That Rayn was an enemy to the English was not important now. He was the only one both Perce and the thugs
feared and who could prevent the blowing of the bridge.
But how to get word to him?

She wrestled unsuccessfully with that question until she
returned to Perce's residence. Mercifully, both the commissioner and Sir Edward had gone out to dine with Colonel Malcolm and his senior officers. Merial picked up the
skirts of her riding habit and ran up to her rooms, where
Jassmina was waiting for her.

Jassmina had fallen into a doze but started awake when
Merial came into the room. "You are late," she scolded
gently. "I was worried about you, *piara.*" Then she saw
Merial's face, and her eyes narrowed. "What is it?"

Merial said, "I must get a message to Baranpur. Can
you help me?"

Jassmina's eyes seemed ready to pop from her skull.
"Are you raving?"

Merial knelt down beside her nurse's chair. Looking
steadily into the worried old eyes, she explained what she
had seen and heard. "Perce intends to start a war between
England and Baranpur. I must warn Prince Rayn."

The puzzled look in Jassmina's eyes was replaced by
a knowing expression. "So he is the one."

"What are you talking about?"

"Narayn of Baranpur is the man you cry for in your
dreams. No," she added sternly, "do not lie to me, who
cared for you since you were a babe. You are dearer to
me than my own life, and I understand your heart. I
thought it was a young *Angrezi,* left behind in your own

country, that you loved. I did not know it was the Tiger who had stolen your heart."

Impatiently Merial said, "This is nonsense, Jassmina. I only want to prevent a war." Then, unable to stare down the certainty she saw in her old nurse's eyes, she got to her feet and walked over to a window that fronted the gardens. Far away, masked by the darkness that covered Sri Nevi, rose the Pir Panjal mountains and the valley kingdom. She thought of Baranpur's beauty and peace, the prosperity and happiness of its people, those people who turned to Rayn as flowers turn to the sun.

"I must warn him," she repeated.

Jassmina protested, "We of Sri Nevi fear Prince Narayn as much as the *Angrezi* sahibs do. He is said to be merciless."

"He's not!"

Jassmina frowned at Merial's involuntary cry. "Did he force you to be his woman? Was that the way it happened?"

The scent of sandalwood and attar of roses, Rayn's arms around her, his kisses sweet on her lips. "This is our choice, also," he had said, and she had chosen. Now she chose once again.

"He helped us escape at peril to his life. For his country's sake, he said, but when Afridi raiders attacked us, he told me to ride and not look back. He saved my father's life—and mine." Merial's eyes had filled with tears, but she dashed them away and demanded, "Can you help me, Jassmina?"

The old woman sighed deeply. "Perhaps I can. Padma's cousin's nephew's son, Gulab Fateh, is a *shikari* for the sahibs. He knows every inch of the Pir Panjals. If you will write a letter, I will put it into his hands. We can trust him to elude Perce Sahib's men and see it safely delivered across the border. Quickly, *piara,* for he must go at once."

But how to word that letter? If she wrote in Hindustani, Gulab Fateh—or others here or in Baranpur—might be tempted to read it. It might be waylaid by thugs or by Ibrahim's police.

Finally Merial sat down at her desk and wrote in English: "H.P. and the thugs plan to dynamite the bridge when it is completed." Then, without signing it, she sealed it and handed it to Jassmina.

"Tell Gulab Fateh that he must avoid *Kotwal* Ibrahim's police at all costs. This letter mustn't fall into their hands."

Jassmina nodded. "I will go now and see that it is done."

Merial felt somewhat relieved. No one in Baranpur but Rayn would be able to read the English script. Of course, there was the possibility that it could be confiscated by garrison soldiers, but Jassmina had assured her that Gulab Fateh was a skilled *shikari.* He'd know how to avoid capture.

And even if the letter were intercepted, she had neither addressed nor signed the cryptic note. It would mean nothing to anyone—except Perce. Merial felt sickened when she thought of him. She could not believe that there was an Englishman so vile that he would destroy his own countrymen's lives and plunge two countries into war simply because of greed. Perce had boasted that in India a man could live like a king, and he wanted Baranpur for his kingdom.

Thoughts of Perce remained with Merial even after she went to bed, and kept her awake long into the night. She heard her father and his superior return to the residence, heard her father's slurred, drunken voice and Perce's laughter. Merial frowned into the darkness. Lately, at Perce's instigation, her father had started to drink as heavily as he had done during those last troubled months in England.

She finally fell asleep near dawn and slept into the morning. By the time she awakened, both her father and the commissioner of railroads had ridden away to oversee their work. "Perce Sahib drives himself hard to complete the bridge," Padma commented innocently when she brought Merial's breakfast.

The irony of that remark took away Merial's already fragile appetite. She wished there was something she could do, but Jassmina reported that she had delivered the note into Gulab Fateh's hands, and with any luck Rayn would have it soon.

The day passed slowly and the afternoon crawled by meaninglessly, endlessly. Outwardly smiling, Merial attended a polo match between the junior officers and barely tolerated Mrs. Fulks's insinuations that Helen Jarris was having an affair with Lieutenant Denning. Inwardly writhing, she sat through the news that engineer Hugh had had another confrontation with Perce and had definitely "gotten the sack" this time. If only Gulab Fateh had reached the border, Merial thought. If only the sentries were speeding her note to Rayn.

Mercifully, the afternoon ended, and Merial was allowed to climb into her waiting victoria and be driven home. Jassmina was waiting for her by the gate and ran to her mistress's side. "Padma has been taken by the police," she wailed.

"My God—*why?* Did something happen to Gulab Fateh?"

Jassmina's lips were trembling. "I don't know. *Angrezi*

soldiers came and took her away, but they wouldn't tell me why."

The two women's eyes met, and Merial felt a thrill of fear. "I'm going to the barracks," she said. "I'll find out what's happened from Colonel Malcolm."

But when she reached the barracks, she found that Colonel Malcolm had gone home. Major Fulks, the adjutant, received her, and his high-nosed, aristocratic face registered distaste when he learned her errand.

"Padma Sitaji—yes," he drawled. "She's been brought in for stealing."

"For—but that's impossible! Padma would never steal—"

He interrupted her. "You don't know what these natives will do, ma'am. I shouldn't worry about it. The girl's been well treated in the garrison lockup."

With an effort Merial halted the impatient words that crowded her lips. "Major, there's been some mistake, I'm sure. Padma was hired for me personally by Mr. Perce. She's completely trustworthy. If I vouch for her honesty, can't she be released?"

The adjutant shook his head. "I can't make that decision without Colonel Malcolm's say-so. He's gone home to his dinner, but you can see him tomorrow."

"I'll go and see him *now*," Merial corrected. "I can't let that poor child stay in jail overnight over a foolish misunderstanding."

Major Fulks had made no mention of Gulab Fateh or the letter he carried. Perhaps Padma's arrest was simply a misunderstanding. Merial was in an agony of uncertainty as she was driven across the military compound to the colonel's residence. A few moments later she was pleading her case to the astonished commandant and his wife.

The colonel was inclined to refuse Merial's request, but Mrs. Malcolm was more soft-hearted. "I'm sure that if Merial says this girl is innocent, she's innocent," she said. "Women understand such things far better than men." She smiled at Merial and added, "Do sign an order of release, Arthur. Your dinner is getting cold."

Some minutes later Merial left the colonel's home. She tucked the precious document into the sleeve of her dress and had just ordered her driver to return to the barracks when a familiar voice hailed her.

"Miss Ashland," Hamilton Perce wanted to know, "what are you doing here?"

Merial's heart seemed to bump into the roof of her mouth as the commissioner of railroads trotted his horse up beside her. "Why are you out alone at this hour?" Perce continued.

She tried for a light tone. "Surely in Sri Nevi I'm perfectly safe."

"In these restless times it's not wise to court danger. Whatever your errand is, I'm sure it'll wait."

He ordered her driver to return to the commissioner's residence, touched his hat, and rode off. As soon as he was out of earshot, Merial told her driver to ride to the barracks.

The man shook his head. "I dare not, Miss Sahib. Not when Perce Sahib commanded otherwise," he whined.

Merial argued, commanded, pleaded. It was of no use. The man was deathly afraid of Perce and would not do anything to anger him. All Merial could do was to sit back against the cushions and try to plan what she would do next.

Back at Perce's residence, she went quickly to her chamber, where she hoped Jassmina would be waiting. She found the rooms empty and in darkness. Ringing the bell that would summon her nurse, Merial tried to light some candles, but her hands shook so badly that she gave up the attempt.

She tossed aside her hat and shawl, and as she did so the colonel's order releasing Padma rustled in her sleeve. Automatically she took it out and put it away in her desk drawer. Then, walking over to the windows that overlooked the courtyard, she looked longingly toward the Pir Panjals.

Twilight shadows stretched over Perce's estate, and a cool breeze caressed her cheek. Birds, settling for the night, were making a racket in the fruit trees below her window, and the scent of roses brought memories she didn't want to examine.

Hearing the sound of a door opening behind her, Merial cried, "Come in, quickly, Jassmina, and close the door."

There was the faint click of the door being closed. "A sensible precaution," Perce said.

Merial whirled about so quickly that her skirts whipped about her legs. "What are you—what is the meaning of this intrusion?" she demanded.

Her defiance seemed to amuse Perce. He locked the door, pocketed the key, and then walked over to the desk to light a lamp. She could hear him laughing softly as a match spurted fire and a lamp glowed into life. "Now, that's better," he said. "I never liked talking to someone whose face I couldn't see."

"Open that door immediately, sir!" Fear of the man warred with disgust and loathing as Merial snapped, "I must ask that you leave at once."

"Meaning that it's highly improper for a lady to entertain a gentleman in her bedroom? But we are in India, my dear, and stuffy English conventions don't apply. And if you're about to call for help, you can spare yourself the trouble. My servants will not come running to assist you."

"If I tell my father—"

"The deputy commissioner of railroads remained behind at the bridge," he interrupted. "Don't fear that we'll be disturbed."

Merial forced herself not to scream as Perce strolled forward. He stopped a few feet away, his pale gray eyes raking over her.

"And anyway," he went on, "it wouldn't matter if Ashland were in the house. He'd either be drunk, or he would be deaf. A sensible man, your father, who understands that the end justifies the means."

"What do you mean?"

For answer he drew a piece of paper from his pocket. Despair filled Merial as she recognized the note she had written to Rayn. "Need I read it to you?" Perce taunted. "No, I see not. I'm very much surprised to learn that the Tiger can read English."

Merial tried to speak, but the words wouldn't come. She swallowed and tasted bile as Perce jeered, "Don't insult my intelligence by telling me you know nothing about this *billet-doux*. I am not pleased by you, Merial, not at all. If this note had reached Prince Rayn's hands, it would have been devilishly awkward for me. I'm happy to say that my people intercepted Gulab Fateh as he tried to cross the border."

"What did you do to him?" she cried.

Perce shrugged. "Naturally my men shot him."

Oh, Padma, I'm sorry. Aloud Merial flared, "By 'your men,' you undoubtedly mean the thugs who've infiltrated the railway workers. I intend to tell Colonel Malcolm about your meeting with Yuir Singh."

Calmly Perce removed a pistol from his belt and set it

down on the desk. "I'm sorry you observed my meeting with those men, Merial, but you will not tell anyone about it. If you did, it would be the end of your father's plans."

"Of course I'll—what do you mean?" she cried.

"If Sir Edward had to choose between creditors who'll throw him in debtor's prison if he ever sets foot in England again and an honorable post as deputy commissioner of railroads, which do you think he'd choose?"

She said furiously, "If he knew what you were doing, my father would be the first to denounce you."

Perce brayed with laughter. "You poor fool."

Striding across the room, he grasped her arms. "Your father wouldn't dare open his mouth. That noble aristocrat, Sir Edward Ashland, is my slave. He's fallen so low that he's sold his own daughter to save his skin."

She struggled against his clasp. She was strong for a woman, but there was power in Perce's wiry arms, and she could not break his grip.

"I need an aristocrat for a wife," Perce explained. "You've seen how that bitch Amanda Fulks turns up her nose at me? To people like her, I'll always smell of the shop. But if I marry a wife with impeccable lineage, that will all change. Sir Edward may be a poor excuse of a man, but his blood is most satisfactorily blue."

She cried, "You're mad if you think I'll marry you. And I don't believe a word of what you're saying. My father would never agree to such filth."

"But he has, my dove."

The heat in his eyes terrified her. "I expected an insipid English miss, not a woman with spirit. So much the better. I'll have fun breaking your will."

To combat a growing faintness, Merial drew a deep breath. It was suffocatingly full of Perce—of his tobacco, of the brandy he'd been drinking, and the cloying pomade he used in his hair. Fury and disgust drove out even her fear of him, and she spoke with a rage that shook in her voice.

"If you lay a hand on me, you will regret it. Your servants may not hear my cries, but there are many English people who will. They'll see you for the cad you are, a common, vulgar gutter rat."

He slapped her hard across the mouth. The vicious blow almost snapped her neck, and if he hadn't been gripping her arm, she'd have fallen. Once again his backhand caught her mouth, and the signet ring he wore tore her lip. "That's enough out of you, my haughty lady. Common, am I? Filthy? Not as soiled as your precious father, though. Do you know why the mob from Sri Nevi pursued you? Why the temple priests wanted you Ashlands caught and torn limb from limb?"

Half stunned by his blows, she watched his face come near, saw his light gray eyes glare into hers as he hissed, "Your father, the honorable and great commissioner of Sri Nevi, had all the gold from the Shaiva Temple loaded into that bullock cart. He *stole* temple gold."

It was a lie—it surely was a lie. But into Merial's reeling brain flashed Jassmina's words about the Shaiva priests inciting the people to riot. She remembered the bullock cart straining along the road in spite of the fact that it slowed them down. And even at the very end, even at the Gujjar Pass, Sir Edward had refused to abandon that cart. Instead, he had left Niall and his father and the other soldiers to die while he took his "belongings" to safety.

"I don't believe it," she gasped.

"But you do. I see it in your eyes. You have remarkable eyes, my lovely. They're like mountain lakes and heat a man's blood."

She cried out as he twisted the arm he held behind her

back and propelled her forward toward the canopied bed.
When she saw what he was doing, she tried to fight him,
but she was powerless in his cruel grip. He tugged at her
chignon, and as her long hair came undone, he wrapped
his free hand in the black curls and jerked back savagely.
She couldn't move or breathe. At any moment she was
sure that her neck would break.

Lips curled into a jeering smile, he bent over her. "I said
I wanted you, and I see no reason to wait for our wedding
night. When you're damaged goods, you'll be glad enough
to marry me."

She couldn't reply, but she could spit in his face. He
cursed her vilely and, with a thrust of his arms, sent her
sprawling up against the bed. Her head impacted with the
wooden frame that held up the canopy, half stunning her.
Next moment he had flung her onto the bed and was tearing open her bodice.

This was a nightmare. This was hell. In horror Merial
found Perce's lips seeking hers. She twisted her head, but
his lips found and sucked down on her mouth. Next moment he pulled back, yelling, as her teeth went through
his lip.

She was off the bed in an instant and running for the
desk, where he had left his pistol. She screamed for help
as he caught her by the waist, screamed again in pain as
he dragged her back to the bed.

"Bitch!"

Once more he flung her on the bed, and a savage hand
clamped down on her breast. From far away she heard
her own voice screaming.

"Calling for him, are you? If you've let him into your
bed, you'll regret it." Perce's face was quivering with rage.
"Answer me, you slut. Did you spread your legs for the
Tiger?"

"He's a finer man than you can ever hope to be!"

His slap sent her reeling, and she was only barely aware that he was tugging up her skirts. "I'm not marrying the Tiger's leavings," he raved. "After I have you, I'll throw you into the gutter. And there's no use calling for help from your prince, my pet. He's far away fr—"

The sentence was never completed. In mid-word Perce was torn away from Merial and flung halfway across the room.

"Don't be too sure of that," the Tiger snarled.

··*Thirteen*··

"HOW BADLY DID he hurt you?"

Merial's bruised lips tried to shape words in response to the barely leashed ferocity in Rayn's voice, but all she could do was stammer, "You're here."

She couldn't believe that he'd come, that he was real. His white tunic and jodhpurs were covered with dust and his boots splashed with mud. His sun-bronzed face was rigid with a lust to kill.

One swift glance at Merial had told Rayn how badly she'd been hurt. Her lower lip was swollen and bleeding, and bruises discolored her cheek and the swell of her breasts above her ripped bodice. But as far as he could tell, Perce hadn't done more than beat her.

Rayn had ridden for a day and a night, ever since his sentries had relayed information that a runner from Sri Nevi had been shot at the border. The man had lived just long enough to tell the sentries that he'd been carrying a letter to the prince from an *Angrezi* woman. When he'd heard that, Rayn had known Mira was in danger.

"You heathen son of a bitch, this is where you die." Perce lunged for the pistol he'd laid down on the desk, but his jeer became a scream of pain as Rayn's throwing dagger pierced his wrist. Clutching his wounded hand, he dropped to his knees and writhed in agony as the bigger man lunged across the room and caught him by the throat.

The commissioner of railroads tried to shout for help, but that cry was squeezed back into his windpipe. His eyes nearly popped from his head, and he made gurgling sounds as inexorable hands tightened on his windpipe. Perce's face was turning purple as Merial tumbled off the bed and clutched Rayn's arm.

"You mustn't kill him," she stammered. "If you do, Colonel Malcolm will attack Baranpur."

But at the moment he wasn't concerned with Baranpur. The killing rage he'd felt when he saw Perce on top of Merial could only be eased by blood.

"According to our laws," he told Perce, "a blow is repaid by a blow."

The force of that blow knocked the commissioner of railroad's head backward. He spat out teeth and blood and tried to shout for help, but his croak changed to a scream of agony as Rayn kicked him in the groin, then slammed a fist into Perce's face. Even above the man's howls, Merial heard the *snick* of Perce's nose breaking.

There were shouts in the courtyard below. Merial ran to the window and saw garrison soldiers racing up the residency stairs. "Rayn, you must go at once!" she cried. "Don't kill him. He's not worth a war with England."

The truth of her words penetrated the red mist in Rayn's brain. As sanity returned, he reluctantly allowed Perce to crumple to the floor.

"Stay behind me." Snatching up the pistol the commissioner of railroads had dropped, he strode for the door and shot out the lock. Next moment they were in the hall, facing a group of servants armed with rifles.

Rayn knocked the first man down and the others scattered as he snarled, "Get out of my way."

In back of them Perce was weeping with pain and fury. "Stop him, you fools," he croaked.

Drawing his sword, Rayn caught Merial up in his arms and raced down the stairs. The garrison soldiers who had been charging through the door were scattered before the slash of the Tiger's sword. In the courtyard Lieutenant Denning was riding up to the front steps. Rayn pulled the Englishman off his horse and tossed Merial into the saddle.

"Stop—or I'll shoot."

Perce was leaning out of Merial's window. His knife-pierced wrist was near useless, but he'd taken a rifle from one of his servants and was steadying it against the sill.

"If you move, I'll shoot," Perce threatened.

His ruined face was a diabolical mask of rage, and Rayn saw what the confused soldiers apparently didn't—that Perce was aiming the rifle not at the Tiger but at Merial. "Drop your weapons and surrender," Perce commanded.

One swift throw of his knife, and he could kill Perce where he stood—Rayn's fingers curled toward the haft of his throwing knife, but he couldn't risk Merial's life. Grimly, Rayn damned himself for not killing Perce earlier, war or no war.

Merial had also seen the direction of Perce's aim. "Don't do what he says, don't," she pleaded with Rayn.

"It's all right, Miss Ashland—I've got the beggar covered." Lieutenant Denning was sitting up on the ground, and he held his pistol trained on Rayn's broad chest.

Perce shouted hoarsely, "I want him alive. He attacked Miss Ashland."

"That's not true," Merial protested. "Perce is the one who attacked me."

But her cry went unheeded as more soldiers came pouring through the residency gates. At Lieutenant Denning's order, they surrounded Rayn. "Drop your weapons," the lieutenant commanded.

Seeing that Perce was still pointing his weapon at Merial, Rayn unbuckled his sword belt. Lieutenant Denning came to help Merial down from her horse, and his face hardened at the sight of her condition. "By God, he'll pay for this," he gritted.

"It wasn't Rayn," Merial tried again, but Lieutenant Denning was busy shouting orders at soldiers who were surrounding Rayn. "Why won't you listen to me?" Merial cried despairingly.

"Poor lady—she's in shock." Bent over with pain, Perce had hobbled through the soldiers to reach Merial's side. He gripped her arm with his left hand as he whispered, "Be silent or I'll expose your father for what he is."

Aloud he added, "Well, Lieutenant Denning, we've finally trapped the Tiger."

"Do you think so?"

The feral snarl with which the Prince asked the question had an effect on the soldiers around Rayn. They looked nervous, and one of them muttered, "Gor' blimey, wot's 'e mean?"

"Surely," Rayn went on, "you don't think I'd be fool enough to come here alone."

Under pretext of supporting her, Perce gave Merial's arm a cruel twist. "Remember," he hissed, "that I can ruin Sir Edward. A word from me, and he'll never be able to crawl out of the gutter again."

Merial felt as though invisible hands were tearing her in two. It didn't matter whether Perce was telling the truth about her father or not. There were too many who'd be ready to believe anything Perce said. Sir Edward would be shunned and disgraced.

But her father's fate paled at what would happen to Rayn if she didn't convince Lieutenant Denning of the truth. Lifting her voice above the commotion she shouted, "Lieutenant Denning—listen to me. Prince Rayn was saving me from rape—"

She broke off, and Rayn saw his Mira's face blanch with pain as Perce was twisted her arm cruelly. Every nerve and fiber of Rayn's powerful body strained with the need to go to her.

There was murder in his heart and in his eyes, but his voice was calm as he spoke in his flawless English. "You think that this trap was of your setting, you fools? Best look to yourselves."

Apprehensive mutters ran through the English ranks. "He speaks English—Gor' blimey, 'e's not scared o' us— Jesus, Mary, and Joseph, sure and he's brought his lancers with him— we're going to die for sure."

Perce's face became livid. "I'll get rid of him now," he swore.

Lifting his rifle, he aimed it at Rayn, who laughed. The deep, full-throated sound echoed through the dark courtyard as Lieutenant Denning lunged forward and grasped Perce's arm.

"No, Mr. Perce—that's not our way, sir. I understand how you feel, but you can't just *shoot* him in cold blood. He's Narayn of Baranpur!"

Perce's battered face contorted furiously. "His lancers may be waiting for a signal to attack us. It'd be wisest to kill him now."

"You fools, you've arrested the wrong man!" Merial screamed.

This time they heard her. But as Lieutenant Denning

turned a puzzled face toward her, Perce said, "She's sustained a shock, Lieutenant, and is obviously deranged. It's understandable, after what this fiend did to her." He paused to take Merial's arm solicitously but forced her away from the crowd. "I'll take you back to your room, dear Miss Ashland. As to this villain—"

"You can be sure we'll keep him safe," Lieutenant Denning interrupted grimly. "The colonel will want to question him before we hang him."

There were two native guards outside her room, whom Perce had ordered there for her "protection" in case the Tiger's men were lurking nearby. The guard outside the residency had been doubled, and a military curfew had emptied the streets. Meanwhile, at the barracks, Colonel Malcolm had ordered a full military alert.

Lieutenant Denning hadn't listened to her when she tried to tell him the truth about Perce. No one had listened. They'd all assumed that she was traumatized and temporarily demented. They'd marched Rayn away to lockup in the old barracks and left her in the hands of her rapist.

All this Merial learned from the talk of the worried guards outside her door. "What is going to happen to us?" she could hear one of them saying now. "I don't care how carefully the *Angrezi* guard that devil. Steel bars won't hold Rayn of Baranpur. He can disappear into thin air if he wants to, haven't you heard? And his *bhaldars* will kill us and our women and babes."

"Peace," the other interrupted. "The Tiger is but a man, and a man can be hanged."

On the other side of the door Merial felt sick. She raged about the room until, stopping at the window, she pounded her fists impotently on the sill. Earlier she'd as-

certained that there was no way she could jump down into
the courtyard, for the window was set too high, and besides, there were English and Indian soldiers everywhere.

Suddenly she heard Sir Edward's voice at the gate and
moments later his horse clattered into the courtyard.
Merial leaned from the window and called to him, and
he looked up at once. "Are you all right, Merial? I came
as soon as I heard."

"I must talk to you," she called. "At once, Father."

He dismounted, tossed the reins of his horse to a groom,
and ran up the steps of the house. A few moments later
she heard his voice in the hallway. "Damn it, I don't care
what you say. She's my daughter!" Merial heard Sir Edward exclaim. "I demand to speak with her now."

There was a pause, and then Perce's voice, dulled by
the heavy door, replied, "Oh, very well. In fact, a talk between you could be useful."

Merial ran to the door as Sir Edward stalked into the
room. His hair had been disarranged by his hasty ride, and
his eyes were wild as he gripped her by the arms. "That
bastard didn't harm you, Merial?" She shook her head
and he sighed. "Thank God he didn't ruin you. Thank
God that Perce was near."

She wanted to vomit. "He's the one who attacked me,
not Rayn."

Sir Edward paled. "What are you saying?"

"It was Perce who tried to rape me," Merial said
bluntly. "Rayn came out of nowhere to save me. Lieutenant Denning only caught him because Perce aimed a rifle
at *me.*" Sir Edward looked sick as she added bitterly, "It's
true. The great Mr. Hamilton Perce is a coward; a rapist
and a traitor, too. He's working with the thugs." Sir Edward began to protest, but Merial cried, "I *saw* him with

them. I heard them make plans to blow up the bridge so that England will declare war on Baranpur."

"Oh, my God." With a groan, Sir Edward dropped his hands from his daughter's arms and staggered to a chair. He sank into it repeating, "Oh, my God."

Merial followed him. "Father," she said sternly, "you must tell Colonel Malcolm the truth. Perce has locked me in for fear that I'd go to the colonel, but you're free to move about. If you don't tell them the truth, they'll hang an innocent man."

Sir Edward massaged his graying hair with both his hands. His pallid face expressed abject despair. "I can't do that," he moaned. "If I do, Perce will—I can't do it, Merial. Besides, this blackguard Narayn is guilty of crimes for which he should hang."

"What will Perce do to you if you tell the truth?" Merial demanded. "Will he refuse to marry me and take away your precious position?"

Sir Edward blinked rapidly like a trapped rabbit. "I don't know what you're talking about."

"Perce said that you agreed to my marrying him in return for being made deputy commissioner of railroads. Is that true?" Sir Edward's expression gave eloquent answer, and she cried, "How could you?"

Sir Edward attempted to pull himself together. "Marriages are arranged all the time in our circles. Why are you making such a fuss?"

Merial rose to her feet and said coldly, "I won't marry that swine. He'll never touch me again, that I promise."

"That was wrong of him. I'll talk to him." A pleading whine crept into Sir Edward's voice as he continued, "Merial, men can be carried away by passion. It's not a subject a father should discuss with his daughter, but if your mother were alive, she'd say the same thing. Perce was blinded by his, er, love of you, don't you see?"

"Perce also said we were forced to leave Sri Nevi that night of the Gujjar because you stole gold from the Shaiva Temple."

Deny it, she prayed. Be angry—say Perce is insane—say anything! But instead of denials or anger, there was a silence that stretched on and on until she heard her own voice say, "So it's true."

"Merial, you don't understand how it was."

He looked so old and beaten that a part of her wept for him even as she raged, "Niall and Major St. Marr died because you were a thief."

With a shuddering sob, he covered his face with his hands. "It's weighed heavily on my conscience all these years," he groaned.

"How noble of you!" But he didn't seem to hear her.

"The Sri Nevi post was such a disappointment. Your mother hated it. She was beautiful and young and needed rich clothes and a fine house. I had a title to give her but no money." Sir Edward passed a shaking hand across his face. "That gold was wasted on that heathen Hindu god. It wasn't doing anyone any good."

"So you stole it. And used it. And lost it. And because of you—because of you—"

Merial turned away and put her face in her hands and sobbed aloud for Niall and his kind father and all the soldiers who had died that day. She wept for what might have been, for the love she'd had for this weak, corrupt creature, and for Rayn, who had come to save her when her own father had sold her to Perce.

Into the tumult of her pain Sir Edward muttered, "I'm sorry, Merial. I know there's no use telling you that, but I am desperately sorry. And I promise you this. Perce will be a decent husband to you. I know some things about the fine commissioner, I can tell you. He treats his workers abominably, and a lot of the money meant for the railroad has trickled into his pockets." Sir Edward's voice grew stronger as he added, "Hugh saw it and tried to discredit Perce, but he had no proof and so was disgraced and dismissed. *I* have proof."

Blackmail on top of blackmail—and one of these criminals was her father. Merial felt as though she were going mad. "Please," she whispered, "go away. Leave me alone."

He tried to put his hand on her shoulder, but she pulled away from him, and after a moment she heard his footsteps dragging toward the door. Then the door opened and closed and locked, and the footsteps went away down the hall, leaving her more alone than she'd ever been in her life.

She didn't know how long she sat there. Minutes—or hours—later there was a woman's voice at the door, and it opened once more to admit Jassmina. She carried a tray laden with buttermilk and a basket of fruit.

"Perce Sahib wouldn't let me come before," Jassmina said briskly. "However, now that he is asleep, the guards let me in. You must be hungry, Meri-*baba.* I have brought you good food."

"Take it away," Merial muttered.

As if she hadn't spoken, Jassmina continued, "It is some hours to dawn, yet, but it will be a special day. It is said that the *burra sahib,* Colonel Malcolm, has pronounced sentence on Narayn of Baranpur. The great sahib has declared that Prince Narayn is to hang at sunrise."

Merial stared dumbly at her nurse. "But—but he deserves a trial. Under English law—"

"The sahibs have already held a trial," Jassmina said

calmly. "I heard that Perce Sahib and your father were also present." She put the tray down on a table as she added, "The colonel sahib fears that if the Tiger is allowed to live, his followers will try to rescue him and lay waste the town."

Merial ran to the door and rattled the locked doorknob. She slammed her fists on the heavy wood and shouted in furious Hindustani, "Release me at once. Sons of noseless mothers, let me out of here—now!"

"It is no use," Jassmina told her. "The guards have their orders from Perce Sahib that they cannot disobey. And—but is it not a disgrace to sit about in torn clothes? You must change at once."

Merial whipped around. "How can you—"

Jassmina lowered her voice. "You must take my clothes and cover your face with my veil. Thus you can go undetected and escape from Perce Sahib. Once outside the residency my son, Adham Khan, will be waiting to help you get away."

Tears flooded Merial's eyes. She went to her nurse and hugged her tightly. "I love you," she whispered, "but I won't do it. Perce would kill you."

But Jassmina was already removing her heavy veil and loosening her sari. "Help me, *piara*—don't stare so," she scolded. "We will play a game on Perce Sahib. You will tie me up and put a gag in my mouth and leave me on that chair, and I will say that you overpowered me. And see—" Here she went to the fruit basket and twisted it cleverly so that it swung apart, revealing a hidden compartment. In the compartment lay a pistol. Merial picked it up and saw with savage joy that it was loaded.

"That," Jassmina explained, "is in case Perce Sahib tries to stop you, but I could not get more bullets. Can you kill him with one shot?"

"Oh, yes." Merial's hand closed fiercely around the pistol. "But I'm not going to leave without Rayn."

Jassmina looked alarmed. "That is impossible. He is locked up in the old barracks, Meri-*baba,* and the soldiers watch over him like jackals over a new kill. They will never let you in."

Swiftly Merial walked to her desk and pulled out Colonel Malcolm's order to release Padma. "This will get me inside the barracks. There I will say that I have come because I heard my cousin, Padma, is ill and also held unlawfully. They'll see the colonel's order and won't suspect me."

Jassmina started to remonstrate, then said in a resigned voice, "I see it is useless to try and stop you. Your fate is tied to that of the Tiger, and what is written is written. Now, hurry—dress in these, and let me knot your hair, so. Stoop your back and keep your voice low as you pass those guards outside the door. Thus and thus—and, *hai-mai,* there is no Miss Sahib anymore, only a poor Indian servant woman."

On Jassmina's insistence, Merial gagged and tied her nurse. Then she kissed her and looked deep into the loving old eyes before veiling herself and shuffling, stoop-shouldered, to the door.

Her guards had no suspicions. The soldiers in the residency compound merely watched her go, and the gateman only commented, "It's very late. How will you escape curfew, Auntie?"

"I have a note signed by the *burra sahib* colonel himself. Good night, now. I'm half asleep already."

As Merial hunched out into the street, a shadow detached itself from the deeper shadows. "Miss Sahib?" a man's voice whispered. "It's Adham Khan, Jassmina's son."

"I will need two horses," Merial whispered back. "One for me and one for Prince Rayn." About to add further instructions, she saw the man shake his head.

"My mother said that I was to help you escape, but she said nothing about aiding the Tiger. Miss Sahib, the soldiers have orders to shoot anyone breaking the curfew."

"I swear on my honor that if you help Prince Rayn escape, he will avenge Gulab Fateh's death," Merial vowed. There was a small silence and she added, "Prince Narayn is Perce's enemy—as am I."

There was another small silence. Then in a more resolute voice, Adham Khan said, "I, too, am the enemy of Perce Sahib. *Jomarzi*—let it be as you wish. I have a cousin who works in the soldiers' stables, in the back of the old barracks which is now the prison. If God wills, I will meet you behind the old barracks with the horses."

As Merial started the mile and a half walk toward the old barracks, she blessed the fact that it was overcast tonight and no moon could give her away. But it wouldn't be too long before reveille sounded, and that would mean the end of Rayn's hopes of rescue. Glancing up at the still-dark east, she knew that she must hurry.

Twice her journey was interrupted by garrison patrols, and by the time it was safe to move again, the eastern sky looked lighter. She ran the last half mile, slowing down only when she reached the old barracks. Here, veiling herself and making the deepest of bows, she begged the young privates on sentry duty to allow her to see the officer in charge about her cousin, Padma Sitaji.

The privates cursed at the supposed Indian's stupidity. "You should be shot for breaking curfew," one of them snarled. "Get out of it now. You can't see the officer in charge until morning. Understand?"

Merial pretended not to understand. Producing Colonel

Malcolm's order of release, she protested, "The *burra sahib* colonel had compassion on my cousin. He bade me come immediately to the old barracks." She paused. "The great colonel sahib said that with this paper I would be permitted to have Padma released."

One of the guards said disgustedly, "I tell yer, Ned, these wogs are getting more stupid by the day. Five in the morning it is, and she wants ter take 'her cousin out o' 'ere." He raised his voice to a yell. "'Op it afore I puts you in gaol, too."

Merial burst into floods of tears and wailed that her cousin Padma was all she had in the world, and that she must see her or die. As her wails rose higher, a burly sergeant came yawning out to see what was going on. When the guards explained, he demanded to see the release order.

"The colonel's signed this order all right," he commented, then raised his voice as though speaking to someone lacking in intelligence. "We can't let your cousin go until the morning, but you can stay here and wait for her, my good woman. Understand?"

She bowed almost to the ground. "Sahib, I beg of you a favor. My cousin is sick and frightened. If I may see her for a moment—tell her that she will soon be free?"

"It's against the regulations," the sergeant began. Then, as Merial began to howl again, he shouted, "God damn all women, anyway. Stop that caterwauling. You can see your damned cousin, but for a minute only, understand?"

Heart thumping, Merial followed the sergeant. Surely the pound of her heart could be heard? But he seemed unconcerned as he escorted her into the barracks. They passed through a guardroom where several soldiers were playing cards and through a barred door to a series of cells. In one cell huddled a number of dispirited Indian prisoners. She couldn't see Rayn anywhere.

"Heaven Born," Merial quavered, "is it true that you hold Narayn of Baranpur here—he who is called the Tiger?"

"That's none of your business." But Merial saw the sergeant's eyes flick toward a cell set back from the others. There, behind a barred door, Rayn lay on a string bed.

He was shackled to the wall by iron chains. More chains bound his feet. Even so, he seemed to be sleeping peacefully. How could he sleep, Merial wondered, when he was about to die?

But Rayn was wide awake. He had been listening, waiting. When he'd seen the guardroom door open, he had known the moment he'd been waiting for had come. To his astonishment, he'd seen a veiled Indian woman instead of Rassul Khan. Then the woman spoke, and his heart clenched like a fist.

How had Merial gotten away from Perce and braved the curfew to come here? And where in the name of the gods had she found the pistol that she now drew from the folds of her sari?

"Put your hands over your head," Merial was saying softly and in English. "If you move or speak, you will die as you stand."

The sergeant stiffened as he felt cold steel in his back. "Why, you little—"

Even in manacles and fetters, Rayn could move swiftly. He was on his feet on the instant and standing at the barred door of his cell.

"The keys are on the ring over the door," he told Merial. "Throw them into the cell."

She obeyed, and the sergeant snarled, "You'll rot in hell for this."

"You will be in hell yourself if you don't remain silent," Rayn said. Swiftly unlocking his fetters, manacles, and the door to his cell, he removed the sergeant's pistol and sword. "Now, get into that cell."

The man hesitated. Rayn shoved him forward, then brought down the butt of his pistol on the back of his head. The sergeant fell as though poleaxed. "He should sleep through the excitement," Rayn commented as he heaved the unconscious man into the cell and locked the door after him.

Merial clutched at his arm. "We must go quickly. Reveille will sound at any minute—"

"When the bugles sound, we'll go through that back window. No one will hear the glass splinter, and we'll be away before the garrison knows what happened."

She started to tell him about Adham Khan, but he interrupted. "You've been a busy young woman," he said crisply, "but Rassul and some of the others are nearby. They'll be waiting for us."

His tone was carefully neutral, hiding the surge of his conflicting emotions. All Rayn wanted to do was kiss Mira's bruised mouth, to tell her how he'd felt when he'd watched her come through the lockup door. With effort, he reminded himself that for her sake and his, he must keep her at a distance.

She wanted him to put his arms around her. Her body and her spirit craved contact with him. But his next words stopped such thoughts. "You should have known my lancers were with me."

Meaning that she needn't have bothered to try and rescue him. She said in a troubled voice, "I couldn't stand by and let you hang for something you didn't do."

Hearing the tremor in her voice, Rayn felt an almost physical ache. The urge to take her into his arms was almost irresistible, and it was with difficulty that he turned his back to her and buckled on the unconscious sergeant's sword. This done he spoke to the prisoners in the nearby cell.

"You know who I am. Make no sound until we have gone."

The prisoners nodded, their eyes wide and awestruck, and Padma pushed herself to the forefront to whisper, "None of us would ever help Perce Sahib. He had my kinsman murdered."

"Unlock the cell door, Prince," a man added timidly, "and we can help. We'll rush out into the guardroom just as you make your escape and confuse the soldiers."

Rayn considered, then unlocked the iron door. As the heavy cell door creaked open, he spoke to Padma. "Your kinsman accomplished his purpose and died like a man. I promise you that his murderers will be punished."

Just then reveille sounded. Rayn smashed the window, and simultaneously the Indian prisoners surged out of their cell into the guardroom beyond. Rayn lifted Merial in his arms and vaulted out of the window.

He landed catlike in the dark below, and a frightened voice hissed, "Miss Sahib?"

It was Adham Khan leading two saddled horses. "Miss Sahib," he stammered, "here are the horses. Go in the name of God, the All Compassionate."

Before she could thank him, he'd melted into the darkness. Rayn lifted Merial onto one of the horses and was about to mount himself when there was a yell. "Bloody hell—the Tiger's escaping!"

Soldiers poured out of the barracks and closed about them but fell back before the cut and slash of the Tiger's sword. Merial caught a momentary glimpse of Rayn's set face before he sprang up into his saddle, grasped her reins, and spurred forward. The animals galloped ahead, scattering the garrison soldiers like autumn leaves. Rayn threw up his head and gave a shout of triumph.

"Look to yourselves, you bastards!" he roared in English. "St. Marr *ki-jai!*"

··*Fourteen*··

LONG LIVE ST. MARR.

As half-dressed English soldiers rushed out of the barracks, Merial twisted in her saddle to stare at Rayn.

"Let's *go!*" Seizing Merial's horse's bridle, Rayn galloped through the midst of the assembled soldiers who went down screaming under his sword. One man raised his rifle to fire, but a grizzled sergeant major struck up the gun barrel, and the shot went wide.

"Hold your fire, idiot!" he bellowed. "You could hit one of our own men. And keep those hell-damned prisoners back. What're they doing out of lockup?"

Reinforcements pounded out of the garrison, stumbling over the escaping Indian prisoners, who milled about and managed to get in everyone's way. For a few seconds the normally disciplined garrison was in chaos, and Rayn made the most of those moments to spur toward the main road. Disorganized bands of soldiers ran after them, cursing and firing ineffectively.

Suddenly several mounted shadows materialized in the dawn-murk. "Lord," Rassul's voice exclaimed, "we've come too late to free you!"

"We're not clear yet. You've found a way out of the city?"

"This way, lord." Rayn's *bhaldars* split forces, half of them riding to guard their prince's rear, the other shielding his advance.

"Keep your head down," Rayn ordered Merial.

The fact that she might be killed didn't trouble her as much as the memory of his one exultant shout. Niall's battle cry. How could Rayn have known—why should he have uttered it?

As Rassul led toward a side alley, Big Fanji's bulk loomed out of the shadows. "Lord, are you unharmed?" the giant boomed.

There were shouts and the sound of booted feet in the near distance. "The soldiers have seen us!" Merial cried, but Fanji grinned and winked at her.

"Don't worry, girl. They won't get far."

He plodded over to a cart piled high with bricks and single-handedly shoved it across the entry of the alleyway. As Merial watched, other *bhaldars* moved wheelbarrows, rubbish, and tree branches that effectively blocked the approaching soldiers' path.

Rayn now spoke to the residents of the alley. "Go back to your houses and remain hidden. Perce will be furious when he learns you've helped me, but I won't forget this."

As the residents of the alley melted away, Big Fanji commented, "They fear the Tiger more than they fear Perce."

But *who* was the Tiger? The question echoed through her mind as the *bhaldars* mounted silently and followed their prince down the alleyway. They then turned up another narrow street and back onto the main road. The gate guards, most of whom had gone to help the soldiers break through the blockade, shot ineffectively as the Tiger and his followers galloped through the Elephant Gate.

Rayn turned his horse to the northeast, and they galloped into the sunrise. Merial strained her ears for sound of pursuit, but all she could hear was the sound of the wind. As the rim of the sun pushed itself clear of the Pir Panjals, Deen and several *bhaldars* met them.

Deen gave a shout of triumph. "I was beginning to worry that Rassul and Fanji had botched things, lord. We were about to ride into that flea-bitten place to rescue you."

"Rescue *us?* That'll be the day," Big Fanji scoffed.

"But the danger isn't over," Merial interrupted. As she recounted Perce's meeting with Yuir Singh and his thugs, the lancers' grins disappeared.

Rayn listened without comment, but his men swore bitterly. "I'll carve him into buzzard meat," Big Fanji vowed, and Deen pleaded, "Lord, can't we ride into Sri Nevi now and capture that son of a diseased whore?"

Rassul, who had been assessing Merial's bruises, added that anyone who slew the unbelieving dog would be assured of paradise. "It is an evil deed to hurt defenseless women—to say nothing of daring to lay hands on you, lord. Perce should be flayed alive."

Rayn replied grimly, "I share your sentiments, but we don't have time. Mira's news merely confirms what we've suspected all along—that the thugs and Perce were somehow linked together." He turned to Deen. "Take twelve men and patrol the Afghan border. Anyone crossing into Baranpur, be they Afridi, *Angrezi,* or thug, is to be questioned. Failing that, he's to be killed." As the lancer captain saluted, Rayn went on. "Chetak, take six men. Infiltrate the railroad workers; get into Sri Nevi. If Perce so much as sneezes, I want to know. We need to know exactly when he's going to blow that bridge."

Rassul asked, "And I, lord?"

"You and the remaining *bhaldars* return to Baranpur at once. Tell General Jaga that he's to mobilize the army."

"Am I to tell him about Perce's meeting with the thugs?"

Rayn shook his head. "Remember there's a traitor amongst us."

Big Fanji spat and growled, "That bastard Ibrahim."

"So far we have no proof," Rayn warned. "The rana trusts the *kotwal* implicitly. I'm hoping that in my absence Ibrahim may grow careless and betray himself."

The lancers looked at each other and Deen questioned, "Where are you going, lord?"

Rayn said, "For obvious reasons, Mira can't go back to Baranpur. I'm going to take her to Kumar."

"I'll take her, lord," Big Fanji offered, but Rayn would not have it.

"I must talk to Daiyal-Raja personally," he said.

Rayn paused only to change horses and to acquire saddlebags full of provisions. "I know you are tired," he told Merial, "but we can't afford to slow our pace. The garrison may be after us."

She could no longer hold back the question that had been tormenting her. "Why did you use that war cry?" she challenged.

"What war cry?" he asked impatiently, and she suddenly doubted her own memory. So much had been happening. Was it possible that she'd been mistaken? Tensely she searched his hard, sun-bronzed face.

"You said, 'St. Marr *ki-jai.*' It was Niall's war cry and his father's, too. Why did you use it?"

"Who can tell what I said in the heat of battle?" He

was looking back toward Sri Nevi as he spoke. "Come—we must ride. Safety is miles away."

Avoiding the path of the railroad, they forded the Indus River farther upstream and rode steadily into the full morning. They rode through the heat of the day and by late afternoon were climbing into the hills again. The narrow, stone-choked mountain road led through fresh-scented deodar pines. Monkeys coughed their warnings in the branches, but there was no sign of any human presence.

"Not far from here there's a place where we can make camp." Rayn broke a silence that had lain heavy between them during the long ride. "We'll rest the night and reach Kumar by tomorrow noon."

Merial looked at him and wondered. *Had* she been mistaken?

Her mind sifted back to the tense moments of their escape. Once more she could hear the soldiers' shouts and the bellowed commands of their officers, the crack of rifle fire. She could smell gunpowder and taste the bitter fear-phlegm in her throat as they spurred through the half-dressed, frantic English soldiers. and then Rayn had uttered that triumphant shout.

No, she hadn't imagined it. The memory of that moment was so real she could almost hear his deep voice echoing against the hills.

Rayn misinterpreted the look on her face and said, "Don't worry, you'll be safe in Kumar."

She tried to concentrate on what he was saying about Kumar.

"Baranpur and the city-state of Kumar have been allies and trade partners for many years. We sell them tea, hemp, and the best of our Baranpur wool, and in exchange we get more Kumari horses than any other kingdom or principality."

"Is that so important?" she asked absently.

"The Kumari horses are very costly. They're durable, swift, intelligent, and make excellent battle horses." Rayn patted his own cream-colored stallion's neck as he added, "Badshah, here, is worth a king's ransom. He was a gift from my friend, Daiyal-Raja of Kumar. We were hunting tiger once, and he insists I saved his life."

Merial said slowly, "You saved my life, too. I don't mean from Perce—I'm talking of that day at the border. When I left you I was sure you'd been killed."

"I don't die easily," Rayn said. He added, "Ibrahim did his best to poison the rana's mind against me, naturally. He's sure that I helped you escape from prison. But Panwa swore by all the gods and demons that I was fighting Afridi raiders on the border."

"And the Rana believed him."

"Panwa's a favorite of my father's. Besides, when we rode back to Baranpur, my lancers and I had many Afridi prisoners."

Silence fell between them again. Though deeply troubled, Merial was still conscious of the beauty around them as they rode higher into the mountains. A shy, white-faced stag peered from the tracery of pines before them, then bounded away with his shy doe. Small game rustled in the underbrush, and a hawk, riding the air currents in the blue sky, dropped like a stone. There was a squeal of terror and pain, and the great winged predator sailed away with its prey.

Even in these peaceful mountains there was death. As the thought touched Merial's mind, the trail forked. Rayn took the left fork, riding into what seemed to be an impenetrable tangle of trees. He dismounted and pushed aside some branches to disclose a clearing. "Here's where we'll rest this night."

He led the horses forward, and she saw that the clearing was surrounded by wild cherry trees and watered by a spring-fed pool. The water bubbled up through rocks that were fringed with rushes and wild roses. When she dismounted and drank thirstily, Merial found that it was icy cold and tasted faintly of iron.

Rayn was meanwhile seeing to the horses. He removed his saddlebags, looked inside, and grimaced. "Bread and hard cheese—unappetizing fare," he commented. "Now, when I last made camp here, this pool was teeming with fish."

Despite his long hours in the saddle, he moved with a spring to his step. Merial felt a stir of curiosity as she watched him cut down a green sapling.

"What will you use for a line and hook?" she wondered.

"You'll see."

Using his belt, he lashed his knife to the staff. Then, kicking off his boots, he rolled up his trousers and waded into the pool. For a moment he stood poised, his face knotted in concentration. Then his arm plunged down.

"Baju would say that taking life is a sin," he commented as he tossed a silvery fish at her feet, "but one more sin on my conscience won't trouble me."

Such as the sin of murder. Thoughts of Niall haunted Merial as she gathered sticks and branches and set the pile of kindling afire with Rayn's flint. The Tiger had admitted to killing Niall as he'd killed so many others in battle, but he didn't look like a warrior now. His face was silhouetted against the setting sun, his hair glinted with copper highlights. The way he stood, poised over the water, tugged at half-formed, elusive memories.

No, she thought, *it's not possible.*

With passionate intensity, she watched Rayn's movements. There was something in the set of his shoulders, in the clean, hard line of his cheek and jaw and neck.

Impossible.

"Are you as hungry as I am?" Without waiting for her answer, Rayn waded out of the pool and began to gut and fillet the fish with swift, economic movements. Then he crossed over to the fire, skewered the fish on a green stick, and positioned the makeshift spit over the fire. She watched the flames emphasize the sharp lines in his face and the fleeting memories she had thought to grasp ebbed away. It was the Tiger, no one else, who knelt before the fire.

"How did you come to know Niall's battle cry?" she demanded.

He turned the fish before replying coolly, "He shouted it before I killed him. I used it this morning to confuse any soldiers who might have known St. Marr."

It made sense. Her heart twisted with old pain and a new, inexplicable sense of loss as he continued, "There's no use tormenting yourself with the past. It's the future we have to worry about. If Perce blows up his bridge, it'll be disastrous for both our countries."

But she wasn't interested in the fate of nations. "He taught me to ride a horse. Did I tell you that?" she murmured.

"Perce?" he asked, astonished.

"I'm talking about Niall. The boy you killed."

He pulled a fish off its skewer and handed it to her. "We've been through all this before," he told her. "Eat now, before the fish becomes cold."

"Niall used to order me around, too," she said.

He laid down his fish. "Let it *alone,* woman."

But she was like a dog with a bone that she couldn't help gnawing.

"I followed him everywhere and must have tried his patience, but he never sent me away. He'd tease me and call me 'highness,' and I loved him with all my heart. That is why—that is why—" Her voice faltered into silence.

Rayn couldn't bear her pain. Without thinking, he reached out and drew her into his arms. She came to him with the blind trust of a child, and he whispered, "It's all right, Meri. I have you safe."

"What did you call me?"

Rayn had used the old nursery name that only old Jassmina remembered. Breath and even heartbeat stopped as Merial pushed away and stared searchingly into Rayn's face.

And suddenly it was as though she were seeing him for the first time. The darkness and her own tears had blurred the image of the man's hard countenance and softened it, changed the shape of the mouth, gentled the eyes.

"Niall?"

For the space of a heartbeat he was silent. Then he said, "You've gone mad."

He would have released her and gotten to his feet, but she clutched at his arms until her fingers dug into his flesh. "You weren't killed at the Gujjar Pass. You're *alive!*"

"Niall St. Marr is dead," he told her harshly. "I'm Narayn, Prince of Baranpur."

But she wasn't even listening. She was looking backward, remembering, understanding as all the scattered threads came together to fashion an incredible tapestry. Her elusive memories—the inexplicable way she'd been drawn to him even from their first meeting—and that night of love. When he'd told her that they had loved each other in another life, he'd meant what he said.

She raised her trembling hand to trace his hard jawline. He jerked back but not before her searching fingers had found a scar under his ear.

"You got that scar falling from your horse, don't you remember? It was bleeding so much, and the garrison doctor cauterized the wound. He called you a proper soldier because you didn't make a sound. Your father was so proud of you."

Don't look back, Rayn told himself, but Mira's voice continued to call to him across the years and to unlock the memories he had hidden even from himself.

"You gave me your mother's amulet," Merial insisted. "I gave it back to you before we rode away. I heard you shouting your battle cry and then shots. I was sure that you'd be killed. I wanted to die, too, Niall."

He spoke thickly, as though the words were torn out of him. "Niall St. Marr died at the Gujjar Pass many years ago. Do you understand? I—*he*—must stay in his grave." He shook her, glaring down at her, noting that her pupils were so dilated that her turquoise eyes appeared almost black.

"Do you understand?" he repeated.

"Yes—no—I don't know," she stammered. "Tell me!"

With that swift feline movement that was uniquely his, he rose and walked away from her to stand outside the rim of light shed by the campfire. There, with his face in deep shadow, he told her that under Major St. Marr's orders, the small band of English soldiers had hidden themselves behind rocks. They'd held off the mob from Sri Nevi until there was no ammunition left. Then bayonets were fixed.

"The mob had rifles and plenty of ammunition. I saw my father get shot through the head. I was trying to get to him when an ugly brute came after me with a knife.

As he knifed me, I sank my bayonet in him. He collapsed on me and covered me with his blood. I lost consciousness, and his comrades must have thought me dead."

He'd come to his senses hours later and seen vultures circling in the dawn sky. He'd stumbled off to try and get help, but in his confusion had gone in the opposite direction from Gandari.

"Old Baju found me collapsed by the roadside. I was barely conscious. My clothes were ripped to shreds, but my mother's amulet was still around my neck. Baju thought I was a fair-skinned Kashmiri prince who'd been ambushed by bandits. Later, when I became delirious with fever and talked in English, he understood the truth but kept my secret."

Baju had taken Niall back to Baranpur. But because of Khem-Rana's known dislike for the English, Baju had made Niall swear not to disclose the truth. "He invented a noble lineage for me and brought me up as his protégé," Rayn continued. "Niall St. Marr died, and Prince Narayn Shivpuri, orphaned son of a royal Kashmiri house, was born. Baju had some idea of turning me into a doctor, but he soon saw that I was a soldier, so he introduced me to Panwa's father. Under Bhupinder Puar's patronage, I entered the rana's army as a junior officer, and it wasn't long before I proved myself in battle against the *Angrezi.*"

"You fought against your own people?"

Savagely he corrected, "They were my *father's* people. My mother was a royal princess, but to you English she was always inferior. And I had other reasons to hate the *Angrezi.*"

In a low voice she interrupted, "I know that my father stole gold from the temple of Shiva. Perce told me."

Even without touching him, she could sense his tension. His voice thrummed with it when he said, "The gold he stole caused many deaths. Edward Ashland's greed murdered my father! Besides, the story of the commissioner's corruption was well known in Baranpur. I have hated Sir Edward Ashland all these years."

"And so you hated me, too," she mourned. "Otherwise you'd have told me who you were. But, Niall—"

"Niall is dead," he reminded her.

"Rayn, then. We were friends. Could you forget our friendship so easily?"

In a hard voice he said, "No. But you are no longer Meri-*baba* but a grown woman and Ashland's daughter." She bowed her head. "That first day in my tent, when I realized who your father was, I was too angry to think clearly. We must think clearly now for both our sakes."

Striding back to the fire, he knelt down beside her to grasp her shoulders. "What you've learned must never be repeated. If the rana finds out that his heir is a half-caste *Angrezi,* he'll disinherit me. I want to accomplish a great deal for my country, Mira. I can't let that happen."

Merial protested, "I can keep a secret."

She sounded so young that it nearly broke his heart. Her pale face was raised to him, and hurt made her eyes seem enormous. She had loved him through the years, and she loved him still. Rayn had to remind himself sternly that her discovery in no way changed the realities with which they both had to live.

He said abruptly, "Let's hope you can."

She couldn't bear his coldness. After all these years of mourning, she'd found Niall alive. Flinging her arms around him, Merial clung close.

"Niall—Rayn—what do I care what you call yourself? I'd die before hurting you. I love you. I've always loved you."

Her low voice throbbed like music, and against its

magic he had no defense. All his resolutions vanished as though made of mist. For a moment he caught her tight against him, and she registered the tremor in his arms. Her heart exulted as she raised her mouth for his kiss.

His mouth found hers hungrily, drinking from her lips as a parched man drinks from a pure mountain spring.

Rayn could feel her love in the way she clung to him, and his own heart and body answered. Her hair had come loose, and as the black, unbound silk fell about them and curtained them from the rest of the world, he knew the depths of his longing. He had tried to cut Merial out of his thoughts after her escape from Baranpur. He had told himself that it was the only sane course since she was Ashland's daughter and an *Angrezi.* Yet in spite of everything she had remained a part of him.

"Easier to cut away my shadow, or my soul," he muttered.

"Rayn," she whispered, "love me. Love me now. Make me forget."

There was so much to forget. So many years. So much loneliness and loss and betrayal. But there were other things that could not be forgotten, Rayn knew. The treachery of Ashland and Perce still threatened them both. At any moment Perce and his accomplice could plunge Baranpur into war with *her* people—

The savage rage that filled Rayn at the thought of Ashland and the commissioner of railroads was like a cleansing wind. This was no time—there could never be time—for *this* love. With mingled anguish and fury, Rayn looked down at the woman in his arms.

"We can't do this," he muttered.

Deliberately breaking the clasp of her arms around his neck, he sat up and looked down at her bleakly. "What we had is over. It has ended, Mira. Let's leave it at that."

Getting to his feet, he strode away to pick up blankets which he tossed beside the fire.

"It's late and we're both tired and overemotional. Sleep, for the love of the gods. We've far to ride tomorrow, and I must get back to Baranpur as soon as I can."

Dawn found them riding in a valley between rounded hills. They had already been riding for several hours, and when they chanced on a convenient rivulet, Rayn stopped to water the horses.

Mcrial wandered some distance upstream to wash and, kneeling on the grassy bank between tall water reeds, gazed down at her reflection in the water.

The woman who looked back at her had little resemblance to Miss Merial Ashland who had recently drunk tea with the memsahibs of Sri Nevi. In Jassmina's sari, with her dark hair in a long, thick braid, she looked like a servant girl. To complete the picture there was the bruised mouth and the look of desolation in her eyes.

"I'm a pretty sight," she murmured.

There was a rustle in the reeds nearby. Merial looked up apprehensively and found herself staring at a monkey. "What are *you* doing here so far from the trees?" she wondered.

The animal chattered its fright but didn't run away, and, looking more closely, Merial saw that the monkey was tethered to a stake. The rope wasn't long enough to reach the water. Apparently, someone had caught the little creature, bound it, and left it to die.

Repelled by such cruelty, Merial approached the monkey cautiously. It gibbered and chattered in fright as she loosened the knots that held it prisoner. "There, little brother," she said. "Go home to your people."

Freed, the monkey darted off toward the nearest tree.

Then, suddenly, it gave out a terrified coughing sound. But why was it frightened? Merial wondered. Surely, now there was nothing to fear—

Her thoughts broke off as she found herself staring at a tiger crouched among the reeds near the stream.

Everything in Merial's brain clamored that she run, but terror rooted her to the spot. Only her vocal chords seemed able to function, and she screamed again and again.

The tiger gathered itself to spring. Simultaneously Merial was shoved aside and Rayn took her place. Just as the great beast leaped, Rayn dropped to his knee, raised his rifle to his shoulder, and fired.

It all seemed to happen at once—the blur of black and gold, the crack of the rifle, and a snarl that turned into an unearthly shriek of pain. Then the great tawny beast crashed down amongst the reeds at Rayn's feet. It was dead.

"Oh, my God," was all Merial could say.

Rayn emptied another shot in the felled beast's brain before turning on Merial. "Are you mad to go wandering off like that? If I hadn't come looking for you and heard the monkey, you'd be dead by now."

His voice was rough with fear that he hadn't yet had time to feel. Now he realized what would have happened to her if he hadn't been near. He caught her by the shoulders, gave her a little shake. "What were you doing here alone?"

Eyes as tawny-gold as the tiger's own searched hers. "That monkey," she gulped.

"An old hunting trick. The staked monkey sounds a warning which alerts the hunters. Then, while the tiger's attacking the ape, he's captured and killed."

She glanced at the great carcass at her feet and shivered

uncontrollably. "Please," she whispered, "let's get away from here."

But his eyes had narrowed. "Someone's coming."

Catching her by the waist, he backed soundlessly into the tall grass. Then, reloading his rifle, he held it at the ready as several men on foot came along the other side of the stream. When they saw the dead tiger, they began to point and shout.

"What is this hubbub?" an impatient voice demanded, and a slim, bearded man rode into view. Both his bearing and the creamy white horse he rode proclaimed noble birth, as did the diamond in his saffron turban and his necklace of tiger claws set in gold. He was dressed all in black, as were the entourage of horsemen who followed him.

"It's Daiyal-Raja himself." Merial heard the relief in Rayn's voice as he rose out of the concealing grass. "Majesty," he said, "I seem to have spoiled your hunt."

The young man stared. "By the beard of Vayu the wind god, it's my friend Prince Rayn!" he exclaimed, and Merial noted that he spoke in a dialect that was not unlike Kashmiri. Since she'd learned to speak Kashmiri as a child, she had no trouble understanding the raja as he continued, "Did you spring from the very earth?"

He splashed his horse through the stream, exclaiming, "Have you again slayed a tiger to save a life? Is another now in your debt?"

Rayn smiled. "I'm honored if you think I served you in some way."

The young raja bowed courteously and insisted, "The honor is mine—that is, if you have come on a visit. If you'd given me some warning, I'd have met you with the splendor befitting your rank."

Rayn nodded to Merial, who bowed deeply to the staring raja. "May I introduce Mira-Bai, an *Angrezi* lady in need of your royal protection?"

"May Your Majesty live for a thousand years," Merial said in Kashmiri, and there was a mutter of surprise from the rajah's black-clad followers.

Daiyal-Raja blinked hard. "Sahiba!" he exclaimed. "My kingdom is yours. If you'll follow me, we will return to the palace, where my senior rani will treat you with all honor."

He signaled Rayn to ride beside him, leaving Merial to follow as befitted a woman. She was grateful, for she was too shaken by all that had happened in the last forty-eight hours to make polite conversation.

She rode numbly, unaware until they reached the well-fortified and guarded gates of the city-state. But here Merial couldn't help but see that Kumar was decorated for a holiday. The city gates were festooned with garlands of marigolds, roses, and fragrant ginger, and similar wreaths hung from rooftops, windows, and trees along the way. Everywhere women were lacing more flowers and tinsel.

"We are preparing for my cousin Joginder Bundi's wedding," the raja explained.

Even more flowers and tinsel marked their progress to the raja's palace, a graceful building of pale pink marble surrounded by gardens of surpassing loveliness. Here Rayn was escorted with great pomp into the raja's palace while, following the custom of *purdah,* Merial was conducted to the women's quarters.

As soon as the gates of the women's quarters closed behind her, Merial was greeted by the raja's principal wife, a young princess called Parvati. Tall and exquisitely molded with sloe eyes and a rosebud mouth which always seemed to be smiling, Parvati was swift to assure Merial that her coming was a joyful event.

"For," Parvati said cheerfully, "it is seldom our good fortune to encounter a lady from another part of the world. When you are rested and massaged, we will all ask a thousand questions!"

Parvati ordered a bath to be prepared, and when Merial had washed the dust of her journey away, servants shampooed her long black hair with sweet-scented herbs. Then a large smiling woman was called in to massage the English guest.

"The strokes always lead away from the heart," Parvati explained. "thus the massage improves the circulation. The cream used by the masseuse is made of fresh-ground almonds and will invigorate you." She paused. "Is it true that you have come all this way from Sri Nevi?"

Merial assented, and the young queen lowered her voice. "It is said that a wicked man called Perce lives there and that he intends to bring his railroad through Prince Rayn's country. Do you know this evil man?"

Instinctively Merial's hand rose to her hurt mouth, and the young rani's eyes narrowed. She clasped Merial's hand and assured her, "You'll be quite safe here in Kumar."

"Thank you, Majesty," Merial said. The massage had left her feeling relaxed and refreshed. "I'm very grateful."

"What need for gratitude? You are my lord's guest. And as such, Mira-Bai, we must prepare you for the evening. Since you're *Angrezi* and need not keep close *purdah* as we do, my lord has requested that you take the evening meal with him and Prince Rayn." She gave an unqueenly giggle as she added, "I think he's as curious as we are about you."

Merial didn't protest as she was arrayed in one of the rani's exquisite saris, but she felt apprehensive. Since last night Rayn had hardly noticed her. Except for the time when he'd shot the tiger, they'd barely spoken. He must be fretting about Perce and Baranpur's safety and regretting the fact that he'd had to waste time by bringing her here to Kumar.

Daiyal-Raja had condescended to set aside the compunctions of caste so as to dine with his English guest. Dressed in a brocaded tunic and white trousers, his head swathed in a turban of royal saffron hue, the young ruler received Merial courteously and tried hard not to stare when, at his request, she put back her veil.

In spite of the bruise that marred her mouth, Mira-Bai was beautiful. Parvati had dressed her in a flowing sari of silver-edged turquoise, and a magnificent turquoise at her hairline emphasized the unusual color of her eyes. Daiyal's interest increased as he saw her eyes turn instinctively to Prince Rayn.

Merial hadn't meant to look at Rayn, but she couldn't help herself. He was wearing a royal half-turban set with a blazing emerald. With his powerful muscles straining a borrowed tunic of saffron brocade and white jodhpurs, he was an imposing figure. But she neither saw nor cared for his splendid clothes. She was only aware of the look in his eyes.

She'd been right. She was a nuisance to him. She'd delayed him when all he wanted was to see the last of her. Merial tore her eyes away from Rayn and looked bleakly at the floor until Daiyal begged her to be seated.

"I am honored that you seek refuge in my household, Mira-Bai," he said. "No harm can come to you here."

Daiyal watched Prince Rayn's eyes narrow at that and knew he'd been right. His friend was deeply in love with this *Angrezi* woman, and she with him, but for some obscure reason they were taking great pains to hide this fact from each other. A pity, since love had been invented by the gods to give mortals pleasure.

When the raja asked what had brought Mira-Bai to Kumar, Merial remained silent and left it to Rayn to give an abridged version of the truth. Daiyal was obviously intrigued.

"Shabash!" he exclaimed, when Rayn described their escape from Sri Nevi. "Perce must be as furious as a dog who has lost his bone."

"Perce is plotting against the security of my country," Rayn pointed out. "I must thus return to Baranpur immediately."

She had expected this, known it, and yet pain lanced through Merial. Tomorrow, perhaps even tonight Rayn would leave Kumar. What they had together was over. He obviously felt she was a part of the past he needed to bury, and she'd probably never see him again.

"But surely you'll stay with us for my cousin's wedding?" Daiyal-Raja was protesting.

"It's not possible, Majesty."

"The festivities will begin tomorrow and last for only five days. Your presence at this auspicious occasion would be an honor."

Rayn hesitated. Refusal might offend the raja, and yet he was in an agony of haste. But while his conscious mind was on Perce and Baranpur's safety, he couldn't help glancing at Merial.

He'd never seen her look so beautiful. In her shimmering sari she was like an exquisite flower. Her eyes were the exact shade of the jewel that hung low on her forehead, and her lips were like the petals of a pomegranate flower. The shadow of the bruise at the corner of that mouth brought a longing so strong that Rayn was shaken by it, and thoughts of Baranpur dulled over as if by mist.

"Prince Rayn, I insist," Daiyal was saying. He added in a confidential tone, "Besides, I'm eager to consult with you about trade. Your father has long insisted that I raise my quota of Kumari horses, as you know, and I'm ready to negotiate with you."

Listening to the young raja, Rayn knew that there was no possible way he could refuse this offer. Besides, a favorable trade agreement might make Khem-Rana more ready to listen to reason. Perhaps he could even be made to realize that Ibrahim was not above suspicion.

Rapidly Rayn reviewed the situation. Deen was patrolling the border, Rassul was in Baranpur, and tough little Chetak had Perce under close observation. If the commissioner of railroads so much as blew his nose, the former bandit would know of it. For now the situation was under control.

With his eyes on Merial, Rayn bowed to the inevitable. "In that case," he said, "I accept Your Majesty's hospitality."

·· Fifteen ··

"THERE IS NOT one cloud in the sky," Parvati-Rani commented. "Truly an auspicious day for marriage."

It was the last day of the wedding festivities and the most important, since tonight the raja's cousin and his bride would exchange vows. The royal party had arrived at the house of the bride some time ago. With appropriate pomp the raja and Prince Rayn had been conducted to a raised dais and seated at low tables of ivory and inlaid mother-of-pearl. The bride's mother herself had greeted the royal women and led them to the gallery overlooking the hall where, screened from view of the men, the women of the household could enjoy the festivities.

The gallery to which the rani, Merial, and Daiyal's junior wives had been conducted was garlanded with jasmine buds and roses. In fact, Merial thought as she sat beside Parvati and looked down below, the entire great hall had the look of a garden.

The stone arches that led to the great hall were wreathed with colored paper and tinsel, and the guests were like brightly colored blossoms. Men in sumptuously embroidered and brocaded achkans wore turbans of every shade, so that the women hidden behind the *purdah* screen could look down on a sea of lavender, rose, amethyst, blue, and emerald. The guests were seated by degree of importance, and behind them stood servants wielding peacock fans.

In the center of the hall were four gilded posts canopied with thousands of marigold-heads strung together. "That is where the priests will light the sacred fire," Parvati explained. "There the bride and groom must perform *satapadi*—the seven steps around the sacred fire—in order to be truly married." She put a shapely hand to her bosom and added, "I remember that my heart fluttered like a butterfly when I took those steps."

Involuntarily Merial's eyes went to Rayn, who was sitting beside the raja. Fitting raiment had been brought to him from Baranpur, and he was dressed in black and gold. A priceless diamond glinted in his royal half-turban, another on the chain around his neck. His splendid physique and his proud, sun-bronzed face were that of a warrior prince. Try as she would, Merial could see nothing of the boy she had once known.

He was smiling at something Daiyal was saying, but as though he knew she was watching him, Rayn's eyes turned almost reflexively toward her. The golden gaze seemed to penetrate the screen that shielded the women, and to touch her physically.

But there was no softness in that look. Since they had come to Kumar, Merial had seen him often at a distance but had not had the chance to speak with him. Even so, she knew that he was in a fever to be gone. Outwardly he seemed absorbed in the new strain of Kumari horses that Daiyal-Raja had bred, but Merial could sense his tension and anxiety.

He was probably cursing himself for bringing her to

Kumar. Merial drew a deep breath of flower-drenched air and tried to pay attention to what Parvati was saying.

"The bride has been praying all morning for a hundred sons and a hundred daughters," the young rani was explaining. "She has been bathed and perfumed, and her eyes rimmed with kohl." She glanced sideways at Merial to ask, "Is it so at a *shadi*—a wedding—in your country?"

"No," she said truthfully, "it's not. A wedding in England is a very formal affair and is conducted in a church."

Before Parvati could ask more questions, there was a burst of music. Proceeded by acrobats on stilts, musicians, and a bodyguard of the raja's own lancers, the raja's cousin rode an elephant up to the house of his bride. As the bridegroom walked into the great hall, Merial noted that he looked tired and very serious.

"Joginder is forty—much older than is usual for a bridegroom," Parvati whispered. "He and Lacchi have loved each other for years, but his family didn't think Lacchi's family was rich or noble enough. They tried to marry Joginder to a princess from Kulu instead. Tell me, Mira, are marriages arranged thus in your country?"

Merial thought of Perce. "Sometimes," she replied.

"Traditionally, a son must obey his parents, but Joginder refused any wife but Lacchi. When the parents realized that their son resolved to have Lacchi or die wifeless, they gave in."

As she spoke, the bride appeared. Kneeling before Parvati, she allowed the rani to bedeck her with the traditional pieces of jewelry. There was a *tikka* on her forehead which bade her walk in the straight path, the earrings which forbade her to listen to gossip, the heavy necklace of gold that bowed her head in humility, the bangles that urged her to be charitable, and the anklets that would remind her to put her feet forward on the path of virtue.

Finally there was the diamond nose ring, a stern warning not to spend more than her husband could afford.

"May you wear these in peace and happiness," Parvati told the bride.

Lacchi wasn't in her first youth, either, nor was she beautiful, but she had a sweet, open face that was so happy the air around her seemed to shimmer. Even veiled in the *shela,* the scarlet brocade shawl that traditionally covered the head of the bride, her radiance shone through.

Merial watched entranced as the veiled Lacchi walked toward the bridegroom to place a garland of flowers about his neck. Joginder looked suddenly young and eager, and Merial wished the lovers well with all her heart. Then, to the accompaniment of drums and wailing flutes, the feasting began.

Lacchi's parents had spared no expense. Servants passed around exotic wines and such delicacies as seed pearls crushed and mixed with honey, sweetmeats, and pungent concoctions of betal nut wrapped in thin leaves of gold. The smells of rich cooking mingled with incense, flowers, and the perfumes worn by the royal women. Though the ladies were served their own feast, Merial's appetite waned before the onslaught on her senses. She noted that Rayn also ate little and drank even less.

Several hours passed in feasting, watching acrobats and professional dancers, and in listening to a *kavi* or poet who came forward to recite witty verses especially composed for the occasion. All this took a long time, and darkness had fallen before the priests lit the sacred fire under the marigold canopy and the actual ceremony began.

Merial concentrated on the man and woman who stood before the priests. Beside the groom, Lacchi looked like a tiny doll in her gold and scarlet sari, but her responses were given in a clear, joyous voice. She exuded happiness when, her sari knotted into her bridegroom's sash, she took the seven sacred steps around the fire.

"It is done. Now nothing can undo their marriage except death." Parvati paused to add thoughtfully, "In former years even death did not undo the marriage vows, and widows followed their lords onto the funeral pyre. The old raja outlawed this practice, but I have often thought that I wouldn't want to live as a widow. I can't imagine being separated from Daiyal-Raja."

Merial thought bleakly of never hearing Rayn's voice again, of never again feeling the touch of his hand. Impatiently blinking away the tears that filled her eyes, Merial concentrated on the black-and-gold figure by Daiyal-Rajah's side. This could be the last time she saw the man she loved.

It was very late when the royal party took its departure. Merial had assumed that she would return in Parvati's luxurious palanquin, but the rani had other plans.

"The raja wishes to join me on my journey home, so another palanquin has been summoned for you," she told Merial. Then she sighed and added, "Is it not a night for love?"

Loneliness twisted deep in Merial's heart, and it grew worse when she stepped into her palanquin and leaned back into the silken cushions.

Stop this, she told herself sternly. There was no use regretting things that couldn't be changed. Perce was far away, and an ocean of tears couldn't alter what Sir Edward had done. As for Rayn, he owed her nothing. They had loved each other as children, and that childish love had flared briefly. Now the flames had died forever.

She closed her eyes. Perhaps she dozed, for it didn't seem long before her bearers halted. Merial lifted the curtain and looking about her realized that they hadn't come to the raja's residence. Instead, they had stopped before a house that was built on the shore of a pond. The lush gardens that surrounded the house were lit by flaring lamps, and more lamps glowed on the veranda.

"What is this place?" she demanded of her bearers.

They didn't reply, but an elderly servant woman now appeared beside Merial's palanquin. "You are at the House of Roses, Heaven Born," this servant said. Bowing deeply she added, "Parvati-Rani felt that as an *Angrezi* lady accustomed to privacy, you might relish some time apart from her and the other royal women. If you will come this way, you will see that all is ready for your comfort."

It was true that tonight the chatter and noise of the women's quarters would have been hard to bear. Blessing Parvati's sensitivity, Merial descended from the palanquin and followed the woman up the steps to the veranda and through latticed doors of fragrant sandalwood into a marble hall. A waterfall had been built into one wall, and water splashed down over stones into a pool below.

"How beautiful!" Merial exclaimed.

After the noise of the wedding, this exquisite house offered blessed silence and peace. Gladly Merial followed her guide to a room that overlooked the water. Here a simple repast of fruit and sherbet had been placed on a low Indian table.

"If you wish to bathe first, here are garments suited for your comfort." Smiling, the woman displayed a kaftan of rose-colored silk. "And if you are too weary to eat, a place of rest has been prepared."

As she spoke, she slid open a latticed door disclosing two rooms. One was a sleeping chamber, with a low couch piled high with silken cushions and curtained by gossamer netting. The other room looked like a garden. Merial could see roses and ferns surrounding a marble pool shaped like a teardrop.

Drawn by the beauty of the place, she walked over to investigate and realized then that she was in a bathing room fashioned to resemble a garden. Near the pool were benches and marble tables laden with thick towels and various jeweled vases of oil and perfume. She knelt down and tested the water and found it warm.

"I'm told that the water never goes below a certain temperature," Rayn's voice said behind her. "The old raja liked his comforts."

She looked up swiftly and saw that he was standing in the doorway of the garden room. Something in his stance told Merial that he was as surprised to see her as she was to find him there, and the wild, hopeful leap of her heart died in disappointment. Meeting her here hadn't been Rayn's idea.

"Daiyal told me that a night at the House of Roses would refresh me, but he said nothing about your being here," he was saying.

Merial remembered Parvati's comments about lovers and realized that the romantic young rani had thought that Merial and Rayn had been pining to be together. It wasn't Parvati's fault that she'd been wrong.

She managed a smile and said, "We seem to be the victims of a royal conspiracy." He was silent and she asked, "When do you leave?"

"At dawn." He turned abruptly and strode back into the room where the refreshments were. "Well, since we're here, we may as well avail ourselves of all this hospitality."

She followed him, and he held out a hand to help her take her seat. His grip was impersonal and his expression was preoccupied, yet even so a flood of memories crowded close.

Rayn watched her as she sank gracefully into the silk cushions. Mira was lovely in her borrowed sari of peach silk. Parvati's luminous pearls had been coiled into the thick, dark braid of her hair. She looked like a queen, but her eyes were sad, and though she tried gallantly to smile, her soft mouth trembled. The need to kiss those rosy lips brought almost physical pain.

For want of something to do, he picked up a gold fruit knife and quartered an apple. "Would you care for some fruit?" he asked.

"Thank you, no." They could be strangers, she thought, perfectly polite and indifferent to each other.

"This place happened to be the old raja's favorite retreat," Rayn went on. "Daiyal told me that his father and his favorite wife would leave the palace and come here, accompanied only by trusted servants. It's a mark of Daiyal's regard that he's allowing us to use it."

Under the music of his voice, Merial's treacherous pulse had begun to race. Desperately needing to break the silence that followed Rayn's words, she commented, "It is so peaceful here in Kumar. What is happening in the outside world?"

"Chetak's men have joined Perce's railroad work force but haven't as yet isolated the thugs." Impatience warred with frustration in Rayn's deep voice as he added, "Chetak himself is in Sri Nevi and watching Perce carefully, but so far the man has done nothing, said nothing. Rassul reports that Ibrahim is also passive. I don't like it. If only—" He broke off.

"If only you hadn't had to bring me to Kumar," she finished.

"None of us knew there'd be a royal wedding in progress, and the trade treaty I've concluded with Daiyal is definitely important." He set down his uneaten apple, adding, "For the rest, General Jaga has the army on alert status. Unfortunately, we're not the only ones ready for war."

Her lips felt dry. "The Sri Nevi garrison?"

His dark brows drew together in a frown. "I was talking about the Afghans. The situation with the raiders has become extremely volatile, and Deen sends news of increased border clashes. I suspect that the thugs are involved in this. If only Ibrahim would betray himself so that I could stamp out the trouble at its source."

Rayn didn't tell Merial the rest of Rassul's report. That the chief of police was even higher in the rana's favor wasn't reassuring. More to himself than to Merial, Rayn continued, "Of course, Perce has been busy, too. Messages have been sent to the viceroy in Delhi demanding the men and firepower needed to 'rescue' you from my clutches."

Merial bowed her head. "I'm sorry."

"Because you resisted rape—or because your father is involved with Perce?"

Restlessly Rayn got to his feet and went to the stone-latticed window. As she watched him staring out into the darkness toward Baranpur, a resolve filled her heart. "I'll go back to Sri Nevi," she announced.

He turned swiftly to stare at her. "Are you insane?"

But it made perfect sense. "I'll return to Sri Nevi and tell Colonel Malcolm what Perce is planning. I'll tell him that Perce tried to rape me. The colonel will listen to me."

A memory, fleeting and shadowed, touched Rayn's mind, and he thought of a small, skinny, pigtailed child ignoring her own terror to thrust the moonstone amulet back into his hands. "It will keep you safe," she had said—

Conflicting emotions harshened his voice as he reminded her, "You helped me break out of prison, held a pistol on one of the queen's soldiers. No one will take your word over Perce's—they'll think you're my accomplice."

"I don't care what they think." Merial rose to her feet to add earnestly. "I'll try to convince them. If I succeed, Perce will fail. If I fail—well, that's a risk I'm prepared to take."

Swiftly he crossed the room and gripped her hands in his. "But I'm not. God in heaven, when I think of you in Perce's hands—"

She caught her breath at his tone, and in the blaze of those fierce, golden eyes she read fury and grief and a longing that matched her own. "Oh, Rayn," she whispered.

Just that, just his name, and the universe around them seemed to stop its eternal movement. Merial heard Rayn curse under his breath as he caught her to him in an embrace that threatened to crack her bones. She didn't care. She pressed herself closer to his hard strength and drew his remembered scent into her lungs.

Mine, she thought fiercely.

"Why can't I stop loving you?" It was said in a groan that unleashed a flood of longing within her.

Her bones seemed to be melting under his heat as she whispered, "Do you want to?"

"I must. Mira, we are from different worlds which will soon be at war. I will very likely kill your friends at the garrison. Your father's blood will stain my sword."

She flinched at his deliberately brutal words. "That needn't happen."

"I must ride for Baranpur at dawn. This is good-bye."

He looked down at her for another moment, then let go of her and strode toward the door. In another minute he'd be gone. Desperately Merial ran in front of him and positioned herself between him and the door. "Take me with you."

He shook his head impatiently and would have set her aside, but she flattened her back against the sandalwood door. "You said once that we chose to love each other. What's happening in the world—with Perce and my father and the thugs—isn't of our choosing. What we can do is choose tonight to part as strangers—or we can stay together."

In the silence of his intent gaze, she could hear the sigh of the pool waters, the beat of her heart. She wanted to throw herself into his arms, but she held herself back. She had said all she could say. It was his choice, now, to go or stay.

At last he said, "If I stay here with you, it will be for this night only. I won't make promises I can't keep." She nodded, and he raised his hand to touch her cheek. She turned her head to kiss his hard swordsman's palm.

She understood all that he had said and more. Between this man who had once been Niall St. Marr and Edward Ashland's daughter, there was no future beyond a single night of love. Yet even as she registered this hard truth, she knew that one night with Rayn was worth a thousand lifetimes of loneliness.

In a low voice she murmured, "Jassmina once told me that God bids us to take what we want from life and pay for it. I'm ready to pay."

Gently he drew her to him and rested his cheek against her hair. "Not if the payment brings grief for you. Mira, think—"

But she refused to think. Twisting her face, she met his lips with hers. "I love you."

His lips sought hers as a thirsting man seeks a fountain of lifegiving water. He savored her sweetness, deliberately prolonging the kiss until she was dizzied and faint with desire. "You are the heart of my heart," he said against her mouth, "the princess of my soul."

He bent his head to hers, and her eyelashes came down to veil her eyes as she raised her lips to his. His mouth was sweet, deliberate, yet his kiss seeped through her veins like fiery wine.

"Your throat is warm ivory," Rayn murmured against her neck. His practiced hand released the coils of her hair, tumbling them around them both. "Your hair is a dark waterfall in which a man could drown."

Their lips met again, long and hungrily. Merial's body, so long starved for Rayn's touch, came alive as he began to caress her over the delicate silk of her sari.

"You are as beautiful as a bride," he continued. "As fair as the stars. Your skin is like sun-warmed silk."

He slid his hands down the bodice of her sari, his fingers circling the firm, clothed mounds of her breasts before they slipped under the fragile silk. Merial sighed as her delicate garments were stripped away.

She had dreamed of his touch, of lips that trailed leisurely kisses from her mouth to her throat, over her breasts. Reality was better than dreams. Lightly, tantalizing her, his tongue laved her nipples before his warm mouth covered them. She felt as though he were drawing her heart from her as he sucked first one then the other of the taut peaks.

Still kissing her, Rayn lifted her into his arms and strode with her into the sleeping chamber. Then, setting her down, she began to work loose the buttons of his clothes. He shrugged out of his ceremonial achkan, and she raised her arms to allow him to slip loose her bodice and unclasp her sari so that it slid to the floor in a whisper of silk.

He found her lips once more. His tongue relearned the satin secrets of her inner mouth while his hands rediscovered the tantalizing curve of her buttocks. Her breasts were rising and falling against him, and her aroused nipples teased his bared chest with shadow-kisses.

He let her go and sat down on a chair by the bed to remove his boots. Kneeling before him she helped him and, when he protested, smiled up at him, whispering, "The Prince of Baranpur must be served by his woman."

Rayn felt his heart constrict into a tight knot of passion and tenderness. Even in the richness of jewelry and silk, Mira had never looked so beautiful as now. Her ebony hair cloaked her like deepest night, and her body gleamed like a pearl. When she breathed, her coral-tipped breasts rose and fell, and her much-kissed mouth was like a flower.

"You're more beautiful than the goddess of dawn," he told her huskily.

"And you're a lovely man." Dropping his boots she bent forward to touch her warm mouth to his flat male nipples, the hard planes of his chest and belly. She kissed the white scars of old battles, old betrayals, as though her lips could bring healing.

She loved every part of Rayn—his scars, the strength of his muscles shoulders and neck and chest, the curl of his dark hair against her fingers, the whipcord-lean belly and the pride of his manhood which would fill her body with its gift of love. The familiar salt taste of him filled her with such longing that she felt herself ready to shatter with desire.

He got to his feet and, lifting her into his arms, strode with her to the bed. There he laid her down on the silken pillows and, unfastening his *kamerband,* impatiently wrenched off his jodhpurs. But he didn't immediately lie down beside her. Instead he knelt beside her, saying, "I am the words, Mira. You are the melody."

Joy swelled through Merial's heart as she realized that

Rayn was speaking the ritual words of the marriage ceremony they had just witnessed. She whispered the words she had heard the happy bride say today: "I am the melody, and you are the words."

He took her hand and drew his lips across each finger before turning it and burying his mouth in her palm. "I take hold of your hand for good fortune so that with me you may attain to old age."

Old age with Rayn—for a moment she allowed herself to dream of years that could lie ahead, golden years in which they could love and work and be together. Then the dream was lost in the reality of Rayn's kisses. It didn't matter, Merial thought as she returned those kisses. She would trade one night with Rayn for anything that life had to offer her.

The thought slid away under his kisses as he lay down beside her, courting her body with delicate caresses that became steadily more insistent. When she sighed with pleasure, his lips followed the pathway of his hands, traversing her breasts and belly and the warm silk of her parted thighs. As if she were his goddess, he worshipped her, but when his hot, open kisses tormented the honey of her inner thighs, she twined her fingers in his thick, dark hair and drew him back to her.

"Come to me," she pleaded.

He kissed her as he cupped her buttocks and raised her hips to receive his gift of love. She gave a long sigh as he entered her, his hard, eager flesh filling her completely. But instead of beginning the dance of love, he paused with his loins tight-fused against hers to look deep into her eyes.

"Become my partner as thou hast paced all the seven steps with me. Apart from thee I cannot live."

Her reply was a murmur of rapture so deep as to be pain. "Rayn, I love you. Apart from you I *will* not live."

Slowly they began to move together, trying to spin out moments that might never come again. But the heat within them was too strong. Their whispers became gasps of pleasure, then cries as their bones, their blood, their nerves and sinews fused in a rhythm older than time. "My queen," he called her, "my life—"

Together they soared into the sun.

"I take it," Rayn commented, "that you're pleased with the House of Roses."

Pressed tight against him, Merial giggled. She felt as though she had drunk too much wine. In fact she'd had none. She kissed his throat lightly, then his chin. "And you're not?" she teased.

He loved the sound of her laughter. Like a fountain of light, it bubbled out of her and transformed them both. But then, the night had left them irrevocably changed. They had loved and talked and dozed only to wake to more loving. Sometimes their coming together had been passionate and abandoned. At other times they had laughed together, teasing playfully in the midst of their desire. Never before, not even at the Bagh Mahal, had he felt so close to her.

"I'm happier now than I've ever been." His deep voice held a note of wonder, and she broke away to sit cross-legged on the bed and look down at him. In the lamp that burned by the bed, her white body gleamed like mother-of-pearl. "The gods must be jealous of so much happiness," he went on.

But she wouldn't let him be serious. She stretched, and the arch of her breasts made desire stab through Rayn again. He reached for her, but she slid down from the bed and out of his reach. Tossing back her black hair, she danced out of his grasp toward the garden room. For a moment she stood poised on the edge of the pool, and then, with a splash, dived in.

A moment later she emerged. "The water is *still* warm. How can that be?" she exclaimed.

"The old raja had his engineers perfect a system by which the pool is heated underground." He'd followed her and was grinning at her from the edge of the pool. "You look," he told her, "about ten years old."

She made a little face. "Does that mean that you are robbing the cradle? *Shabash,* Prince. There is little merit in such a deed, and you must pay the penalty."

Before he realized what she was doing, she had reached out, caught his ankle, and tugged. Caught off balance, he fell into the pool. Huge waves of displaced water sloshed over the marble rim of the teardrop. He came up, spluttering and laughing. "You little vixen, you'll pay for laying hands on a prince of the blood."

He put his arms around her and she melted against him. "How will I pay for my crimes?" she challenged.

"I'll think of a way."

Opening like a flower to the sun, her mouth welcomed the bold invading stroke of his tongue. He could feel the caress of her erect nipples against his chest, and desire for her became so strong that it was almost physically painful. He bent to kiss the upthrust coral peaks, licking off the water droplets till she moaned with pleasure and went limp against him.

"I like your way of making me suffer," she whispered.

Against her flank she could feel his man's hardness, and she gloried in his want of her. She loved the tickling feel of his chest hair against her breasts, and the tremor in his great arms which spoke of desire held back. She had tamed the Tiger—*her* Tiger—by becoming wholly his. Merial sighed deeply with satisfaction and then chanced to look up at the high window that faced east. Far on the horizon the sky was turning gray.

Dawn was coming. In spite of the warmth of the water, Merial felt chilled. Rayn was riding away today, and perhaps their people would soon be at war.

She had sworn she wouldn't say the words that burst from her lips. "Take me with you?" she begged.

"It wouldn't be safe for you in Baranpur. There's my father and Ibrahim." Recalling the chief of police's hot eyes made her shiver, and Rayn's face grew grim as he divined her thought. He wanted to shout that he would keep her safe forever, but he checked himself. He mustn't make promises he might not be able to keep.

Holding her tight against him he tried to think of words that could comfort and heal her. "Whatever happens after this, nothing can change last night or what we mean to each other." He paused and added reluctantly, "You knew it would be like this."

He was going. She could hear it in his voice. She could not let him go quite yet, so she clung to him whispering, "Love me again, my prince. Love me now."

His kisses smothered her words, but when he would have lifted her out of the pool, she wrapped her legs around his loins and held him prisoner. With a growl of pleasure, he lifted her leg against his flank and thrust into her satin heat.

She took him deep, and undulations of pleasure began at the core of her and rippled outward as he moved within her. His movements seemed almost lazy, and so were the lips that stroked her mouth and throat, tongued her nipples taut before sucking them. In her turn she kissed his shoulders, and the broad expanse of his chest, ran her hands over his shoulders and back and the hard musculature of his buttocks.

Gradually his thrusts became swifter, and she cried out at the sweet ferocity of his movements within her. Leaning back in his arms, her hair spreading behind her like the petals of a dark sea-flower, she moaned out his name. The spirals of fire within her expanded until she was aflame with desire, and it seemed as though she must shatter into him. Yet she wanted more. She needed to be consumed by him. She wanted to merge her flesh with him, not for this one convulsive moment but for all time.

The water churned and roiled about. Their cries mingled into a paean of love as she drew the honey of his seed deep into her.

For a long moment they leaned against each other, still entwined. Then, drawing a deep breath that was almost a sigh, he lifted her away from him and onto the edge of the pool.

She knew it was a moment of parting but couldn't help pleading, "It's not quite dawn yet."

He kissed her on her thigh, then sprang lithely up onto the lip of the pool. Water droplets clung to his strong-muscled body as he strode over to the towels, draped one about her, then held her wordlessly close to him for a moment.

"Sleep for a while," he said. "You'll be quite safe here, my love."

Careful not to show by any sign or word that her heart was breaking, Merial dried herself and followed him into the other room. She slipped on the rose-silk kaftan and was plaiting her hair when there was a timid cough at the door.

"Lord," the woman servant's voice said, "forgive this intrusion, but one of your *bhaldars* wishes speech with you."

"From the border or from Rasgani?" Knotting a length of cloth around his waist, Rayn went to the door.

"I do not know." The woman looked anxious. "His name is Captain Rassul Khan and he says he must see you at once. Did I do wrong?"

"Send him in and leave us." The woman hurried away, and almost immediately there were footsteps in the marble corridor outside. Merial went to stand beside Rayn, and his arm curved protectively around her waist as Rassul came striding to the door.

He bowed deeply to them both and said in his quiet way, "I am sorry to intrude upon your rest, but there is urgent need. Lord, Khem-Rana is dying."

··*Sixteen*··

"WHY WASN'T I informed that he was ailing?" Rayn's voice hardened. "An assassin?"

Rassul shook his head. "No, lord, not according to Baju. The King of Kings was in counsel with his ministers when he collapsed, and Baju says that the evil is in the rana's own blood. I came myself because I didn't want another to bear the news."

"I'll leave for Baranpur immediately," Rayn said.

When Rassul had gone, Merial asked, "Did you suspect Ibrahim of trying to assassinate the rana?"

"I wouldn't put it past him," Rayn said grimly. "Perce may think he's using Ibrahim to get his hands on Baranpur, but he's underestimating his ally. Ibrahim has the power of the police and the thugs behind him, and now's a perfect time to try and seize power."

She cried, "He wouldn't dare! He knows the people love you."

"Remember that I'm not Khem-Rana's blood son. He broke tradition to adopt me as his heir, and some of the ministers didn't like it. Even now there are a few who'd swing around to Ibrahim's side if it were to their advantage."

Putting her arms around him, Merial implored, "Rayn, if you return now you may be riding into Ibrahim's trap."

"Nonsense." Rayn buckled on his sword belt as he added, "General Jaga is loyal, I have my lancers, and Panwa will let me know if any of the ministers are intriguing with Ibrahim." He drew her to him, kissed the top of her head. "Don't be afraid, Mira."

Another thought came to her. "You want Ibrahim exposed for what he is. If I were to confront him unexpectedly, tell him what I heard Yuir Singh say to Perce—"

"You're going to stay here in Kumar," Rayn interrupted. He drew the moonstone amulet over his head and set it around her neck. "Let this keep you safe, my love."

He left at once, and Merial watched from the window as he strode down the steps of the House of Roses. But before he could mount his waiting horse, a small group of black-clad horsemen, headed by Daiyal himself, rode up.

Before the astonished Rayn could greet him, the raja leaned down from his horse and extended his hand.

"My friend, I'm here because I've learned the bad news about your father. I grieve for the health of my brother ruler and wish to enable you to return swiftly to Baranpur. I want you to choose two dozen of my horses as a gift."

In spite of his fever to be gone, Rayn was impressed, but Daiyal waved away such thanks.

"It would look well if Baranpur's crown prince returns to Rasgani surrounded by horses worth a king's ransom. Certainly it would silence would-be detractors." He paused to add significantly, "I'm acting in Kumar's best interests. In these troubled times, we need a friend in Baranpur."

Put that way, there was no refusing. Rayn bowed deeply. "Majesty, I'm grateful."

Merial watched him ride away with the young raja, feeling even more troubled than before. Daiyal, too, felt that there might be trouble over the succession. "Ibrahim must be brought down," she mused.

The more she thought of it, the more she was sure that the shock of seeing her would trick the chief of police into revealing his connections with the thugs and with Perce. But Rayn would never consent to her going back to Baranpur with him. Unless—

Suddenly Merial knew what she had to do. Dressing hastily, she summoned her palanquin. When it carried her back to the palace, she went in search of Parvati.

The rani was sitting in her rose gardens amongst her women. There was a dreamy look in her eyes signifying that her own night had been one of love. She turned to Merial with a smile, but when she saw the Englishwoman's distress, she sent her attendants away.

Taking Merial's hands, she said, "Prince Rayn has gone, and you are grieving. I wish there was something I could do to ease your sorrow."

"Then please help me to go with him," Merial said.

Parvati was astonished. "I thought you were going to stay here in Kumar, Mira-Bai."

"If the rana dies, there will be much danger for Rayn." Merial lowered her voice. "He believes that Ibrahim, the chief of police, is in league with enemies of Baranpur. I must go to Rasgani and expose him for the villain he is."

Looking even more bewildered, Parvati demurred, "How can a mere woman do such a thing?"

Merial explained, adding, "If Ibrahim isn't stopped, there'll be war between Baranpur and England, and that would affect Kumar. You'd eventually be drawn into the conflict."

Parvati turned pale and Merial knew that she was thinking of her handsome young husband. "But you are not only a woman but an *Angrezi,*" she protested. "Khem-Rana would never believe you."

"I'll *make* him listen to me." Merial sank down on her knees before Parvati. "Please help me go with him," she pleaded. "If something happens to Rayn while I'm safe here, I wouldn't want to live."

Tears filled the rani's dark eyes. "I understand how you feel. But if he finds you in his entourage, the prince will surely send you back."

Merial had her answer ready. "Daiyal-Raja has given Prince Rayn two dozen Kumari horses. Surely they are special steeds that need the utmost care—and more than one groom to care for them?"

Parvati looked astonished, then gave one of her unexpected giggles. "What a clever idea!" She threw her arms around Merial and embraced her. "I will help you arrange things."

When Rayn and Rassul rode out of Kumar a half hour later, two dozen horses from the raja's private stables went with them. Along with the splendid, cream-colored beasts came a groom and a horse-boy, specifically trained to administer to the precious animals. The head groom, Gopal Nath, had been sworn to secrecy by the rani herself. He made sure that his "assistant" kept out of the prince's sight, and Rayn, absorbed in his thoughts, did not notice that the slender young horse-boy had little to say for himself.

They rode swiftly through the morning, and by late afternoon were climbing into the Pir Panjals. As they approached Baranpur's border, another of Rayn's lancers came spurring down the slope toward them. "What news?" Rayn called.

"I come from Rasgani, lord, where Khem-Rana lies on the point of death," the man replied. "Ibrahim has been spreading rumors that you, too, are dead, and police are everywhere in the city under pretext of keeping order."

Rayn's voice was grim. "What else?"

"Made bold by rumors of your death, the thugs have begun acts of sabotage in our northern cities. After conferring with Minister Panwa, Lieutenant Fanji has taken the *bhaldars* and gone in pursuit. He's left six of our comrades behind to guard the Bagh Mahal, and General Jaga and the army are on alert in case violence erupts in Rasgani."

Rayn approved. "Couldn't Panwa discount the rumors of my death?"

"He has denied your death publicly and loudly, but the poison spreads. Panwa reports that Ibrahim is reminding the ministers that you are not blood-heir to the house of Raoshad."

In his calm way Rassul suggested, "Lord, let's just waylay Ibrahim and slit his throat."

Rayn pounded the pommel of his saddle with his clenched fist. "We need proof to convince my father of Ibrahim's connection with Perce and the thugs." Rassul nodded somberly, and Rayn ordered the *bhaldar* messenger to return to Rasgani immediately. "Tell your comrades at the Bagh Mahal that I'm returning. Then join Fanji in the north."

They had reached a mountain stream, and Rayn called a halt to water the horses. As the Kumari groom and the supposed horse-boy led the horses to drink, Merial noticed a crude altar made of stone. On it lay the eviscerated and bloody carcass of an animal.

Hastily turning away from the gruesome sight, she

started as she heard Rayn's voice at her back. "A very recent sacrifice to Kali. Thugs have been here." He turned to Merial, adding, "Hurry with the horses, boy. We must travel more swiftly, and—*gods above!*"

A big hand caught Merial's chin and turned her face to the light. She'd never seen Rayn look so angry. "What in hell's name are you doing here?"

With equally fierce determination, she met his gaze. "I'm going to help you expose Ibrahim."

"You're going back to Kumar." He turned to shout an order, but she caught at his arm.

"If you try and send me back, you'll have to tie me to the horse. The minute I can, I'll get away and ride back to you. I know the way, you see." Rayn swore bitterly, and she said, "I mean it, Rayn."

Rassul now came hurrying up. "Your order, lord?" he began, then broke off to stare at Merial.

"You don't have any time to lose," Merial pointed out. "I will be safe with your aunt, Rayn. I swear that I will not leave her side until it's time to testify against Ibrahim."

Conflicting emotions were warring in Rayn. The sight of his Mira here filled him with fear for her, and he wanted nothing more than to send her back to Kumar. But he also knew that even if he sent Rassul with her, there was a chance that the fanatic thugs might ambush her and kill her—or worse. Better to take her to Baranpur, where, as she said, she would be safe with Rukmiri-Bai.

"Mount one of the Kumari horses and stay beside me," he barked. "I don't want you out of my sight."

He didn't say another word until they had covered several miles. Then, finally, she broke the silence. "I know you are angry and worried for me. Don't be, my love."

About to snap out an angry answer, Rayn saw that

Mira's turquoise eyes were smiling up at him. The lilt in her voice caught at his heart, and exasperation crumbled into love for the brave, stubborn woman at his side. "Do you know what danger you're in?" he demanded.

"Of course I do," she replied. "I'm no fool. But I couldn't stay away when there was a chance I could help you. Besides, it is as you said last night. Without thee, I cannot live."

Rayn said grimly, "If anyone recognizes you and reports you to Ibrahim, you may not be alive for very long."

Twilight found them spurring down the steep road that led into the valley kingdom. Here they were met by a deputation of armed riders who wore the livery of Panwa's household. Their leader saluted Rayn and exclaimed, "Highness! I can't tell you how relieved and grateful we are to see you."

"Did your lord send you to meet me?" Rayn asked.

"Yes, Highness. Your *bhaldar* brought news of your arrival to our master, and since your other *bhaldars* are away in the north, he sent us as an escort for you." The man lowered his voice to add significantly, "There are some in Rasgani who would not welcome your safe return."

To take Merial into the rana's palace would be madness. Rayn spoke quietly to Rassul. "We'll ride up to the city together. Then you will take the horses and go to the Bagh Mahal. Stay there until I come."

They rode up to the gates of the city together, and Merial experienced a sense of déjà vu. That first time she had entered Rasgani, she and her father had been captives and the people had come out as much to jeer at them as to welcome their prince. Now long lines of shadowy figures were standing with their faces turned in the direction of the Silver Palace. Their silence, the moonlight shining down on their light-colored *dhotis* and saris, gave a surrealistic touch to the scene.

"They're waiting for news of Khem-Rana," Panwa's officer volunteered. "They have stood here like this since he became ill."

Beyond the gates their roads diverged. Merial could hardly speak openly to Rayn, but she watched him, her heart in her eyes.

Once more Rayn spoke to Rassul. "Make sure my orders are carried out," he said, and the *bhaldar* raised his unsheathed sword to his lips.

"On my life, lord."

Merial forced herself not to look back as they separated, with Rayn riding toward the rana's palace. "Do you think he'll be safe?" she asked Rassul.

"God alone knows that," he replied, and she realized that under his habitual calm manner, he was worried, too. "Stay close to me, Sahiba."

Both Merial and the nervous Kumari groom followed Rassul closely as they rode down the street. They had gone barely a mile when they were challenged by a group of police. "Who are you and where do you go in defiance of the *Kotwal* Ibrahim's order?" their leader demanded.

Rassul identified himself. "I'm taking these horses to the *Bagh Mahal* by order of Prince Rayn," he added.

It seemed to Merial that something like amusement flickered the policeman's eyes, but he saluted with military precision. "In that case you are free to go as you wish. Forgive me for detaining you, but this is an unsettled time, and the *kotwal* has ordered us to disperse the people."

Apparently, the police hadn't been successful, for there were people everywhere. Not only were the roads full of people, but the mosques and temples were also jammed with devotees praying for the rana's recovery and for the safe return of Prince Rayn. Chants and prayers and the sound of gongs filled the night as did the heavy scent of incense. The Kumari horses, well trained as they were, snorted uneasily.

Suddenly, in the distance, there came a faint shout. "Is the rana dead?" Merial wondered fearfully.

The people around her craned their necks and muttered between themselves. Then, like a ripple carried by currents of water, the news was passed down from those closest to the Silver Palace. It eddied through the crowd until the people around Merial were saying the words.

"The gods be praised—the Tiger is back. Prince Rayn's alive!"

With something like awe, Merial watched the people's mourning turn to joy. Men yelled out thanks to the gods and embraced each other; women clutched their children and wept joyful tears. The priests and *mullahs* at the temples and mosques raised their hands heavenward to give thanks. Ibrahim's police stood by sourly, unable to control these outpourings of joy.

"Prince Rayn is much loved," Rassul remarked proudly. "By the beard of the prophet, he will make a rana men will die for."

Merial wished that Rassul hadn't spoken of death. As they took the lakeside road, a cool, damp breeze rolled in from the water, and she shivered.

As they went farther from the rana's palace, the crowds began to thin out, and they rode the last mile to the Bagh Mahal in silent, deserted darkness. Merial felt a spurt of relief as they approached the main gate, but Rassul checked his horse. "Something's wrong," he muttered.

Now Merial saw that the gate was guarded not by *bhaldars* but by men wearing Panwa's livery.

"Stay here," Rassul ordered Merial. He then rode

ahead and called, "I am Rassul Khan, captain of the prince's lancers. Where are the *bhaldars* who were sent to guard my lord's palace?"

The gate guards saluted and one of them replied, "Captain, they've gone to join the rest of their comrades in the north."

Rassul demurred, "They wouldn't leave our lord's palace in anyone's hands."

"There was no choice. There's news that the Afridi army is massing for war, so General Jaga is ready to march our forces out. The remaining *bhaldars* were needed to reinforce their comrades on the border."

It sounded logical, but as the guard spoke, an exclamation of surprise came from the courtyard. "By Vayu's beard," a rasping voice exclaimed, "Kumari horses! Where did they come from?"

Merial started as though stung as the gates opened, and Yuir Singh strolled out. "You, horse-boys, don't just sit there," he commanded. "Bring in those animals."

"Don't do it—he's one of the thugs!"

As Merial cried out, Rassul whacked the rump of one of the Kumari horses with his whip. The startled beast surged toward the gate, scattering the guards, and Rassul shouted, "Get out of here!"

Merial spurred her horse back the way they'd come. Behind her, she could hear the whinnies of confused horses, Gopal Nath's outraged yells, and the bellows of Yuir Singh. "After them, you imbeciles," the thug leader was shouting. "The minister will have our heads if they get away."

Riding a few feet behind Merial, Rassul drew his sword. "Keep going and stay low in the saddle." As rifle bullets whizzed past her head, Merial's mind worked feverishly.

So Ibrahim hadn't been the one manipulating the thugs—
or at least, it hadn't been Ibrahim alone.

"And Rayn went with Panwa's men!" she cried. "He's
ridden straight into a trap!"

"Not if we get word to him," was the grim reply.

As Rassul spoke, there came the sound of pursuing
hoofbeats. "Our friends are gaining on us," the lancer captain remarked. "Mira-Bai, you must reach our prince and
warn him."

"What about you? One against so many—Rassul Kahn,
they'll kill you."

"My place is here—yours is with our lord," was the
stern rejoinder. "May God, the All Compassionate, go
with you."

"Rassul—" But he'd turned back to face Yuir Singh
and Panwa's men, and there was nothing to do but gallop
on. Merial chewed on her lower lip till she tasted blood
as behind her she heard shots and the harsh screams of
dying men.

She knew that Rassul meant to fight to the death. He'd
sacrificed himself to save his prince, and she couldn't let
that terrible gift go to waste. With tears streaming down
her cheeks, Merial rode like a fury. She passed the lake
road and then came up to the fountains, where Ibrahim's
men were forcibly dispersing the crowds and arresting
those who protested.

What to do, what to do—she slowed her horse and tried
to think past the pounding in her head. There was no way
she could just go riding up to the Silver Palace—not with
Ibrahim's police everywhere. Besides, even if she managed
to evade all her enemies, how could she gain entry to see
Rayn?

Her only chance was to mingle with the crowd and
make her way to the palace on foot. Merial slid down from

her horse, slapped its rump, and sent it on its way. With any luck, Yuir Singh's minions would continue to follow the riderless steed.

"Get a move on, you!"

A big policeman was behind her, shoving and lashing about with his whip. Merial fell to her knees as a small man was pushed against her.

"May all Ibrahim's men be carried off to hell," he muttered. "Are you hurt, sister? But—by the beard of the prophet—it can't be you, Mira-Bai!"

Merial recognized the little flower seller, Ahmed Ibin Amin. His eyes were as huge as an owl's as he stammered, "What are *you* doing here, Sahiba?"

The big policeman with the whip was advancing on them, threatening, "Get moving, or by order of the *kotwal* I'll have you thrown into prison."

Ahmed Ibin Amin timidly touched Merial's arm. "It's not safe here," he whispered. "Come with me."

But she wouldn't budge. "Help me to get to the Silver Palace," she begged. "I must help the prince."

The flower seller's eyes now nearly popped out of his head. "The *prince?*"

But there was no time for explanations as the police moved in, swinging whips and clubs. In the confusion of cursing men and women and crying children, the flower seller grasped Merial's arm and dragged her into a dark alleyway. "My house isn't far, Mira-Bai. You'll be safe there."

Ahmed's house turned out to be little bigger than a shack. The furniture consisted mainly of a bed on which a large fierce-looking woman was sitting. The child in her arms began to wail as the woman shrilled, "Who is this you bring here, shameless one?"

"Peace, Fatima. It's Mira-Bai, the prince's lady." Ahmed shut the door and bolted it.

The big woman looked scared. "She's wanted by the police. If they find her *here,* we'll be punished." Angrily she added, "I told you not to go out tonight. I warned you. But do you ever listen to me?"

Ahmed began to argue with his wife, and the child's crying became louder. "Be still," Merial commanded them all. "Just tell me the quickest way to the Silver Palace, and I'll leave." When they didn't listen to her, she raised her voice. "There's no time to waste. Prince Rayn's in danger."

Both Ahmed and his wife stopped their wrangling, and Fatima demanded, "Who would want to harm our prince?"

"Ibrahim, for one, and also his so-called friend, Panwa Puar. Thugs now control the Bagh Mahal, and Rukmiri-Bai is undoubtedly a prisoner." Merial paused to draw breath. "Captain Rassul, who accompanied me, has been killed, and the prince himself is in the gravest danger. I must get word to him."

Fatima heaved herself off the bedstead. "Worthless one," she shrilled at Ahmed, "what are you waiting for? Go quickly and fetch the *Jamadar* Ram Gunga." She gave her small husband a push, adding, "He's a military man and will know how to get to the bottom of this."

Merial slumped down onto a stool in a corner of the narrow room. Her legs had begun to shake, and there was a tight feeling in her chest. Fatima thrust a cool herbal drink into her hands, but she pushed it away. "I can't stay here!" she cried. "I must go to him."

"I can hear them coming now." As Fatima spoke, the door creaked open to admit many men. By their dress some were Muslims, some bearded Sikhs, some Hindu.

Merial recognized a prosperous silk merchant who had brought his wares to the Bagh Mahal, a *mullah* from the Mosque, and the boatman who'd ferried Rayn's boat. All these and more squeezed into Ahmed's shack until the walls creaked in protest.

But the crowd somehow managed to part for a gray-haired *jamadar,* a retired soldier who carried himself militarily erect. He had buckled on his sword, and he rested one gaunt hand on its hilt as he faced Merial. "I am Ram Gunga, formerly an officer in the army of Khem-Rana," he announced. "I served under the Shield of the Kingdom. I also recognize you as the *Angrezi* lady who helped at the hospital. Now, Sahiba, you say that the prince is in danger?"

Merial again gave an account of what had happened. As she described Perce's meeting with the thugs, a growl arose from the listening men. The old soldier interrupted to say, "Prince Rayn and Panwa Puar have always been friends, Sahiba. How do we know that what you say is true?"

Merial displayed the amulet that Rayn had placed around her neck. "The prince gave this to me as proof that *he* believes in me. Do you recognize it?"

Her voice rang with authority, and her audience was impressed. "It's the prince's amulet, the one he always wears," Ram Gunga ascertained.

"That's good enough for me." Fatima planted big fists on her hips. "Well? How do we help the prince?"

A powerful man whose lips were red with chewing pan, betel leaf, demurred. "The palace is guarded closer than a jealous Turk's harem. There's no way any of us can get in."

"Perhaps I can do something," the elderly *jamadar* said. "I have many old comrades amongst the palace guard, and they'll let me through the gates. I'll leave at once."

Merial would have liked to go with him, but she knew that her presence would do more harm than good. It was hard to wait in the cramped hut with the others until the *jamadar* returned, a half hour later.

"I saw the prince at a distance," Ram Gunga reported. "He was speaking with General Jaga in the courtyard of the palace."

At least Rayn was safe for the moment. "Did you talk with him?" Merial queried.

The old soldier shook his head unhappily. "Alas, Sahiba, no. There is talk of war on the Afghan border, and at the prince's order, the army is moving out. There was so much confusion I couldn't get close to the prince."

Merial's heart sank. With Fanji and his contingent of lancers dealing with the thugs to the north, with Deen and the army on the Afghan border, Rayn stood alone. Terror filled her, the same blind, unreasoning fear she'd felt when she'd left her sick father alone in his tent and hurried down that long-ago pathway. She had prayed then for a miracle and had found Rayn with Niall's amulet at his throat—

"But of course!" she exclaimed. "The amulet!"

She whirled on the old *jamadar.* "You must take this amulet to General Jaga at once. See the general personally and tell him what's happened. Explain that the prince needs him back in Rasgani."

She placed the moonstone amulet in the *jamadar*'s gnarled hand, and the old soldier carried it to his lips. "I will go as quickly as I can," he promised. "I will convince the general even if I die for it. But the army may not return in time to—to—"

His words faltered, and his stern old eyes were suddenly

afraid. Merial spoke stoutly. "The army will be on time. Meanwhile, I'm going to the Silver Palace."

"But the police will arrest you," Ahmed protested. "That's madness, Sahiba."

"If I'm arrested, Prince Rayn will hear of it and be warned that something's wrong."

The old *jamadar* pursed his lips while he considered this. "You are a brave woman," he approved. "But supposing the police arrest you—and kill you—quietly? Supposing the prince never learns that you came looking for him?"

That possibility had occurred to Merial, but she only said, "This is war. We all must be prepared to take some risks."

"Well spoken!" Ram Gunga drew his sword and raised its blade to his lips. In a firm voice he spoke the formal oath of fealty. "From this moment on, I am Prince Narayn's man. I am his child. My head and my sword and my life are at his command. Now, brothers, you say it."

With one voice, the men in the room repeated the solemn pledge. When the echo of their voices had died away, the *jamadar* saluted Merial.

"We belong to the prince. We are his army. Anyone who dares to raise his sword against the Tiger will answer to us." His voice rolled like a kettledrum as he exhorted, "Go, Sahiba, and may all the gods watch over you."

··*Seventeen*··

BY THE LIGHT of the late-risen half moon, Merial made her way toward the Silver Palace. Ibrahim's police had dispersed the crowds, and silence, broken only by the mournful gonging of a nearby temple bell, lay over Baranpur's capital.

There was a rustling sound by the roadside, and a horse snorted. Merial's heart seemed to leap into her throat until she heard a low voice mutter, "Be still, pearls of my heart, be still, my lions. We must not be seen or heard by these evil men."

Both the voice and the Kumari dialect were familiar. Merial peered into the shadows and saw, between the trees that bordered the roadside, the unmistakable glint of cream-white horseflesh.

"Gopal Nath?" she queried.

After a moment's frightened silence, the groom's face peered out from behind a tree trunk. He had lost his turban, his face was scratched bloody, and he looked both terrified and angry.

"Mira-Bai!" he exclaimed. "By all the gods, I thought you'd been killed like poor Captain Rassul."

She'd known Rassul was dead, of course, but hearing the words said aloud made it worse. Silently Merial said farewell to the *bhaldar* who had always been her champion.

"I'm glad you got away, Gopal Nath," she managed to say around the lump in her throat.

"Those filth-eating hyenas, may they be reborn in torment, stole more than half of my beautiful darlings." The groom seemed ready to cry. "How can I face His Mightiness the raja and tell him I only managed to save ten of his horses?"

Behind Gopal Nath, shadowy forms tossed their head and snorted. Ten Kumari horses, Merial thought, and felt the stirrings of an idea.

Abruptly she announced, "I'm taking the horses with me, Gopal Nath!"

"What do you mean?" She told him, and the groom made the sign against the evil eye. "The gods forbid," he stammered. "You are going to take these horses to the Silver Palace *now?* But—but, Mira-Bai, those evil men will kill you and keep the horses, and I'll never be able to face the raja again."

"On the contrary, you'll be hailed as a hero for aiding Prince Rayn." Merial went up to the nearest horse and began to stroke its milky neck. "Daiyal-Raja will be the first to say you've acted wisely in giving me these horses." Gopal Nath still didn't look convinced, so she added, "If Baranpur falls to 'the evil men,' so will Kumar."

Muttering and shaking his head, the groom helped her mount one of the horses. "Kumari horses are unlike any other," he lectured. "On no account must you allow any unskilled groom to lay his hands on them." He swallowed hard, shut his eyes, and made the supreme sacrifice. "I—I will go with you to the Silver Palace, Mira-Bai."

But she was afraid that he might lose his nerve and give them both away. After instructing the groom to remain hidden, Merial urged her horses forward. Now her spirits lifted for the first time that night. There was still a chance that—

"Stop where you are."

Merial drew rein at once, and the well-trained horses stood waiting as several policemen, hard to spot in their olive and gray uniforms, approached her out of the darkness.

"There's a curfew in Rasgani," their officer said sternly. "I should order you shot."

"I didn't know about any curfew." Careful to keep her voice low, Merial threw in a Kumari accent for good measure. "I've come here by order of His Mightiness Daiyal-Raja of Kumar, who sent these horses as a gift to Khem-Rana."

One of the policemen whistled. "They're Kumari, all right. Worth a fortune, I'd say."

Taking heart from the awe in the man's voice, Merial continued, "It is Daiyal-Raja's express command that I deliver these horses to the Silver Palace."

"All right," the officer in charge said. "You can leave them with us."

Merial pretended horror and outrage. "Impossible! The raja will have my head if I don't deliver these priceless animals myself." The officer wavered, and she added with a confidence she didn't feel, "That is, unless you'll take responsibility for offending the ruler of Kumar."

The police officer stared so hard at Merial that she was sure he could see the color of her eyes in the darkness. Finally he snapped, "You two—Mulraj and Govind—fall out and escort this fellow to the palace. The palace guard will know what to do with him and his *precious* horses."

Inwardly quaking but outwardly self-possessed, Merial followed her escort. It was a short ride to the Sun Gate, where the policemen explained matters to the palace guards. An officer of the palace guards was summoned.

"I've never seen finer Kumari horses!" he exclaimed. "I myself will take charge of them."

Merial's heart sank. Rayn was still as far away as the moon, and the great, closed doors of the Silver Palace looked ominously like the jaws of a predator that had clamped shut about its prey. The courtyard was swarming with police and Panwa's men, and from what Merial could see, they greatly outnumbered the white-and-silver livery of the palace guard.

"I can't leave these precious horses without at least speaking to Prince Rayn," Merial protested. "It's the raja's order that I hand these horses to no one but him."

"That's impossible," the officer spluttered. "He's with the King of Kings and can't be disturbed by such a paltry matter."

It had worked before, so she tried it again. Feigning a boldness she was far from feeling, Merial planted her fists on her hips. "So, Captain, are you willing to take responsibility for insulting my master, the raja of Kumar?"

She watched conflicting emotions war in the officer's face before offering a compromise. "At least give him the message that a horse-boy has ridden all the way from Kumar. Then he can decide whether or not to accept the horses personally."

Glad to have found a way out of a ticklish situation, the officer ordered a guard to carry the message to the prince. "Meanwhile, you can take the horses to the stable," he added.

Merial's heart jolted all the way to the stables. Surely

Rayn would understand her message and come. Or he would come if Panwa hadn't already—

"You say that this Kumari horse-boy is alone?"

There was no mistaking that deep voice, and Merial almost wept with relief as the palace guard burst into apologies. "He says he comes in the name of the raja of Kumar. I told him you couldn't be disturbed, Highness, but he insisted."

Next moment Rayn strode into the stables. He went to Merial and, catching her by the shoulders, looked anxiously into her face. "What's happened? Where's Rassul?"

"Dead." She was so grateful that he was unharmed, so thankful for the hard clasp of his hands on her shoulders, that she was barely coherent. "Rassul was murdered by thugs who control the Bagh Mahal. You're betrayed, Rayn—really betrayed. It's Panwa who controls the thugs—"

His grip tightened. "What are you saying?"

As she told him, all the tangled threads of past events fell into place for Rayn. He'd trusted Panwa too much to suspect him before, but now he could see clearly. It had been Panwa who'd taken Mira home that night of the storm, Panwa who'd led her into the thugs' ambush. Later it had been Panwa who'd brought news that Ashland had been arrested, Panwa who'd deliberately given Mira his ring so that she'd try and rescue her father.

"He used the thugs to draw Fanji and my *bhaldars* away from Rasgani." Rayn gritted the words through his teeth. "And tonight he supported my decision to send the army to the Afghan border. Oh, *shabash,* Minister. Well done, indeed."

Merial was tugging at his arm. "You must get out of here, now."

"I can't leave my father."

That was true enough, but how could he protect the ailing rana? The only forces that remained loyal were the palace guard—and the guard was far outnumbered by the combined forces of Ibrahim's and Panwa's armed men.

"Rayn, *please!*"

At least he could get Mira out of here before all hell broke loose. "Go back to the flower seller's house," Rayn commanded. "Remain there until I come for you. I'll send someone with you, who—"

He broke off as a step sounded outside. "Are you there, my prince?" Panwa's voice drawled.

A moment later the minister sauntered into the stable. Merial felt his eyes flick over her disinterestedly before he turned to Rayn. "I was told you'd gone to the stables. Is there trouble, Highness?"

"No trouble. Daiyal-Raja sent some Kumari horses to cheer my father, and I'm accepting delivery." Rayn moved casually toward Panwa as he added, "Have you ever seen such magnificent horseflesh?"

Panwa appeared shocked. "This is no time to talk of horses, Highness. You must return to your father's side."

"First I'm going to escort this horse-boy to the Sun Gate. After bringing me these beauties, he deserves that much courtesy."

"One of my men will do it." Panwa turned to walk toward the stable door, then stopped short as Rayn's sword-point dug into his back.

"Kill him," Merial urged. "Kill him now."

At the sound of her voice, Panwa whipped around. His eyes widened, and his face twisted in astonished fury. "Shaitan! What's *she* doing here?"

"Mira has brought me some interesting news from the Bagh Mahal." Rayn caught Panwa by the throat of his jeweled tunic, lifting him several inches off the floor. "If you've hurt my aunt, I'll kill you myself."

Panwa showed his white teeth. "She's no aunt of yours —*Prince.*"

All traces of the polished, languid aristocrat had disappeared. He spat out a virulent obscenity and sneered, "Shield of the Kingdom, they call you—you who are nothing but a nobody from nowhere. You think you're going to rule Baranpur, but you won't. You'll be dead— you and your precious foster father—and Ibrahim and I will be in control."

Rayn's eyes were like flint. "And Perce?"

Panwa's eyes blazed with contempt. "As soon as he explodes his bridge, his usefulness ends. The thugs will kill him for us, and then I will help Colonel Malcolm destroy the thugs. Thus with the *Angrezi*'s blessing, I will ascend the Silver Throne."

"Someone's coming," Merial warned as footsteps approached the stable.

Rayn dragged Panwa back into the shadows. "If you say one wrong word, you'll die. Mira, look after the horses."

Merial pretended to groom the Kumari steeds as the stable doors opened and a man came in. "The missing Kumari horses, by the gods!" a hoarse voice exclaimed. "*Angrezi* bitch, I've found you at last!"

Yuir Singh's pistol was hardly drawn before Rayn ran him through. But in that fragment of time Panwa twisted away. Rayn lunged after him, but he wasn't quite swift enough. He stopped as he saw the tiny, razor-sharp throwing dagger that Panwa was pressing against Merial's throat.

"Do you value her life, Prince?" Panwa taunted.

"Let her go," Rayn snarled, "or I'll make you pray for death."

Panwa's lips curled back over his teeth. "Who are you to give me orders? *My* blood connects me to the House of Raoshad. My father was Bhupinder Puar. Do you think I'd let you rule Baranpur—you and your *Angrezi* whore?"

Rayn felt nausea crawling through his veins. "Let her go," he urged. "Mira has nothing to do with this—it's between you and me."

"On the contrary, your woman and I have unfinished business. After you're dead and rotting, I may enjoy her before giving her to Ibrahim." Panwa began to drag Merial backward toward the stable door, adding, "I'm going to call my men, and if you so much as move, your Mira will die. You might as well face it, my baseborn friend. You've lost."

Merial saw the truth of this in Rayn's eyes. Once again he was powerless because of her. But this time the stakes were the kingdom and the people of Baranpur. Heedless of the dagger-point at her throat, she urged, "Stop him, Rayn. He mustn't rule Baranpur."

"Be silent, bitch." Merial could feel the heat of Panwa's breath against her cheek but continued desperately, "He'll kill us both anyway. Stop him while you have a chance. It doesn't matter about me. Ah—"

She gave an involuntary gasp as Panwa's knife dug into her skin, and watching the bright blood on her white throat, Rayn went beyond rage to icy calm. He knew without doubt that Panwa meant to kill both him and Mira. He knew that if he killed Panwa now and marshaled the loyal palace guards, he'd have a chance, but that once Panwa alerted his men and the police, even that fragile hope was gone.

He looked deep into Merial's eyes. *Do it,* those turquoise

eyes urged him. *Don't think of me. Think what Panwa and Ibrahim will do to Baranpur.*

He knew that she was right, but he couldn't bear to stand there and watch her die. His nostrils flared in a deep breath as he spoke quietly.

"You unspeakable filth, it's me you want. Let her go and I'll do whatever you say."

As though his words were some kind of signal, there was a shout outside the Sun Gate. "What in Iblis's name is going on?" Panwa swore. "I told that fool Ibrahim to disperse the crowd."

He was interrupted by another shout, louder than the first. "Open the gates!" Fanji was bellowing. "Open it in the prince's name!"

Panwa jerked his head around. "Impossible. He's away in the—"

His words ended in a gurgle as Rayn sprang across the stable, knocking Merial aside and catching Panwa by the throat. The minister tried desperately to stab his enemy, but his dagger was shaken loose.

"I should kill you now," Rayn snarled, "but I need you alive—*friend.*"

There was a confused sound of shouting, and then the crack of rifles. "Lord! Where are you?" Fanji was yelling.

Merial ran to the stable door and flung it open. "Over here!"

Flinging the half-conscious Panwa aside, Rayn grasped Merial by the waist and hauled her back. As he did so, Panwa's men and squadrons of police opened fire on the *bhaldars.* Through this hail of bullets, Rayn's lancers rode up to the stable.

Fanji tumbled out of the saddle and ran to Rayn. He grasped his prince by the arms as if making sure he was still alive, meanwhile stammering, "Thank the gods you're not hurt, lord. We rode like sons of Shaitan himself, but we thought we mightn't be in time."

Panwa snarled, "You'll all die anyway. My men are everywhere in the courtyard and so are the police. You're outnumbered, and Jaga is still far away."

Ignoring him, Rayn said, "Fanji, I'm taking your horse. Watch over Mira. Ghazni, take charge of our honored minister. The rest with me."

He swung up on Fanji's horse and spurred out into the courtyard. The lancers followed him and one of them shouted, "There he is!"

Ibrahim had appeared on the steps of the palace with a detachment of police at his heels. "Surrender!" he ordered.

Rayn laughed and rode his Kumari horse up the steps toward Ibrahim. Meanwhile, his *bhaldars* plunged amongst the police and Panwa's men. The confused palace guards were still assessing the situation when Merial heard Rayn's exultant shout.

"Surrender, hell!"

"They're outnumbered fifty to one," Merial groaned as a contingent of police, armed with rifles, surged out from the dungeon doorway.

"One *bhaldar*'s worth fifty of them any day," Fanji snorted. He was grinding his teeth with excitement and the frustration of having to miss the action, but he now paused to brag. "It's a good thing I captured one of those thugs up in the north. After some persuasion, he told us all about Panwa's treachery."

Merial scarcely heard him. Her attention was riveted on the unequal battle that seethed through the courtyard, up the palace steps, and up to the still-closed silver doors. As loyal palace guardsmen fell before the disciplined *crack* of rifles, she could see Rayn fighting in what seemed to be a sea of enemies. The *bhaldars* were battling overwhelming odds, and Fanji roared his frustration.

"By the balls of Ravanna, I want to fight, too!"

Just then another sound rose over the clamor of battle. A deep-throated roar from beyond the gates demanded, "The prince—the prince! We demand to see that the prince is safe!"

Hundreds of people—thousands—were at the gate. Fanji grinned. "Will you look at that!"

People—the people that Ibrahim's police had whipped and clubbed a few short hours ago—Rayn's people—were pouring through the ruined Sun Gate. Heedless of the shots fired at them, they surged into the courtyard, and, wielding hoes and rakes, old muskets, steel-rimmed staves and boat poles, they went after Ibrahim's police.

A howl of triumph rose as Rayn's powerful form was seen amongst the fighting, and Merial saw the little flower seller, Ahmed, in the forefront. "There's our prince. Let's help him, brothers!"

But Ibrahim's men and Panwa's followers were too disciplined to give way. Rifles cracked, and the vanguard of the people's army went down. As more scantily armed figures dropped to the ground, Merial heard a new sound. She grasped Big Fanji's arm. "I hear trumpets!"

The giant gave an exultant yell and, hugging her, lifted her high in the air. "It's the army! Jaga's on his way."

After that the battle ended swiftly. Ibrahim's and Panwa's men surrendered, while tattered remnants were chased down by both the army and the citizens of Rasgani. Within the hour the courtyard was full of prisoners guarded by grim palace guardsmen, and Ibrahim and Panwa were dragged forward to kneel before Rayn.

They were filthy with blood and grime, but they glared

at Rayn, who decreed, "Take them away. They'll be tried for their crimes and sentenced."

Fanji didn't like that. "With respect, lord, they're responsible for Rassul's death. Give them to us."

A growl of agreement rose from the *bhaldars,* and General Jaga suggested. "The royal elephant should crush their heads immediately. Thus justice would be served."

"By Shaitan, I will not die a dog's death!"

Panwa's turban had been lost, and his face was ghastly gray. There was nothing left of the aristocrat who had almost become the next ruler of Baranpur. Yet his eyes met Rayn's squarely as he said, "We are both men, and men vie for power. I took a gamble and lost. Remember that we were friends once."

"I also remember that you threatened my aunt's life—and the life of the woman I love," Rayn reminded him sternly.

Almost in tears Fanji pleaded, "Lord, *please* let us have the bastard."

Panwa kept his eyes on Rayn. "Meet me sword to sword, Prince."

Merial cried, "No!" and General Jaga shook his head. "Why should the prince risk his life battling with a condemned criminal?"

Panwa raised his voice. "Hear me, all of you. I am connected by marriage to the house of Raoshad and am entitled to die with a sword in my hand." He twisted his head to look around him. "Isn't that the law?"

No one would meet his eyes. "You're finished, Panwa," Rayn said.

Panwa insisted, "It is my right. Tell him, General."

General Jaga shifted uneasily but had to say, "It's true that anyone with royal blood can demand to die fighting. But you'll not fight the prince." His mustaches bristled as he added, "By the gods, I myself will meet this criminal in combat."

Panwa interrupted, "Has the great Tiger of Baranpur lost his teeth that he has to hide behind his generals? Perhaps it's because he has no royal blood that he is afraid."

Rayn recognized that Panwa had created a problem. If he didn't accept his challenge, there would be whispered rumors. Malcontents could point to the fact that Prince Rayn hadn't dared to meet Panwa Puar face to face. Such talk could erode confidence in his future rule.

But that wasn't the only reason. Rayn could still see the well of Mira's blood on her white throat. The urge to kill Panwa roughened his voice as he snarled, "Give him a sword and clear the way."

He unsheathed his tulwar as he spoke. Light glittered on the curved blade as he advanced to the center of the courtyard. Grasping a borrowed sword, Panwa did likewise, and the two men met face to face.

"Watch yourself, Tiger of Baranpur," Panwa taunted, "or I'll have your hide."

Rayn said nothing. Watching the man she loved, Merial saw that his face seemed older, almost gaunt as mind and body coalesced into one concentrated effort. The stink of blood and gunpowder seemed to intensify, filling her nostrils until she felt physically ill.

Panwa and Rayn began to circle each other. The courtyard had become deathly silent, and only the scuff of boots on the cobblestones could be heard. Then, suddenly, Rayn lunged forward and the clash of steel against steel broke the silence.

Panwa was a skilled and strong swordsman, but he was no match for Rayn's skill and ferocity that drove his opponent back, step by step.

Parry, feint, and lunge—and Panwa broke the silence

to taunt, "Can you feel the royal cushions under your backside? You who don't have a drop of the rana's blood in your veins?"

Rayn's sword sliced through his shoulder, and Panwa cried out and went deathly pale. Even then he panted, "Gutter rat, what honor will you bring to the Silver Throne?"

Each word that Panwa said was calculated poison; Rayn knew he needed to end it quickly. He feinted, lunged under Panwa's guard, and the former minister yelled as his sword was knocked from hand.

There was a shout from the onlookers, and Fanji hammered his huge fists on his thighs. "*Maro*—kill him, lord!"

Suddenly Panwa's hand snaked to his boot.

"A knife—he's got a knife—"

Almost before the words could leave Merial's lips, Panwa rushed toward Rayn, yelling, "You'll never wear the crown!"

His shout became a howl of agony as Rayn parried the blow, grasped Panwa's arm, and twisted it, causing the knife to graze Panwa's own chest.

Panwa slumped gasping and choking to the cobblestones. Fanji stepped forward, squatted down beside the dying man, and examined the knife that Rayn had dropped.

"*Zahr*—poison!" he exclaimed. "The dog dipped his weapon in venom."

Panwa's eyes had begun to glaze. His face worked with agony. Even so he managed to gasp, "You are finished, too, Shield of the Kingdom. You'll never live to enjoy—"

His voice ebbed away, and General Jaga drew a deep breath. "It's over."

But that wasn't true, Rayn knew. Panwa had poisoned

more than his blade, and that virulence could still destroy Baranpur.

The sun was rising as Deen and Big Fanji and two other lancers escorted Merial to the liberated Bagh Mahal. The old *jamadar,* Ahmed the flower seller, who'd been wounded in arm and chest, and many others fell in behind them, so that their progress through the main street was like a triumphant march. Everywhere they went, Rayn's name was being shouted, and several voices called Merial's name as well.

Big Fanji rolled his eyes. "The people love you, girl."

The *jamadar,* who looked ten years younger and whose narrow chest was swollen with importance, made answer. "She is a courageous woman. She went to warn Prince Rayn while I hurried to General Jaga. The general received me as soon as he knew I carried the prince's amulet. 'Ram Gunga,' he said to me, 'the country will never forget that you risked your life in the prince's cause.' "

Rukmiri-Bai, regal in a gold-edged sari and still quivering with the insult of being held prisoner in her own home, met Merial at the gate of the Bagh Mahal. "My dear, your throat!" she cried in horror. *"Hai-mai,* but the wound must be tended to at once."

She called for Geeta and began issuing orders. In the midst of this familiar and friendly tumult, Merial sank down into a chair and fell asleep.

When she awoke, she was in her own bed. She had a dim recollection of Geeta and Rukmiri-Bai bathing her and putting her to bed. Now the sun was low in the sky, and from a nearby mosque a *muezzin* was calling the faithful to prayer. How long had she been asleep?

"You've slept through the day." Merial turned quickly to see Rayn standing by the window. With a glad cry, she jumped out of bed and ran to him, pressing herself against him.

"How long have you been here—why didn't you wake me?" she whispered between kisses.

"You needed your rest." She leaned back in his arms to look at him and saw that there were lines of weariness etched into his hard face.

"You haven't rested at all," she charged.

"There wasn't time," he admitted. "A council of the ministers just convened, and a new *kotwal* has been chosen. Rasgani is quiet now under martial law, but some of the thugs have gone underground and must be ferreted out. Panwa's poison may yet start a war."

She shuddered at his choice of words, and gently cupping her chin, he ran a fingertip along the bandage Rukmiri-Bai had fastened around her throat.

"War with the Afghans, you mean?" she questioned fearfully.

"That was no war, only trouble inflamed by Ibrahim's thugs. Deen managed to convince the Afghan leaders of this, and they joined forces in routing the thugs." He added, "I meant that Panwa sent messengers to Perce last night. Ibrahim confessed to as much."

Instinctively she knew that the possibility of Perce's blowing the bridge wasn't the only thing troubling him. "How is the rana?" she asked.

"He's unconscious and Baju says that it's only a matter of time." He took his arms away from her and went to stand by the stone-latticed window as he added, "He's a harsh man, but in his way he cared for me, and we both love Baranpur."

She ran to him and kissed his mouth and his chin and the hard line of his jaw. "Come to bed, now, beloved. You need to rest." He shook his head, and she saw for the first time that he was dressed for travel. "Surely you're not thinking of riding to the border now?"

He nodded. "I must join my lancers."

But she protested this. "Not until you've rested."

When Rayn looked at her, rest wasn't what came to his mind. Through the thin transparency of her nightdress, the late sun tinted her nipples to darker coral, splashed gold over the creamy satin of her breasts and stomach and the tantalyzing dark shadow between her thighs. A wave of desire mixed with tenderness hit him like a physical blow.

With some difficulty he said, "I have to go, Mira."

"Stay," she whispered.

He was lost. In unthinking response he crushed her against him, imprinting her softness against his hardness. Their lips met in a kiss that dissolved physical boundaries. They breathed with each other's breath, their tongues tasted the secret recesses of each other's mouths. Like shipwrecked sailors who'd languished without food or drink for days, they supped greedily from each other's lips until they felt drunk with the sweet wine.

Rayn knew that no human force could tear him away from the soft arms that held him. As his hands caressed Mira, he felt the heat of her love seep into his blood and bones. He trembled with hunger for her.

She felt the tremor in his great arms as she slipped her hands under his loose tunic and caressed his back. Her fingers, feather-light, traced old scars and the bruises of today's battle. Then, working loose the buckle of his belt, she pushed down his jodhpurs so that she could cup his hardness in her hand.

Unfettered by clothing, they sank down on the bed together, but when he would have drawn her under him, she rolled away from him and knelt astride him. Bending, she kissed his throat and flat male nipples, the hardness of his belly, then roved lower to savor his manhood with lips and tongue.

"Are you an houri from paradise or a demon sent to torment me?" Rayn's laugh was unsteady. Tremors of longing racked him as he felt the flick of her moist tongue against his heat.

"I am your woman—the Tiger's woman." Her voice had a fierce pride in it, a joy that negated all the ugliness of what had gone before. Again she teased him, her tongue laving and stroking, her mouth cradling him.

"Enough." Rayn drew her down beside him, calling her every name of love he could think of as he kissed her mouth and drew the honey from her breasts.

He knew exactly how to please her now. Merial felt her body expand under his expert caresses, yet even in the mind-drugging ecstasy that enveloped her, she sensed that today's lovemaking was different from all others. Today they were coming together not only with desire and tenderness but also with wonder. It was a miracle that they were here, that in spite of everything, they were together.

Every kiss was a loveword, each caress a poem from Rayn's heart. His Mira was fragrant with roses and sandalwood, her nipples were cool against his tongue, the sweet taste of her belly and thighs were familiar and yet new and wonderful. Rayn felt that he could love her a hundred times and possess her—be possessed—anew each time.

In his silent adoration she felt a strength grow in her. She felt invincible. Nothing and no one could hurt or separate them. Merial's universe contracted, coalesced into a pulsating golden world that held only Rayn—his scent, the way his dark hair curled at the nape of his neck, the taste of his skin, the hard insistence of his passion.

With an inarticulate cry, she opened her thighs to him and with them her heart, her soul. He sank deep into her honeyed fire.

"Promise me"—she was trembling under him as she panted the words—"promise me we'll never be apart again."

They began to move together, but even the ancient rhythm was different today. It was a promise, a vow more solemn than marriage.

"Never again, Mira."

His mouth covered hers, drawing her soul from her body into his, giving her his own heart and spirit in return, as they burst into a single flame.

·· *Eighteen* ··

WHILE RAYN WAS dressing for travel, a summons came from the Silver Palace that the rana was conscious and wished to speak to his son. The messenger added that the King of Kings also commanded the presence of the *Angrezi*, Mira.

Merial was apprehensive, and Rayn tried to reassure her. "After yesterday, anyone in the city who is not blind, deaf, or senile knows your name. They revere you as the brave woman who helped defeat Ibrahim and Panwa."

This was attested to by the cheers that followed them as they rode to the palace, where workmen were repairing the damage to the Sun Gate, and servants were scrubbing the grime and blood from the courtyard. Many of the palace guards wore bandages like badges of honor, and they saluted smartly as their prince trotted by on his stallion.

Merial's apprehension rose as Rayn helped her dismount from her palanquin. "What is it?" he asked.

She didn't know how to explain that she felt alien and somehow unacceptable, so she simply shook her head. "It's nothing."

"Don't be afraid of the rana." He held her for a moment and then let her go. "He's just a very sick old man."

But the rana's power was still very apparent inside the palace. The atmosphere held the still, charged quality that comes before an electrical storm, and servants had been enjoined on pain of death not to speak or make any sound that could offend the ear of the dying monarch.

Silent courtiers and senior military officers crowded the outer corridor, and inside the Hall of Audience Baranpur's ministers and generals stood in silent vigil on either side of the empty throne. Heavily armed guards barred the way to the stairs that led up to the rana's private quarters, and as Merial followed Rayn up the stairs, she noted that one fierce-looking guard was standing at attention with tears streaming down his cheeks.

The rana's door was also heavily guarded. At a sign from Rayn, these guards swung open the great carved doors disclosing a sickroom that was like none Merial had ever seen. Carpets of finest Persian wool covered the marble floor. The walls were hung with priceless tapestries and with ivory and sandalwood panels. The court painter had covered the ceiling with jewel-studded figures of the gods and scenes of battle in which Khem-Rana figured as the victor. The windows were stained glass, and the largest of them bore the golden emblem of the sun.

In the middle of the room was a bed of ivory and gold, and there, attended by Baju and the court physicians, lay the rana. Canopied with cloth of gold encrusted with diamonds, pearls, and rubies, the King of Kings looked small and shrunken, and his gray hair hung lankly around his pallid face. There was a pinched look about the royal nostrils, and his fierce eyes were closed.

As Rayn went to kneel beside the bed, Baju, looking

almost as gaunt as the rana, whispered, "Be careful, Highness. He is sleeping."

"You sent word that he wanted to see me," Rayn replied in the same low tone.

The court physician began to speak, but Rayn waved him silent, and it was Baju who answered gravely, "The King of Kings is 'seeking the forest' for his soul's salvation."

This was a Hindu euphemism for one who was a step away from death. But just then the rana's eyes fluttered open, and in that death-pale face the eyes above the proud beak of a nose were alive and full of intelligence.

"My son," he gasped. "I'm told that as soon as I became ill, the kingdom was plunged into ferment and that Panwa and Ibrahim tried to seize power. Is it true?"

"True, Majesty." Rayn knelt to kiss the rana's hand as he added, "But it is also true that Panwa Puar is dead, that the former *kotwal* awaits execution, and that Baranpur is at peace for the moment."

He explained succinctly, without softening any of the dangers that faced the country. The rana's fierce eyes demanded complete honesty. "When will you march against this dog Perce?" he demanded.

"The army and cavalry are ready to march on my order, but that must be a last resort. War is what Perce wants." The rana frowned as Rayn added, "We can destroy the Sri Nevi garrison, but we won't be able to hold out for long if England declares war on us. My lancers and I will take care of Perce personally."

"Bring me his head. I wish to feast my eyes on that pleasant sight before I leave this life." Intolerant, hooded eyes swung toward Merial. "But now, there is another matter. What is this runaway slave doing back in Baranpur?"

Merial had knelt beside Rayn. She kept her head bowed as he replied, "She came because of love for me. It was she who first discovered Panwa's treachery and who recalled General Jaga. She also roused the people against Ibrahim and Panwa."

Impatiently the rana flicked his hand. "I have heard all of that. Remember our law, my son, that commands us to beat an escaped slave to death. I'll spare her life for the so-called service she did you, but she must leave Baranpur at once before I repent my generosity. By the gods, I'll have her slain if I see her face again."

"Mira is going nowhere, Majesty. She remains here with me as my wife."

As Rayn hurled this thunderbolt, Merial gasped aloud. Under the folds of her sari, she could feel Rayn's hand gripping hers, and the silent pressure was reassuring. Not so the rana's fury. His eyes blazed in his death-mask of a face, and he half rose to a sitting position.

"You are demented. I'll never give you permission to marry an *Angrezi.*"

Rayn got to his feet. Dark eyes locked with golden ones as he said bluntly, "I will marry her with or without your permission, Majesty."

Purple spots rose into the rana's cheeks. Like a malignant bird of prey he screeched, "I'll have your head for that!"

He sank down, panting, onto his pillows. Rayn said nothing as his foster father grated, "To marry an *Angrezi* is to marry an outcaste. Would you break your caste and descend into hell?"

"There were marriages between our people in the past," Rayn shot back. "Great men have sprung from unions between noble *Angrezi* and the best of our people."

"You would defile your line with impure blood. Do you think Baranpur will follow an outcaste prince?"

"Our people know I'd never abuse their trust. They'd follow me anywhere," Rayn retorted. "As for Mira, they love her and respect her for the brave and lovely lady that she is."

Reaching down, he raised Merial to her feet. Holding her eyes with his own, he spoke as though no one else were in the room. "I know that it is the custom in your country for a man to ask the lady of his heart to be his wife. In Baranpur there'd be lengthy negotiations between our families and a haggling for your bride price. But we do not need any of this meaningless ritual."

Her eyes filled with tears. "Rayn, it's not necessary—"

"I love you, Mira," he interrupted. "Will you be my wife?"

Once again the rana struggled to lift himself to a sitting position. "If you persist in this unforgivable behavior, you'll forfeit the crown of Baranpur. I've raised you up as my heir, and I can cast you down again."

Before the full impact of what the rana was saying reached Merial, Rayn spoke. "I will die defending you. In everything but this, my sword is at your feet." His voice deepened with emotion as he continued, "I've always worked for Baranpur's good, and when Ibrahim gave you evil counsel, I incurred your wrath by speaking against him. I will not lie to you now. If marriage to Mira means that I must renounce the Silver Throne, so be it."

"Rayn, you must not do this!" But the two men ignored Merial's protest.

"Your mind is fixed?" the rana demanded harshly. "You're willing to lose your *izzat*—your respect and honor—because of an *Angrezi* woman?"

"It's she who honors me," Rayn replied.

"Then leave my presence," the rana snarled. "You've betrayed my trust in you."

His words trailed away, the fierce eyes closed. Baju bent over him anxiously and whispered, "He has exhausted his strength. You must leave, Highness."

Merial shot a look of agony at Rayn as they left out of the royal sickroom. "Go back to the rana—tell him you didn't mean what you said." When Rayn didn't respond, she grasped his arms and tried to shake him. "Why do you want to throw away all you've worked for?"

Instead of answering, he looked searchingly into her eyes. "You didn't answer me back there. Will you marry me?"

She cried, "Is it necessary to ask me that? But as you said, rituals and formalities aren't necessary between us I love you and will be yours forever."

He took her hand from his arm and raised it to his li "I meant what I said last night. I don't intend to lose you.

"But you love this country," she protested. "Think what you are giving up!"

"I'm giving nothing up." He smiled down at her, adding, "Crown or no crown, I intend to serve Baranpur. I was a general in the rana's army once. I'll be one again."

Before she could respond to this, a man came striding up the stairs. He whispered to the challenging guards, who let him pass. Merial recognized one of Rayn's lancers, and Rayn descended swiftly to meet the *bhaldar*.

"Report," he ordered.

"News from Sri Nevi, lord. Chetak has captured one of Panwa's messengers, and the son of Iblis taunted us saying that Perce knows what has happened here in Rasgani. Captain Deen has been advised of this and will join us on the Sri Nevi border."

"There's one thing left to try," Rayn said. "I'll ride for the border at once."

He raced down the stairs, Merial at his heels. "What is your plan?"

"To warn the garrison troops." Rayn's laugh was a harsh bark of sound. "I hope Colonel Malcolm appreciates the irony of their arch enemy warning them against one of their own."

"I'm going with you," Merial said.

"Impossible—" But she faced him squarely.

"Surely I've earned the right to be at your side."

"Do you think this is a game?" he snapped. "We'll ride hard and fast. We must reach Perce before he explodes that bridge." As she swept resolutely down the stairs with him, he added, "I forbid it, Mira."

"If you truly want me for your wife, you must know that I won't submit meekly to your orders. I can't give you blind obedience, Rayn." He glared at her, and she cried, "I'm English, remember? Colonel Malcolm will never listen to you, but there's a chance he'll listen to me."

Rayn registered the truth of what she said even when he wanted to deny it. Reading his indecision rightly, Merial urged, "It's for the safety of Baranpur."

Both of them knew this was true. "Very well," Rayn said sternly. "But you must swear to obey me unquestioningly. I want your sacred oath on that, or by the gods I'll tie you up and put a guard on you."

A Kumari mare was saddled and male clothes found so that Merial could travel more comfortably. Thus dressed, she rode behind Rayn and the lancer who had brought the news. As they galloped out of Baranpur, shouts of acclaim followed the prince. Each salute seemed an added reproach to Merial. Whether Rayn was successful in stopping Perce or not, because of her he might never rule the people he loved.

Once they were outside the city limits and away from prying eyes and ears, Rayn broke a long silence by saying, "Mira, you know, of course, that Perce isn't in this alone. Your father is his accomplice."

In spite of the sudden ache in her heart, she met his gaze steadfastly. "I've chosen my allegiance, Rayn."

His lips quirked into the smile she remembered. "It seems that we are both outcasts." He reached out a hand to her, and she took it, welcoming the strong, decisive clasp. She felt absurdly happy. No matter what danger awaited them, they'd face it together.

Her buoyant mood wasn't dampened by the killing pace Rayn set. Stopping only to water their horses, they rode through the night, never slackening their pace as the dawn broke. There, at a point near the border, Deen and many other *bhaldars* r ps. em.

The young cap oked unusually grim. "Chetak reports that so far the explosive charges haven't been placed, lord. As yet, Perce hasn't made a move."

His words trailed off into surprise as he realized that Merial had accompanied their prince. Merial was too weary to even smile in response to the bow he gave her. She was grateful when Rayn ordered a brief rest.

She leaned into his arms as he helped her dismount and heard him swear under his breath. "I must have been mad to let you come."

"You didn't have a choice," she reminded him.

He held her close to him and complained, "Gods above, what a shrew I'm marrying."

"The Tiger can't have a weakling for a mate," she retorted.

Deen, overhearing these words, approved. He and the

other *bhaldars* agreed as they watered their horses that here was a woman that was worthy even of their lord. She could ride like a *bhaldar*, she was as loyal and brave as she was lovely, and she'd proven herself a mistress of state-craft. When they took to horse again, Merial saw in their eyes a reflection of the adoration they had hitherto reserved only for their prince.

"My men have shifted allegiances," Rayn commented. "They've placed their swords at your feet."

In a few hours they'd reached Baranpur's northwest border. The cut trees left the countryside looking scarred and naked, leaving little cover. The Tiger's men seemed able to blend into the scenery, but they went more carefully now, riding through a countryside that was littered with refuse left by Perce's workers. Careless cooking fires had left charred gashes in the green slopes and meadows, and trees had been hacked down for kindling. Rayn's eyes smoldered as he surveyed the damage. "Perce has a lot to answer for."

They crossed a stream, muddied and soiled with rubbish, and took cover in a thick copse of trees that overlooked tents clustered on the riverbank and workers toiling on the bridge itself. Here Chetak and the remainder of the *bhaldars* were keeping watch.

"Ashok and Chander are down there working on the bridge," Chetak reported. "Lord, there's a different feeling in the camp today—hard to explain, but definitely there."

"Then the charges will be placed tonight." Rayn dismounted and held out his arms to help Merial down. "Best rest while we can."

Merial admired the discipline of Rayn's lancers, who watered and fed their horses, posted guards, then lay down on the hard ground and calmly went to sleep. Rayn spread a blanket some distance from the others. "Come and rest, sweetheart."

Exhausted, she fell asleep with her cheek pillowed against his chest. The even sound of his breathing, the strong, steady beat of his heart, lulled her to rest. But when she awoke, he was gone. She sat up to look for him and saw him talking to his officers and two muddy, half-naked men.

"The explosives have been placed, lord," one of them was saying. "Chander and I saw this, but we could not remove the charges in daylight."

Nodding, Rayn glanced up at the sky. "It's half an hour to sunset. There are sentries patrolling the bridge at all times and more near the camp, so we'll split our forces."

The other *bhaldars* assembled to receive their orders, but first Rayn nodded to Deen. "You're to stay here and guard Mira. If I'm killed, get her to Kumar."

Looking unusually grim, Deen promised, "Lord, my life for hers."

Over the heads of his hard-faced lancers, Rayn's eyes met Merial's, but there was no time for words. Merial could only wait and watch as Rayn divided his *bhaldars* and explained his strategy.

Silently she waited while the sky filled with sunset colors. Bands of scarlet and gold gave way to shades of lavender, salmon pink, then the sun sank and the swift Indian night fell.

She'd sworn to obey him in this, and she would not by word or gesture show her fear for him. But as Rayn mustered his men, Merial couldn't help whispering, "My love, be careful. Come back to me safely."

He didn't hear her, of course. Merial stood close to Deen feeling nervous and frustrated as the shadowy forms of the *bhaldars* followed Rayn across the now dark plain. "God grant the sons of dogs don't hear," Deen muttered.

Merial kept her eyes on the shadows until they melded with the darker shades of night. Though she could make out the figures of the sentries patrolling the uncompleted bridge, no challenge came out of the darkness. Suddenly a dark form slid up over the bridge and caught one of the sentries by the throat. The man crumpled to the ground and was lowered into the river.

Deen's teeth flashed in an approving grin. "A very neat piece of work."

Other sentries were being disposed of. Merial wanted to turn away, but a horrible fascination held her transfixed. She couldn't take her eyes away as one after another, the dead sentries were lowered into the river.

"It's terrible," she whispered.

Deen shrugged philosophically. "It's war. Those who are slain only wait to be reborn. And as deaths go, it's a mercifully quick way to go."

Unlike the death Perce had planned for Rayn—or the torments Ibrahim and Panwa would have inflicted on their prince. Sickened by the greed that drove human beings to plot against and to murder their own kind, Merial had started to turn away when she heard the sound of voices.

Deen caught her by the arm, but she shook him off. "They're speaking English. I must hear what they're saying. We must go closer."

The young captain hesitated, and Merial whispered, "It was for this I came with the prince." She added, "There seem to be only two of them. There won't be any danger if we go softly."

"All right." Deen drew his knife and held it ready. "Follow me."

Stealthily they crept through the trees. On the outskirts of the woods stood two shadowy figures smoking cigars. Their cigars glowed like fiery eyes for a moment, and then one of them said, "A pity, after all that work, to destroy the bridge."

Merial's flesh crawled as she recognized Perce's voice. And she nearly cried out as a familiar voice replied, "You're sure it's the only way?"

She couldn't believe that her father had become embroiled in this filthy plan, also. Merial held her hands tight over her trembling mouth as Perce chuckled.

"The only way, no. The most expedient, yes. Even you should see that this will finish the Tiger once and for all. Besides, I must cover my tracks."

There was so much vindictiveness in his voice that Deen's knife-hand twitched. "Does that son of a jackal dare to speak ill of the prince?"

Merial held up a hand enjoining silence as Perce went on. "I know your daughter ran off with the Tiger, Ashland. It must make you want to get your hands on the scum—eh? Ironical, isn't it, that after everything Narayn of Baranpur's done to stop the railroad, the railroad will be the cause of his destruction? And he won't have anything to do with it."

Sir Edward spoke the question that was burning in Merial's mind. "When will it be?"

Instead of responding, Perce said, "I've left my matches in my tent. Go and get them for me." Sir Edward stiffened, and Perce jeered, "Still giving yourself grand airs, are you, honorable hero of the Gujjar Pass?"

"Oh, God—" The words were said in a low, sick tone, and Merial felt her hardened heart suddenly begin to bleed. "Why do you keep throwing that up in my face?"

As if the other man hadn't spoken, Perce continued,

"Originally I'd intended to blow up the bridge during the completion ceremonies. Colonel Malcolm and half the garrison would have been there to see the show." She was sure that he was smiling as he continued, "It would have created an uproar in all the English papers—so many dead, so much destroyed. But even now the dynamite will give one hell of a blast. Go and get the matches for me, there's a good fellow, and tell Gunga Dass to light the lamps."

Slowly, as though robbed of every ounce of will, Sir Edward turned to obey. As his bowed figure walked down the hill, Perce laughed softly and sucked on his cigar. "Bloody weak fool," he said.

The words died in a croak as Deen caught him around the throat and dragged him into the trees. "Don't kill him," Merial warned. In English she demanded, "When are you going to explode the bridge?"

Perce's eyes had widened at the sight of her. "I don't know what you mean," he rasped.

"I'll make him talk once we get him someplace where his screams won't be heard." Deen swiftly bound and gagged Perce, then searched his pockets and handed a pistol to Merial. "Now we'll see."

But Merial was shaking her head. "The prince must be told that we've captured Perce. Go quickly."

Deen was undecided. "I do not wish to leave you alone with this offal," he demured.

"He's bound and gagged and I have this." Merial held the pistol to Perce's head. "Tell Rayn—"

She was interrupted by an explosion that knocked her to the ground. It was as if a thousand thunderclaps had been rolled into one. "Rayn!" Merial screamed.

With an oath, Deen sprang away into the darkness, and

Merial rounded on Perce. "If Rayn is dead," she vowed, "I will kill you."

He glared at her triumphantly, and with a sick kind of finality, Merial realized that Rayn had lost. War was now inevitable—war that would destroy the valley kingdom. She'd never hurt anyone in her life, but now her finger itched to squeeze the trigger and send Perce to the hell he deserved.

"But I won't kill you," she told him. "I'll leave that to Rayn."

If Rayn was alive—if his *bhaldars* had survived—Merial tried for a bracing breath and drew in the acrid stink of gunpowder and smoke. The wind carried terrible sounds to her—agonized screams and terrified shouts and curses. Rayn, she prayed, be alive.

There was a rustle in the underbrush, and his voice spoke out of the darkness. "Easy, Mira."

She turned with a glad cry that changed to a gasp of horror as she saw him. He was black with gunpowder and covered with blood, his hair had been singed, his wet clothes clung to his powerful frame like a second skin. When he saw Perce, his eyes blazed with the need to kill.

"You're hurt—" she cried, but he didn't hear her.

"You swine," he said to Perce, "you filthy swine."

The gagged man's eyes narrowed as Rayn continued, "We didn't have time to remove all your charges. Five of my lancers lie dead in the river along with hundreds of your railroad workers. The tents by the river are in flames, and most of the people who lived there have been killed."

Smoke and the acrid scent of scorched flesh wafted toward them, together with the sounds of pain and terror. When Rayn reached out, Merial thought he was going to strangle Perce, but he only tore the gag from the commissioner of railroad's mouth.

Perce spat, "I assume you're going to kill me, but you won't get away with this. The garrison will be after you for this terrible crime."

"No, because you're going to tell them the truth." Rayn grasped the still-bound Perce by the throat and lifted him up to eye-level. "You're going to sign a confession for Colonel Malcolm."

"Don't move, or I'll shoot you!"

Sir Edward was standing a few feet away. In his trembling hand he held a rifle aimed at Rayn's chest. Sir Edward continued, "Tell that man with you to cut the commissioner loose and—my God! *Merial.*"

"Never mind the girl—shoot the bastard," Perce commanded.

Merial ran between them and Rayn. "You'll have to kill me first!" she cried. "Well, Father? Are you going to pull the trigger?"

As Sir Edward hesitated, Rayn was thinking swiftly. Were he alone, he could easily take Sir Edward down. But there was always the chance of a stray bullet hitting Mira.

Besides, killing Perce and Sir Edward wouldn't prevent the English from attacking Baranpur. Rayn sifted through options and possibilities and resolved on one.

"We seem," he said, "to be at an impasse, so here's a proposal. I want to send Commissioner Perce to hell. He wants to kill me. Since you English are fond of sport, I will meet you, Perce, with sword or pistol. If I win, I will expose you for the scoundrel you are. And if I lose—"

"What makes you think I'd meet you in a duel?"

Rayn shrugged. "My *bhaldars* will be here shortly, and they're not as sports-minded as I am. They'd avenge their comrades' death by flaying both of you alive."

Sir Edward paled, and Perce snarled, "Damn you—I'll do it. Untie me and I'll fight you."

"Stop where you are!" Merial cried as Sir Edward stepped forward. "Father, you must help us bring Perce to justice. The colonel will believe you if you tell him the truth."

"You've gone mad. Why should I help your lover?"

"Do you remember the Gujjar and the men that died there because of your greed?" Merial interrupted. "The man you call the Tiger is really Niall St. Marr."

Sir Edward stared. So did Perce. In a strangled voice Sir Edward repeated, "Impossible. Niall St. Marr is dead."

Rayn taunted, "Ghosts have a habit of returning to life, Ashland." He touched the moonstone amulet. "Do you remember this?"

Sir Edward stared and moaned, "It *is* him. Oh, my God, have mercy on me."

"Get a hold of yourself, you pathetic fool," Perce snarled. "Don't you know this is your chance to wipe away the past? If he really *is* St. Marr, he can ruin you."

"Then you'd better silence me, too," Merial vowed. "I will tell everyone what you are—both of you."

"Ashland! Untie me quickly, man. His men will be here at any moment."

Galvanized by the urgency in Perce's voice, Sir Edward moved. As though jerked by marionette strings, he cut Perce free.

"I no longer have a father," Merial mourned.

He gave her an agonized look. "You don't understand."

Perce got to his feet and flexed his arms and hands. "You'll kindly remember the terms of our bargain— *Prince*. If I win, you'll surrender to me."

"Swords or pistols?"

Perce chose pistols. With his eyes on his adversary, Rayn spoke to Merial in the Kumari dialect. "If he kills me, make your way to Colonel Malcolm and try to explain who's to blame for this. It's the only chance we have for averting war."

Then, switching to English, he said, "Perce, we will stand back to back and then walk away from each other. Mira will count till ten. On the count of ten we turn and fire."

Perce snarled. "Get on with it."

Rayn met and held Merial's eyes for a long moment. *It's all right, love.* But it wasn't all right, and she drew a long, sobbing breath as the men went back to back. Perce was shorter, not as powerful, but the determination in his face matched Rayn's.

"One," Merial counted.

The men began to walk away from each other. Rayn's easy stride contrasted to Perce's jerky movements. He was nervous. Would he be nervous enough to miss?

"Two."

Surely she was dreaming this. It was a nightmare like the nightmares she'd had of the Gujjar Pass and the Bridge of Winds. Desperately Merial prayed that she could wake up.

"Three."

Sir Edward gave a little moan. He looked broken and old—he looked beaten. "Four," Merial stammered.

As the word left her lips, Perce turned on his heel, raised his pistol, and took aim at Rayn's broad back.

"Look out—" But that scream was all Merial had time for before Perce pulled the trigger.

·· *Nineteen* ··

RAYN FELL.

Still screaming, Merial started forward intending to shield him with her own body. But before she could take more than a step forward, Rayn rolled aside, raised his own pistol, and fired. Perce screamed as Rayn's bullet pierced his right arm.

As Perce dropped his pistol, Rayn came to his feet in a crouching lunge that knocked Perce to the ground. "*Now* you bloody coward," Rayn snarled.

His left shoulder was bleeding, but he didn't feel any pain. All he could think of was Perce's throat between his hands.

At that moment there was the sound of running feet, and Rayn's *bhaldars* came up. They, too, were covered with blood and grime, and Big Fanji had a crude bandage wrapped around his thigh. "Lord, mounted *Angrezi* soldiers are coming from Sri Nevi," Deen reported.

Perce choked, "Now you're trapped—*Prince.*"

Reluctantly Rayn let go of the commissioner of railroads' windpipe. "You're going to explain that the bridge was blown at your bidding."

Perce spat. It was an eloquent, contemptuous gesture, and pure hatred blazed from his eyes.

Deen bounded over to Perce, jerking out his dagger as he went. "I'll make him talk."

Rayn ordered him back. "A confession forced by torture wouldn't be believed. Our commissioner of railroads must willingly admit to his crimes."

"Meanwhile, we can fight!" Fanji bellowed, and the other *bhaldars* shouted assent.

Merial had torn off her head-covering and was bandaging Rayn's shoulder. Fortunately, it was a clean flesh wound. "Leave it," he told her impatiently. To his men he added, "Fighting won't help us now. Our only chance is to get the commissioner to tell the truth."

Perce glared defiance. Sir Edward hung his head. "I'll tell them," Merial offered. "I'll tell them that Perce tried to rape me—his involvement with the thugs—everything."

Sir Edward croaked, "Don't do it, Merial," then averted his eyes from the scorn that blazed in her eyes.

"Hopefully, they'll listen." Rayn's voice was grim as the sound of horses' hooves neared. "Get into battle position," he ordered his men, "but hold your fire. I'm going to attempt to parlay with the colonel. Fanji—lend me your turban."

Rolled out, Big Fanji's scorched headgear became a white flag. Merial walked forward to join him, but Rayn stopped her. "Remember that you're still under my orders. You're only to accompany me while we parlay. If there's fighting, Deen will get you out of it. Do exactly as he says."

Fanji handed Rayn a lamp, and Merial took another. On foot, carrying the white flag, they walked forward toward a clearing. Here it was even more evident that the night sky was lurid with the flames that were engulfing the ruined bridge. Merial's heart sank. The English would never listen to her after this!

Rayn had the same thought. "If you fall into English hands, tell them that I kidnapped you and threatened you with death if you didn't cooperate."

"You forget that I held a pistol on a soldier of the queen," she retorted. "There's no turning back for me, either, Rayn."

But her defiance faltered as they waited. In the silence of that waiting, Rayn's makeshift flag of truce snapped in a burning wind. She reached for Rayn's hand, and they stood linked together as the pounding of hooves came closer.

Colonel Malcolm had mustered out his entire garrison, and against the backdrop of flames it seemed to Merial that an endless wave of soldiers was rolling toward them. Suddenly a rifle cracked, and a bullet whistled past her ear. "Stop firing!" Merial screamed. "Can't you see the flag of truce?"

There was another shot and then the barked command to hold fire. "Who is there?" the colonel's voice demanded.

Rayn answered, "I am Prince Narayn of Baranpur and wish to parlay with Colonel Malcolm. Miss Ashland is here with me."

There was an instant's shocked surprise before a series of angry oaths filled the night. "So you're hiding behind a woman's skirts, now," Colonel Malcolm snarled. He urged his horse forward crying, "If you're any kind of man, you'll let her go unharmed."

Merial loosed Rayn's hand and took several steps forward. "I'm not a prisoner, Colonel. I'm here of my own free will. I've come to explain who really blew up that bridge—"

Her words were drowned in a chorus of angry protests that burst forth from the colonel and his officers. "Enough!" Rayn's deep voice cut through the babble. "I haven't come to parlay with fools. I'm here only because I don't want my people to be blamed for this senseless destruction. I was led to believe that Englishmen observed the flag of truce."

Colonel Malcolm barked, "Say your piece."

In a few terse words Rayn described the events that had led to the explosion. His sparse eloquence held them until he came to Perce's name. Then Colonel Malcolm interrupted. "That's enough!" he cried. "Where is the commissioner? I'll stake my immortal soul that you murdered him."

Rayn called an order, and Perce, together with Sir Edward, was led forward. "You can see that he's very much alive."

The colonel shifted in his saddle. "I also see that he's wounded. Let those two Englishmen go at once," he commanded, "or flag or no flag, I'll order my soldiers to fire on you."

Perce immediately shouted, "The Tiger blew up my bridge. The murdering swine acted with the full knowledge and agreement of his government, so—"

"You're a liar!"

Merial turned in amazement as the words seemed to explode out of Sir Edward. "Perce is lying," Sir Edward continued. "The bridge was destroyed under his orders."

The colonel gaped. "You must have gone mad, Ashland. Why should the commissioner of railroads destroy his own work?"

"Because he wants power," Sir Edward panted. "Perce

wants to see England pull down Khem Raoshad and his son so that *he* can rule Baranpur."

"He's raving," Perce snarled, but Colonel Malcolm held up a hand.

"Something's odd here, and I mean to get to the bottom of this." He turned to Sir Edward, saying sternly, "If what you're saying is true, you're Perce's accomplice."

Merial saw her father's pallid face twitch like a hunted rabbit's. "God help me," he groaned, "I'm that—and worse."

"You cowardly son of a bitch," Perce roared. Next moment he had twisted free of the *bhaldars* who held him and lunged for the pistol strapped to Deen's side. Before anyone could move, he turned the weapon on Sir Edward. The pistol barked once, and Sir Edward fell, clutching his chest.

Deen dealt Perce a stunning blow, and the commissioner of railroads collapsed onto the ground. "Guard that man," the colonel ordered his soldiers.

Dismounting, he hastened to where Merial bent over her father. "Is he dead?"

Rayn, also kneeling beside Sir Edward, replied for her. "He's still alive."

As he spoke, Sir Edward opened his eyes. "Merial. Get the colonel. Must—tell him everything."

"I'm here, man." Colonel Malcolm knelt down beside Sir Edward and spoke sternly. "You're minutes away from death, Sir Edward. Tell the truth."

"I mean to," Sir Edward panted. "Perce *had* to destroy the bridge because he'd skimped on costs and used the money to line his pockets. He planned it for months. I know because I helped him, and I also carried the signal to detonate the charges tonight. I told Gunga Dass to light the lamps. He's one of the thugs, and that was the prearranged signal—"

Rayn watched Merial gnaw her lip in agony. She'd lifted Sir Edward's head into her lap and with trembling hands was smoothing back his hair. "Oh, Father," she mourned.

In a urgent whisper Sir Edward continued, "Perce planned to blame Narayn of Baranpur for the destruction of the bridge. He knew we'd go to war. Once the English soldiers destroyed Baranpur, he intended to use his influence to be appointed its governor."

Perce had regained consciousness. He tried to get up, but English soldiers surrounded him now, and they pushed him back. "You murdering swine," one of them said.

Rayn was asking sternly, "What was your reward for helping him, Ashland?"

Merial felt her father's whole body jerk as he sighed, "His silence."

"Tell them," Rayn commanded, and Colonel Malcolm scowled.

"You don't give the orders here, *Prince.*"

Sir Edward cried, "He's not Prince Narayn Raoshad. He's Niall St. Marr."

This time the silence was absolute. Then a voice rose out of the ranks of garrison soldiers. "I knew it! When I heard that old war cry, I knew—my God, it's the captain's lad come back from the dead."

Stunned, the colonel stared at the man he had considered his arch enemy. "I don't believe it," he stuttered. "If you're really Niall St. Marr, why make war on the English?"

Once again Rayn spoke to Sir Edward. "Tell the rest."

"He makes war on us because I betrayed his father,"

Sir Edward panted. Merial closed her streaming eyes as, with agonizing slowness, the story was told. When she heard her father confess to the theft of the temple gold and the cowardice that led to the death of Major St. Marr and his men, she felt riven with grief.

"All these years—I hid the truth," Sir Edward whispered. "Then Perce heard about it from the Shaiva priests in Sri Nevi. He—made inquiries and found out." He looked up at his daughter, tried to smile. "Merial, forgive me. St. Marr, forgive—"

The labored voice sobbed into silence. In a voice scarcely recognizable because of tears, Merial whispered, "He's dead."

Rayn knelt down and felt for a pulse. Then he closed the staring eyes. In the ruddy glare of the burning bridge, his face was stern.

"Edward Ashland has atoned," he said. "May his God have mercy on him."

"The problem is, what are we to do with you?" Colonel Malcolm wanted to know.

It was noon of the next day. The fires of the ruined bridge had burned down, and though the wind from the east still carried the acrid stink of smoke, the wounded had been attended to and garrison soldiers were shifting through the rubble to try and account for the dead.

Leaning back in his chair, the colonel surveyed the powerful man who sat across from him. "Perce has confessed. I'm tempted to give the blackguard short shrift and a long rope, but there'll be a trial in England first. He defrauded the company he worked for, after all, and they'll want his hide."

"Defrauding the railway company is much worse than killing a few Indian workers," Rayn agreed.

The irony in Rayn's deep voice caused Colonel Malcolm to frown. Most of the time he couldn't see anything of Captain St. Marr anywhere in that hard-planed, sunbrowned face. But when Prince Rayn spoke as he had now, when he moved his head or curled his lip, the colonel caught a glimpse of the man who'd been one of his most promising young officers.

"Perce is disposed of," he said. "Ashland is dead. Which leaves you, St. Marr."

"My name is Prince Narayn Raoshad of Baranpur." Rayn paused before adding, "Let's look at some facts. My adoptive father, the rana, is dying and I am his heir. War with my country would not only be costly, but also an embarrassment to your government."

"You're talking as if you were one of *them!* Are you or are you not Niall St. Marr?"

"Niall St. Marr is dead," Rayn corrected. "It is with the prince of Baranpur that you need to formalize a treaty of peace."

Colonel Malcolm shifted uneasily in his chair. "I've made enough concessions as it is," he growled. "I've let your lancers ride away as you demanded. I've given you safe conduct so that you could accompany Miss Ashland into Sri Nevi for her father's burial."

"So you did." Rayn got up from his chair and went to the window. Through it he could see the church beyond the parade grounds. "But that is in the past, Colonel. The present reality is that you can't afford Baranpur as a hostile neighbor. Better by far to sign a treaty with a rich and powerful kingdom."

Colonel Malcolm harrumphed loudly. "But the terms, St.—er, Prince Rayn, are unheard of. A standing army of your own controlled solely by the ruling house of Baranpur. Trade talks to be opened with terms of *your* choosing. And a government completely autonomous from the British crown—it's outrageous."

"Considering the heinous acts committed by Perce against my country and my own person, I feel that my terms are more than generous. We don't seek reparations for the damage Perce has done to land within Baranpur, and in exchange for the privilege of building your railroad close to our borders, we only require favorable terms for trade. Tea, hemp, and the finest wool anywhere—these are commodities that England needs." Rayn smiled and added significantly, "Besides, your country surely wouldn't want to blacken its name and its reputation in the world community."

Listening to this smooth flow of words, the colonel sighed. The fellow didn't sound like the Tiger at all—he sounded like an English politician. "I'm not empowered to act on such matters," he said stiffly. "The viceroy—"

"Since His Excellency is in Delhi, I'm sure he'll listen to your recommendations," Rayn pointed out.

Colonel Malcolm surrendered. "I couldn't shake Captain St. Marr once he'd taken a stand," he said, "and I'd be mad to try to argue with you now. Besides, what you say makes more sense than I care to admit." He paused. "You're going to return to Baranpur immediately?" Rayn assented. "What," the colonel then said, "of Miss Ashland?"

"What of her?"

Noting the subtle shift in the big man's voice, Colonel Malcolm cleared his throat. "I couldn't help noting that there was some, er, fondness between the two of you." He met the cold steadiness of the Tiger's eyes as he added, "Dash it all, St.—I mean, Prince Narayn, my wife is very fond of Merial. So am I. We'll try to shield her all we can from the unpleasantness that's bound to come out at

Perce's trial. And we have friends in England who'll look out for her."

"She doesn't wish to return to England."

"Oh, come, man, of course she does. She's English, born and bred. Besides, she can't want to stay on in a country that has brought her nothing but sorrow."

"Is there no sorrow in England?" Rayn challenged, and the colonel flushed.

"At least she'll be with her own kind," he said earnestly. "Oh, I know what you're thinking. You want her to go back to Baranpur with you. But the future you can offer her is uncertain. You know that she'll always be an *Angrezi* in a land that has no love for English people."

"My people love and revere Mira." About to continue, Rayn suddenly realized that they were no longer *his* people, that by now the rana would have surely appointed another heir. Perhaps that successor would be as hostile to the English as Khem-Rana himself, which would mean that the future was even more uncertain than even the colonel thought.

He was silent as the colonel continued, "You're English—well, *half*-English, anyway—so you'll understand what I have to say. No one of English blood could think of throwing away her precious heritage." The colonel leaned forward and regarded Rayn with earnest eyes. "I'm speaking as a friend of your late father's. If you take Merial with you to Baranpur, she may regret it for the rest of her life—and so might you."

"I am the Resurrection and the Life and whosoever believeth in Me shall never die."

How long she had been standing here, Merial didn't know. The minister's voice droned on and on, conducting the funeral service, but the wind caught his words and blew them away. It was a wind that still stank of smoke and death.

Jassmina, standing some distance aside, wiped her flowing eyes with her sari as Merial walked slowly forward to lay a wreath of roses and marigolds on the plain pine coffin. The English community, learning of Edward Ashland's involvement in Perce's plans, had largely ignored his funeral. Only the colonel's lady was there to walk over to the slender figure kneeling in the dust beside the open grave.

"It's time to go, dear." Mrs. Malcolm put a motherly arm around her shoulders, coaxing, "Come home with me, now, and I'll make you a nice cup of tea."

"Thank you—you're very kind, but I'll stay here a little longer." Merial's white lips tried to smile, then quivered into stillness as the colonel's wife left the cemetery.

Jassmina was not to be fobbed off so easily. "*Piara,*" she begged, "come and rest." When Merial shook her head, she muttered, "Where is *he* that you should suffer alone? After all that has happened, his place is by your side."

The old woman withdrew, shaking her head, and Merial felt a nagging ache in her heart. She wanted Rayn here with her. She needed his strength and his comfort. But Rayn was with Colonel Malcolm and had been with him all day. Merial knew that they were discussing some kind of treaty—something to do with Baranpur's future— but she didn't know the details. She hadn't followed much of what Rayn had said to the colonel on that long and terrible ride back to Sri Nevi last night.

Merial's eyes were swollen with crying, but her heart was heavy with tears that still hadn't been shed. Tears for the waste of it all, for what might have been had not Sir Edward Ashland prized gold above his family and love and honor. And yet, as Rayn had said, he had finally atoned for his crimes.

She heard a step and looked up to see Rayn walking across the dried earth toward her. He was bareheaded but booted and spurred for travel. Her cry of welcome was stilled by the look in his eyes, and instead of going to meet him as she'd wanted to do, she remained on her knees by Sir Edward's open grave.

"You look exhausted." Rayn's hands were warm as he drew her to his feet, but he let go of her almost immediately. "I thought you'd have gone back to the colonel's house."

She shook her head. "I needed to be alone for a few minutes. To—to think."

"I understand." Merial's senses were too dulled to notice the brief pain that flickered in his eyes. "Of what were you thinking?"

But she couldn't discuss her father now, not yet, while the pain was too sharp. "How was your meeting with the colonel?" she parried.

"We've agreed on a temporary treaty to respect each other's borders. We will make no more raids on his people, and he'll make sure that the railroad is diverted away from our boundaries." He paused. "I'm hoping that the new rana of Baranpur will see reason and honor this agreement. Later, a formal treaty can be drawn up."

So it wasn't Baranpur's fate that made him look like that. "Is something wrong?" she asked. "Is it about Perce?"

"No. Hamilton Perce will be tried for his crime, including the murder of your father, and I have no doubt he'll be duly executed according to English law."

He looked down at the coffin as he spoke, and she asked in a low tone, "Can't you forgive him even now?"

"The colonel asked me the same question." Rayn's mouth twisted wryly as he added, "The poor fellow was uncomfortable throughout the whole interview. Imagine having a bitter enemy turn into a possible ally and the son of a brother officer." He searched her pale face as he added, "He asked me whether I was ready to return to my 'own kind' now that I've been vindicated."

"What did you answer?"

Instead of replying, he looked over her head toward the Pir Panjals. Obscured by the late afternoon haze, the mountains seemed far away.

As his silence continued, Merial's heart felt a new soreness. It was as if a crack had appeared in the hard ground at her feet and that the fissure was widening between them. She had feared this from the moment that Sir Edward made his confession. No matter how much they loved each other, Sir Edward would always stand between her and Rayn.

His father, his friends, now Rassul and many of his *bhaldars* had been sacrificed to Sir Edward's greed and cowardice. Merial wanted to put her arms around Rayn and tell him that she loved him more than her own life, but she held herself in check. Her family had been responsible for much of the grief in his life. Now Rayn must choose his future, without constraint.

"I understand," Merial whispered.

She'd unconsciously spoken in English, and her words sent desolation lancing through Rayn. Her tear-swollen eyes, the black European clothes that she wore mourning her father—all these proved that the colonel had been right. Mira's heart was and would always be English.

With an effort, Rayn kept his voice even. "Do you want to return to England, Merial?"

For the first time he used the Anglicized version of her

name, and she understood what he was trying to tell her. He was sending her away. Words of denial rose to her lips, but she pushed them back and forced herself to say quietly, "Is that what you want me to do?"

"It's your choice."

This, too, we have chosen. The echo of his voice sighed back to touch her like the ghost of a caress. She could hardly bear to think of that happy time in her present desolation, but the memories crowded close. Bleakly she realized that from this day forward she'd have nothing but those memories to fill her life.

"I'll do whatever you wish," she said, but her voice broke on the words.

He turned suddenly, and she saw that his eyes were the most unhappy she'd ever seen in a man's face. "No, it must be as *you* wish. If you want to return to England, we'll go."

She couldn't believe she'd heard right. "We?" she repeated stupidly.

"I'm no longer crown prince. If we return to my—to Baranpur, your life may be difficult. I couldn't promise you happiness or anything else."

She tried to concentrate on what he was saying, but her usually swift mind wouldn't rise to the challenge. "But," she stammered, "you love Baranpur."

"It's dear to me," he admitted, and though he attempted to speak indifferently, she could sense the battle that he was waging in himself. "It's been home to me for many years, but a man's home is chosen by his heart. *You* are my heart, Merial."

"Don't call me that!" she cried. She threw her arms about him, saying passionately, "I'm Mira, your Mira, and where *you* are is my home. I don't want a crown or— or England—or an easy life. I want *you*."

He gazed into her eyes as though he were trying to gauge her deepest thoughts, and she whispered, "Don't you know that by now, my love?"

He caught her to him, holding her so hard that she could hardly breathe. "Are you sure?"

When she nodded, his mouth claimed hers with fierce triumph. "What does a kingdom matter?" he whispered against her lips. "I have my sword. We are young, Mira, with all our lives ahead of us. My *bhaldars* and I will carve out a kingdom for us—and for our children."

"Yes!" she cried, and he looked down at her with all his love shining in his eyes.

"To hell with England and the crown of Baranpur!" he shouted exultantly. "We'll be together, beloved. We'll *live.*"

He kissed her again, long and hungrily, his mouth remembering the sweet perimeter of her lips, the silken lining of her mouth. "I can't wait to get you alone so that I can strip these damned English clothes off you and make love until the dawn comes," Rayn said.

There was the sound of hoofbeats behind them, and a familiar voice called, "Lord?"

Deen was sitting his horse some distance away. Behind him, leading the bridles of two horses, was Big Fanji. The lancers were accompanied by a man dressed in formal court clothes.

"I'm sorry, lord," Deen continued apologetically. "I know your orders were for us to wait for you in the hills. But this man rode up some time ago with an army escort. He brings news from the palace."

Rayn asked quietly, "The rana is dead?"

"Last night the King of Kings left this life. May he be reborn in bliss." The messenger dismounted, knelt down, and bowed until his forehead touched the ground. "In the name of the departed rana, Highness, I bring you this."

Reverently he extended a gold casket. Rayn opened it to disclose the King's ring and a single sheet of paper. Merial watched Rayn's face change as he read the paper.

"Read it," he said.

" 'To my son Narayn, heir apparent of the Princedom of Baranpur,' " Merial read aloud, " 'known also as the Shield of the Kingdom, Commander of the Armies, Favored Son. I, Khem Raoshad, descendant of the sun god, rana of Baranpur, send greeting. We have disagreed on matters of policy in the past, and your decision to marry an *Angrezi* rankles. Nevertheless, I honor you as a truthful and courageous man. I am convinced, therefore, that you will rule Baranpur well. My day is done. Do not falter as you take your place upon the Silver Throne.' "

The letter was written by the court scribe and witnessed by the rana's chief ministers. "Then you're the new rana of Baranpur," Merial whispered.

Deen and Fanji had also dismounted and were kneeling before their new ruler. Merial would have followed suit, but Rayn caught her to him and held her close.

"This is your place," he told her firmly.

"Always."

For a moment they gazed wordlessly into each other's eyes. Then Rayn took his Mira's hand. "Come, my queen—my friends. It's time to go home."